MORAL
DEFENSE

MORAL DEFENSE

A Samantha Brinkman Legal Thriller

MARCIA CLARK

THOMAS & MERCER

Published by Thomas & Mercer, Seattle

www.apub.com

Amazon, the Amazon logo, and Thomas & Mercer are trademarks of Amazon.com, Inc., or its affiliates.

ISBN-13: 9781503939776 (hardcover)
ISBN-10: 1503939774 (hardcover)

ISBN-13: 9781503938694 (paperback)
ISBN-10: 1503938697 (paperback)

Cover design by David Drummond

Printed in the United States of America

PROLOGUE

Stephen pushed the hair off his wife's clammy forehead and stroked her cheek. Paula's skin was pale and tinged with green. The Uber driver'd had to stop three times to let her throw up. When he finally pulled into the driveway, Stephen gave Paula a worried look. "You sure you don't want to go to the ER?"

Paula turned toward the open window and gulped some more of the fresh, rain-soaked air. "It's just food poisoning; I'll make it." She gave him a wan smile as the driver parked the car. "Happy anniversary." The smile fell away as she clutched her stomach, pushed open the passenger door, and vomited onto the driveway.

Stephen saw the driver's disgusted expression in the rearview mirror and threw him a dirty look before jumping out and running around behind the car to help her. Paula was leaning halfway out, trying to catch her breath. He put a hand on her shoulder. "Can you make it to the house?"

She spoke in a weak voice. "Think so." She put her right foot on the ground, then her left. Holding on to the doorjamb with one hand and the car door with the other, she started to pull herself up.

Stephen put an arm around her waist. "Let me carry you."

Paula shook her head. "Just . . . hurry."

Stephen helped her out as he said to the driver, "Please put our bags on the porch."

The driver opened his door with an irritated sigh. Stephen glared at him as he bent down to steady Paula, who was doubled over. They hobbled up to the front door, their bodies bumping against each other, out of sync. When they reached the porch, Stephen held her against him with one arm as he fumbled for the key. "Damn!" he sputtered as the key ring fell to the ground. Behind him, he heard the Uber driver back out of the driveway and take off.

When Stephen managed to unlock the door, he shoved it open so hard it banged against the wall. Paula ran for the bathroom.

Stephen turned around and saw that the driver had left their suitcases at the end of the driveway. He shook his head. The jerk. As he stomped down to get their bags, it began to rain again. A sudden, cold wind drove the icy drops straight into his face. Stephen dipped his head and shivered as he walked back to the house. The image of the romantic fireplace in the bungalow where they'd planned to spend the night flashed through his mind. Oh well—next time. And next time he wouldn't let Paula order that damn Dover sole in cream sauce.

Stephen hurried down the hall to their bedroom and dropped the bags just inside the door. To his right, he heard Paula retching in the master bathroom. The sound made his stomach seesaw. Sympathetic nausea. He wondered whether that was a real thing. He called to her through the door. "Need help, hon?"

Paula coughed twice, a harsh, jagged scrape. Her voice was raw and barely audible. "No. Thanks."

He shook his head. Poor Paula. "I'll get you some water."

Stephen started back down the hall, stopped at the door on his left, and looked at his watch. One thirty. Cassie *should* be asleep. He cracked open her door and peeked inside. All good. He moved farther down the hall, then noticed that Abel's door was slightly open. But there was no light on.

The more he fit his door open, Stephen peered into Abel's room. "Abel? You okay, kiddo?"

He stepped inside. Rain was blowing straight through the open . . . wait, *broken* window. What? It took a moment for his eyes to adjust in the darkness. Clothing spilled from the open drawers of Abel's dresser; books were strewn around the room; the drawer of the nightstand lay on the floor. His heart gave a quick, hard thud as his gaze moved to the bed. And stopped. Stephen recoiled, unable to process the sight. The blood-soaked body; the dead, staring eyes. His son. No. It couldn't be right. Stephen fumbled on the wall for the light switch.

At that moment, he felt a rush of air. A sharp pain exploded in his throat. He screamed and grabbed at the side of his neck. He tried to breathe, but something was in the way; he choked as he gasped for air. The killer abruptly yanked out the blade and stepped back. Stephen heard his own voice make a strange, gurgling moan.

Out of the corner of his eye, he caught a flash of blue as he fell, facedown on the floor. Stephen put a hand to his throat to staunch the blood that was flowing from the gaping wound. Paula. Cassie. He had to help them! He tried to push up, reach for the killer, but as he raised an arm, he felt the blade plunge into his back. His arm fell. The blade drove into his back again. Stephen's brain screamed, *Warn them! You've got to warn them!* He mustered all his strength, lifted his head, and tried to shout. But all that came out was a thin, high-pitched wail. Then the killer drove the knife into his back again. Stephen collapsed. He was gone.

Paula clutched the sides of the toilet, the tiled floor cold and hard against her knees as her stomach heaved for the hundredth time. There was nothing left of the Dover sole. Now it was just bile. As she gulped for air, a strange sound penetrated her fog of misery. It seemed to come from somewhere inside the house. A yell . . . or a scream? But that made no sense. Paula rested her cheek against the rim of the toilet and listened. The cool porcelain felt good against her skin. She didn't hear anything. But where was Stephen? He should've been back with her water by now. Paula waited to see whether her body had finished wringing out the last dregs of dinner. After a few seconds with no heaves, Paula pushed herself up and flushed the toilet. Holding on to the sink with one hand, she used the other to splash water on her face and rinse her mouth. She stood there, doubled over at the sink, and listened again. Nothing.

Her insides aching, stomach muscles already sore, Paula held on to the wall for support as she moved to the door of the bedroom. She peered down the hallway. "Stephen?" No answer. Her stomach lurched again, and she felt the acidic burn of bile rising in her throat. She closed her eyes and leaned against the wall, forcing it back down. When the wave subsided, Paula glanced to her left, saw that Cassie's door was closed, no light showing under it. She looked down the hallway. Abel's door was standing open. Something wasn't right. "Abel?" No answer.

Another wave of nausea almost made her drop to her knees. She wanted to lie down right there. But what if Stephen had fallen? What if he was unconscious? Paula flipped on the hall light and listened again. What was that? It sounded like heavy breathing. "Stephen?" Nothing. Frightened, unsure, Paula hesitated. What should she do? Her head swam as she gazed toward Abel's room. Her mind was too numb to work it out. She heard herself whisper, "Go see; you have to go see." Paula leaned against the wall as she slowly crept down the hall, one hand on her stomach.

Paula stopped in Abel's doorway. Rain-soaked curtains flapped in the wind that whistled through the broken window. She stared, confused, into the darkness; then her eyes moved down to the bed. She screamed. "Abel! No! Oh God, no!"

Paula stumbled into the room. But before she could reach the bed, she tripped over . . . something on the floor. She lost her balance. As she fell, she looked down and saw her husband's body. She let out a shriek, but it was cut short as something sharp and cold plunged into the back of her neck.

Cassie stood at the doorway of Abel's room, white-faced, the echo of her mother's scream still ringing in her ears. The wind that now howled through the shattered window sprayed her with freezing rain, soaking her hair and long T-shirt. A streak of movement made her look out through that window. Then, in flashes, she took in the bloody scene. Her brother, vacant eyes fixed on the ceiling. Her mother, head resting on her father's stomach, body curled, knees to chest. Blood . . . so much blood. She sagged against the doorway. Too much. It was too much.

Cassie shook her head back and forth, trying to shake the images out of her brain. Tears streamed down her face.

Then she sank into a crouch and began to scream, a deep animal wail.

ONE

Earlier that same night

I leaned toward the black lens of the camera. "Sheri, if it's true the FBI recruited a fifteen-year-old kid to work as an undercover drug dealer, a lot of heads should roll. And the kid—well, now he's an adult—but he definitely shouldn't *still* be in prison."

Sheri, the host of *Crime Time*, turned to my worthy adversary for the evening, Lonnie Miston, a former prosecutor who'd recently come to his senses and joined me on the right side of justice: criminal defense—though he still had that short, conservative prosecutor haircut. "Lonnie, you've got to admit, it does seem a bit over the line to recruit a minor—"

Lonnie jumped in. "No question. But the FBI didn't tell him to start his own cartel. The only reason he's in prison now is because he got caught dealing fifteen pounds of cocaine—"

I shook my head, and the camera came back to me. "Dealing's the only thing he knew *how* to do thanks to the FBI, who yanked him out of high school when he was a sophomore—you know, when most kids are getting their learner's permits and figuring out they're not gonna need to know geometry to get a job."

Sheri interrupted. "Sorry, folks, my producer tells me that's all we have time for tonight. Samantha Brinkman, Lonnie Miston, thank you for joining us. To all of our watchers, join us again tomorrow on *Crime Time*, when we'll talk to the former FBI agent who's blowing the whistle on this case."

I pulled out my earpiece and unclipped the little microphone on my lapel. The guy wasn't my client, but his predicament really did piss me off. The FBI had used him up and then spit him out. And now, although he'd been a model prisoner for the past eight years, he couldn't get paroled because one of the scumbags he'd helped the FBI take down had cronies in high places.

The whole thing reeked of backdoor string pulling and dirty politics.

I headed to the makeup room and ran into Lonnie, who was washing his face with a baby wipe. I looked at him in the mirror as I wiped off the lipstick. "Tell me you don't really think that kid should still be in prison."

"Oh hell no. Matter of fact, I'm hoping they take down the sleazeball agents who recruited him."

I clapped him on the back. "My man. Always glad to meet a recovering prosecutor. Welcome to the side of truth and justice."

Lonnie's smile was a little embarrassed. "It's taking a little getting used to."

I threw my baby wipe in the trash. "Trust me, once you get your sea legs, you'll love it."

"Well, I know I'll love the money, anyway." He adjusted his tie in the mirror. "You up for a drink?"

Was it my imagination? Something in his tone made it sound like this was more than just a friendly gesture. I'd assumed he was married. Hopefully not. I looked at him in the mirror. Lonnie *was* kind of a hunk. Strong jaw, deep-set blue eyes under bushy eyebrows, muscular but not in an obsessive way. "Can't tonight. Next time?"

Lonnie flashed me a sexy smile. Yep, definitely not just a friendly invite. "You got it."

I headed out, wondering why I'd turned him down. I didn't have to work tonight, and I had no other plans. Maybe it was because he still had that prosecutor vibe. Bad enough I had to deal with them on the job. The last thing I needed was to let them ruin my personal time. As I walked out the back door, the security guard motioned for the limo—a nice, gas money–saving perk for doing the show—to come forward. The car pulled out of the garage, but before it could reach me, a fairly new-looking black Escalade with gold trim and custom hubcaps zoomed into the space.

The security guard gave the driver a stern look, held up a hand, and gestured for him to back out. But the car stayed put, and the passenger-side window rolled down. I looked inside, saw the driver, and sighed. The guard started to move between us, but I shook my head. "It's okay. I know him."

I hadn't heard from Deshawn Johnson, my former client, in a while. Generally speaking, this is good news. When clients show up after their cases are over, it's usually because they're in deep shit again. It's never because they want to drop off a box of See's Candies and thank me for the great job I'd done.

And in Deshawn's case, I'd done a miraculous job. I'd gotten him off the hook on a dope case that would've landed him in prison for twenty-five to life. So seeing him pull up in this tricked-out Escalade just had to be bad news. From what I knew, Deshawn's legitimate skill set didn't qualify him to buy a car that pricey. As I walked over to the passenger window, I scanned the street, half expecting to see flashing blue and red lights pull up behind him. "What're you doing here?"

"I need to talk to you. Get in; I'll take you home."

It'd been a long week, and I was tired. I'd been hoping to get to bed early for a change. But he looked and sounded desperate. Just the fact that he'd gone to the trouble of finding me here meant this was serious. I told the security guard to let the limo driver go.

He gave Deshawn a skeptical look. "You sure?"

Unfortunately, I was. "Yeah, thanks."

He sighed and shrugged. "Have a good one." His expression said he thought that was unlikely.

I had a feeling he was right, though probably for different reasons. I got into the Escalade, gave Deshawn the directions to my apartment in West Hollywood, then asked the question I didn't really want him to answer. "So, what's new?"

Deshawn was driving with one nervous eye on the rearview mirror. "Remember that dope you took off me?"

Warning bells went off in my head. This was going to be bad. About three months ago, Deshawn and his buddies, not realizing who I was, tried to jack me. I'd been busting my hump on a motion that stood a good chance of getting his case thrown out. When we recognized each other, I was so pissed off that he was still out capering, jeopardizing everything I was trying to do for him, I'd made him empty his pockets—and found a big baggie of what turned out to be very pure heroin.

I decided to remind him of why I'd taken it. "You mean the dope I never saw you with? The dope that would've landed you in prison for life if you'd been caught with it? *That* dope?"

We were stopped at the light, and his eyes kept bouncing from one mirror to another. "Yeah, that dope. The dope my play cousin, Taquan, fronted me. Which *he* got from a dude who's telling him if he don't bring back the dope or the money, Taquan's gonna be wearin' a Colombian necktie."

My stomach lurched at the image. I'd seen one of those in a big dope case I'd handled last year: they'd slit a guy's throat, then pulled his tongue through the hole. "How come you didn't tell me someone fronted you that dope?"

Deshawn looked at me like I'd just asked why the Easter Bunny hadn't come this year. "Now how's that gonna look in front of my homies? Like a little bitch who can't even afford to buy his own shit." He shook his head. The light turned green, and he glanced at the rearview mirror again as he pulled forward.

This made no sense to me, but it wasn't a point worth debating. "Where's the guy been all this time?" No dealer who moved quantities that big would let three months go by without getting paid.

"In jail. He was up on a murder rap, s'posed to be doing life." Deshawn gave me a pointed look. "But his *lawyer* done put the case down."

So now he was out, and he wanted his money. "How much time do you have?"

"Maybe an hour. Where you got it stashed?"

This, of course, was the problem. Whatever was left of that stash was in police custody now. After I'd taken it from Deshawn, it *somehow* found its way into the hands of my other client, Harold Ringer. Ringer had been facing life in prison for raping and beating a young homeless boy who'd been tricking to stay alive. I'd managed to persuade the jury to acquit the asshole. When he got released from jail, he'd found the baggy of heroin in his pants pocket. He'd overdosed that same night. So the heroin had gone to a worthy cause, but I had a feeling Deshawn wouldn't agree. "I don't have it."

He jerked the steering wheel to the right, pulled to the curb, and stopped. He stared at me, his eyes wide. "What'd you do with it?"

His panic was infectious. When I spoke, my voice was edgy. "Does it matter?"

"Hell yeah, it matters!"

I couldn't tell him the truth, and I was too distracted to come up with a halfway decent lie. "I used it to take care of a problem."

Deshawn was outraged. "You used *my* dope to solve *your* problem? The fuck is up with that?"

He had a point. "I'm sorry. I had no idea."

Deshawn put his head down on the steering wheel. "I'm so fucked." After a moment, he sat up and resumed driving as he muttered to himself. The words *motherfucker* and *dead fuckin' meat* came up a lot.

When he reached my apartment, he parked and stared out the windshield. "Taquan don't deal too good with pain. If this dude squeezes him, my name's gonna pop out like a piece of toast." Deshawn faced me, his expression bleak, terrified. "Which is what I'll be. You got to get me the money, Ms. Brinkman—or the stuff. That'll do."

I started to calculate how much room I had on my credit cards. "What kind of money are we talking about?"

"Like I told you when you took it: a hundred grand."

I hadn't believed him at the time, thought he'd just been puffing in front of his crew. My throat closed. Holy shit. I mustered up a confident look before I met Deshawn's eyes. "I'll find a way to get the money. Just tell your cousin to lay low for a while. And you do the same."

He gave me an incredulous look. "What you think I *been* doin'? This ain't my ride. I got it from—"

I held up a hand. "Don't tell me." I had enough to worry about without hearing who he'd gotten in bed with to score a new Escalade. "I'll be in touch."

Deshawn's expression was grim. "Real soon, right?"

It was the first time I'd ever seen him worried—about anything—and that, even more than what he'd said, told me just how life-threatening this situation really was. "Right." I got out and patted the roof. "I got this."

Deshawn drove off, and I trudged up the stairs to my little one-bedroom. The building only has twelve units, no elevator, no security parking—well, no security, period. But it's situated at the top of a hill that gives me a halfway decent view of the city from the little balcony off the living room.

I let myself in, dropped my briefcase near the door, and looked at my "bar"—the little pass-through counter between the kitchen and the living room—to see what I was pouring that evening. There were about two inches left in my bottle of Patrón Silver tequila. That'd do for now. I threw some ice in a glass, emptied the bottle into it, and took my drink out to the balcony. It was a cool, clear night, and the city lights sparkled against the black-velvet sky. Tomorrow was Saturday. Good. It'd give me some time to come up with a plan. I didn't know how I was going to find a hundred thousand dollars, and I sure as hell couldn't imagine how I'd manage to do it in time to save Taquan and Deshawn. I just knew I had to. This one was all on me.

I racked my brain for the rest of the evening, but by the time I fell into bed, the only ideas I'd had were: 1) hold up a Brinks truck, 2) commit a bank robbery, or 3) rip off a high-end jewelry store. Definitely not Plan A material.

The sound of a loud duck quacking—my cell phone ringtone—jarred me awake the next morning. I looked at the clock. It was only eight thirty. On a friggin' Saturday. Annoyed, I let it go to voice mail.

An hour later, after I'd kicked over my engine with my third cup of coffee, I checked my phone to see who'd been dumb enough to wake me up on a Saturday morning. Tiegan Donner. Talk about a blast from the past. Five years ago, when I was a public defender, I'd represented her older brother, who'd been busted—basically for having won a bar fight. Tiegan had sat in the back of the courtroom every single day, a very pretty, petite blonde who'd asked fairly intelligent questions for a layperson. I'd won the case. The so-called victim had popped off at me during cross-examination, which showed the jury who'd really started the fight. I wondered whether her brother was in trouble again.

Her message didn't offer any clues. She just asked me to please call her as soon as possible. But she sounded upset. Really upset. Only one way to find out. I pressed the call back button.

Her voice sounded shaky but relieved. "Sam, thank you so much for getting back to me."

"Sure, no problem. What's up? Is your brother okay?"

"Yeah, he's fine. It's not about him. Have you seen the news this morning?" I hadn't. "There's been a—a horrible thing. It happened last night. One of my students, her family was murdered. Her mother's still alive, but they don't expect her to make it."

I grabbed the remote and turned on the television. It must've been late last night or I'd have heard about it. "I'm so sorry, Tiegan." But why was she calling me?

She paused for a moment, then said, "I don't know whether you have time for this, but I thought I'd take a chance and ask. I'm her counselor as well as her teacher, and the lawyer for our school told me that Cassie should have some legal representation—a criminal lawyer—to kind of be there for her."

"Why? Is she a suspect?"

"No! Oh no. Actually, Cassie's the closest thing they've got to a witness right now. But she's just a kid, and the police said they can't rule anyone out right now, so the court agreed to appoint a lawyer for her." Tiegan paused again. "Anyway, you did such a great job for my brother. I was wondering if maybe you'd consider taking the case?"

The kid probably should have someone around, if only to hold her hand. And if the court was going to appoint a lawyer, that probably meant the family couldn't afford to hire one. But why was Tiegan the one calling me? "Tiegan, I'm flattered that you thought of me, but her family might want to have a say in all this."

She gave a deep sigh. "Cassie's adopted. The only family she ever really knew is gone now. She's got relatives in . . . Michigan or something, but they're not close. She's basically lost everyone."

That was pretty rough. Abandoned at birth. Now she'd be feeling abandoned all over again. I'd been clicking through the channels looking for the story on the news. I found it on Channel Four. They were showing a million cops and crime-scene techs moving in and out of a small brick-front house with white shutters. Outside the yellow crime-scene tape, I could see that it was a quiet, middle-class suburban neighborhood. A banner across the bottom of the screen said, "Family Stabbed to Death in Glendale."

Pretty gruesome for that quiet place. I was more than a little curious, and I could definitely use the billable hours. It wouldn't even make a dent in what I owed Deshawn. But it might put enough money in my pocket to give him some temporary help until I found a way out of this for him. "I'll call the court on Monday."

Tiegan spoke in a rush. "Thank you so much, Sam! Do you want to meet her? I think it'd be good for her. The more support she's got, the better."

If I could tell the court I'd already met with the client, I'd stand a better chance of getting the case. "Good idea. Tell me where she is."

TWO

For the time being, until her relatives decided who'd be able to take her in, Cassie Sonnenberg was staying with the Reeber family. The daughter, Debbie Reeber, was just a classmate, not a close friend. But Tiegan didn't want Cassie to stay with one of her two BFFs, because they had "inappropriate family dynamics." Tiegan didn't elaborate, and I didn't ask. According to Tiegan, Debbie's family was stable, and her mother, Barbara, was one of those saintly types who was always willing to step up and do the right thing. Plus, they lived just a couple of blocks away from Cassie, so it wouldn't be a big move.

But from what I saw, Cassie neither knew nor cared where she was. She sat scrunched up in a corner of the couch in the Reebers' living room. Barbara Reeber sat next to her, holding Cassie's hand. Even folded up like an accordion, in the throes of earth-shattering grief and shock, she was clearly pretty. She had a strong jaw and high cheekbones, and her cutoff jeans and black T-shirt showed a strong, slender, athletic body. But right now, her short, purple-streaked blonde hair was tangled, the knots stuck up at the back of her head; her blue eyes were vacant; and her face was pale and slack.

After Tiegan introduced me to everyone, I took the chair across from her. "Hey, Cassie. Did Mrs. Donner tell you I'm asking the court to let me be your lawyer?"

Tiegan leaned in and said in a soft voice, "I let all the kids I counsel call me by my first name."

I nodded. Cassie was staring at me as though I were speaking Urdu. I tried again. "If I'm appointed, I'll be on hand to help you out, sit in when the police talk to you, answer questions for you, things like that. Sound okay?"

Cassie wrinkled her brow, tears pooling in her eyes. "You mean the police are going to talk to me again?"

A million times. But she looked so lost, so forlorn, I decided this might not be the time to tell her that. Besides, she'd see for herself soon enough. "They probably will. But at least you won't have to do it alone anymore." I was curious to know what she'd witnessed, but I wasn't going to grill her right now, when she was so obviously grief-stricken and in shock.

Tears spilled over and ran down her face. "I just keep seeing them . . ." She clamped her hands over her eyes. "I keep thinking it's not true, that I'll wake up and it'll turn out to just be a bad dream." After a moment, Cassie dropped her hands and finally looked at me, the misery on her face so deep it was heartbreaking. "But I can't wake up." She began to sob. "And they won't even let me see my mother! She's all I've got left! Why won't they let me see her?"

I glanced from Barbara to Tiegan. "What's her condition?"

Tiegan gave me a warning look and shook her head. "She's in a medically induced coma. I hear they plan to keep her under for at least a week or so." She looked at Cassie with sympathy. "They'll let you go see her in a day or so. But it might be tough, Cassie. She won't be able to talk to you."

Cassie bent over, her arms wrapped around her torso. "I don't care! I just need to be with her!" She put her head down on her knees and sobbed.

Barbara patted her back and made soothing noises. "Of course you do. And the minute they say it's okay, I'll take you to the hospital."

I waited for Cassie to sit up, then asked, "Do you have any questions you'd like to ask me?"

She took a couple of ragged breaths. "When do you think they'll catch the guy?"

"That's hard to say. I heard that you think you saw him. Is that right?" Cassie nodded. "Can you tell me about that?"

Cassie stared at a point on the floor. "I saw him through Abel's window. He was running across the backyard. At first I was so . . . messed up, I didn't realize he might be . . . that he was the . . ." She stopped and swallowed as fresh tears ran down her face.

I tried to distract her. "What did he look like?"

She twisted her hands together, her voice trembling as she spoke. "I only saw him from behind, but he was big, and he had on a blue bandanna."

I figured the police had already covered this ground with her, but she obviously wanted to talk about it, and I didn't see how it could hurt to let her. "What else was he wearing?"

Cassie swallowed. "It must've been something with no sleeves, because I could see his arms. He had tats. I think one looked like a lightning bolt."

Blue bandanna, a lightning bolt. Typical signs of a skinhead gangbanger, maybe a local faction of the Aryan Brotherhood. I wouldn't have expected that in Glendale, though I'd heard rumors that white gangs were moving into some suburban areas. But why would they target Cassie's family? "You only saw him in the backyard, not inside the house?" Cassie shook her head. "So by the time you woke up, it was all over?"

Cassie's face crumpled. She dropped her head into her hands and began to sob again, but now the sobs seemed to scrape up from deep inside. It hurt just to hear them. She couldn't speak for a few moments. Her voice was raw, broken. "N-no. I heard Mom and Dad come home. Then . . . I fell back to sleep, I think. But a little while later, I thought I heard my mom scream. It sounded like she was in Abel's room. That's what woke me up. I was so scared, I hid under the bed! I didn't know what to do!"

I could only imagine. And I could see she felt guilty. "You did the right thing, Cassie. There was nothing you could've done to help anyone. What made you leave your room?"

Cassie seemed lost in misery. It took her a moment before she replied, "I heard the back door close. It was all quiet. I wanted to call the police, but I'd left my cell phone in the kitchen." She began to shake again. "I opened my door just a little bit, so I could see."

"Where's Abel room in relation to yours?"

"Across the hall, a little farther down." Cassie's breathing turned fast and shallow. "I didn't want to go out, but I had to do something. So I decided to run to the kitchen as fast as I could, but when I passed Abel's room, I felt the wind blowing. I stopped to look and noticed the window was broken. That's when I saw him, the guy with the bandanna. He was running through the backyard. Then I saw . . ." Cassie's face screwed up in a tight ball, and she began to sob again.

Barbara Reeber put an arm around her. "Tiegan, would you get her pills? They're in my purse in the kitchen."

Tiegan had been watching Cassie with helpless anguish. "Sure." She hurried out.

I watched Cassie sag against Barbara's shoulder, the pain on her face so vivid it was hard to look at her. "They gave her a sedative?"

Barbara nodded. "I think she needs to rest and try to let go of it all for a little while, if she can. The police have already put her through it so many times. I'm hoping they'll realize she's given them all she's got to give and leave her alone now."

I thought, *Oh baby, they so won't.* But I just nodded. Tiegan came back with the pill bottle and a glass of water. She tipped out one pill and gave it to Cassie, who took it with a big gulp of water. She leaned back against the couch and closed her eyes as she caught her breath. Her face was mottled with red spots from crying so hard.

I stood up and gave Cassie my card. "In case you want to talk or you have any questions."

Cassie took the card, then looked at me with red, swollen eyes. "So if I have to talk to the cops again, you'll go with me."

I nodded. "If you want me to."

Her frightened expression said it all. "I will."

Tiegan walked me out to my car. The day was incongruously beautiful. It'd rained for most of the night, and the air had that fresh, green smell; the sky, washed clean of smog, was a deep, rich blue. The trees that lined the sidewalk dripped fat, heavy drops that sparkled like topaz in the sunlight. I waited until we got away from the house, then spoke in a low voice. "I hear the cops don't think it was a burglar."

Tiegan nodded. "Abel's wallet is missing. But that's not much."

I agreed. If someone were there to steal, they'd take more than just a wallet. The small theft felt like an afterthought. So it had to be personal. "What do you know about the parents? Anyone have issues with them?"

"Not that I know of." Tiegan said that Paula Sonnenberg was a city councilwoman, and her husband was a storage systems administrator at IBM. The son, Abel, a high school senior, was your average suburban white boy: no criminal background or gang ties. Tiegan stared down the street. "I didn't know the parents myself, but from what I've heard, they were really good people."

It always started that way. But "He was such a great guy" and "She was so kind" inevitably gave way to stories that painted a less glowing picture. Even if they were only tales about how "He drank a little too much" and "She racked up charges on their credit cards." But there had to be something wicked gnarly going on for a whole family to be targeted. "So the skinhead angle is the only one that makes sense."

She nodded. "I'm scared for Cassie. This guy's got to be crazy. What if he comes back for her?"

It seemed a little far-fetched—and a lot risky—to me, but someone rabid enough to do a massacre like this couldn't be relied on to do much rational thinking. I told Tiegan I'd spotted a patrol car passing by the house when I'd arrived. "They're obviously keeping an eye out, but I'll check in with the cops and see what they're doing."

Tiegan forced a shaky smile. "That'd be great. Thank you so much, Sam."

"Glad to help." I opened my car door, which gave an embarrassingly loud metallic groan. Beulah, my ancient Mercedes, has more than 250,000 miles on her, and like an old person, she just doesn't care about appearances anymore. She squeaks and burps and farts at will.

Tiegan gave the car a worried look. "I can give you a lift to the station, if you like."

"Thanks, I'm good." I patted the roof. "Beulah likes to complain, but she always gets me there." A big fat lie. Beulah has crapped out on me so many times the Uber drivers all know me by name.

I drove to the station, thinking about why a skinhead would target an average middle-class family like this. True, the mom, Paula Sonnenberg, was a city councilwoman, but that was hardly a high-profile gig. And I couldn't imagine how an administrator at IBM or a high school kid could run that far afoul of a skinhead gang.

The building that housed the Glendale Police Department was small compared with the huge, impersonal Police Administration Building downtown, where my father, Dale Pearson, worked. I hadn't grown up with him; all I'd had was Celeste, a narcissist who'd resented me from the moment she'd learned she was pregnant. She'd told me I was the result of a one-night stand with someone who—like her—had wanted nothing to do with a kid. I'd learned that was a total lie in the most bizarre way possible. Dale, a veteran homicide detective with LAPD, got charged with the double homicide of a beloved actress and her roommate, and I wound up as his lawyer. Let me just say for the record: meeting a parent for the first time after he's been charged with two murders is not the most fun way to explore your family tree. In any case, he and my mother had actually dated for a while, until she found out he didn't have money—which was right about the time she realized she was pregnant. She hit Dale up for abortion money and dumped him. Ultimately she found out it was too late to get rid of me, but she never told him about me. And that's why Dale and I got to find out about each other when he was Suspect Number One for a notorious double homicide.

That I—who'd always been as virulently anticop as they come—could wind up having a father who was an LAPD homicide detective was one of those obnoxious life ironies; funny to those who know me, very *un*funny to me. I suppose it isn't exactly his idea of perfection to have a daughter who defends the criminals he busts, either.

But now, for a change, having a homicide detective for a dad might come in handy. Dale was back on the job, thanks to my getting his case thrown out. He was assigned to Cold Cases, but he had friends in the Robbery Homicide Division—the elite unit that picked up the high-profile murders—and the Sonnenberg murders fit that bill. The case belonged to Glendale PD at the moment, but I had no doubt it'd land in RHD within hours—if it hadn't already.

As I pulled up in front of the Glendale police station, I braced myself for a nasty reception. The local cops hated it when RHD took away their hottest and biggest cases. If RHD had already bounced them out, I was going to get a face full of misdirected bitterness.

On the drive over, I'd thought about the possibility that Cassie was the murderer. I knew the cops had to keep her in the mix, if only because she hadn't been attacked. But it was hard to picture her doing all that. A knife attack, three people, and it looked like the killer had broken in through Abel's window. None of that made Cassie a likely suspect. But I couldn't dismiss the possibility. In any case, I didn't intend to talk about that. First of all, the cops wouldn't tell me anything. Second of all, she was my client. It was my job to steer them away from her. So I wanted to see how seriously they were taking the skinhead theory.

I parked at the curb and stared up at the gray-toned slabs of stone and brick. See, the problem starts right there. Why all that gray? Why all those skinny windows? The place looked like a modern-day gulag. You want people to feel comfortable with the police, think of them as protectors instead of bullies and thugs. So why not make the cop shop at least *look* like a friendly place? Paint a mural on it. Or show you're really cool and hire one of those gang kids with mad artistic skills. And maybe have rap music playing in the lobby. Something classic, like Tupac. I replayed the lyrics to "Changes" in my head. Rap probably wouldn't sell. But the rest was doable. I walked up to the front desk and asked who was in charge of the Sonnenberg murder case. The desk sergeant gave me a suspicious look. "You a reporter?"

I shook my head and slid my card across the counter. "Samantha Brinkman. I'm representing your key eyewitness, Cassie Sonnenberg."

He made a stink face when he looked at my card. A defense lawyer is the only thing they hate more than reporters, but I watched him do the math. I could either help the detectives set up meetings with her, or I could make her real hard to find. Not impossible, but hard.

"Have a seat. I'll see what they say."

I took a seat on one of the minimalist aluminum and plastic chairs and scrolled through my e-mail, answered a few, then checked out my Twitter feed. It's always edifying to see audience reactions after an appearance on *Crime Time*.

@sambrinkman: drug dealer whore #sleazeballlawyer

I hope the FBI shoots you in the back #fuckalllawyers

Nice tits.

Very insightful stuff. But I made a mental note to remember which bra I'd been wearing.

It was a good fifteen minutes before a slender man in slacks, a plaid sport jacket, and a navy tie came out. He wore his thinning brown hair slicked back and had a surprisingly warm smile. "Samantha Brinkman?"

I stood up. "You're the lead detective?"

"Until RHD takes it away." He looked at his watch. "Which should be any second now." He held out a hand. "Westin Emmons." We shook. "I'm a big—well, big is probably taking it too far, but I'm definitely a fan of your work."

"Thanks." Dale's case had gotten lots of coverage. And getting a cop acquitted of all charges had improved my image with the police. Though to be honest, it couldn't have gotten much worse. And the animosity was mutual. "I'm about to get appointed to represent Cassie. Just kind of a standby thing, until you get the guy. She told me about the man in the blue bandanna. He sounds like a skinhead, and her counselor's worried he might come after Cassie. I assume you guys are taking care of that."

"We are, though I think it's pretty unlikely he'll go after her. Come on back; I'll fill you in on what we've got so far."

Never in my life had I been treated this cordially in a police station. I guessed this was what it was like to be a prosecutor. Emmons led me to the modern version of a bullpen, a rabbit warren of gray cubicles, and pulled a chair to the side of his desk for me. "The mom and dad had booked a hotel room for the night. According to the hotel manager—who comped them a bottle of champagne—they were celebrating their anniversary. But the mom got food poisoning—bad fish—so they canceled and came home."

He hit a key on his computer and scanned the reports on the monitor. "Broken window in the son's room looks like the point of entry. That was the only room ransacked, probably because the mom and dad walked in on the killer. We know Abel's wallet was stolen, but we don't believe burglary was the real motive. A burglar wouldn't have taken the time to kill that way—or hung around to kill the parents. No murder weapon. Preliminary exam by the coroner says it was a large, dagger-type knife. None of the kitchen knives are missing that we can tell, so we think the killer brought the knife with him."

"And I take it you found the back door unlocked." He nodded. "You said you don't think burglary was the motive, then I guess you think it's personal. Who hates the family enough to do something like this? From what I've heard about them, it makes no sense."

Emmons pushed back from the computer and faced me with a grim expression. "That's one question we probably can answer. You already know that Cassie's description seems to fit a skinhead." I nodded. "Paula, the mother, is a city councilwoman. The white supremacist gangs in the area have been growing. Even had an arson at a black church a few months ago. We couldn't pin it on any specific gang, but someone painted a swastika on the sidewalk, so . . ." Emmons lifted his hands.

Pretty easy to connect those dots. "Did Paula take action?"

Emmons had a look of admiration. "She got a stiff gang injunction passed about a month ago. Nice work, but ever since then, she's been getting death threats at her office. And last week, someone called in a bomb threat."

That brought things into focus. "I heard skinheads were moving in, but I didn't realize it was that bad."

Emmons nodded with a look of disgust. "PENı's big here. Some Nazi Low Riders have been spotted lately, too. We're hoping that in a day or so, when Cassie's feeling a little better, she can give us more details on the guy."

They'd need it. Public Enemy Number ı and the Nazi Low Riders were two of the bigger gangs under the umbrella of the Aryan Brotherhood. Cassie's general description could probably fit a couple hundred of them. But one thing about the skinhead theory didn't make sense. "You think the mom was the target, then?" Emmons nodded. "But they weren't even home when he broke in. And other than Cassie, the mom's the only one who survived . . . sort of."

Emmons's expression said he'd already thought of that. "They took Uber that night; their car was in the driveway, so it looked like they were home. And the mom . . ." Emmons shook his head. "From what the paramedics said, she looked as close to dead as you can get and still have a heartbeat. I have to imagine he was in a hurry or he'd have stopped to make sure."

"But why break into the son's room?"

"You haven't seen the place, have you?" I shook my head. "He probably didn't know whose room he'd broken into. We found a brick on the floor just inside the window. Looks like that's what he used. My guess is, he picked the son's room because that window faced the backyard, so it was less exposed."

I supposed that made sense—for a boneheaded killer who'd go after a city councilwoman just because she got a gang injunction. "What're you doing about security?"

"We've got a guard posted outside the mom's hospital room, and I've got all units patrolling the house where Cassie's staying, plus one permanently posted outside the house."

I hadn't noticed a black-and-white unit when I'd been there. "Plain car?" Emmons nodded. "How's the mom doing?"

"Not well. She lost a lot of blood, and it seems the stab wound to the back of her neck might've done some damage to her spinal cord. We don't expect her to make it." He shook his head, his expression bleak. "Helluva thing for this little town."

I tried to imagine that crime scene, the fury of the attack that would've left a violent energy lingering in the air, the bodies splayed around the room, the coppery smell of all that blood.

It *was* a helluva thing. For any town.

THREE

When I got back to my car, I called Dale. Emmons had been pretty forth-coming, but he hadn't said much about how they planned to track down that skinhead. Not that I expected him to. He couldn't know for sure whether I'd leak something to the press and tip the guy off. But Dale might have some inside info, and if he did, he'd tell me. Maybe.

Lucky for me, he was on his way home. Unlucky for me, he was on his way home from his anger management class. Those classes always left him in a foul—angry—mood. I asked him whether he had time to talk—but in person, not on the cell phone.

"Yeah, you can come by the house. I've got a couple of hours before I have to start getting ready."

"For what?"

"For a date."

"Another crime victim?"

Dale sighed. "You're not funny."

"Who's joking?" Dale had met Chloe Monahan, the actress he'd been accused of killing, when her apartment was burglarized two months before her death. They'd started dating, but the relationship had already been going sour by the time she was murdered. None of that had helped his case any. It's not illegal for a cop to date a crime victim, but given Dale's track record, why tempt fate?

Dale gave an irritable sigh. "Not that it's any of your business, but no. Sarah's a crime-scene tech. I'll leave the front door open." He ended the call.

See what I mean? Crabby as hell.

I made it to Dale's house in Porter Ranch in just half an hour. I hadn't seen the place since I'd dropped him off the day his case got dismissed. He'd really fixed it up. It was a three-bedroom Spanish style with an enclosed courtyard in front. Dale had painted the exterior wall ochre and framed the stucco around the outer door with Spanish-style colored tiles. It wasn't a big change, but somehow, it gave the house a much warmer, more inviting look. I had to hand it to him, he had an artistic eye.

And he knew how to dress, too. He was wearing a tailored Jared Lang dress shirt, gray with darker gray paisley cuffs, and black slacks with black Italian loafers. You'd never know he was a cop. Except for the regulation haircut.

Dale was in the living room running the vacuum cleaner. I had to yell to be heard over the noise. "Getting the crime scene ready for her?"

Dale gave me a flat look. "It's good you went to law school." He bent down and ran the vacuum cleaner under the coffee table. "No, I'm trying to work through a case." He gestured to the vacuum cleaner. "It helps me think."

"Yeah, me, too." It was weird, finding out that we had little things like that in common. "You want to talk about it, I can listen."

He turned off the vacuum cleaner, pulled the plug, and pushed it into the hall closet. "No, thanks." He gestured for me to have a seat. "Want something to drink?" I shook my head. "You sure? I'm getting a water."

"I'm good." I sat in the wingback chair. Dale came back in with a bottle of water and plopped down on the couch. I knew I probably shouldn't poke the bear, but I had to ask. "How're the anger management classes going?"

Dale's expression turned dark and irritable. Yep, shouldn't have poked the bear. "Yuppie-time, crystal-twirling, pyramid-wearing bullshit." He took a long pull from his bottle of water and set it down a little too hard, a few drops splashing onto the coffee table. "It's ridiculous that they're making me do this. We were both drunk, she hit me, then I shoved her. This makes me a wife beater? Since fucking when?" He swiped away the drops of water on the coffee table with the side of his hand, his expression disgusted. "Goddamn waste of time."

Clearly, the classes were working well. The night Chloe Monahan got killed, she and Dale had had a fight. And it was true, he hadn't really roughed her up. But not everyone in the department was a fan of Dale's. Even though he'd been cleared of the murders, there were some who didn't like the idea that a homicide detective had even been charged—guilty or not. So, to appease Dale's detractors, the brass had decided he should do penance. His fight with Chloe was the only thing he could truly be blamed for. Anger management classes were the answer/punishment.

Dale sighed. "But you didn't come here to listen to me bitch about those stupid classes. What's up?"

I told him I thought I'd probably be appointed to represent Cassie Sonnenberg and what I'd learned about the murders. "You have any inside intel on the skinhead guy? Whether they've got anyone specific they think is good for it?"

"Not so far. But I heard the Robbery Homicide Division is looking at the case. I'm guessing they'll take over today. If they do, I've got sources I can work there. How's the kid doing?"

I remembered her white, pinched face, her racking sobs. "Cassie's a wreck. That was the only family she really knew."

"Yeah, I heard she was adopted." Dale shook his head. "Poor kid. What a tough break."

"Definitely. And I guess they can't really rule her out yet, but . . ."

Dale had a pained expression. "They will eventually. What about friends? Is there somebody she's close to who can take her in?"

That was even sadder. "Not that I can tell."

"How'd you wind up with the case?"

I told him about Tiegan's call. "Right now, the only adult supervision Cassie's got is people from school . . . and me." The thought made me stop. I'd had a rough childhood myself, but that was the one thing I'd been spared. "You know, it just occurred to me. Why didn't Celeste put me up for adoption?"

Dale frowned, then shook his head. "I don't know. But you can bet it had nothing to do with what was good for you."

No doubt about that. Celeste had treated me like a walking tumor all my life, dragging me from one boyfriend to the next, in search of the good life she felt she deserved but wouldn't dream of working to get on her own.

But I found out that life could get worse—a lot worse—when Celeste landed the man of her dreams: a billionaire real-estate mogul who lived in a mansion, a virtual castle, in Bel Air. The day we moved in with Sebastian Cromer, she was ecstatic. She'd achieved her life's goal of climbing into bed with all the money she could ever want. My life, however, became a living hell, because Sebastian the Magnificent was a raging pedophile.

I spent my thirteenth year on this planet in an escalating spiral of abuse that started with lascivious looks and ended with nightly rapes. I'd been afraid to tell my mother. I knew she wouldn't want to hear that her Daddy Warbucks was really a Sandusky. But I finally couldn't take it anymore, so I told her. She called me a liar, a jealous little bitch who couldn't stand to see her happy. And it wasn't until I actually managed to get a photo of him attacking me and threatened to take it to the police that she finally moved us out of there.

Dale and I talked a little longer about Cassie and the possibility that the murderer was a skinhead out for revenge. I told Dale that Glendale PD was giving Cassie and her mother protection. "But Emmons doesn't think they're really in danger."

Dale polished off his water and screwed the cap back on. "Me, either. I don't see the perp coming back for Cassie, and the mom's probably not going to make it." He glanced at the clock on the side table. "I'd better get going. If RHD takes the case, I'll let you know what I find out."

Dale walked me out to the car. When he saw Beulah, he shook his head. "When are you going to let go of this thing? You need money? I can help you out."

I glared at him, then patted the hood. "Don't listen to him, honey. He can't help it. You know how superficial men can be."

Dale chuckled, but he winced at the screech of rusty hinges when he opened the driver's door for me.

I backed out of the driveway, mentally begging Beulah not to embarrass me. Luck was with me—or maybe Beulah realized her days were numbered with Dale around. I pulled away without a hitch. When I made it to the freeway, I called Tiegan to find out how Cassie was doing.

"She's sleeping. Those pills really knock her out."

"Probably for the best." I told her what I'd heard about Cassie's mother being the likely target.

Tiegan sounded resigned. "I guess that makes sense. In a sick, demented sort of way."

I wondered how much Tiegan knew about this family, about Cassie. "How long have you been Cassie's counselor?"

"Five months. At the beginning of the year, I was just her English teacher, but when her counselor went out on disability, Cassie asked me to fill in."

"I didn't know teachers doubled up like that."

"They don't usually. But I've got experience as a counselor, and the school was shorthanded, so I agreed to help out."

"Then you've gotten to know her pretty well."

Tiegan hesitated before answering. "To an extent. She's not the most . . . forthcoming student I've ever had. But I did notice in her file that she'd bounced between foster homes until she was four. By the time the Sonnenbergs found her, she was on the brink of being a foster child for life."

"At four?"

Tiegan's voice was sad—and somewhat bitter. "Everyone wants a baby. Very few want toddlers. And no one wants them after that."

What a hard, cold reality that was. "Does Cassie know her birth mother? Or father?"

"It would've helped a lot right now if she did, but no. It was a closed adoption."

I thought about that. I'm not sure it's all fluffy unicorns and rainbows when a child gets to meet the mother who gave her up. But to have that door forever slammed in a child's face, to know she can never even find out who her mother was, must be a whole new vista of hurt and abandonment. "Did Cassie seem happy at home?"

Tiegan gave a grim little laugh. "Are any of them happy at home at this age? Let me put it this way: she didn't seem *un*happy. But we didn't talk about her family much. We mainly talked about how she was getting along in school, her friends, what she wanted to do when she graduated. That sort of thing."

"And what did she want to do?"

"She wanted to be an actress."

Of course she did. The little girl who'd been abandoned craved a massive, adoring audience to fill the gaping hole in her heart.

FOUR

I spent the rest of Saturday doing boring chores and errands. By six o'clock I was starving and ready to sit down. I called Michelle Fusco and asked her to meet me at our usual fave, Barney's Beanery, a legendary bar and diner where old-school rockers like Jim Morrison and Janis Joplin used to hang. It's practically walking distance from my place. Not far from hers, either.

Michelle had been my best friend since sixth grade, and she was a crack paralegal. I'd begged her to come work with me, because she was the best in the business. But to be honest, it was a little scary—kind of like having a friend become a lover. We were closer than most sisters, and we both knew that working together could ruin that. But I'd had a feeling it was meant to be. And I'd been right. We'd had some lean times and some scary times. But most of all, we'd had good times.

Michelle was already nursing a bottle of Stella Artois and a basket of French fries when I got there. The smells of old grease, spilled beer, and charred meat were thick, and the crowd at the bar was cheering and yelling at a hockey game on the television. I scanned the crowd and saw they were all wearing T-shirts that had pictures of the Hollywood sign and logos like LA's THE PLACE! Out-of-towners. It figured. I'd never seen anyone in

LA give a damn about hockey. As I sat down, I waved to the waiter and pointed to Michelle's beer. I took a handful of fries. I'd already told her about trying to get myself appointed to represent Cassie. Now I filled her in on Emmons's theory that the killer was a skinhead. "I guess it fits."

Michelle looked noncommittal. "It's all anyone *can* think at this point, right?"

That much was true. "According to the cops, the Nazi Low Riders really had a hard-on for Paula. Death threats, a bomb threat. It's not a big stretch to think they'd do something like this. But I'm going to check my own sources on the skinhead angle."

"Tuck?"

I nodded. Tuck Rosenberg—not Jewish, just very German—was a former client and current shot caller of the Los Angeles branch of the Nazi Low Riders. "If they put out an official hit on Paula Sonnenberg, he'd know about it." I noticed Michelle's golden-brown hair was swinging freely tonight. "How come no Scünci? They all in the wash, or something?" Michelle, who looked a lot like Jessica Biel, always wore Scüncis. And I always gave her shit about it.

Michelle threw a fry at me. "Shut up."

The waiter delivered my beer, and we ordered cheeseburgers. I took a sip. "Wait, I got it. Brad doesn't like them." Michelle's sour expression told me I'd nailed it. "I'm right, aren't I?"

Michelle's latest love interest was an associate in a white-shoe law firm. The kind of law firm that makes billions and pays its associates bubkes. I'd been skeptical about Michelle dating a guy who'd work in a place like that. But when he'd stopped by the office to pick her up, I got the attraction. He was a nice guy and handsome—in a white-bread, super-straight, squeaky-clean sort of way.

She gave me a flinty look. "No, you're not right." Michelle pushed the fries away. "Ugh. Stop me. I can't afford to grow out of my jeans. I don't get paid enough." She gave me a meaningful look. I pointedly turned and stared out the window. "But this case should be pretty easy money."

"Easy. But not much. I'm out of a job the minute they make an arrest."

Michelle took a sip of her beer and raised an eyebrow. "Unless it's her. I know it seems too weird, a fifteen-year-old girl doing all that, but is there any chance?"

I shrugged. "Never say never. And she was the only one who survived. But . . ." I just didn't think so.

Michelle shook her head. "It doesn't feel right to me, either." Her features grew sad. "That girl has got to be one giant mess."

"She really is."

Michelle peeled the label off her bottle of beer. "Well, for the time being, the case is good publicity. And you could use some. Your shine's been fading, since you've been out of the limelight for the past few months."

"True." Dale's case had made me momentarily famous enough to pick up some high-profile cases. But none of them wound up going to trial, so I'd been out of the public eye for a while. It's not about wanting to be famous, per se. It's all about building the client list. Famous lawyers get big cases. Big cases mean big money. Usually. Well, sometimes. "Anyway, even if I don't make much on the case, I don't mind helping her out for a little while. The girl's had a rough life." I told her about Cassie's childhood.

Michelle studied me. "You can probably identify with some of that."

Other than Dale, she was the only one in my life who knew what I'd been through. But I hated talking about it. "So I guess that means there's hope for Cassie. Look how well I turned out."

Michelle rolled her eyes. "Eat your cheeseburger."

The problem of what to do for Deshawn plagued me. I considered my options. The only thing I could do for him right now was hide him somewhere. If I maxed out my personal credit card, I could put him up in a two-star hotel for a couple of weeks. I just needed to buy some time so I could think of a solution. I called him, but it went straight to voice mail. I tried not to think about what that might mean.

With nothing to do except worry, I tried to distract myself by staying busy for the rest of the weekend and managed to bring my caseload up to speed. By eleven o'clock Sunday night, I was dead tired. I closed my laptop; took a steamy, hot shower; and fell into bed. I was asleep within seconds.

But it didn't matter. I had the dream anyway.

It's always the same. I thrust the knife into his chest again and again and again. I stand back and wait for him to fall, but he doesn't. He smiles. That same sick, leering smile that always made my stomach lurch. I stare, confused. How can he still be standing? In an agony of frustration, I jam the knife into his stomach again and again, sobbing with the effort. But as I pull back and wait for him to fall, he turns into a giant, and he pins me against the wall with hands that feel like steel clamps. I close my eyes and try to wrench free, twisting my body back and forth, my heels kicking against the wall. Then I feel a blast of hot, fetid air. I open my eyes to see that his mouth is open wide, and it's a huge, cavernous black hole. I feel myself being sucked into the darkness. Trapped, terrified, I scream and scream.

And I wake up to the sound of my own rasping croak, a pounding heart, and a T-shirt soaked in sweat. I used to believe the dreams would stop, that the real-life nightmare that fueled them would fade with time. But it's been years since the Sebastian Cromer chapter of my life ended, and the dreams still come—almost every night. I stared out the window at the still dark sky and wished I could go back to sleep. But I knew better than to try. The nightmare always left me feeling sick and jittery. The only way to wash out the memory was to get up and get moving.

I pounded two cups of coffee standing at the kitchen sink and headed into the office.

Unlike my old digs, which were in the heart of gang territory in the San Fernando Valley, my new office is in West Hollywood, not far from my apartment. My "suite" consists of two offices and a reception area. Michelle's desk is in the reception area. My investigator, Alex Medrano, has the smaller office on the right, and my office, which is maybe five feet bigger, has what they call a "partial view." Meaning that if you stand on tiptoe and tilt your head all the way to the right, you can see a sliver of Sunset Boulevard.

It was only seven o'clock when I got in, but Alex was already there. Like Deshawn, Alex Medrano is a former client. Unlike Deshawn, he had not been a lifelong devotee of criminal enterprise. He'd just used his insane computer skills to steal money for his family when they were going through a really bad time. I'd managed to get him a sweetheart deal in return for his agreement to show the DA how he'd done it. And he'd turned out to be the best investigator I'd ever seen—anywhere. If he couldn't find something, it didn't exist.

On top of all that, he was gorgeous. Huge dark eyes with enviable lashes; thick, wavy black hair; and high cheekbones. When he dressed up, he looked like something out of *GQ*. Could he be that beautiful and also be straight? Alas, no. But that didn't keep him from working it with the ladies when the need arose. And they routinely melted like ice cubes on a hot stove.

I quickly brought him up to speed on the Sonnenberg murders. "I'll call the court when they open up in half an hour and ask for the appointment. But since I already met with Cassie and the lead detective, I shouldn't have a problem."

Alex was excited. "I heard about that on the news. It's crazy. What can I do?"

Now that I knew the cops were running hard on the skinhead theory, I'd decided to explore other possibilities. "Check out the family. I'm looking for any other enemies they might have."

"I'm on it." Alex headed to his office.

At eight thirty sharp, I called the court. It turned out I'd had a little competition for the case. A couple of other lawyers had e-mailed the court and asked for the appointment. But the school's lawyer had also e-mailed. And he'd explained how I was already "on top of the case." I got the appointment.

Five minutes later, I got a phone call from Dale. "Keep this to yourself, Sam. They spotted a Nazi Low Rider on surveillance footage from a liquor-store parking lot. They should be bringing him in any time now."

"Did RHD take the case?"

"Yeah. And I know what you're going to ask, but I can't—"

"Yes, you can. They love you at RHD. Get me in to watch the interview."

Dale sighed. "I'll try."

Ten minutes later, Dale called me back. I was in.

FIVE

The Nazi Low Rider was handcuffed to the table, but he still managed to look relaxed as he slouched down in the chair and glanced around the interrogation room. He looked like a biker in his worn, dirty jeans and beat-up motorcycle boots. I supposed there was no reason a skinhead couldn't be a biker, too—though I'd guess some bikers might disagree. His shoulder-length black hair lay flat on his head, and the ends were frizzy and jagged. My hand itched to take a pair of scissors to it. He looked into the one-way mirror—our viewing window—and raised his free hand in a one-finger salute.

I returned it and whispered to Dale. "I don't remember Cassie saying the guy had long hair."

Dale shrugged. "She said he was wearing a blue bandanna."

Right. I'd forgotten that. At a fast glance in the dark, the blue bandanna was probably all she'd had a chance to see. Detective Westin Emmons and a tall, beefy man entered the interrogation room. His red-blond hair had shrunk to a monk's fringe that barely made it all the way around his large head. Both were dressed in shirtsleeves and slacks. The bigger detective made the introductions. "I'm Detective Rusty Templeton, and this little guy here is Detective Westin Emmons, come from Glendale PD to help us out. Thanks for talking to us, Mr. Horrigan."

He gave them a cold, lazy smile. "You can call me Dominic. Seeing as we're having a friendly chat." He yanked his cuffed hand against the chain. "Though I don't usually wear these when I'm with friends."

Rusty Templeton took the lead. He returned the cold smile. "Funny, that's not what I heard."

Dominic stared at the detective, his expression deadpan. "God, you cops are so *fucking* funny."

Rusty ignored him and went straight at it. "We've got surveillance footage that puts you at a liquor store just a mile away from the Sonnenberg house on the night of the murders. Where'd you go when you left the parking lot?"

Dominic sniffed, then made a hacking sound as though he were dredging up something from the bottom of his gut. He looked around, and I thought for sure he was going to spit on the floor, but he decided to swallow whatever it was instead. My stomach lurched. "Where'd I go? Home, that's where. That liquor store's right by my house. Notice I didn't ask you which liquor store? That's because I go to the same friggin' place every time. Ask Tio. He's the owner. He'll tell ya." Dominic made that hacking sound again.

Even Templeton looked disgusted. "We know you and your buddies got mighty pissed off about that gang injunction. We've got information that there was talk of putting out a hit on Paula Sonnenberg."

A gang injunction is basically a restraining order that lets the cops bust members of the named gang for doing just about anything—walking too slow, walking too fast, standing in one place too long. You name it, the bangers can get busted for it. If an injunction is enforced seriously enough, it can practically clear a gang out of the covered area. So the injunction in Glendale would really cramp their style.

Dominic snorted. "There's always some young peckerwood with more mouth than brains talking shit."

Templeton raised an eyebrow. "You saying there was no hit?"

"If there was, I sure as hell never heard about it. Look, I hated that bitch and I don't mind that someone wasted her. But I didn't do those fucking murders. If I had, she wouldn't be in no hospital. She'd be in a morgue."

Templeton shrugged. "People get sloppy."

Dominic looked at him with contempt. "Not with this shit they don't. I'm doing this, I go straight at the bitch. Put her down fast and hard. No mistakes. And I don't bother with the rest of the family."

Templeton leaned back and looked at Dominic through narrowed eyes. "Unless you had to. And I can see you thinking that wasn't so bad. Since she targeted your family, you've got the right to take out hers. An eye for an eye."

A fair point. But Dominic shook his head and gave a mighty snort. "I didn't do it, man."

Templeton gave him the typical skeptical-cop look. "Then tell us who's been talking about the hit."

Dominic tilted his head and looked at Templeton like he was an idiot. He spoke in a flat, hard voice. "There was no talk, and I never heard about no hit."

Templeton kept at it for a while longer and tried to squeeze names out of him, but he got nowhere. Ten minutes later, he pulled the plug. "I'm gonna go talk with my partner here for a bit, so you sit tight."

Dominic yanked the chain on his cuffed hand and gave him a dirty look. "Fuck off."

Seconds later, Templeton opened the door to the viewing room and waved us out. We stepped into the hallway. I introduced Emmons to Dale.

Templeton glanced at me, then focused on Dale. "What do you think? Anything here?"

Dale shook his head. "You covered it. And unless you got his prints somewhere, I don't know how you hold him."

Templeton looked at me. "You got any bright ideas, Counselor?"

"No. You've got nothing. You have to cut him loose." But Dominic's point about going after Paula first had made me curious about one thing. "Do you know in what order they got attacked?"

Emmons answered. "Looks like the boy, Abel, was first, since that's where he broke in. The mom and dad were both found in his room, so they probably heard something and came in to check. That's when the suspect got them. I'm guessing they came in one at a time, with the mom being last—looked like she fell on him. Also because the killer didn't take the time to make sure she was dead."

That made sense. "So you think he didn't go after Cassie because he was pressed for time?"

Emmons shrugged. "Or he didn't know she was there. She never came out of her room."

"Sure would help if the mom made it," Dale said.

"Ya think?" Templeton had an exasperated look.

I wasn't sure how much help she'd be even if she did survive. "She got attacked from behind, right?"

Emmons nodded. "Right. We're hoping she got a look at him before she passed out."

I didn't want to tell him that even if she did, with the kind of injuries she had, she might not remember what she saw. "So the door knock didn't pan out?"

Templeton shook his head. "Middle class suburban 'hood, after one a.m. No one saw or heard a damn thing."

I thought that was kind of weird. "On a Friday night? With a window broken out? You'd think at least some teenagers would be up."

Emmons shrugged. "It's a pretty quiet town. And it's not as though there were shots fired."

"So what's your next step?" Dale asked. "You going to check out the rest of the family?"

Templeton nodded. "We'll look into the son and the dad, see if they gave anyone a reason to off them."

I wasn't about to let them know it, but I was way ahead of them.

When I got back to the office, Alex came out and sat on the edge of Michelle's desk. His cologne wafted through the air. He always wore Acqua di Gio. It was wonderful. "I think I've found a little hint of something on Stephen."

I set down my briefcase on her desk. "What is it?"

Michelle looked up from her monitor, annoyed. "Will you two get off my desk and go yammer somewhere else?" She pushed away my briefcase. "Or don't you care whether your sentencing memo on Graveman gets done? 'Cause I'm good either way."

I grabbed my briefcase before it fell on the floor and motioned for Alex to follow me to my office. "She been like this all day?"

Alex shook his head. "Worse."

Michelle folded her arms and glared at us. I wiggled my fingers at her and smiled. "Kidding." We went into my office and closed the door.

I plopped down on the couch. It was just a plain beige number I'd cadged at a low-end office-furniture warehouse, but it was a new, plush feeling to have a couch to lie down on, and I did it as much as possible. "So what've you got on the dad?"

Alex pulled over one of the chairs that faced my desk and sat down. "I don't know if this guy is going to qualify as an enemy who'd hate Stephen enough to kill the whole family, but it seems there was some kind of issue at work. Stephen got the guy fired, and the guy bitched about it like crazy on Glass Door."

Glass Door is a website where people can vent or crow—mostly vent—about businesses and bosses. I frowned. "Kind of don't see how getting fired adds up to mass murder. Especially after he bitched about Stephen in public."

Alex gave a little smirk. "Where do you think the term *going postal* came from?"

I shrugged. "I suppose. Anyway, the more you know . . . Got any idea how to flesh it out?"

"I'll have to social engineer it."

No one was better at working the phones and the people who answered them than Alex. "Sounds good."

"I also have some of Abel's friends for us to talk to."

I thought about that for a moment. "Hold off on them for now. I want to talk to Cassie first. See who she thinks knew him best."

And who liked him least.

SIX

I had to be in court for a hearing that afternoon. The cop who'd taken my client's statement claimed he'd read him his rights. My client and his dim-witted cohort claimed otherwise. Even assuming everyone showed up on time and didn't dick around with meaningless questions—which happens so seldom it's frightening—the earliest I could get to Cassie would be four o'clock.

As predicted, the cop was late, and the DA decided this was his career-making case. I didn't get out of there till four thirty. I called Barbara Reeber and asked whether I could come by and see Cassie.

"I'm okay with it, but I'm not sure about Cassie. She's been holed up in her room all day."

"Why don't I drop over and see? If she's not in the mood, I'll take off."

Barbara was good with that. On my way there, I wondered what kind of shape Cassie would be in. It was hard to imagine the kind of hell she had to be going through. When Barbara let me in, she said in a low voice, "I told her you were coming, and she didn't seem to mind. But let me go get her."

Barbara turned to head down the hall, but I stopped her. "Maybe it'd be better if I talked to her alone. She might be more comfortable if it's one-on-one." And I didn't want Cassie to worry about what she said. If we were alone, I could promise her confidentiality.

Barbara looked a little uncertain. "I guess . . . if that's what Cassie wants."

I gave her a reassuring smile. "Only one way to find out."

Barbara led the way down the hall and stopped at the first door on the left. She knocked and said, "Cassie? Samantha Brinkman is here to see you."

Cassie's voice floated through the door, weak and thin. "Okay."

Barbara opened the door. Cassie was sitting on her bed, her back against the wall, knees drawn up to her chin. The shades were drawn, and the room was fairly dim, but I could see that her eyes and nose were red and her face was splotchy. The air smelled salty, like freshly shed tears. I tried to give her a supportive smile. "Would you like to talk to me here in your room, just the two of us?"

Cassie looked at Barbara uncertainly, then nodded. "Sure."

I patted Barbara's arm. "I won't keep her long." Barbara clearly didn't love the idea, but she left, and I closed the door behind her. "Before we start, I want you to know something. I'm a lawyer and you're my client. That means everything you say to me is privileged, and I can't repeat it to anyone. Ever. Got it?"

Cassie tilted her head and paused briefly, then said, "Okay."

I sat on the rocking chair next to the bed. "What's it been like staying here? From what I hear, you and Debbie weren't that close."

Cassie swallowed and picked at a thread on the knee of her jeans. "You really can't tell anyone what I say?"

"I really can't. Or I lose my bar card. That means I can't be a lawyer anymore."

Cassie blew out a breath and rubbed her eyes with the heels of her hands. "It totally sucks. I mean, they're nice to me and all, and I know they don't have to do this." She gave me a plaintive look. "But why couldn't I stay with my friends? Tawny says her mom and dad would be okay with it."

"I'm not sure." That'd been Tiegan's call, but I didn't want to hang her out to dry. "This is only temporary. We'll figure something out." It sounded lame, but I didn't know what else to say. "How are you doing otherwise?"

Cassie put her hands over her eyes. "I miss them all so much!" Tears rolled down beneath them, and she bit her lip. After a few moments, she collected herself and wiped her face with the back of her hand. "You know I was adopted, right?" I nodded. "I was in a horrible foster home before they adopted me. I still remember how happy I was when Mom and Dad took me out of there. And they . . . they told me if they hadn't, probably no one would ever have adopted me."

They did *what*? Why on earth would they say a thing like that? I was glad the room was dark. I tried to keep my voice even. "I guess you were pretty grateful to them."

"Totally. Mom always used to say how lucky I was."

Again, why? Why say a thing like that? But I'd caught a hint of an edge in Cassie's voice. "That must've sucked, to always have to be saying you're grateful for something most kids take for granted."

Cassie stretched out her legs and stared at her feet. "Yeah, it kind of did. But she wasn't trying to be mean. I know she loves me." She gave me a tiny, tremulous smile. "I'm so glad I get to talk to you."

Her situation was different from mine. By the time I was Cassie's age, I'd long since faced the fact that Celeste neither loved nor even liked me. But I could definitely relate to her. "Me, too."

She spoke in a soft voice. "But what was really hard was when I wanted to find out who my birth mother was. She got so upset. She was like, 'We're your family. Your birth mother never gave a damn about you. Why do you care about her?' I told her I was just curious, you know? Like, where did I come from? Did I have brothers or sisters somewhere? I tried to tell her that it didn't mean I didn't love her and think of her as my mom, but . . ."

It seemed to make her feel better—or at least distract her from her misery—to talk about her problems as the adopted kid. I finished the thought for her. "But she didn't get it."

Cassie shook her head. "And she didn't get how hard it was for me with other kids. Everyone could always tell I was adopted. I don't look anything like them."

That was certainly true. Cassie was medium height, a little on the tall side, blonde, and blue-eyed. The Sonnenbergs were all on the short side, with dark hair and eyes. "How did you get along with Abel?"

Cassie bit her lip. "We had some . . . issues. He was jealous because he thought Mom and Dad did too much for me, that they were always bending over backward for me."

"Was he right?"

"No!" Cassie stopped and took a deep breath. "I don't know why he thought that. I just hoped he'd get over it and move on. Like maybe when we got older, he'd stop being so jerky and we'd be friends. I'd have a big brother to hang out with." Cassie put her hands over her eyes again. "Now I'll never get to!" Her chest heaved with silent sobs.

I felt awkward; I didn't know what to say. "I'm so sorry, Cassie."

Finally, she dropped her hands to her lap. Her eyes were red, but there were no tears. Probably all cried out. She leaned against the wall again, pulled her knees back up under her chin, and wrapped her arms around her legs. "Can I ask you a question?" I nodded. "Barbara said that they arrested a guy."

"Not exactly. They detained him for questioning. But they don't think he's involved." At least, not yet. Cassie looked disappointed. I didn't blame her. I was, too. "Can I ask you a question?"

"About the . . . ?"

"No. You've had enough of that, I'd guess." Cassie gave me a grateful look. "Do you know who Abel used to hang out with?"

Cassie frowned. "I know a few guys, I think. We really don't . . ." She paused and swallowed. "I mean *didn't* hang together." Cassie took a deep breath. "He used to hang out with Tommy Deerfield a lot. And maybe Eric Asner."

I pulled out my pocket-size notepad and wrote down the names. "What about enemies? Did he have problems with anyone?"

Cassie thought about it for a moment. "I know there was a girl who got into a fight with him at a party." She looked up at the ceiling. "I think her name is Janessa . . . I can't remember her last name."

"Not a problem." The first name might be distinctive enough to get us there.

Cassie tilted her head and peered at me. "You think somebody did this because of Abel?"

"I'm just looking into all the possibilities." Emmons had said the killer probably chose his room to break into because it was the best point of entry, since his window faced the backyard. But all avenues had to be explored. And although Templeton had said they'd be looking into the possibility that Abel or Stephen had been the target, they were busy running down the skinhead angle right now. So for the moment, I figured I'd have the field to myself, and I wanted to make the most of it.

"But what about that guy I saw running away? They're saying he was probably one of those skinhead gangbangers. You think Abel was involved with those guys?"

I wasn't sure whether she knew her mother had been targeted. If not, I sure didn't want to be the one to tell her. I dodged the question. "Not so far. But I'm sure the cops will find out."

Barbara knocked on the door, then opened it. "I'm sorry to interrupt, but it's time for dinner. You're welcome to join us, Sam."

I stood up. "Thanks, that's very kind of you, but I've got to head back. Cassie, remember: You can call me whenever, okay?" She nodded.

It was after six by the time I left, and the freeway was still a bumper-to-bumper nightmare. There was no point in going back to the office.

As I inched along the 405 freeway, I thought about Cassie and how, in some ways, I identified with her. Was it just because of our messed-up childhoods? For some reason I didn't think so. It felt deeper than that. I tried to figure out what it was about her that resonated, but I couldn't put my finger on it.

I gave up and thought about what Paula had said to Cassie, telling her how lucky she was and that no one else would've adopted her. What the hell was up with that? It sure didn't fit with the caring, kind Paula people had described. I wondered whether maybe Cassie had exaggerated. She obviously had abandonment issues; who wouldn't, with her childhood? Maybe those issues had colored her memory, filtered innocuous comments through a damaged lens. I'd had a couple of clients who'd been adopted, and I knew how common it was for them to have serious, sometimes debilitating feelings of worthlessness. For my clients, those feelings had run deep enough to land them in prison. But if Paula really had said those things to Cassie, she was either an incredibly insensitive jerk or she was an emotional sadist. And I wondered about the rest of the family; what was the story with the dad or Cassie's brother, Abel, who'd gotten into a fight with that girl . . . Janessa?

There definitely was more to this than met the eye, but that was nothing new. Even the most mundane liquor-store robbery has a few layers beneath the pointed gun and the emptied cash register. But I had the feeling this one was more layered than most.

As I pulled off the freeway, I got a call on my cell phone. I didn't recognize the number, so I let it go to voice mail. When I listened to the message, I was so light-headed with relief that I had to pull over and park the car. I leaned back in my seat and closed my eyes.

It was Deshawn. He was alive. So far.

SEVEN

I called him back and asked him how he was doing.

He huffed. "How the hell you *think* I'm doing? Runnin' for my life is how I'm doin.' Leo's people be lookin' for me everywhere. You got my money?"

I deduced that Leo was the drug-dealer-slash-nemesis. "I'm sorry, but no. Not yet." I told him about my idea to put him up in a hotel for a little while.

He sounded suspicious. "Where?"

Seriously? He was getting picky at a time like this? "Anywhere you think they won't look for you. But the budget's tight, and you may have to be there for a couple of weeks, so be reasonable."

A few seconds passed. I heard car horns blasting in the background, then he asked, "How about Oxnard?"

"Kind of far north for you, isn't it?"

"Yeah. For Leo, too. He stays down in Riverside."

Good thinking. I told Deshawn I'd set him up. "But go easy on the room service, will ya? This is going to max out my credit card."

He huffed. "How come I wind up with the broke lawyer? I thought y'all were s'posed to be rich."

Yeah, me, too. We ended the call, and I hooked him up with a room at the Stay Inn. Which I hoped he'd take as a game plan. Then I texted him the information and told him to get up there ASAP and that I'd be in touch. It was just a temporary fix, but at least he was safe for now.

I called Alex when I got home. "Want to go see new sights, meet new people, expand your horizons?"

He saw right through me. "You mean door knock the crime-scene neighborhood? Didn't the cops already do that? The book says that's the first thing—"

"I'm going to buy every copy I can find of that damn book and burn them." Alex, being the driven Type-A that he was, had decided to compensate for his lack of experience as an investigator by reading every book on the subject he could get his hands on. But he'd found his bible in one book in particular, *The Professional Guide to Private Investigation*. And no matter how many times I threatened to smack him in the head with it, he kept citing crap like this at me. "Did that damn book tell you how often the cops find no one home and move on? Or how often they just walk away when someone says, *'No hablo inglés,'* even when it's obviously bullshit? Or that some folks just prefer not to talk to cops?" A lot more of them preferred not to talk to defense lawyers, but that was beside the point.

"Okay, okay. When?"

"Tomorrow. Late afternoon." That way we'd catch the kids and stay-at-home parents and still be around when people got home from work.

"Dress code?"

I'd taught him that. Dress for your audience; make them feel at ease. If you're talking to a bunch of stoners, don't show up in a three-piece suit. "Dress shirt and jacket, no tie. We're going for middle class, suburban. And don't forget your recorder."

Lesson number one when doing witness interviews: never do it alone. If a witness takes the stand and decides to "forget" some juicy nugget from our interview, I can't testify about what he really said. Lawyers can't testify in their own cases. But Alex can.

And the recorder stays hidden because it's just for my own benefit. I always make a show of taking notes in front of the witness, but I can't do a good job of questioning if I'm constantly scribbling.

Also, if I decide to call the witness, I have to turn over those notes to the prosecution. So I don't necessarily write everything down. It's a nifty little trick, but it only blindsides the prosecutors who don't talk to the witnesses before they take the stand. It always amazes me that there are prosecutors who don't interview their witnesses ahead of time—some because they're lazy, others because they're afraid it might look like they've coached the witness. I say, talk to your witnesses, squeeze them for every last drop of information, and don't worry about that coaching nonsense. It's more important to know every inch of your case, and it avoids nasty surprises. As far as I'm concerned, putting any witness on the stand without knowing exactly what he'll say is as dumb as it gets.

I got off the freeway at Woodman and headed toward Ventura Boulevard. I was on my way to the Chimney Sweep, a dive bar in Studio City. The name alone says, "Why go there?" But two things made it perfect for my purpose: the ambience—sparsely populated and so dark you have to hold on to your drink to find it—and its location, tucked into a dingy, aging mini mall and sandwiched between a ballroom dance studio and a Middle Eastern restaurant. It was a place where no one would recognize the Nazi Low Riders' shot caller, Tuck Rosenberg. Neither one of us wanted to be seen together, but it was really life-threatening for him. The press had mentioned that I was helping Cassie. As far as the Nazi Low Riders were concerned, that put me in the enemy camp.

From the moment I walked in the door, I wished I'd worn latex gloves. But the truth was, nothing short of a hazmat suit would've made me feel okay in that place. I refused to feel my way through the maze of small tables, afraid of what I'd touch, so I bumped into more than a few of them in the inky darkness before I made it to the bar. I ordered a club soda but passed on the offer of lime—the pathetic excuses I saw in the plastic condiment tray were so dry and shriveled they looked like dead worms—and took my drink to one of the few booths. The middle of the cheaply shellacked table was a lot lighter than the six inches around the perimeter, which probably hadn't been wiped since The Clash broke up. The damp air was heavy with layers of booze sweat, cake disinfectant that smelled like urine (and maybe was, but I tried not to think about it), and that musky old-building smell. I couldn't see the water stains on the walls, but I knew they had to be there.

The good news: there were only three other people in the place. Two older men, hunched at a small table, their heads bowed over their beer bottles, and one older woman who sat in the back and worked a crossword puzzle book, an unlit cigarette behind her ear. None of them seemed even remotely interested in me—or anything else.

Five minutes later, Tuck showed up. It's hard not to notice him, and even the three sad sacks in the place looked up for a moment when he walked in. Six foot four, long blond hair, built like a Viking, and tatted like the Illustrated Man, Tuck filled the doorway as though the bar was some kid's dollhouse. I waved him over.

The booth creaked as he lowered himself into the seat. He glanced around the room, then spoke to me in a low voice. "Nice to see you."

I waved him off. "No it isn't, so thanks for doing this." I nodded at the bar. "If you want a drink, I recommend . . . nothing."

His eyes slid to the side, took in the bar, and came back to me. "You heard they picked up Dominic on those murders?"

Heard and saw. But telling him I'd actually been at the cop shop wouldn't help matters. "He says there was no official hit put out on Paula Sonnenberg." I looked into his eyes.

Tuck met my gaze with a solid ice-blue stare. "It's true. And believe me, if anyone ordered a hit, I'd know about it."

"You sure about that?" The white gangs weren't known for their commitment to organizational management structure. They got into a lot of random shit because basically, they were a bunch of violent, low-IQ misfits. Not that other gangs weren't. They just tended to be a little more amenable to the corporate hierarchy.

Tuck sighed, an implicit acknowledgment that a wolf pack was more organized. "I can tell you for sure there was no official hit in the works. That shit doesn't happen without my say-so. But can I promise you some dumbass didn't decide to go rogue?" He shook his head, his expression resigned. "No. No one can do that."

I pressed on. This might be my only chance to talk to him. "Anyone been bragging?"

Tuck shook his head. "And something this big, I'd definitely hear about it. They'd want to take credit."

True enough. One thing all gang members seem to have in common is the need to yap about their exploits. "If you hear anything, can you let me know?"

Tuck shook his head. "No promises. I don't hang my own people out to dry. But I can say this much: it doesn't feel like a Rider."

"Because?"

"Too risky. Breaking into a house in the middle of the night, expecting to get away with offing a whole family—especially a white family." He shook his head. "Not our style."

Not *his* style, anyway. Tuck was pretty smart. But the same couldn't be said for his BFFs. "For your sake, I hope you're right." If it were a Nazi Low Rider, Tuck's operation would be in the crosshairs of every cop shop in town for a long, long time.

Tuck blew out a breath. "Got that right." He gave me another one of his solid stares. "We done?"

"Yeah." I stood up. "I'll leave first."

I wove my way through the empty tables, arms and shoulders scrunched together to avoid touching anything. I didn't let myself take a full, deep breath until I got into my car.

As I headed down Ventura Boulevard to the freeway, I saw an In-N-Out Burger. My stomach saw it, too, and started grumbling. Now that

I was out of that sinkhole of a bar, I realized I was starving. I pulled in behind a long line of cars—I've never seen an In-N-Out that wasn't packed—and took out my phone to check my e-mails. I'd deleted a bunch of junk when my phone rang. It was Michelle. "What's up?"

"You're going to be in the office tomorrow morning."

"Says who?" Not that I wasn't planning to be there, but it was my go-to reaction to any order.

"Those creepy Orozcos are coming in. Arturo called to give me the heads-up."

My heart gave a hard thump. "What'd you tell them?"

"That I'd see if you were available. But he'd already hung up." Michelle gave an irritable huff. "I'd really appreciate it if you'd wrap it up with them."

I'd represented Ricardo Orozco on an ugly gang shooting. He and his fellow Grape Street Boyz dickweeds had shot up a house that was supposedly the *casa* where the shot caller for the rival gang—the Southside Creepers—lived. Except he didn't and never had. And Ricardo had fired the shots that killed a six-month-old baby in his playpen and maimed a young girl for life. He'd laughed about it, said the baby would've just grown up to be a Southside Creeper piece of shit, and made foul remarks about the "gimp-assed *puta*" who'd "never get laid now." In short, I'd say Ricardo was a sewer rat, but that was unfair shade to throw at sewer rats.

Unfortunately—I say that because I'd actually wanted to lose this time—the case went belly-up when the gang found a way to shred the sole eyewitness's credibility. All that was left was an illegal weapon possession charge. Ricardo wound up with a low-term state prison deal that, for him, was nothing more than a vacay with old homies.

Injustice is a fact of daily life. Whether it's a jerk who steals your parking space or a judge who screws you with a bad ruling. You don't like it, but you move on. You deal. But there's a line, a point after which you don't deal. At least, there is for me. And that case had crossed it.

Just before Ricardo's guilty plea, while the court was busy with another matter, I sidled up to the custody list—a printout that shows where prisoners are supposed to be housed—and made a slight change. Ricardo wound up getting assigned to the Southside Creeper section of the jail. Half an hour after he got to his cell, they found his body. He'd been shivved at least a dozen times. No witnesses.

Ricardo's father, Ernesto, and his brother, Arturo Orozco, asked me to look into the murder. They had a civil lawyer working on the money side of things, but they wanted to find the *pendejo* who'd sent Ricardo into the death trap. They didn't believe it was just a mistake, and they didn't trust the cops. Since I'd done such a great job on Ricardo's case, they asked me to take care of it. I couldn't afford to say no. I needed to control the situation. And I needed to find someone I could blame for altering the custody list to keep my neck off their chopping block. That meant someone who'd have access to the custody lists *and* someone who deserved to be the object of the Orozcos' wrath.

But it'd been a few months, and the Orozcos were getting impatient. It wouldn't be long before someone pointed out that I'd been one of the people standing next to the bailiff's desk, where the custody list had been that day. And if the Orozcos got wind of that, they'd turn their sights on me. They wouldn't care that no one had actually seen me make the change on that list. "Beyond a reasonable doubt" meant nothing to them.

I tried to sound reassuring, though my mouth had gone dry and my heart was beating like a metronome on crack. "Don't worry, Michy. Their case should wrap up pretty soon."

By the time I got my food, I'd lost my appetite. I threw the bag onto the passenger seat and took a long swig of my soft drink.

I'd have to come up with a story to back them off, buy myself some more time. Then I'd have to drill down on that fall guy.

Or the Orozcos would drill down on me.

EIGHT

I had the nightmare again that night. This time I woke myself up with actual screams instead of my usual strangled croaks. I peered at the clock on my nightstand. Four a.m., early even for me. But I didn't try to go back to sleep. I couldn't take the risk. The Orozcos were beyond punctual—probably their only virtue—and I couldn't leave Michelle to deal with them alone. I took a long, hot shower to clear my head, then forced myself to have some toast with my coffee. I thought about how much longer I could push them off. Probably not much. The last time I'd seen Arturo, he'd gotten up in my face. Old Man Ernesto'd had to pull him back. But he'd let me feel the wrath for a few seconds before he'd yanked Arturo's leash.

I drank my fourth cup of coffee on the balcony so I could check out the day. A thin white layer of clouds covered the sky like a gauze bandage. The sun shone through them and bathed the sky in a pale, silvery light. I would've appreciated something dark and ominous to go with my mood—or a bright blue day, for contrast. Friggin' weather.

I finished my coffee and headed out. It was only eight o'clock when I got into the office, but Michelle was already there. I noticed she was wearing a black Scünci. A pretty funereal theme for her. She usually favored patterns and bright colors. "You trying to send me a message?"

Michelle gave me a hard look, "Yeah, get rid of those guys, or I'll kill you."

"You don't have to be here. I can handle them."

Michelle's face softened a little. "I didn't want you to be alone with them. Alex is here, too."

I noticed his door was open. He always closed it when he was working. Except apparently when he was worried about my well-being. It was reassuring that everyone was watching out for me. Especially since Alex really knew how to fight. But I didn't think the Orozcos would make a move on me here in the office with so many people around. Not when it was so much easier to get to me in my very *un*secure apartment. Those two were at the helm of the Grape Street Boyz gang, and they didn't get there by singing Christmas carols. Ernesto was from Honduras, where the gangs made ISIS look like a Cub Scout troop. And he'd trained his sons well. They didn't have to do the dirty work themselves anymore, but they wouldn't mind getting back into that game if need be, just for shits and giggles. Still, I appreciated the effort. "Thanks, guys."

She flapped a hand at me. "Just make them go away."

I went to my office and took my .38-caliber Smith and Wesson out of the left bottom drawer, made sure it was fully loaded, then put it in my top left drawer, which I kept open for easy access. I tried to focus on casework. I had a search-and-seizure motion that was due on Friday, but I was straining so hard to hear the buzzer at the outer door that I couldn't concentrate. By the time it did sound at eight thirty, I was almost relieved. I wiped my sweating palms on my pants legs and took a deep breath, hoping it would make my pulse slow down. I heard Michelle buzz them in.

I came out and stood near her desk with a big, fake, confident smile. As they entered, I gave them a big, fake, hearty welcome. "Ernesto, Arturo, so nice to see you. Please, come in."

A black cloud of menace always seemed to hover around them, and I don't think I'd ever seen either of them, father or son, crack a smile—which, when I pictured what that might look like, struck me as a good thing.

They didn't smile now, either, as I turned and led them back to my office. I stood behind my desk and gestured to the two chairs in front of it. They actually match now. So uptown. Ernesto moved slowly on thick, heavy feet. From past experience, I knew his hands felt like blocks of concrete. I bet his fist would feel like a pile driver. His son, Arturo, had the beginnings of a tire around the middle, but the muscles in his biceps and chest strained against the fabric of his shiny, cobalt-blue shirt. He leaned forward in his seat, and the sickly sweet smell of his cologne and the greasy goo he used to slick back his hair filled the room. I had to breathe through my mouth to settle my stomach.

I did my best to channel a calm voice. "I have an update for you."

Arturo rubbed his right fist with his left hand. A habit of his. "We already heard that bailiff who was in court said he didn't write nothing on the custody list."

They'd apparently been doing some digging on their own. A very bad sign. "That's true. But apparently there were quite a few handwritten scratch-outs and notes on that list. And it got passed around to a lot of people. All the bailiffs on the floor, the jail deputies who work transportation. Even some of the prison guards. But I just got a tip yesterday. It's from a source who's in tight with the shot caller of the Southside Creepers. According to my source, there's a deputy sheriff who might be the shot caller's homie—"

Arturo cracked a knuckle. "Who is this *pinche* source of yours?" His lips twisted in contempt.

I shook my head. "I can't tell you that. And you don't want to know. Because if anything happens to him, they'll be looking at me. And you. And then you'll never get that deputy's name."

Ernesto looked at me through eyes that were slits in his fleshy face. He was the only one who could handle any semblance of rational thinking. He slowly nodded, "When will you get us the name of this deputy sheriff?"

"I'm working on it. My source wants a favor from me first. Some legal help. It'll take me a little while to get it done—"

Arturo gave me a narrow-eyed glare. "How long?"

How long could I push it? "Three months, max."

Arturo shook his head, his eyes still fixed on me. "Too long."

Ernesto frowned at him. "My son is not a patient man." His eyes shifted to me, and he fixed me with a flat stare. "But we have waited a long time already. We would like you to get us the name in one month. If you cannot do it by then, you give us the name of this pig who is friendly with the Creepers. We will find a way to persuade him to give us this deputy."

I forced a calm smile, though I could barely hear him over the roaring in my ears from the throbbing headache that'd been mounting ever since they walked in. "I will do what I can, of course. But it would be best if you let me handle this. We don't want any more bloodshed, right?" Ever since Ricardo's murder, a gang war had been raging between the Creepers and the Grape Street Boyz. The body count was reaching epic proportions. This struck me as a win-win for the rest of us, but the two vipers in front of me were unlikely to share that view.

Ernesto stood and stared down at me. "No one wants bloodshed. But it can't always be avoided."

Arturo joined him. His eyes shone like polished knives. "One month, *Abogada* Brinkman."

I kept the smile on but spoke in a firm voice. "I'll do my best."

As I walked them to the door, I noticed Alex was sitting on Michelle's desk. He made it look casual, but I saw that he was sizing up the Orozcos, ready for action. Seeing him made me cocky. "Oh, and I meant to tell you. We've just about run through my retainer, so you'll be getting a bill for my time starting Friday."

Ernesto turned sideways and nodded. Arturo opened the door for him, and they left. I let out an exhale that went on for so long I didn't know how I'd been breathing all this time.

Michelle looked mildly impressed. "You go, girl. Way to show 'em you're the boss."

I strutted over to her desk. "I know, right? Anyhow, their money spends the same. May as well get it while we can." As in, while I was still alive. "And thanks, Alex."

He gave me an innocent look. "What? I was just hanging out, talking to Michelle."

I gave him a knowing smile. "Then thanks for that."

I went into my office, closed the door, and dropped onto the couch. I was pissed at myself. My little bullshit story about the Creeper snitch had only bought me one month. I'd have to move fast. But I didn't have time—or the kind of access I needed—to dig up a credible fall guy. How the hell was I going to get out of this?

Then it came to me. *I* didn't have access, but I knew someone who did. Dale. If there actually were a jail deputy with a connect to the Southside Creepers, Dale could find out. I reached him on his cell phone and gave him a version of the Orozco situation. One that—of course—omitted my part in Ricardo's untimely demise. "So the Orozcos want to know which deputy had connects to the Southside Creepers."

Dale paused for a moment. "Maybe there is no connect, Sam. Maybe it's just a screwup. It happens."

Which was the story I'd counted on selling to the Orozcos. Unfortunately, they weren't buying. I had to admit, messing with that custody list was one of my bigger mistakes. I know I can be impulsive, but this one was an all-time low, even for me. I told Dale that if he couldn't find a connect, that would be the end of it.

He sighed. "Fine. But if I do come up with a dirty jail deputy, you keep it quiet until we get him some protection."

I told Dale I had no problem whatsoever with that. "Hey, by the way, thanks for those reports." He'd slipped me a copy of the police reports that'd been generated so far on Cassie's case. It was strictly on the down low.

Dale cleared his throat. "I have no idea what you're talking about." He ended the call.

I smiled at the phone, then stood up and stretched. If Dale did come up with a name, I'd still have to do my own digging to figure out whether the deputy was sleazy enough to deserve being set up as my fall guy. But at least now I'd put some wheels in motion.

Of course, that still left me with my Deshawn problem.

I sighed. One step at a time.

NINE

I had a couple of appearances to take care of in Van Nuys, and when I got back to the office I found Alex ready and waiting for our excursion to the crime scene—otherwise known as Roberta Avenue in Glendale, California.

Glendale wasn't far, distance-wise, but it was a world away in feeling. Being there was like traveling back in time to Anytown, USA: wide streets lined with trees grown so big their roots buckled the sidewalks in some places; tidy, postage-stamp-size lawns in front of small but well-kept ranch-style houses; a little mom-and-pop mini grocery in the middle of the block, where I could picture mothers sending their grade school kids to pick up a loaf of bread—or go buy themselves an ice-cream cone on a hot summer day. The vibe felt like *Everybody Loves Raymond*—or just about any of those average-guy sitcoms, where neighbors still dropped by to borrow a cup of flour. Glendale had its sketchy areas—which was where the skinhead factions were encroaching—but for the most part, it still had that innocent, small-town thing going for it.

At four o'clock on a Tuesday afternoon, kids were straggling home from school, bent forward by the weight of their backpacks. Some young boys, no more than eleven or twelve, giggled as they shoved and pushed and danced around one another. Groups of little girls with pink and bedazzled backpacks side-eyed the boys and one another as they spoke in low tones. I knew from vast personal experience that those little rapier-like tongues were slicing and dicing everyone and everything they saw.

I pointed to a small house, second from the corner. "That's it." Alex parked across the street, and we both stared at it. Other than the shredded remnants of crime-scene tape that still clung to the trees near the sidewalk, the house looked like any other. It had a beige stucco exterior, white-trimmed windows, and a small porch with a potted fern that was already turning brown. The lawn was showing patches of yellow and brown. But given the drought, that was probably not a new development. The mailbox at the curb had one of those metal flags that tell the postman there are letters to be picked up. This one was painted to look like an American flag. Probably the mother's idea. It seemed like a politician thing to do.

Just an ordinary home in an ordinary suburban neighborhood—that happened to be the site of a massacre. We got out, crossed the street, and stood on the sidewalk. I noticed that the backyards were deep and that the fence between them was barely six feet—easily climbed. "Let's start next door."

A middle-aged woman in pale-blue sweats and white Skechers—the rocker kind that promised a better, tighter, firmer butt—answered the door. Her curly brown hair framed a face with a harried look. According to the police reports Dale had slipped me, her name was Malia Trevanian. She looked from me to Alex with a confused, wary expression. "Yes?"

For a change, I could be completely honest about who I was and what I was doing. "I'm Samantha Brinkman, the lawyer who's helping Cassie Sonnenberg, and this is Alex, my investigator." We gave her our cards. "We just wanted to ask you a few questions about that night."

The harried look turned sad. "That poor little girl. And that family. Such good people! They'd do anything for you. Last month, when my husband was away on business, a pipe burst at the side of the house. It was like a geyser, and you know how expensive water is now. I was freaking out, didn't know what to do. But Stephen came running over. He took care of everything." She paused to blink away tears and shook her head. "Anyway, I'd be glad to help you, but I already told the police everything I know."

Which was absolutely nothing. "What about earlier that day? Did you happen to see anyone hanging around the neighborhood who seemed out of place?"

"Out of place?" She shook her head slowly. "No. I mean, I'm sure I saw people on the street. But I don't remember noticing anyone who stuck out."

I tried a few more questions, but Malia was a dead end. I thanked her for her time.

She nodded with worried eyes. "I sure hope they find the guy who did this. I know they think it's some white supremacist guy who was angry with Paula. But what if it wasn't? What if it's some maniac just randomly targeting families?"

I thought that was highly unlikely, but there was no point arguing. Besides, who knew? Anything was possible. "I understand. It really is scary. But I do know the police are working on this night and day. I'm sure they'll catch him soon."

Malia did not look the least bit reassured. I didn't blame her, but in my case, it had more to do with my dim view of the cops than it did with the fear of a random, uncatchable psycho with a bloodlust for suburban families. We headed to the next house.

Alex paused at the edge of the walkway leading up to the front door. "If Malia's any indication of the level of paranoia, I'd guess these neighbors were pretty cooperative with the police."

"Agreed. But I never thought they were deliberately holding out. It's not that kind of 'hood." My only worry was that the cops hadn't asked the right questions. Like "did you see anyone hanging around earlier that day who didn't belong here?" I hadn't seen even one statement in the reports that showed a response to that question. But especially if the killer were a Nazi Low Rider, he might want to get the lay of the land before launching a mass murder—if only to plan an escape route.

An older man and his wife at the next house, who wore matching pale-yellow cardigan sweaters over white turtlenecks and beige slacks, were also big fans of the Sonnenbergs. "Paula is such a dear," the woman said. "When Robert went in for his knee replacement, she brought over a tuna casserole because she knew it was our favorite. And Stephen came over to mow the lawn every week until Robert recovered." She cast a fond glance at her husband. "Bless him, he still likes to do it himself."

But they hadn't seen or heard anything that night. We hit six more houses on both sides of the Sonnenbergs' house and *nada*. Everyone loved the Sonnenbergs, had little stories to tell about their neighborly generosity, but no one had seen or heard anything. It wasn't until we'd knocked on four more doors across the street that we got a glimmer of a possible break.

Phillip Bryer was a retired Loomis guard who lived directly across the street from the Sonnenbergs. "I keep my eyes open by training. Can't seem to stop old habits." He sighed and shook his head. For a moment, he frowned, then he stared over my shoulder at the sidewalk. "You know, I do remember a young man I'd never seen before. He was standing in front of my house that afternoon."

I pushed down the shock at finally getting something that resembled a lead. "What was he doing?"

His brow knitted. "Nothing. Just stood there. Seemed to be looking at the Sonnenbergs' house, but I can't be sure. His back was to me."

Maybe a Nazi Low Rider? But I didn't want to steer him. I made my question open-ended. "Can you describe him?"

Phillip thought for a moment. "Clean-cut young guy. Jeans, T-shirt. Nothing that special about him except he had longish black hair. Wore it in a ponytail. But that's no big deal these days. I only noticed him because he was right in front of my house, and he stood there for a little while."

Didn't sound like a Nazi Low Rider. "How long? Five minutes? Ten?"

"I'd say somewhere in there, between five and ten."

"Did you ever see him go and knock on a door?" That might show he had legitimate business in the area. Phil shook his head. "Do you remember what color T-shirt he was wearing?"

Phillip frowned. "White? Yeah, I'm pretty sure it was white. Didn't see the front, though."

Nothing about this guy sounded like an Aryan Brotherhood gang-banger. I let Alex chime in with a few questions, but we'd gotten all we were going to get from Phillip. It was a lot more than we'd gotten from the other folks here in Mayberry.

When we reconnoitered on the sidewalk, Alex looked back at Phillip's house. "What do you think?"

"I think it's interesting, but I'm not sure what it means. It doesn't jibe with a Nazi Low Rider or any of the other AB gangs."

Alex nodded. "Want to keep going?"

"Not really." But then two houses away, I saw a teenage girl come out to check the mailbox. Even from where we were standing, I could tell she was the high school hottie. Long, sandy-blonde hair that fell over one eye, a cropped sweatshirt that said I WOKE UP LIKE THIS, and skinny jeans—the kind that only models and anorexics who lie about it can rock. I'd bet the boys loved her and the girls hated/envied her—but hung out with her anyway because she was where the boys were.

I waved to her, and she studied us with a curious expression as we approached. When we reached her, I held out my card and introduced us. She glanced at the card and looked up at me briefly before her eyes slid away to land on Alex. And stayed there. Alex, wonderful slut that he is, went to work.

He held out his card with a ͏͏͏͏͏ warm ͏͏͏͏͏ way ͏͏͏͏͏ smile "Nice ͏͏͏͏͏ to meet you "

She took the card and returned his smile. "Heather Ruskin. Nice to meet you, too." She held up a hand to shield her eyes from the sun. "You guys here about the murders?"

Alex nodded. "Did you happen to see or hear anything unusual that night?" Heather shook her head. "What about earlier that day? Did you notice anybody hanging around on this street who didn't belong here?"

Heather paused, then shook her head. "I went to a friend's house after school that day, and I didn't get back until dinner. So I really didn't have the chance to see anyone." She blinked rapidly, then dropped her head and looked away. I saw a few tears glisten in the air as they fell to the ground. "I never hung out with Abel, but we'd bump into each other every once in a while. He was so nice. I just can't believe . . . what happened."

I kicked myself for not bringing Kleenex. I usually do. For some reason, it makes people feel like they owe me. "Where did you usually see him?"

"In school. Sometimes around here, back when I took the bus."

And he was nice to her. But that was no surprise. I'd get a more accurate reading on Abel from someone who didn't look like Heidi Klum and Chris Hemsworth's love child. "Did you know Cassie?"

Heather swiped a finger across her cheek. "Not really. I'm a senior, and she's just a sophomore."

"What about Cassie's parents?"

She shook her head. "I'd see Paula around, but I didn't really talk to her. Just 'hi' and 'bye.'"

"And Stephen?"

Heather hesitated, and a weird expression crossed her face. She was about to speak when her mother opened the front door, looking agitated. "Heather, why haven't you left yet? I told you I need the chicken right away. If dinner's late, your father will have a fit."

Heather turned around and called out to her. "I'm going right now." She began to back away from us. "Sorry. Um, good luck. I hope they get the guy." Heather turned and trotted to the older-model Jetta in the driveway.

As Heather drove off, the mother came out and gave us a suspicious look. "Excuse me, but who are you?" I moved up the walk and told her who we were and why we were talking to Heather. She sighed and nodded. "Well, I've already told the police I didn't see or hear anything that night."

"Did you happen to notice anyone who seemed out of place hanging around on this street earlier in the day?"

She looked irritated, but she gave it a second of thought before shaking her head. "No. I'm sorry, but I've got to get dinner ready."

She was a busy mom. She didn't have time to be checking out the goings-on in the neighborhood. "Not a problem. I understand. Have a nice evening."

Alex and I headed back to his car. As he pulled away, he glanced up at his rearview mirror. "Do you think that retired Loomis guard really gave us something?"

I'd been wondering the same thing. "Maybe. And I was kind of wondering what was on Heather's mind, too."

"You mean when you asked about the dad?"

I nodded. I didn't know whether it meant anything, but if the case wasn't solved soon, I'd try to get back to Heather and find out.

TEN

Next stop: Abel's buddies. Alex had lined up the interviews for that evening, since we were going to be in the area.

They'd agreed to meet us at Tommy Dearfield's house. Based on Alex's Facebook and Instagram research, Tommy was Abel's closest friend. He lived a little more than a mile away, at the west end of Glendale. Alex parked in front of a two-story house with a dormer window on the second floor that faced the street. A huge, old jacaranda tree dominated the front yard, but the house had a newer feel, with a fresh coat of pale-yellow paint and window fittings that looked like they'd recently been redone.

Tommy himself answered the door. He had thick, wavy brown hair that fell across his forehead and a semicute freckled face, but it currently wore a cold expression. When I introduced us and offered a card, he ignored it. "Yeah, come in. Everybody's in the living room."

He led us down a short hallway, then turned right into a medium-size living room with French windows that gave a view of the street. Ethan Allen furniture in gray and rose hues gave the room a traditional but still homey feel. The pink plastic flowers in a wicker basket on the coffee table ruined it.

Two other boys in jeans and faded Affliction T-shirts slouched on the pale-gray linen sofa. The one with the shoulder-length black hair said his name was Foster Trumble. The one with the crew cut who was built like a football player was Eric Asner. Neither of them seemed happy to see us.

I thanked them for making time to talk to us, then explained that I was just looking into this as Cassie's support person. This did not help our cause. They grunted and gave us sullen looks. I decided I may as well jump right in. "Did Abel have any enemies? I mean someone who was really pissed at him?"

Eric seemed stunned by the question. "Pissed enough to do all that? No way."

Foster was a little more collected. "There're probably some guys out there who don't like him. But I never knew of anyone who had that big an issue with him."

Tommy had been glaring at us since he opened the door, and he still was. When he spoke, his tone was defensive, hostile. "I don't know of anybody who didn't like Abel. He was a great guy. There's no way this is about him. No way."

All righty then. Alex lobbed a few more questions their way about Abel's extracurricular activities. He was mainly into video games. He'd wanted to make the basketball team, but he wasn't tall enough. And he'd tried out for the baseball team, but he didn't make the cut because, according to Tommy, the coach was a jerk. Eric hinted that Abel just wasn't good enough. But a hard look from Tommy cut off any more comments. All in all, based on what they said as well as what they didn't say, I got the impression that Abel was a wannabe, a guy on the fringes of the "in crowd." Closer to the hip kids than any of these guys were, but never really a part of their group.

I was about to wrap up when a woman with wavy brown hair similar to Tommy's came in. "Mrs. Dearfield?" I asked.

She had a dish towel in her hands, but she looked like she'd just come home from the office. She wore tasteful makeup, a long bob that was neatly styled, and she was dressed in business-appropriate slacks and blouse. "It's Ms. Tucker now. I'm divorced. I just wanted to say a quick hello. Didn't I see you on TV? You were representing that man who turned out to be your father, right?"

This still made me wince. I tried to turn it into a smile. "Yes, that's me."

"You did a great job. Cassie's very lucky to have you."

I thanked her, and she left, saying I should take as long as I needed.

I told her I appreciated that and turned back to the boys, who now had the air of hostages. I decided to try another tack. "Look, we're just trying to help Cassie. She's obviously having a very hard time right now—"

Tommy cut me off. "Cassie's a drama-queen bitch. Abel was always having to deal with 'poor Cassie this' and 'poor Cassie that.'" He gave a look of disgust. "She was a pain in the ass. She lied about pretty much everything, just to get attention."

I kept my voice neutral, though I wanted to smack him in the mouth. Really hard. "What did she do, exactly?"

Tommy shrugged. "She always had some big problem. Her teachers weren't fair, the other kids were mean to her, her parents wouldn't buy her the right clothes, blah, blah, blah." He tossed his hair again. "And everything that happened to her was, like, the worst thing ever. No one could ever have a problem like hers."

Sounded to me like typical teen angst, if a little exaggerated, which figured given Cassie's background. But it had clearly gotten under Abel's skin. I hated to say it, but that sounded pretty typical, too. The bird with the broken wing often does suck up all the attention. But it sure didn't sound like Paula was the monster Cassie had described. "So she and Abel didn't get along?"

Tommy snorted and made a face. "Nobody *could* get along with that whiney little bitch."

I asked Eric and Foster for their assessments of Cassie. Their memories were similar to Tommy's but hazier. They hadn't hung out with Abel at his house as much as Tommy had, so they didn't know as much as he did.

Alex was primed to ask the follow-up on Cassie's information. We decided it'd go over better if a guy asked it. "Did any of you hear about a problem Abel had at a party with a girl named Janessa?"

Eric rolled his eyes. "It's a BS story. He supposedly got pissed off at her because she wouldn't go out with him or something. She's such a friggin' tease."

Alex gave him a "just us guys" smile. "Were you there?"

Eric shook his head with a look that said it didn't matter. "But I know her."

It was the same with Tommy and Foster. They'd heard about the story, but Abel had given it his spin, and they were happy to go with it.

We wound down after a few more minutes. I'd heard enough about Saint Abel. It was time to get to the other side of things. Alex had found the girl.

Janessa Wagoner lived a few miles south of Tommy. We were there in less than ten minutes.

"He was a total asshole." Janessa, an African American cutie with sparkling brown eyes, made a sour face. "He hit on me at Trudy's birthday party, and I was like, 'No, thank you.'"

Janessa's frank, no-bullshit style was refreshing. "So you didn't like Abel?"

"No." She paused, then shrugged. "To be fair, I didn't really know him. I just didn't dig his vibe, you know?"

I smiled. "I really do."

Janessa gave me an appraising look. "Yeah, you're pretty hot." She gave Alex the once-over. "You guys hooked up?"

I let myself smile. "No. We just work together."

Alex was amused. "And I'm gay."

Janessa gave a resigned nod. "Figures. Anyway, I was totally polite and all, said, 'Thanks but no thanks,' but he just lost it. Called me a conceited bitch, said I wasn't that hot and I was too fat and he was too good for a whore like me."

Janessa was curvy but by no means fat. I shook my head, disgusted, and spoke with sarcasm. "Seems a tad over the top."

She rolled her eyes. "Ya think?"

I gave a short laugh. I loved the fact that Janessa wasn't in the least crushed by his obnoxious remark. Some—too many—girls would've flown into an anorexic tailspin. "So what'd you do?"

Janessa smirked. "I dumped my drink down his pants."

Now I really laughed. "You soak him?"

The smirk widened. "Oh, totally. He had to leave. It was great. After that, he tried to talk me down at school, but everyone heard about the party, so he had to let it go." Her mood shifted, and she got serious. "I got lucky. Ginnie, not so much."

A new name. And judging by Janessa's expression, a new and much worse situation. "Ginnie?"

"Didn't anyone tell you about Ginnie Miller?" We both shook our heads. "Yeah, come to think of it, that figures. She hardly told anyone about it. I know some of what happened, but you should really talk to her. I'll get you her num . . . wait. I think I'd better call her and find out if she wants to talk about it." Janessa stood up. "Be right back."

Alex leaned toward me. "We're still going after Ginnie if she says no, right?"

"Of course."

One minute later, Janessa was back. "It's cool. She'll talk to you."

A pleasant surprise. "Now?"

"Yep." Her voice was firm but upbeat. In fact, that described Janessa in general. "Here's her address."

She handed me a piece of paper with the phone number and address. I liked the way this girl worked. If my practice expanded like I hoped it would, I'd hire her in a heartbeat if she was willing. "Thanks, Janessa." I asked her whether she knew Cassie, but she, too, was a senior, which meant their paths didn't cross.

We got to the end of our questions, and I told her we appreciated her help. As we headed to the door, Janessa's mood shifted again. This girl was fast in thought, word, and deed.

Now she looked worried. "I hope you catch the killer soon. It's been pretty scary around here."

I started to tell her we weren't the cops, but the truth was, we were doing their job for them. "Don't worry. We'll get him."

Alex gave her a reassuring smile. "And we don't think it's the work of some random serial killer. He won't be back."

As we headed for the car, I elbowed Alex in the ribs. "Nice cop impression, Joe Friday."

Alex stared at me. "Seriously? Ms. We Always Get Our Man?"

I sniffed. "That's different. I really am a Royal Canadian Mountie."

Ginnie lived farther east, in Burbank. When her mother ushered us in, we found her at the kitchen table, surrounded by schoolbooks. "If you have a test or something, we can come back another time."

Ginnie gave us a shy smile and shook her head. "It's okay. I'm just doing some review stuff, getting ready for my GED."

Her mother gestured for us to have a seat. "Can I get you anything to drink?"

I was thirsty, but I didn't want to have to take any bathroom breaks. "No, but thank you."

"Okay, let me know if you need anything." She started toward the door, then paused. "Say, aren't you the lawyer whose father—"

Not again. I forced a smile. "Yes."

She looked pleased with herself. "I thought I recognized you." She started to leave, then stopped and turned back. "You were terrific, by the way."

I felt like a schmuck. "Thank you."

She left, and Ginnie pushed aside her books. Homeschooling took a lot of discipline. I wondered whether I could've pulled it off. Probably not. Wait. No. Definitely not. The lock on the liquor cabinet was too easy to pick. "I guess Janessa already told you that we wanted to ask you about Abel?"

Ginnie nodded without looking at us. She seemed nervous, and her short blonde pixie cut and long, slender neck gave her a delicate, vulnerable look. It made me worry about what I was about to hear.

She took a deep breath, her brow furrowed with pain. "I went out with Abel a couple of times. The first time, we went to a movie and that was okay. But the second time, we went to a basketball game at school. Afterward, on the way home, he tried to get me to . . . make out and stuff. I did for a minute, but then he got too . . . intense, and I didn't want to anymore. I told him I was sorry, that I wasn't into it. He just lost it. Called me a cock tease and a bitch and a whore." She paused and took a deep breath. "It was scary. He was so . . . out of control he was, like, spitting."

There was something really wrong with this guy. "Did he hurt you?"

"You mean, like, hit me or something? No. But the way he screamed at me and pounded on the steering wheel . . . it was scary. I didn't know what he was going to do. I was about to jump out of the car, but then he took me home. I was so relieved. I thought, 'Thank God that's over.' But it wasn't."

"What happened?"

"He posted all kinds of lies and crap about me on Facebook. Said I hooked up with a bunch of the guys on the football team, that I gave them—" Ginnie choked up, and she stopped. After a few moments, she continued. "He even Photoshopped my face on some other girl's body and claimed I was sending out nude pictures."

What a complete piece of shit this kid was. "What'd you do? Did you report him?"

"Yes, but he denied it all." She sighed, her expression showing utter despair. "And he'd used a dummy Facebook page, so they couldn't trace it to him." Ginnie swallowed hard. "My friends knew it was a bunch of lies. But all the guys would laugh when they saw me in the hallway." She stopped and took a deep breath. "It just got to be too much. So I asked the principal for permission to do home study."

It would've been bad no matter who he'd done it to, but it was even worse that it'd happened to someone so delicate. "I'm sorry, Ginnie."

She dipped her head and sighed. "Thanks. But to be honest, I was having problems before all that. I have a panic disorder, depression. Abel made it worse, but . . ." She gave me a wan smile. "My mom's been wanting me to do homeschooling for a while. And I'm doing much better now, so it was probably all for the best."

I was starting to think that Abel's shuffling off this mortal coil was probably for the best, too.

ELEVEN

Michelle shook her head, her expression disgusted. "Wow, Abel's a real dick." She threw her empty coffee cup into the trash. "It blows my mind how fast social media turned into a pipeline for chickenshit assholes."

Alex, who'd perched on the edge of her desk, folded his arms. "For sure, but I don't see either of those girls going after him in any way, let alone taking out the parents."

No doubt about that. "But I think we should take a look at their families. A father or a brother with a screw loose might've gotten fired up enough to do it." Michelle gave me a skeptical look. "I said *might*. Look, all I'm saying is, it couldn't hurt to check them out, see if they have alibis."

"Should be easy enough," Alex said. "And even though it's a long shot, it is important to keep an open mind in an investigation and not get married to any one theory until all the evidence is in."

I glared at him. "You're quoting that damn book, aren't you?"

Alex gave me a stubborn look. "It's right, isn't it?"

"Big whoop. That line's been in every homicide detective manual since friggin' Wyatt Earp."

Alex sighed and headed to his office. Michelle gave me a tolerant smile. "By the way, Deshawn called."

For a flash of a second, I let myself hope that he'd found a way to appease the drug dealer. Then reality set in. "Did he leave a message?"

"Just said to tell you it's getting tough, and that you'd know what he meant." Michelle looked worried. "Someone giving him a hard time?" She liked him. We all did. When he wasn't jacking people, he was a charming guy.

"You could say that. Did he leave a number?"

Michelle shook her head. "Said he'd call back."

It felt like a lead weight had dropped into the pit of my stomach. "Thanks, Michy."

I walked into my office, closed the door, then grabbed a pillow off the couch and held it over my face to muffle my scream. When I'd finished, I lay down and tried to figure a way out of this mess. I had to bail him out, and fast. But I didn't have a clue how to get that kind of money, and I sure as hell couldn't get my hands on that much heroin. And—not to be selfish about this—but if his cousin cracked and gave up Deshawn's name, how long would it take for Deshawn to buckle and point the finger at me?

I went to my computer and opened my file of current cases. I knew I didn't have any dealers working at that high a level, but maybe one of my clients had connections. I pored over each case, searching for possibilities. An hour later, I'd come up with nothing. I sat back and drummed my fingers on the desk. I could look into my closed cases, but finding those clients would be almost impossible. And what few I could find would be unlikely to help me. Either because they're in prison and having buyer's remorse over the deal I made for them (and probably hoping someone's roasting my body over an open pit) or because they're on the street once again, up to no good and in no mood or position to do any favors. So I was glad for the distraction when Alex knocked.

He had that gleam in his eyes that said he'd hit a rich vein. He sat in front of my desk, notepad in hand. "I got some follow-up on Stephen, the dad."

"This about him getting someone fired?" I wasn't crazy about this lead.

"It's better than you think." Alex looked down at his notepad. "William Everleigh worked under Stephen. He fired Everleigh for supposedly dummying up his time sheets. But Everleigh claims it wasn't true, that Stephen set him up to get him fired."

I sat up, alarmed. "You talked to Everleigh?"

"No, to the other employees."

This worried me. We couldn't let anyone know we were talking to Stephen's coworkers—including the coworkers. It was one thing to knock on a few doors and ask neighbors whether they'd seen or heard anything. The cops had hit them up so many times, they wouldn't think to complain about it. And I hadn't been worried about talking to the kids. I was legitimately on board to help Cassie, so I could just say I was getting to know more about her. Plus, the kids wouldn't bitch about it. But adult coworkers might. And the cops would jump our shit big-time if they found out we were digging around in Stephen's life. Alex was smart enough to "social engineer" his way into the phone calls with Stephen's coworkers. I didn't know who he'd pretended to be, and I didn't want to know. I just wanted to make sure we wouldn't get caught. "You covered your tracks, right?"

Now Alex looked annoyed. "Of course, duh. Do you or don't you want to know why Stephen set the guy up to get fired?"

"Okay, hit me."

"Because Stephen was having an affair. At least that's the rumor. And he wanted to push his girlfriend—his twenty-one-year-old, extremely new and unqualified girlfriend—into Everleigh's position."

I leaned back in my chair and thought about that. "So says the disgruntled employee who got fired. Does anyone back him up?"

"Yes." He looked down at his notepad again. "Suzanne Chalmers says Stephen was always a little too interested in young women, and he did spend a lot of time with this one—Lilliana Wiley—in particular." Alex looked up. "It was a huge promotion for her. I got three others who backed that up."

"Anybody have proof he was having an affair with this Lilliana? Catch them in the act of . . . anything?"

Alex flipped his iPad closed. "No. Everyone who worked in that department thought they were hooking up, but no one could say for sure."

That figured. Unless someone caught them banging in the mail room, it'd be hard to say one way or the other. Still, it was interesting. "Did you talk to her?"

Alex spoke irritably. "No. I couldn't figure a safe way in."

I gave him a little smirk. "You mean that wasn't covered in your book? Shocking." Alex threw me a mock glare. "Don't beat yourself up. She'd never admit it anyway. Does she have a boyfriend or husband? Or, please God, a jealous ex-husband with a really bad temper?"

Alex pointed at me. "You nailed it. The coworkers didn't know, but I found out that she'd left her fiancé, who coincidentally was more than twice her age, about a week after she got the promotion."

"Nice. You check out his alibi?"

Alex nodded. "Working on it."

I wasn't optimistic about this lead, but it couldn't hurt to check it out. Sometimes lousy leads send you to the right ones. "Not that I expect this, but have you had a chance to check out friends and family for those two girls, Janessa and . . ."

"Ginnie. Not yet. But I should have that and their alibis by tomorrow afternoon."

"Nice job, Alex." I looked at my watch. It was almost eight o'clock. "Take the rest of the night off."

Alex raised an eyebrow. "Gee, thanks, boss."

I shut down my computer and pulled on my blazer. "Think nothing of it."

"Believe me, I do."

We walked out to the reception area where Michelle was still typing away. She looked up at me. "You're going to be late. You gas up Beulah?"

"I'm gonna Uber." I didn't want to spend the night drinking club sodas.

Alex looked incredulous. "You have a date?"

I sniffed and tossed my head. "Like that's so unbelievable?"

Michelle gave me a look and shook her head. "She's meeting Tiegan for drinks."

The killjoy. "Thanks for the backup."

Michelle gave me a saccharine smile. "Any time. Let us know what you get."

I shot her a death ray and headed out. I intended to ask Tiegan what she thought about my meeting with Cassie's friends and get her take on how Cassie was doing. I also wanted her opinion of what we'd learned about Abel. She'd said she didn't know much about him, but maybe our information would trigger a memory.

We'd picked Firefly, a hip lounge and restaurant in Studio City, which was sort of a midway spot between the San Fernando Valley, where Tiegan lived, and my apartment. I wouldn't have chosen it on a Saturday, when it was a "scene." But on a weeknight, it'd be pretty calm. I liked the way the bar area was set up like a cozy library, the walls lined with bookshelves and the comfy seating—all overstuffed couches, wingback chairs, and ottomans.

When I got there, I was glad to see I'd been right. The lounge area wasn't packed, there were a couple of quiet corners available, and the music—a pop/rock mix—wasn't blasting. I wanted to order their fried olives, but this wasn't a night to get distracted by food. I was here on a mission.

Tiegan was at the bar, nursing a glass of red wine, when I arrived. I could see that the bartender was enjoying her company. That was no surprise. Tiegan was girly-girl pretty: petite, with honey-blonde hair that was parted on the side and framed big, blue eyes and full lips. And I'd bet she got carded at every bar. She could easily pass for a high school senior. "Is that pinot noir? If so, is it any good?"

Tiegan smiled. "Yes and yes."

I told the bartender I'd have the same, and we took our drinks to a pair of armchairs in the corner. There were a few couples on the couches, but no one so close that I had to worry about what we said. "How's Cassie doing?"

Tiegan sighed and stared down at her wineglass. "A little better. Barb says she's not sleeping fifteen hours a day anymore, but she watches television constantly. I don't blame her for needing the escape, but it's going to be a while before she can think about rejoining the world."

"Have we heard any updates on Paula?"

"She's still in a coma. I hear they plan to keep it that way for at least another week or two to reduce the brain swelling."

"Has Cassie been to see her?"

"Yes, Barb took her yesterday." Tiegan took a sip of her wine, then balanced the glass on her knee.

Tiegan seemed a little bit jittery, nerves maybe. We'd never met in a social situation before. "I went to see Cassie yesterday evening."

She looked somewhat surprised, but she simply asked, "To talk about the . . . the crime?"

I sipped my wine. "No, actually. We talked about personal stuff. There was one thing in particular she mentioned that I wanted to ask you about."

She looked concerned. "What was that?"

"She told me about her home life. Mostly her mother. She said her mom talked a lot about how lucky she was to get adopted by them. She told Cassie that if they hadn't adopted her, she'd probably have wound up in a foster home for good. Did Cassie ever say anything about that to you?"

Tiegan's expression was confused and a little taken aback. "The only thing I remember Cassie telling me along those lines was that her mother accused her of being ungrateful when she wanted to find her birth mother. But I don't remember her ever telling me that Paula said . . . what you just said." She took another sip of wine, her expression troubled. "That's pretty awful."

"Do you think it's true? Or is it possible Cassie's negative filter twisted things a little?"

"Could be the latter, or both." Tiegan swirled her wine and seemed to consider that. "Cassie has her issues." Tiegan looked at me pointedly. "As you've seen. And she did complain about not fitting in anywhere, about always feeling like an outsider."

I remembered what she'd said about not looking like the rest of the family. "I'm sure it didn't help that she's so blonde and fair." And tall.

Tiegan stared off for a moment. "Definitely not. I remember seeing her with her family when we had our open house at the beginning of the year. She looked so awkward and uncomfortable, like she didn't know what to do with herself."

I wanted to check out what Abel's friends had said about her. "If you had to describe Cassie, would part of that description include drama queen?"

Tiegan gave me an ironic little smile. "Well, she *is* a teenage girl." Her expression turned serious. "Why? Who told you that?"

I wasn't sure I should name names. "Some of Abel's friends. According to them, she was always complaining. Her teachers weren't fair, other kids were shitty to her, that sort of thing."

Tiegan shrugged. "Not to me she didn't." She paused as a couple hovered nearby, waiting for the hostess to seat them. When they passed through, she continued. "Cassie could be needy. But that kind of chip on the shoulder? No. And I never thought she was that much more dramatic than any of the other girls."

Tiegan would certainly have a more realistic perspective on Cassie than Abel's posse. I'd go with Tiegan's assessment. "Did you ever hear about Abel being abusive toward anyone? I'm talking girls specifically."

Tiegan had been swirling her wine. Now she stopped and knitted her brow. "No. But I assume you have. What did they say?"

I told her what we'd learned from Janessa and Ginnie. Tiegan's expression said that was all news to her. "I'm guessing you never heard about any of that?"

"Definitely not, or I'd have done something about it. At least reported it to the principal. That's just terrible." She tilted her head and peered at me. "You think Abel could have been the target?"

I shrugged. "Could be. I think it's at least worth considering." But since Tiegan seemed to know less than I did about him, I moved on. "Did Cassie ever talk to you about Abel?"

She tucked her hair back behind her ear. "Not really. Why?"

"She seemed pretty broken up about losing him. I didn't get the feeling from his friends that he would've felt the same if the tables were turned."

Tiegan raised an eyebrow, but she didn't seem surprised by that. "It's pretty common for the natural child to resent the new kid on the block. Especially if the parents bent over backward to make her happy."

"Which, according to Abel, they did." I watched Tiegan to see whether she'd try to explain the discrepancy. She didn't, she just nodded, so I continued. "But that's not the way Cassie made it sound. Obviously, I never knew Abel, so I can't say whether he's a reliable source, but I don't think he'd feel that way for no reason. And if he were right, if Stephen and Paula did bend over backward for Cassie, why would she be so resentful of them? Especially Paula?"

Tiegan took a sip of her wine and thought for a moment. "Do you have any experience with adopted kids?" I told her that I did, but only after they'd committed crimes. She nodded. "Right. Of course. Well, I think a lot of adopted kids have mixed feelings about their parents. They love them, they're grateful to them, but at the same time, they resent having to feel grateful."

I wasn't sure that made sense. "Even when the parents don't demand their gratitude?"

"They can feel the pressure to be grateful even though no one suggests that they should." Tiegan spoke matter-of-factly. "And they very often send mixed messages. They're pleasers one minute, and then the next minute they're aloof and unreachable."

I'd noticed that in my clients. Now I put it together with what Tiegan had told me. "So they detach before someone else can abandon them. Again."

"Exactly."

I looked down at my wineglass and thought about how to broach the next subject. The soft lighting made the purples and reds in my wine look deep and rich—an optical illusion because it tasted like vinegar. Note to self: next time, don't let Tiegan pick the wine. "I was thinking of talking to Cassie's friends. She mentioned a girl named Tawny. Do you know of any others?"

Tiegan's mouth turned down. "Yes, Rain Frankel. I can put you in touch with them."

I noted the obvious. "You're not crazy about them."

She shrugged. "They're a little too wild, in my opinion. But from what Cassie's told me, it's not their fault. They have really messed-up home lives."

"Do you think Cassie would have a problem if I talked to them?"

"I can't see why she would." Tiegan looked a little puzzled. "But why would you want to?"

It was a fair question. I wasn't supposed to be digging into the family's lives or trying to find the killer. I was just supposed to be helping

Cassie deal with the cops. "Just trying to understand her a little better."
I tried my disarming smile. "So I can be a better support person."

Tiegan look doubtful, but she said, "If you want, I can ask her if
she minds you talking to them."

"Thanks, that'd be great. I don't want her to feel like I'm going
behind her back." Even though I kind of already had. "One last question. Do you know whether Cassie had a boyfriend?"

Tiegan seemed to be searching her memory. "I think she did, but I
don't remember her talking about him during our sessions, so I'm not
sure. Tawny and Rain can probably fill you in on that score."

I'd gotten what I'd come for, so I let Tiegan grill me on the progress
of the investigation. I told her what little I knew and tried not to ham-
mer the cops for what little *they* knew.

I asked her how she kept her sanity dealing with teenagers and
how many times a day she fantasized about hauling off and pounding
them. She confessed she felt tempted at least once a week. From there,
the conversation veered into the kind of world the kids were going to
have to deal with and how college campuses had turned into shooting
galleries where no one felt safe.

I couldn't help thinking that for Cassie, that grim reality had already
climbed right into her home.

TWELVE

I was tired and buzzed when I got back to my apartment, so I took a hot shower and put myself to bed. And for a change, I didn't have the dream. I woke up at seven, with a throat that wasn't sore from scream-ing—or trying to. It's a rare reprieve for me, and every time it happens, I think, *This is how normal people wake up every day.* No T-shirt soaked with fear-sweat, no shakes, no pounding heart. And then I think, *What would it be like to not be afraid to fall asleep, to wake up and feel this way every day?*

But this time those thoughts made me flash on Cassie. Made me wonder what it was like for her to see kids with families who looked like them, kids who took it for granted that they were wanted, that they belonged there. And I wondered whether she ever tried to imagine what it was like to get to live that way.

Now she had a whole new world to compare herself to. A world where kids didn't wake up in the middle of a killing field, with the bodies of their father, mother, and brother splayed on the floor in a pool of blood. A world where kids got to wake up in their own beds and worry about kid things, like whether Mom would let her get those sexy, pricey new jeans all the girls were wearing or whether Greg would ask her to the prom.

I pushed myself out of bed to stop those thoughts and headed for the shower. I was feeling kind of hungry, but I wasn't in the mood to make breakfast. Maybe I'd get some fast food at a drive-thru on the way to work. It was junk, but it was tasty. I had one foot out the door when my home phone rang. It was Dale. "What's going on? You got news for me?"

"Kind of. Want to meet me for breakfast?"

"Your timing's perfect. I'm starving."

We decided to meet at BLD on Beverly Boulevard. Good food but no frills, i.e., no tablecloths, lots of hard surfaces, so lots of clatter and noise. Not the best place for a confidential chat. But on the other hand, the din might give us cover. I got there before Dale. The smells coming from the kitchen made my stomach grumble like an old airplane engine. I decided not to wait, and when the waiter showed up, I ordered coffee and a wild mushroom omelet.

I'd just finished ordering when Dale rushed in. He got the fried egg sandwich that came with Gruyère and bacon, potatoes on the side. It sounded fantastic. But if I ate all that, I'd have to go home and change into sweats.

I waited for the server to bring his coffee, then asked, "What've you got on the Orozco situation?"

Dale glanced at the nearby tables. Everyone was busy with their food and one another. He leaned in. "So far, I'm not seeing any connections between the deputies or bailiffs and the Southside Creepers."

Shit. "But you're not done yet," I said with hope.

"Not quite. But the ones who have given interviews all say they didn't change Ricardo's cell placement, and they're willing to take polygraphs."

It took every ounce of willpower not to groan out loud. If those deputies all wound up passing their polys and the Orozcos found out about it—a distinct possibility, since the local press was following the investigation—it wouldn't be long before they took another hard look at me. "One of them must be lying."

Dale peered at me a little suspiciously. "I guess we'll find out soon enough."

My omelet arrived at the same time as Dale's sandwich. But my appetite was gone. I forced myself to take a bite as Dale tucked in to his breakfast. He noticed I was barely eating. "Want to send it back?"

"No, it's good. I just drank too much coffee."

"You shouldn't have caffeine on an empty stomach." He pushed his plate toward me. "Have some of my potatoes."

It always drove me nuts when he did this "dad" thing. He'd dived into it headfirst with his other daughter, Lisa, who was a junior in high school. Dale and the mother had divorced when Lisa was a baby, and she'd moved to the East Coast. But he'd kept in touch, and now that they were back in Los Angeles, he was seeing Lisa on a regular basis. And he was really grooving into being a dad.

That was fine. For them. I just wanted him to leave me out of it. "Thanks, but I keep a bottle of Scotch and some Xanax in the car. That usually takes the edge off."

Dale sighed and pulled back his plate. "I'm just trying to help."

"You didn't ask to meet me just to say you haven't got anything yet. What's up?"

Dale finished the last of his bacon, then wiped his mouth. "I need a favor. A friend of a friend got beefed for excessive force. Kevin Hausch. He swears it's a bullshit claim, but the so-called victim is making a lot of noise about going to the press. Kevin knew about you and asked me if you'd be willing to help him out."

"Why's that a favor? Tell him to call Michelle for an appointment. I'll give him a good deal." I took another sip of coffee, but it burned like acid. I pushed the cup away.

Dale tucked his napkin under the plate and didn't meet my eyes. "He says he doesn't have the money for a retainer."

I put my hands on the table. "He wants me to do this for free?" Dale nodded. I waited for him to look at me. "That's one *hell* of a favor. Why should I do it? Are you tight with him?"

Dale dropped his eyes back down to the table and traced the edge of the saucer that held his coffee. He was clearly not happy to be having this conversation. "No. But he's got a lot of friends in the department, and I could use a few more of those." Dale forced himself to look at me. "Besides, we're not talking about a trial or anything. He just needs you to get the victim to back off."

I didn't like anything about this. I didn't like the idea of representing a cop, and I especially hated the idea of having to represent a cop who'd been charged with excessive force. "Who's the victim and who's his lawyer?"

"I think he said the victim's name is Julio Valenzuela. And he doesn't have a lawyer."

I stared at Dale in disbelief. "No lawyer? Then it can't be a righteous beef, or some ambulance chaser would've sunk his teeth into Julio's neck by now. Why's Kevin so worried?"

"Because Valenzuela's saying he doesn't want money. Apparently lawyers were circling, but he turned them all down. He gave their names to Internal Affairs, and they checked it out. He's telling the truth."

I'd never heard of a victim refusing to lawyer up or talk settlement. No wonder Kevin was freaking. "So the guy sounds that much more legit."

Dale's expression was grim. "Exactly." He took a long pull on his coffee.

I never represent cops. Dale had been an exception. But Dale did need some goodwill in the department, and he was doing me a big solid—or at least I hoped he would—on my Orozco problem. "I'll talk to Julio, see if I can make him go away. But I'm not doing any departmental hearings, and I'm sure as hell not taking the case to trial."

Dale popped the last bite of sandwich into his mouth. "Deal. I'll get you Kevin's contact information. He's got all the paperwork on Julio and his beef."

I looked at my watch. It was after nine. "I'd better bust a move. I've got to be in court by ten thirty."

Dale flicked his fingers at me. "Go. I've got the check."

I took my purse off the chair and slipped it onto my shoulder. "Thanks."

Dale flagged down the waiter and motioned for him to bring the check. "By the way, you talk to your buddy Tuck Rosenberg about the Sonnenberg murders?"

I'd started to get up, but now I sat back down and stared at him. How did Dale know Tuck Rosenberg? Did he know about my meeting? Or was he just guessing? "I don't know what you're talking about."

Dale raised an eyebrow, his mouth turned up at the corners in a smirk. "I know you got him to watch my back."

When Dale was in custody in Twin Towers, an asshat drug dealer who didn't like the questions I was asking got someone to shank Dale. Tuck was doing the short-term sentence in Twin Towers I'd negotiated for him, so I'd asked him to get his Aryan Brotherhood buddies to watch out for Dale. "Who told you?"

Dale gave a little smile. "One of your many jailhouse admirers. You have quite the fan club."

I raised an eyebrow. "And some of them might even have been my clients."

Dale laughed. "Anyway, thank you. Again."

I stood up and slung my purse over my shoulder. "*De nada*. Thanks for breakfast."

As I trotted out to the car, I wondered who'd told him about my arranging for his protection. It had to be an AB guy. I supposed it didn't matter anymore. My thoughts drifted back to Cassie's case. I'd heard the cops had branched out from the Nazi Low Riders—by the way, one of the dumbest gang names I'd ever heard, which is really saying something—and were checking into every white supremacist gang in Southern California. The theory being, you shake enough trees, something's bound to fall out. But it hadn't happened yet.

I barely made it to court on time, but my worthy co-counsel on the eighteen-count robbery case was late. The judge kicked it over to the afternoon. I had to hang out through lunch, a time suck I could not afford. To top it off, my client was refusing to take the twenty-year deal the DA was offering, even though he was facing more than 120 years. When I finally got out of court, I wound up in traffic so ugly I could've walked faster. By the time I got back to the office, it was almost four o'clock, and I was an irritable mess.

Michelle saw my ugly mood. "Hey, Sunshine. He wouldn't plead?"

I dropped my briefcase on the floor and picked up the mail she'd sorted and left on the side table for me. "No. Of course he wouldn't plead. That'd make too much sense."

She leaned back and stretched her arms. "About the same sense it made for him to knock down twenty liquor stores with his half-wit brother."

"Eighteen liquor stores."

"Whatever. Alex has some 4-1-1 for you."

I finished sorting the mail. It was mostly junk. "No one says 4-1-1 anymore."

"No? How about bite me? People still say that, don't they?"

We exchanged middle-finger salutes, and I stomped over to Alex's office. As usual, the door was closed. "Knock knock. I've got your boxes of Thin Mints and Do-si-dos." A lie and we both knew it. If I had those cookies, they'd be tucked away in my kitchen.

I opened the door to find Alex at his desk, wearing a pained expression. "Do you always have to say stuff like that?"

"Apparently." Alex sat down behind his desk, and I flopped down on the folding chair—there wasn't room for anything bigger—across from him. "Michelle says you've got something."

"Yeah, I checked out Ginnie and Janessa. Ginnie's got no brother, no dad, and her mom was tweeting nonstop on the night of the murders about the Gloria Estefan concert that had blown her mind. Ginnie herself—"

I held up a hand. "Nonstarter." She was so frail, she probably couldn't cut her own steak, let alone three people.

Alex nodded. "Janessa has a younger brother, but he lives with her dad in San Bernardino."

"Which is where they were on the night of the murders."

"Yep. And Janessa—"

I shook my head. "Didn't give two shits about Abel. You're done with them. What about the guy Stephen got fired for dummying up his time sheets?"

"I haven't found him yet. No worries, I will. When I do, you want to meet with him?"

His confidence was always a breath of fresh air. No one had ever been more secure in his abilities. But it was more than justified. "Maybe. If we can come up with a good cover story. You know, something better than 'We're thinking you might've tried to kill the whole family.'"

"We will. But assuming we rule him out, then what?"

I hated to say it. "Then I think we let the cops figure it out."

Alex nodded and sighed. "I'm not optimistic about that."

I put my hands on my knees, then stood up. "I never am. The only way they solve this case is if something drops in their laps."

I headed back to my office, wishing I really had tanked up on Scotch and Xanax.

THIRTEEN

The next day, for no reason but pure, dumb luck, my first case wrapped up early. I'd arranged to meet Dale's sort-of-not-really buddy Kevin Hausch at the Code Seven, a cop bar and diner on Main Street, just a couple of blocks from the courthouse. I had forty-five minutes before my next case, so I had a little extra time to enjoy the walk.

I strolled out into the watery sunshine of the early spring day and wove my way through the motley crew that crowded the sidewalk. The assortment of humanity around the criminal court building in downtown LA was always a diverse mix. Hookers, cops, office workers, lawyers (hookers in suits), city and county pols (hookers in shirtsleeves), and the homeless.

For a change, I wasn't trying to beat the clock, running from the jail to the courthouse to the parking lot and then the next courthouse, so I got to look around at the world, take in the trees, the pale-blue sky, and the closest thing LA had to city bustle. But that also meant I got to watch a homeless guy pee against one of those trees outside city hall, listen to the Cup Man—an old guy who stood on the corner every day with a plastic cup on his head—spew about the coming apocalypse, and smell the belching exhaust of old buses and the gag-heavy perfume of the trannie who seemed to be following me a little too closely.

When I got to the diner, I saw that Kevin wasn't there yet. The place smelled like onions and old cigarette smoke. I felt the carpet crunch under my feet as I headed for the table at the far end of the dimly lit room. The drapes that framed the soot-stained windows looked like they hadn't been washed since Carter was president, and the wood tables were battered and chipped. It was only eleven o'clock, but two detectives were already pounding shots at the bar. I noticed a few uniformed cops at the tables, but otherwise, it was pretty quiet. An older woman wearing tight slacks and a small apron, whose eye makeup looked like it'd been applied with a canoe paddle, asked for my order. Actually she asked, "Whadda you want?" I ordered coffee.

She'd just left when a heavyset man in slacks and a dress shirt that strained around a beer belly walked in. He paused and peered around the room, squinting as his eyes adjusted to the dim lighting. Probably Kevin. But I took a few seconds to size him up before waving him over. He looked like he was in his late forties, maybe early fifties. His thick brown hair was starting to go gray at the temples, and his bushy mustache had flecks of white and gray. He had a heavy face, the flesh under his brows hung low over his eyes, his nose was thick and wide, and his jowls were starting to sag into his neck. I raised my hand and waved. He nodded and headed to my table in a rolling, bearlike gait. The hand he held out looked like an oven mitt. "Thank you for taking the time."

His voice was a deep baritone, the kind that'd make you jump when he ordered you out of the car. I shook his hand and noticed that it was surprisingly soft. "Sure, no problem," I lied. The chair squealed in protest as he sat down.

Up close, I saw that he had big, round brown eyes under heavy eyebrows. I was willing to bet a hundred bucks that he had a hairy back. "We'd better get to it." I glanced at my watch. "I've got to get back to court in about twenty minutes. How'd this whole thing start?"

Kevin folded his arms on the table and looked around before he spoke. "I pulled the guy over for a broken taillight."

I took out my notepad. "His name?"

"Julio Valenzuela. As I was walking toward the car, I saw him reach toward the passenger seat. I told him to put his hands on the steering wheel where I could see them."

I could've recited this story in my sleep. "Did he?"

Kevin gave a curt nod. "Yeah. But when I got up to the driver's window to ask for his license and registration, I saw the edge of a plastic baggie on the floor under the front passenger seat. So I told him to step out of the car. He got out and started hollering at me about how he didn't do anything wrong and I had no reason to stop him. Shi—I mean, stuff like that. He was waving his arms around and getting more and more agitated. I told him to back off, but he wouldn't listen, kept getting in my face, so I turned him around and cuffed him. Then I put him in my patrol car—"

"You didn't call for backup?"

He straightened up and squared his shoulders. "No. He's not that big, and he calmed down once I got the cuffs on him. I put him in the backseat of my patrol unit and went over to his car to get a better view of the baggie. I saw a white powdery residue in the corner—"

A line I'd read in so many police reports I couldn't even listen to it anymore. "So you pulled it out and it was, what? Coke? Meth?"

Kevin's jaw tightened. "Coke. Just a small amount."

"Did you take him in?" He nodded. "What happened on the way to the station?"

He gave me a heavy-lidded stare. "Nothing. I took him to booking and walked away. I think they OR'd him."

Let him out on his own recognizance. "So he got released that same day?"

He gave another curt nod. "Yeah. And he didn't say anything about excessive force. About a week later, I found out he was claiming I'd roughed him up in the field, cuffed him too tight, didn't belt him up in the backseat, and I purposely drove like a 'wild man' so he'd get thrown around. It's all bullsh—sorry. A bunch of lies."

Their stories sure didn't jibe; I'd give him that much. "How do his booking photos look?"

He snorted. "Nothing. You can't see a damn thing."

"Anyone take photos of his body?"

Kevin turned his palms up and shrugged. "There was no reason to. He didn't tell anyone he'd been bounced around." He gave me a firm look. "Because he hadn't been."

I'd be interested to hear what Valenzuela said about that. "What happened with the possession charge?"

"Pending. It's just a misdemeanor. He'll probably plead guilty and get probation."

"But he hasn't yet?" Kevin shook his head. "I hear he's not asking for money, so what's your take on why he's beefing you?"

Kevin frowned, his brows meeting in the middle. "Honestly, the only thing I can think of is that he's trying to get the dope case thrown out."

If that really were his goal, it'd be a lot better to let his public defender claim the search was bogus than to pursue an excessive-force claim. Unless his public defender had already told him he had no shot. "Okay, Dale says you have the reports on this?"

"Yeah, and the booking photos." He pulled out his cell phone. "Give me your e-mail address."

I gave it to him and waited while he typed it in. "You still working?"

Kevin made a face. "Yeah, but they have me riding a desk until this is resolved." He shook his head, looking more depressed than angry. "I hate it. I need to be on the street. It's the whole reason I stayed in patrol."

It wasn't the first time I'd heard a cop say that. I imagine there's a kind of freedom to working the streets, and a constant excitement in ferreting out the puzzle pieces that don't fit: the new Mercedes rolling around in the housing projects, the too-young girl leaving the fleabag motel with a too-much-older man. "I'll do what I can. But I won't be able to represent you in any formal capacity. I'll meet Valenzuela, see if I can shake him off, maybe get you some ammunition to fight with if he won't back down. But that's it."

Kevin gave me a full nod this time. "Understood."

I got up. "Okay, I'll get back in touch when I have something to report."

Kevin stood, and we shook hands. "Thank you, Ms. Brinkman. I want you to know I really appreciate this."

I couldn't really say it was my pleasure. "Sure. We'll talk soon."

The waitress finally showed up with my coffee. I looked at her. Seriously? "You're a little late." For a whole lot of things, I had a feeling. I nodded at Kevin. "He can have it."

Kevin held up a hand. "No, thanks."

I headed out, but Kevin stayed. As I glanced back through the window, I noticed him move toward the bar.

When I got back to court, I checked my e-mail. Kevin had already sent me everything. I looked at Valenzuela's booking photo. Granted, the resolution on my cell phone wasn't great, but I didn't see a scratch. Then again, it was only a head shot.

I'd finished my business in court and was on my way to the parking lot when I got a call from Alex. "What's up?" I wove around a young Asian couple holding hands and strolling.

"I found the guy Stephen got fired."

"Where?" I headed for the stairs with dread. When I'd had to park on the upper level, I'd told myself the stairs would be good exercise. Now I wanted to tell myself to screw off.

"He lives up in Silicon Valley, but he's down here for a company training program."

"Can we snag a meeting with him?" My steps were getting slower and heavier with every stair.

"Yeah, he agreed to meet us in that little concrete park behind the Hall of Administration when he gets out for the day. Should be around four thirty."

Ugh. That meant another trip downtown, and I barely had enough gas to get back to the office. I had to pause and catch my breath on the second-floor landing. "We'll take your car. What's our cover story with him?"

"We're reporters, covering background on the victims. Hey, you okay? You sound like you've been running."

"I had to park in the sky." Also known as the third floor. "Okay, see you when I see you."

But after I ended the call, I started to have reservations about this meeting. Too many people still seemed to recognize me, even though it'd been three months since Dale's case was dismissed.

When I got back to the office, I told Alex I thought it might be too risky for me to meet this guy, and he should do it alone. "But I want to check him out for myself. So I was thinking: while you do the interview, I could be nearby. Just don't let him sit near the fountains." Because Alex was going to record the conversation, and the noise would screw up the sound.

Michelle rolled her eyes. "What're you going to do, Sam? Wear dark glasses and a scarf on your head?"

I shot her a look. "Yeah. And a trench coat. Like Carmen Sandiego."

She pulled off her Scünci. "Here, wear this and your sunglasses. That should do it."

"I'd rather wear a set of antlers. No offense."

"None taken." She pulled back the Scünci like a slingshot and fired it at me.

It turned out not to be a problem. It was the end of the business day for just about every county employee in a three-block radius, and the weather was nice enough to enjoy coffee and a snack in the park before heading home. I had plenty of people to blend in with.

Alex took a table just eight feet away from where I was nursing a big cup of green tea. At a quarter to five, Alex waved, and I saw a short man whose body looked like a stack of circles waddle over to his table. William Everleigh, I presumed. When he sat down, I saw that he had a young face. I pegged him somewhere between midthirties and early forties. Alex had positioned the chairs so I'd get enough of a side view to read his expressions and hear their conversation.

William—who, of course, told Alex to call him Bill—started by saying that he wanted to be able to decide when something was off the record. Alex assured him that wouldn't be a problem. Alex asked him some general questions about Stephen Sonnenberg, how long he'd worked for him—three years—what it was like to work for him—okay, he guessed—and what Stephen's reputation was at the office. Bill hedged on that one, and I could tell he was dying to unload. So could Alex. He baited Bill with a question about why he'd left the company. But Bill just shrugged and mumbled something about wanting to move up north. So Alex threw out bigger bait and hinted that he'd heard Stephen had kind of a thing for young women. That did it.

Bill leaned in. "This is off the record, okay?" Alex nodded. "He got me fired so he could move in his twenty-year-old squeeze who barely knew how to program."

Alex feigned surprise. "How'd he do that?"

Bill was already breathing hard. He bit off his words as though he were snapping the necks of baby chicks. "He claimed I was reporting false hours on my time sheet. A total fucking lie! I'd never do a thing like that! But he was the boss, and I was just a nobody, and I didn't have an angel in senior management to protect me. So I got dumped. And that idiot, Lilliana, got my job." He sat back and stared off with narrowed, angry eyes. I could practically see the steam coming off him.

Even from where I was sitting, I could see Alex oozing sympathy. "That's really shitty. Do you think he was having an affair with the woman?"

Bill exploded. "Of course he was! I can't prove it, but it was totally obvious." He shook his round head. "I always knew there was something not right about Stephen. It wasn't just Lilliana, either. He liked young women a little too much. And I mean *young* young. Not like junior high or anything, but I remember he'd watch the summer interns. You could practically see the thought bubble over his head: 'I'd like to get my hands on that one.' High school kids! It was disgusting." Bill made a face. After a few moments, he shook his head again. "You know, I'm really sorry about what happened to the rest of the family. It's a terrible thing. But screw that guy. The world's a better place."

"How'd you hear about the murders?" Alex was easing Bill into the final issue: his alibi.

Bill's tone was bitter. "Not from anyone at work. I haven't spoken to them since I left. I heard it on the news. I was at the airport on my way back down here to pack up my stuff. I'd just gotten the job up in Silicon Valley."

I slouched down in my chair, disappointed. So he was probably in Silicon Valley at the time of the murders. Damn. So much for Everleigh. After another few minutes, Alex wrapped it up. I headed to the car, and Alex joined me thirty seconds later. We got in, and he leaned back against the seat and blew out a breath. "Man, he really hates that guy."

"You could see that from space. But if he's telling the truth, he has a solid alibi."

Alex started the car. "It'll be easy enough to check out. I just wonder how much of his stuff about Stephen being a perv is believable."

"Me, too. Seemed a little over the top to me." But not impossible. Pervs did walk among us.

As I well knew.

FOURTEEN

Since we were already downtown, I decided to drop in on Cassie and see how she was doing. "Can you give me a lift, Alex? I'll just Uber home."

Alex lifted his hands off the steering wheel. "See how they're shaking? That's because I fear what Michelle will do to us if she finds out you spent money on Uber."

That was, unfortunately, no exaggeration. And Michelle didn't even know I was footing the bill for Deshawn's hideaway. Yet. "But I think Cassie's more comfortable talking one-on-one, and I don't want you to get stuck waiting for me."

"I'll 'wait' at the Americana. Take your time."

The Americana at Brand was a great mall in Glendale, the kind that was like a Disneyland for shoppers. Alex really knew how to make the most of a situation. When he dropped me off, I said, "Let me know if there are any good sales."

But Cassie wasn't home. Barbara was apologetic. "I didn't know you were coming. She asked if she could go see her friends, Tawny and Rain. I thought it'd be good for her to get out and do something normal. I'm so sorry."

"No, no, Barbara. My bad. I just assumed she'd be here, which was silly of me." But now that I was here, I might as well make the most of it. I'd been meaning to talk to her daughter. "Would you mind very much if I spoke to Debbie? Just to get her view on things?"

Barbara didn't mind at all.

I knocked on the door and heard Debbie tell me to come in. Whereas Cassie's room had been a typical guest room—clean, tidy, but spare, no personality—this room very obviously belonged to a teenage girl: posters of Meghan Trainor, Nicki Minaj, and One Direction; no stuffed animals, but lots of powder-blue and pink pillows; framed photos of Debbie with various girlfriends in goofy poses; and hanging over the mirror above a dressing table, a multicolored, pop-bead-style necklace that said "Holly 2015"—Holly's birthday commemorative, I surmised.

Debbie was lying on the bed, watching television. It looked like *South Park*.

Debbie herself was one of those girls you overlook in every group photo. Her brown hair was long, thin, and parted in the middle to frame a fair-skinned face with no discernible bone structure and pale-brown eyes. She looked at me with a gaze that was flat and uninterested.

"Hey, Debbie. Mind if I ask you a couple of questions?"

She looked annoyed. "I already told the cops I don't know anything."

And they'd obviously left it at that. I kept my voice light. "But sometimes you remember different things when you hear different questions. Just a few minutes, I promise." Debbie shrugged. I pulled out the small wooden chair that'd been parked in front of a small desk and turned it around to face her. "Has Cassie ever talked to you about feeling scared of anyone?"

Debbie sighed, then lifted the remote and turned down the volume on the television. "She did at first. But not lately."

"Do you guys ever hang out?"

She shook her head, her tone peevish. "She mostly sits in her room all day, watching TV."

"So you guys don't do much talking?"

"No." An irritable look crossed her face. "You should ask my mom. She's the only one Cassie talks to. Well, my mom and whoever Cassie's texting constantly."

Hadn't the cops taken her phone? Apparently not. "You don't know who that is?"

Debbie rolled her eyes and gave a petulant sigh. "When I asked her, she just said she deserved a little privacy, she had a lot to deal with, and went to her room." Debbie finally clicked off the television and looked at me. "I know she's been through such a horrible thing, and I totally expected her to be sad and crying all the time. But I never thought she'd be mean."

I was—and wasn't—surprised by this. "Does she act like that a lot?"

Now I could see that hurt, not irritation, was the real issue for her. "To me, yeah. Not to my mom."

I was fairly sure that Debbie was getting the snotty treatment because Cassie was jealous—probably as a rule—but now more than ever. "I'm sorry, Debbie. That's a drag. All I can say is, don't take it personally. People who go through terrible things can act mad so they don't have to feel sad. Cassie doesn't know what's going to happen to her now. She's really scared, and I think she's coping by being angry at the whole world."

Debbie shrugged and traced the flower on her bedspread with her finger as she thought about that. "Makes sense, I guess." After a moment, a worried expression settled on her face. "But she really leans on my mom a lot, and it's wearing her down." Debbie looked up at me, contrite. "I know it sounds terrible, but I hope Cassie's relatives find a place for her soon."

"It doesn't sound terrible. It sounds perfectly normal. And I'm sure they will. Cassie can't stay here permanently." I stood up, then thought of one more question. "Did it seem like Cassie was texting a guy?" I wasn't sure how she could tell, but it was worth a shot.

Debbie tilted her head to one side. "Kind of. Only because they'd go at it for a long time, and she seemed a little happier afterward."

"Did you ever see her with a boyfriend in school?"

"I didn't really see her much at all. I'm a junior. Cassie's a sophomore."

And when I asked her about Abel, I got the same answer. It was interesting how segregated these kids were. I didn't remember being roped off that way when I was in high school. But I wasn't exactly representative of your average high schooler. And given the kind of shit I got into with the older kids—and a couple of teachers—it probably would've been better if there had been a little more division among the ranks. "Okay, thanks, Debbie."

She sat up and spoke with urgency. "But I hope she'll be okay. I mean, I do feel sorry for her and all."

I gave her an understanding look. "I know."

I thanked Debbie and left her to the *South Park* rerun. I texted Alex that I was ready to go, and he texted me back that he'd decided to wait outside and save himself from bankruptcy.

Barbara was in the kitchen, wiping down the counter with a paper towel. I told her I appreciated her letting me talk to Debbie. "Did you happen to notice that Cassie's been texting a lot?"

She raised her eyebrows. "A lot? No. I know she gets texts every day, but I assumed it was just her friends checking up on her, and I was glad." She finished wiping the counter and threw the paper towel into the trash can under the sink.

"So you don't know who she was texting with?"

"No, she'd always go to her room to answer them, and I never asked who it was. Didn't want to pry." Barbara paused. Her eyes filled with tears. "She seems so lost, so frightened. And who can blame her? If it were me, I'd be curled up under the bed." She pulled a Kleenex out of her sleeve. "But Cassie's such a sweet girl. Always telling me how she doesn't know what she'd do without me, how grateful she is for all I've done for her—really to all of us for taking her in. Can you believe that? After all she's been through, all she's going through, and she manages to be thankful." Barbara dabbed at her eyes.

I nodded, but I had a feeling that being thankful, being grateful, was Cassie's default mode. I told Barbara I'd be in touch and wished her a good night.

When I got back in the car, I asked Alex whether he could get me Cassie's cell phone records. "I want to find out who she's texting non-stop. I've got her number."

Alex gave me a smug look. "Not a problem."

"And cell towers." If I knew what towers were accessed by the calls, I'd also have some idea where that person was.

"That might take a little longer."

FIFTEEN

On the way back to the office, I told Alex about my freebie case—Kevin Hausch, the cop who'd been beefed for excessive force. "This should be quick and dirty. We talk to the alleged victim, poke holes in his story, persuade him to back off, and we're out."

"And if he won't?"

"Then Kevin's got himself a problem, 'cause he won't have us." I wasn't just unhappy about representing a cop, I was also unhappy about wasting time on a freebie. We were doing better, but the bills were still coming in faster than the money, and it was about time to give Michelle and Alex a raise. And Deshawn's hotel bill was climbing. I'd be maxed out in another week.

Julio Valenzuela worked in an auto body shop on La Brea, in Hollywood. We decided it'd be best to drop in unannounced tomorrow.

Alex merged onto the 101 freeway. "What's our cover story?"

"Let me think about that." I would've posed as a lawyer who wanted to take his case, but since he'd made a point of telling Internal Affairs he'd shut down all the lawyers, I figured that wouldn't be a winning gambit.

It was after six o'clock by the time we got back to the office.

I felt my cell phone buzzing in my purse as we walked in. I pulled it out and looked at the number. Niko Ferrell. He was the very defini- tion of *hunk*. I'd met him when I stumbled into a Krav Maga class a few months ago. He was, of course, the teacher. Bald, with a trim beard and mustache and an incredibly lean, muscled body, he made all the women in the class—plus a few of the men—go slack-jawed when he walked in.

But I'd gotten too busy and had to drop out after the second class. Niko had called to find out why I stopped coming and wound up ask- ing me to have coffee with him. I didn't even try to play it cool. So far, I'd only managed to squeeze in one early-morning coffee date on my way to work, but it'd been really fun.

Michelle gave me a wise look. "You're smiling. Who's the guy?"

I smiled some more. "Niko."

"The hottie with the body? You finally gonna go on a real date with him?"

Alex put a hand to his chest. "Wait, I need to sit down." He perched on Michelle's desk. "A date? You're actually going to do something human? I've got to see this guy."

I gave a little laugh. "You really do. He's a work of art." Should I take the plunge and see whether we could find enough to talk about to make it through dinner? I had no time or patience for even one more of those boring dinners with forced small talk and awkward silences. The last time I'd been stuck on one, I'd gotten bombed on margaritas just to numb the pain. The ensuing hangover had convinced me life was too short for that much agony. So I wasn't sure I wanted to risk it. This attitude *might* have something to do with the reason I was still single. "I'll see. Maybe."

I went into my office and listened to his message. He had a deep, sexy voice that got me distracted, so I had to play it twice. He was asking about dinner at a Moroccan restaurant on Sunset. It sounded like fun. Fun. I couldn't even remember what that was like. At least, not that kind. I called him back and got his voice mail. I hesitated.

Did I really want to do this? *Beep.* Time was up. I gulped. And said I'd love to.

With that daring, reckless move behind me, I got to work and sent Alex the paperwork and photos on Kevin Hausch's case, then read through it all myself. I'd known Julio's story would conflict with Kevin's—but now that I'd read the reports, I saw that they were 180 degrees off. I'd be interested to see how it held up when Alex and I pounded on—uh, questioned him.

At eight o'clock, Michelle stopped in to tell me she was leaving. I gave her a look of disbelief. "What, already?"

She deadpanned, "You're such a riot."

"I know, right?"

Michelle rolled her eyes. "And tomorrow we need to catch up on billing. The rent's due next week. So we sit down at ten o'clock. No excuses."

I could feel the tension building in my chest. This was why fun was never on my radar. It wouldn't fit in the budget. I held up two fingers. "Scout's honor, I promise."

When I got home, I poured myself a healthy shot of Patrón Silver on the rocks. I'd gone ahead and splurged and bought a bottle. I took my drink out to the little balcony and gazed at the downtown skyline in the distance. From here, it looked like a real cityscape.

I went back inside and turned on the television. *The Usual Suspects* was on—one of my favorite films of all time. When I finally put myself to bed, I thought I might be able to sleep in for a change. But when I woke up, it was still dark outside. I hate the lonely feeling of being the only one awake. It reminds me of my childhood—all of it. I tried to go back to sleep, but after fifteen minutes, I gave up and headed for the shower.

I made it to the office by seven, with a tray of Starbucks coffees for us all. Mainly me. One for Alex, one for Michy, and two for me.

Alex showed up at seven thirty, wearing a worn-looking blazer and slacks. Exactly what I'd have suggested. "Good choice. Have a coffee." I'd worn an old brown skirt and my oldest black blazer. It even had frayed cuffs. I wasn't hugely worried that Valenzuela would recognize me. The police reports showed that he'd been out of the country during Dale's trial. But just to be on the safe side, I'd pulled my hair back and put on a pair of fake glasses with heavy black frames.

He looked down at his suit with disgust. "It's hideous. I had to borrow it from my cousin." Alex scanned my outfit and circled a finger in the air. "And that's unthinkable. Seriously, is this really necessary?"

"Yes, it really is. We're lowly civil servants. We need to look the part."

Michelle rushed in ten minutes later and grabbed a coffee without even saying hello. She took a long slug, then exhaled. "That is good. Very, very good." She took in our outfits. "Wow, congratulations. You guys really managed to look like hell. You about to head out?"

I nodded. "I'll call you from the road if anything crazy happens. Otherwise, see you by ten."

The body shop where Valenzuela worked was just a few miles east of the office, but morning crosstown traffic being what it was, it still took us fifteen minutes to get there. Disco Auto Body was a dingy, grimy, little two-bay shop. An old—and I mean thirty or more years old—faded red Audi sat on blocks near the front of the lot. And in the far corner, next to a tent, there was a collection of husks of cars, body parts, and even the disembodied cab from an ancient Ford pickup truck. Judging by the multicolored patches on the inside of the tent, I imagined that was where they did their spray-painting.

The service bays held the only cars that looked even remotely drivable: a beat-up black Mustang with the front bumper torn off in the first bay and a white Nissan Maxima with a smashed-in driver's-side door in the second bay. The whole place smelled like heavy oil, grease, and chemicals so toxic they'd burn off your eyebrows. It was like a car hospital for the underprivileged. A wiry, Armenian-looking man in dark-blue overalls with an unlit cigarette dangling from his lips was on the phone in the tiny, filthy office—which, of course, had the obligatory pinup calendar. Ms. March looked very fetching in her size DDDs and crotchless pink panties.

Alex wore a stink face as he looked around the lot. "Do you see Valenzuela?"

"Nope. And I don't see any disco balls, either."

Alex gave me a puzzled look. I pointed to the sign. He rolled his eyes. I moved toward the office, thinking I'd ask about Valenzuela. Then I heard a toilet flush and saw a man who matched the photos Hausch had sent me coming out through a small door on the left, wiping his hands on a dirty paper towel. He was a little guy, about five foot six—my height—with slicked-back hair, eyes that sloped down at the corners, and heavy lips.

I held my purse in front of me with both hands so I wouldn't have to shake, and I went over to him. "Mr. Valenzuela?"

He frowned at us and stopped just outside the office. He spoke with a heavy Spanish accent. "Yes. Who are you?"

I gave him our fake names—Cheryl Heathman and Esteban Ibarra—and told him we investigated claims of excessive force for the State Department. He demanded to see our identification. We gave him our cards that showed we were liaisons for the attorney general's Special Investigations Unit. It's so cool what you can make on the computer. The cards even had a picture of the state seal—a nice touch, I thought. He studied the cards, then put them in his breast pocket. "What do you want to know?"

The man in the office was still talking—loudly—on the phone and pacing around in circles. "Do you mind if we step away so I can hear you?"

Valenzuela looked at me suspiciously, but he moved with us to the far side of the lot. Better. "We need to get your side of the story and make sure it's been accurately reported by Internal Affairs. The officer says he stopped you for a broken taillight. Was your taillight broken?"

"*Sí.* I was meaning to fix it, but . . ." He spread his hands.

Kind of ironic that a body-shop guy couldn't fix his own light. But they do say the cobbler's kids go barefoot. "Then he says he saw a baggie with white powder under the passenger side front seat—"

"No!" He shook his finger at us. "No, no! I don't do *drogas*. That is a lie."

I pulled out a notepad and pretended to write down what he said. "The officer says that when he asked you to step out of the car, you were angry, and you behaved in a threatening manner."

"*Otra vez*, no!" He shook his finger at me again. "This *policía* lies! He told me to get out and I say why? I gave you my *licencia*, my insurance. It's just a broke taillight. He open my door." Valenzuela put a hand to the collar of his overalls and gave it a hard yank. "He drag me out the car. I fall down, and he kick me in *estómago*!" Valenzuela grabbed his stomach, red in the face. "Then, he put the handcuffs and throw me in his car. I hear him open his trunk, then he go to my car, and I see him bend down on passenger side. He make like he pull out baggie from there, but no!" He shook his finger again. "Is a lie!" He spit on the ground. "*Mentiroso!*"

Alex whispered, "That means liar."

"Yeah, I got that." I finished writing what he'd said and flipped the notebook closed and frowned. "May I call you Julio?"

He narrowed his eyes and folded his arms, chest puffed out. "Okay."

He was still pretty agitated. If he was lying, he was awfully good at it. "Julio, what I don't understand is why he'd do this to *you*. Are you dating his mother or something?"

Julio muttered something that sounded a lot like "fuck his mother" in Spanish and spit out, "Because I look for my sister!"

Huh? There was no mention of a sister in the reports I had. "What are you talking about?"

Julio looked from me to Alex. "I try to tell one of these men in the *oficina*, but he tell me I'm *loco*."

And so, of course, the cop didn't bother to write it down. It was just crazy talk. Not cool, but I could see it happening. "Please tell us about it." I nodded toward Alex. "He speaks Spanish if you have any trouble."

Julio tilted his head and studied us for a moment, still a little suspicious. "My sister is . . . how you say? Wild girl. Not bad. She just make mistakes. She stole *una cosa* from a store in Arizona. I think she say it was color for the . . ." He pulled on his hair.

"Hair dye?"

"*Sí*. The court don't want put her in jail, so they send her back to Guatemala. She call me from cell phone she borrow when they stop in Sierra Vista."

"Arizona?" Alex asked.

Julio nodded. "She tell me they go to Nogales, then Mexico. She say she call me when she get into Mexico, but I wait two weeks and I don't hear nothing. I call *nuestra familia* in Mexico, but they say she no come. So I think maybe she stay in Nogales. I go there; I ask for her. They tell me go to . . ." He turned to Alex and spoke in Spanish.

Alex translated. "They told him to go to the station at the border checkpoint. Nogales PD."

"The *policía* I talk to there is very ugly—"

Alex interjected, "He means nasty, not bad-looking."

I shot him a look. "Got it."

Julio continued. "He call me *tonto*, tell me no one can stay in Nogales. Everyone go to Mexico. He say my sister has to be in Mexico." Julio clenched his jaw, then moved it from side to side. "I can't do nothing, so I come back here the next day because I have to work. And that's when this *policía* beat me and make up lies, put *drogas* in my car."

I'd heard about those deportations in lieu of prosecutions. But I saw where he was coming from. The timing of his inquiry about his sister and the potentially bogus drug bust *was* suspicious. If it was a coincidence, it was an ugly one. "Have you heard from your sister?"

Abruptly the anger ebbed, and tears welled up in his eyes. "No. I talk to her one month before. No one in Guatemala see her. We think . . ."

That she's dead. She might very well be. Clearly, *something* had happened to her after her bus left Sierra Vista. Whether it was connected to Kevin Hausch was a different story.

But now I wanted to find out.

SIXTEEN

"What do you think?" Alex asked as he turned left onto Hollywood Boulevard.

Julio had agreed to keep our conversation to himself until we got back to him. I believed he would—for a little while. We were the only ones who'd taken the story about his sister seriously, and it helped that Alex was Latino. But just before we left, Julio said that his public defender was pushing him to plead guilty to the misdemeanor possession, and though he didn't want to do it, he couldn't afford to spend a year in county jail if he went to trial and lost.

That meant there wasn't much time. Once Julio pled guilty, his complaint against Kevin Hausch and the story about his sister would likely get dismissed as just a bullshit excuse to get out from under a dope charge.

I watched a skateboarder weave through the crowded sidewalk, his hips rolling under his body like ball bearings. "I just don't know. I believe something happened to his sister. But for all we know, she jumped off the bus, and she's hiding somewhere. In which case, what does any cop have to do with it, let alone Hausch?"

Alex hit the brakes and cursed under his breath as a young woman in headphones crossed in the middle of the boulevard, oblivious to the screeching tires all around her. "Yeah, that's the thing: if Hausch has nothing to do with it, I'm not sure I buy Julio's story. There'd be no reason to roust Julio and plant dope on him." He glanced at me as he waited for the girl to reach the sidewalk. "But we were supposed to get him to drop the complaint and walk away."

And we sure hadn't done that. Damn it. More work on a freebie. Exactly what we didn't need. I thought about how we could make this case go away. "The key is the sister. If we can show Julio that Hausch has nothing to do with her disappearance, maybe he'll realize no one's going to buy his story about getting jacked up, and he'll let it go."

"He might. But that's going to take some digging. I'm happy to do it, but I think there's someone who won't exactly be thrilled with that."

"Are you out of your friggin' minds?" Michelle stood with her hands on her hips, looking—as Alex had predicted—extremely *un*thrilled. "We can't afford this."

I couldn't argue, but I could explain. "Yeah, but—"

Michelle shook her head. "There's no 'but' unless it's 'but I don't mind getting evicted.'"

She was right, of course. I didn't mind the long hours. Too busy was just busy enough for me; it kept me from thinking—and feeling. But it wasn't right to do that to Michy and Alex. They deserved to have lives. "Okay, I surrender. I'm officially done with Hausch."

Michelle leaned back and gave me a suspicious look. "What're you up to? That was way too easy."

I raised my hands. "When you're right, you're right. That's all. We said we were going to catch up on the billing, right? I'll just go over my calendar, make sure it's up to date. Back in a sec." Michelle stared at me, still trying to figure out what my game was.

I headed into my office, closed the door, and fished my cell phone out of my purse. I called Dale and told him what Julio had said. "I can't spare the time to go to Arizona and dig around. But if you can get me proof there's no connection between Hausch and Julio's sister, I'm pretty sure I can get Julio to back off on the complaint."

"It'll have to go on the back burner for now." Dale sounded amped up. "I was just about to call you. I've been squeezing my CIs for intel on the Nazi Low Riders, and one of them just came through. Says he heard someone in the gang bragging about getting even with the 'city council bitch' a few days before the murders."

Confidential informants were the bane of my existence. Sleazy, unreliable, but sometimes hard to impeach, they've screwed more than a few of my clients over the years. "How credible is this guy?"

"Very. Relatively speaking. But he didn't have a name, only a description. We're going to hit up all the probation houses."

When a house is associated with gang activity, it gets put on probation. Meaning the cops don't need a warrant to search it. There had to be at least twenty-five to thirty addresses on that list for the skinhead gangs. That could keep them busy for days. "I sure hope this pans out."

"Me, too."

I ended the call and got down to work. When I'd finished, I tucked my calendar book under my arm and walked out to Michelle's desk.

We worked through each client, and an hour later, the billing for February was done.

Michelle heaved a sigh of relief. "There, was that so bad?"

I stood up and stretched. "Yes."

I went back to my office and focused on my paying cases, writing motions, making phone calls, and preparing witness lists for the ones I thought might go to trial. By five thirty I felt like I'd done enough penance for one day. I picked up my purse and walked out to the reception area. "I'm pretty much caught up, so I'm taking the night off." I stopped at Michelle's desk. "I strongly recommend you do the same."

Michelle sat back. "I haven't seen you leave this early in months. Please tell me you finally have a date." Her expression said she had very little hope for that possibility.

I gave her what I hoped was a mysterious smile. "Maybe."

Michelle studied me for a moment, then shook her head. "You're the worst liar ever." She waved me off. "Let me know what you get on Cassie."

I huffed and threw my jacket over my shoulder. "Okay, fine." I'm actually a pretty good liar, but not when it comes to Michelle. I haven't been able to put one over on her since seventh grade.

I had set up a meeting with Cassie's besties, Tawny and Rain. Tawny had volunteered her house. Her parents would be leaving for a party at the country club no later than six, so we'd have the place to ourselves.

It was a tough drive. The days were lengthening, and at five thirty, the sun was just high enough to drill through my windshield at eye level. It was like looking into a laser beam. As I got off the freeway, I remembered that I'd been meaning to get back to Heather, the teenage beauty who lived across the street from Cassie. I'd gotten the feeling she had something to say about Stephen Sonnenberg when her mother interrupted. It might be nothing, but I was already in the neighborhood, and I had a few extra minutes.

I parked in front of her house and had one foot out of the door when a car pulled up and parked in the driveway. Heather got out of the driver's side. Her mother got out of the passenger side looking frazzled. "Heather, you have to yield when you're making a left. That means you wait for everybody! It's not worth a few extra seconds if you kill someone."

This probably wasn't my best timing, but oh well. I stood up and waved to them. Heather waved back and began to approach me. Her mother hesitated for a moment, then followed. We met on the sidewalk, and I reintroduced myself. The mother said her name was Laura.

I shook her hand and gave her a—hopefully—disarming smile. "I just realized the other day that I heard from practically everyone on the block about what they thought of the Sonnenbergs, but I never had the chance to ask you guys." I'd decided to try the open-ended approach. If Heather clammed up, I'd have to find a way to get her alone.

Heather darted a look at her mother. There it was again. That little hiccup. Laura's expression hardened. She spoke first. "I didn't really care for Stephen. Paula was—I mean is—she's still hanging in, right?" I nodded. Laura looked relieved. "I always thought she was basically a good person. A little on the ambitious side for my taste, but her heart was in the right place. Stephen just rubbed me the wrong way."

Heather put a hand on her mother's arm. "But you didn't feel that way until I told you . . ."

Laura shrugged, then nodded. "I suppose that's true. But I saw it, too."

I looked from Laura to Heather. "Saw what?"

Laura covered Heather's hand with her own. "The way he looked at Heather." She paused for a moment, and her eyes tightened. "A little too much interest, a little too much energy. It wasn't a big deal. I didn't think he'd ever do anything, but it felt . . . wrong, you know?"

Oh boy, did I. "Did he ever say anything to you, Heather?"

She looked away, uncomfortable. "Nothing bad, really. It's just, whenever he saw me, he'd come up to me and want to talk."

"About?"

Heather shrugged, but the way she rolled her shoulders looked as though she were trying to get something off her back. "Just, how was school, what was I going to do on the weekend, what were we reading in English class. Dumb stuff like that." Her face reddened. "But he always got too close to me. He'd stand, like, right here." She put a hand in front of her nose and made a face. "It gave me the creeps."

I could well imagine. "But you never said anything to Paula about it?"

Laura shook her head. "Heather didn't want to. She thought Paula would dust us off as paranoid." She sighed. "Which was probably true. And I didn't want to cause friction. So I told Heather to walk away whenever she saw him and not to worry about being rude."

Wow. A mother who believed her daughter, who cared about her daughter. Imagine that. I tried to picture Celeste saying something like that to me. It almost made me laugh out loud. "Did you ever hear any of the other neighbors complain about Stephen?"

"Not that I know of," Heather said. "You, Mom?"

Laura shook her head. "And I know that if you ask other people on the block, they'll say he was a good guy. Maybe he was—with them. But they don't have pretty teenage girls. Heather's the only one on this block. The other kids are either much younger or much older."

Laura chatted for a moment about the influx of young professionals and how it had changed the neighborhood, then excused herself. "I've got laundry to fold." She turned to Heather. "And you have homework to do." We said good-bye, and Heather followed her mother up the front walk.

I got back into my car, thinking about what Heather and Laura had said. It fit with what Stephen's coworkers had said, that he liked younger women. But a woman in her twenties felt a lot different to me than a seventeen-year-old girl who still lived at home.

I had not one doubt that Heather was telling the truth. I just wasn't sure how far to take it, what exactly it meant about Stephen. It wasn't a crime to give off a lech-y vibe, smile a little too widely at a pretty young girl, or watch young interns with a little too much interest.

I'd just pulled away from the curb when a baseball rolled out into the street. A little boy in a baseball uniform ran after it. I waited for him to get it, and he waved a thank-you to me. I smiled and waved back.

I drove off thinking how very different life in suburbia was from anything I'd ever known. I'd never even lived in a house until Celeste moved us in with that piece of shit, Sebastian Cromer. Until then—and again after we'd moved out—we'd always lived in apartments. And as close to Beverly Hills as she could manage. Not because Celeste cared about good schools or safe neighborhoods, but because she wanted megabucks and a fancy life filled with luxury in an enviable zip code. None of those things was on offer in a middle-class suburban neighborhood like this one.

SEVENTEEN

I headed east on Mountain Street, toward the old-money part of Glendale. The trees on Tawny's block were so broad and leafy they formed an almost complete canopy over the entire road, and the houses were only barely visible above high, thick hedges or walls. Some of the homes had been newly rebuilt in a Mediterranean or modern style, but many were the original two-story brick and Tudor styles. Tawny's house, a two-story brick mansion with wings on either side, was set back a good fifty yards from the street. It was on a rise that I'd bet gave the upper floors a view of the city. Green, rolling hills stretched out behind the mansion. I pulled up to the tall iron gates at the bottom of the long driveway and rolled down the window to press the call button. The smell of grass and dirt, along with a skunky odor that I recognized as wild onion, floated in on damp air. I pulled my jacket closed. It was a lot chillier here. A young girl's voice asked for my name. I gave it, and the gates opened.

I parked off to the side of the circular driveway—which sported the obligatory three-tiered fountain in the center—in case Mom and Dad decided to come home early. The heavy wooden door opened before I could ring the bell. I was kind of disappointed. I wanted to hear whether it played "Hail to the Chief" or something. A very sexy-pretty, slender young girl with long, dirty-blonde hair and pink streaks that reminded me of Cassie's 'do stood in the doorway. In fashionably torn jeans and Uggs, she clung to the door as though it were a favorite teddy bear. "Tawny?" She nodded and stepped back. I walked inside. "Thanks for seeing me."

"Sure. Rain's in the family room. Esmé made us a fire."

As she turned to lead me there, I mentally thanked Esmé, who I assumed was one of their housekeepers. It was icy cold in the house. We crossed a marble foyer and entered a high-ceilinged, richly furnished room with complementing leather couches, wingback chairs, and otto-mans, where a fire roared in an oversize fireplace. In front of it, on a large, fluffy burgundy pillow, sat a young Goth-looking girl, her skin so white it seemed translucent against her inky-black hair. When she turned to face us full-on, the gemstone piercings in her nose and upper lip flashed in the firelight.

I smiled and held out my hand. "Hi, Rain. Thanks for seeing me."

She stared at my hand for a moment, then reached up and briefly folded her hand around my fingers. Hers were cold and clammy. "Sure, no problem."

It struck me that neither girl had even cracked the tiniest smile yet. Tawny grabbed two more plushy pillows from a stack to the left of the fireplace and put them on the floor near Rain. I noticed they were color-coordinated in floral patterns of burgundy, hunter green, and dark blue, to match the furniture. We sat down.

Tawny spoke first. "We're happy to talk to you. But like I said when you called, we already told the police everything we could think of."

Or rather, everything the police could think to ask. The cops were still working on the skinhead theory. I'd decided to leave them to it and dig into the Abel-as-target theory. "I might have some different ques-tions, though. I heard you guys saw Cassie recently."

Rain looked at the fire. "She's totally wrecked. I feel so bad for her."

"Yeah," Tawny said. "It's, like, really hard to even imagine what she's dealing with."

I told them I felt sorry for her, too. Then I asked whether they minded sharing what they knew about Cassie and Abel. They didn't. I started with Cassie. "Does Cassie have a boyfriend?"

Tawny frowned. "Now? No, I don't think so."

"She was kind of hanging with this junior at the beginning of the year," Rain said. "Waylon Stubing." She looked at Tawny. "Remember?"

Tawny looked puzzled for a moment, then the clouds cleared. "Oh, yeah. He's in drama, really cute. I thought he was gay until Cassie started hanging out with him."

"But they're not together anymore?"

Tawny leaned back on her hands and stretched her feet toward the fire. "They broke up around Christmas."

Just a few months before the murders. Maybe she'd gone back to him now. I could see her needing all the moral support she could get. "Did you guys know Cassie's parents at all?"

Tawny's expression showed she didn't get the relevance, but she answered anyway. "Not really. We mainly knew what Cassie said about them—"

Rain rolled her eyes at Tawny and cut in. "They were total assholes, and they made her feel like shit every single day, like she constantly had to bow down to them because they did her the big favor of adopting her. Mutts from the pound get treated better than those jerks treated Cassie."

Tawny very obviously didn't agree. "Come on, Rain. They weren't that bad." She gave Rain a pointed look. "At least they weren't drunks."

Rain looked away, and we all fell silent for a moment. One mystery solved: why Tiegan hadn't wanted to let Cassie stay at Rain's house. I exchanged a look with Tawny to let her know I got it. "What did you think of them, Tawny?"

Tawny moved closer to the fire and hugged her knees. "They could be clueless sometimes. And her mom did get kind of bent when Cassie said she wanted to find her birth mother. I think that's when she told Cassie she should be grateful and all that. I don't know that it was a constant thing."

I leaned toward Rain. "But you think it was?"

Rain shrugged and looked chastened. "I don't know. Maybe not."

I studied her. Did she want to talk about it? I gave it a sideways shot. "Did any of your parents get to know Cassie's mom and dad?"

Rain's expression turned bitter. "My dad left when I was seven, and my mom wouldn't remember who she met yesterday."

Tawny gave me a sardonic smile. "*My* parents? They don't even know *Cassie*, and they barely even know Rain."

Rain gave a short bark of a laugh. "And Tawny and I have been friends since fifth grade." She gave Tawny a sarcastic smile. "But at least you have Esmé."

Tawny gave a humorless little laugh and explained. "Esmé's our tenth housekeeper. She barely speaks a word of English."

I gave her a sympathetic look. Second mystery solved: why Tiegan wasn't crazy about Tawny's family.

And now I understood what all three girls had in common. "How long have you guys known Cassie?"

"Since freshman year," Tawny said.

So, not that long. "Did you both know Abel?"

Rain made a face, and her voice was filled with contempt. "He's a wannabe and an asswipe."

Tawny seemed to agree with that. "It was so pathetic. He was always sucking up to the jocks."

"So it wasn't an in-crowd thing?" I asked. "More of a jock thing?"

Rain sneered. "Yeah. He was always trying to hang out with them."

"And they'd make fun of him behind his back all the time," Tawny said. She shook her head. "It kind of made me feel sorry for him, in a way."

"Not me," Rain said. "He used to call me Dracula's whore. And he slut-shamed Ginnie just because she wouldn't put out."

Tawny shook her head, but she seemed less outraged. "Yeah, that was really shitty. But so many guys do it."

I was incredulous. "Seriously?" I was very familiar with Internet trolls—I had more than my share of them. But that kind of bullying among students who actually knew one another was worse, to me. I'd heard of it happening, but I'd never known that it was a common occurrence.

Rain nodded, her expression matter-of-fact. "Happens all the time."

I asked Tawny, "What about you? Any run-ins with Abel?"

Tawny stretched out her legs and leaned back against the wall. "No, I never had a problem with him."

That figured. Tawny wasn't in Heather's league, but she definitely qualified as one of the pretty girls. "Were there any other girls besides Ginnie who had a problem with Abel?"

Rain and Tawny exchanged a fast look. Tawny dropped her eyes, but Rain met my gaze. "Maybe. Delia told us he roofied her at a party."

"And raped her?" They both nodded. Why was that "maybe"?

Tawny read the question in my expression. "Delia says a lot of things like that." She looked at Rain. "Remember, she said Mr. Thompson groped her in the hallway?"

Rain shook her head. "Yeah." She turned her back to the fire as she pulled her hair over her shoulder. "He was our freshman English teacher, who's about ninety years old and practically blind. I don't think he could've found her tits if he'd wanted to." Rain inclined her head toward Tawny. "And remember when she said Drake tried to drag her into the boys' locker room?"

Tawny tilted her head. "Right. And she said Trudy tried to kiss her?"

Rain frowned. "Trudy?"

"The softball coach."

"Oh, yeah, right." Rain looked at me. "So it may be true, but it's hard to know with Delia."

"Did she ever report anything to the cops?" The girls shook their heads.

"And she made us swear not to tell," Rain said.

I got why there was a question mark next to Delia's name. But true or not, rape was a plausible motivator. I could see someone—though probably not Delia—getting angry enough to do something about it if he believed her story. "Does Delia have a father who's in the picture?"

"No," Tawny said. "He died when she was little. Like four or five, I think."

"What about a brother?"

There was a beat, then Rain nodded. "Yeah. He got back from Iraq a few months ago. He's kind of hot, but he's a little . . . I don't know . . . extreme."

Bingo.

EIGHTEEN

I'd set up an interview with Delia for four o'clock the following day. But at two thirty, I got a voice mail from Dale. They had the killer. If he was right, this was huge. I immediately called him back. "Does your guy fit Cassie's description?"

"I don't want to talk about this on a cell. I'm at the station."

Delia, like all the other kids, lived in Glendale. The Police Administration Building, which everyone called the PAB, wasn't exactly on the way, but it was doable. Regardless, there was no way I was going to wait until after her interview to find out who they'd busted.

I told Alex and Michelle about Dale's phone call. "Alex, if we take off right now and get a little bit lucky with the traffic, we can see Dale and still get to Delia by four."

Alex was skeptical about that. He rescheduled Delia for four thirty. The story of the arrest had already made the news. I watched it on my phone while Alex drove.

He glanced at my phone screen as we idled at the light on the freeway on-ramp. "Maybe we should cancel with Delia. I mean, if they've got their guy . . ."

I shook my head. "We don't stop digging until the DA files charges."
Because until then, you just never know.

When we got to the PAB, we found Dale at his desk.

He was on a call, and I shifted from one foot to the other while I
waited for him to finish it. The moment he did, I jumped in. "Cassie
said the guy had a tattoo of a lightning bolt on his arm. I couldn't tell
from the photos on the news whether your guy has one." Cassie hadn't
been able to tell whether he was bald, because he'd been wearing a blue
bandanna.

"No, he had a *14* on one arm and an *88* on the other. But a *14* could
look like a lightning bolt when you only get a glance in the dark."

The fourteen stood for the number of words in a scumbag Nazi
leader's speech—and eighty-eight referred to the letter *H*—as in, you
know, Heil Hitler. Such genius. "You going to put him in a lineup?"

Dale shook his head. "Even if she did ID him, I doubt we'd get the
DA to file without some backup. One fast glance in the dark, in the
rain—that just won't cut it. So we're running his prints first. We've got
some strays around the doorway to Abel's bedroom."

"Not at the back door?"

"Nothing that was usable."

"What's he say about your snitch's story?"

"That the snitch is a lying sack, that he never threatened to kill
Paula or anyone else, and that I should know better than to believe a
shit-for-brains CI. Also that he's not dumb enough to make a threat like
that in front of anyone who's likely to be a snitch."

That made no sense. "Wait, what? If this guy could tell who was
likely to be a snitch, then how come your little fink still has his head
attached?"

"Well, there's that." Dale's phone rang. "We about done? I've gotta go."

"Yeah, me, too." I started to go, and he picked up the phone. I
turned back. "Hey."

Dale covered the receiver with his hand. "Yeah?"

I spoke in a low voice. "You get anywhere on Hausch?"

Dale glanced around the room, then gave me a warning look. "Not yet."

I started to go, then turned back again. "Just curious: How'd you wind up on Cassie's case? I thought RHD took it."

"They just needed extra manpower for the house searches." He waggled his fingers at me. "'Kay, 'bye."

Alex and I took off. As he pulled onto the freeway to head toward Glendale, he asked, "So we're going to keep working it till they confirm they've got the right guy?"

"Definitely." I remembered what I'd wanted to ask Alex after my evening with Tawny and Rain. "Did you get Cassie's cell phone records yet?" I had a feeling her mysterious texting buddy was her old boyfriend, but I wanted to make sure.

Alex slapped the steering wheel. "Shit! I got sidetracked with Julio's story. Sorry, I'll get right on it."

This was probably the first time I'd ever seen him drop the ball. Usually, his problem was being *too* on top of things. If ever there was a sign that we had too much going on, this was it. But I could see Alex was upset with himself. "Don't sweat it, Alex. It's no biggie." He sighed. "I mean it. Let it go." He muttered to himself for the rest of the drive.

It was four thirty by the time we made it to Delia's place, as Alex had predicted. Our cover story for Delia was that we were helping the police by talking to everyone who knew the Sonnenbergs. It was a bit of a stretch, but far from the worst lie I'd ever told to get a witness to talk to me. You do what you gotta do.

Delia lived in an apartment complex that was a little village of connected townhouses. A road that reminded me of Autopia in Disneyland wound through it, and there was a grassy expanse in the center where a bunch of kids of all colors and both genders were playing soccer.

Alex parked in one of the visitor spots, and we walked through the winding paths to Delia's place. Even from the outside, I could tell it was a little run-down. The white paint on the door was faded and peeling, and wood showed through the cracks. The brass number on the door was tarnished, and one of the screws was missing.

When Alex rang the doorbell, a dog started to bark. It sounded like one of those little yappy dogs with a Napoleon complex. Running footsteps pounded toward us, and then the door opened. A plump girl in skinny jeans, a purple Obey T-shirt that featured flowers inside a square, and purple ballet slipper-style flats, opened the door. I ventured a guess. "Delia?"

Her mascara had fallen, and her dark eye shadow was smudged, making her eyes look like the proverbial holes in a blanket. But her dark-brown hair was thick and shiny and hung in pretty waves down to her collarbone. She took us both in, then, predictably, smiled at Alex. "Are you the guy who called me?"

Alex gave her a warm smile. "I am." He gestured to me. "And this is Samantha Brinkman."

Delia barely glanced at me before refocusing on Alex. This happened so often with female witnesses I got suspicious when it didn't. She stepped back from the doorway. "Come in. My mom's upstairs, but she said we could talk in the dining room."

I noticed a stairway on our left as we walked through a small living room, passed a tiny kitchen on the right, and finally landed in the dining room. It had sliding glass doors and a balcony that offered standing room only. We sat at the oval table. Delia's laptop and geometry book occupied one end, so we sat on either side of it. She closed her laptop and sat down behind it. I thought it'd be best to slide into her story about Abel slowly. Since she hadn't wanted to report the rape, and Tawny had said she hadn't wanted anyone to know about it, it probably wasn't going to be easy to pry the story out of her. We'd have to start by doing what we could to win her trust. "Are you friendly with Cassie?"

"Not really." She quickly added, "I don't hate her or anything. I just, like, don't hang out with her." Delia's voice sounded like an exaggerated Valley girl imitation, every sentence ending on a questioning note.

I bet she twirled her hair with an index finger when she wanted to flirt.

"You guys didn't have any classes together?" I asked. She shook her head. "What about gym?" It was a deliberate prompt. I wanted to see what she'd do with the opening.

Delia's eyes got bigger. "Do you . . . do you guys know . . . about that?"

I gave her a solemn nod, hoping that was the right move. "If you want to talk about it, we'll keep it on the down low." It couldn't be this easy, could it?

Delia's chin quivered. When she looked up, her eyes slid off me and stuck on Alex. "You promise not to tell anyone?"

Alex nodded. Delia took a deep breath. "Freshman year, the softball coach tried to make out with me."

Alex acted surprised. "Really? A teacher? Wow."

Delia nodded. "She's not the only one. Mr. Thompson, my English teacher, tried to kiss me, too."

This was way too easy. Not to knock the Alex magic, but even that couldn't grease the wheels this fast. My very strong suspicion—no doubt influenced by Tawny's and Rain's opinions—was that Delia was a little bit nutty. Her act was pretty weak. I didn't buy it for a second. But it did make me sad. This girl had serious issues.

Alex shook his head. "How did that happen?"

"In the classroom. He told me to wait after class, and when everyone was gone, he told me he was in love with me and tried to kiss me."

Alex gave her a sympathetic look. "That's terrible, Delia. Did you report them to the principal?"

Delia shifted in her chair. "No. I knew he wouldn't believe me." She looked up at Alex. "Please don't tell my mom! She'll get so upset."

Alex nodded. "If you don't want me to tell, I won't. But this is pretty serious. You shouldn't have to put up with this. What they did was wrong."

Delia leaned forward, her expression grave. "Yeah, I know. But that's nothing compared to what Abel did to me."

Alex looked at her, concerned. "What did he do?"

Delia glanced upward—I guessed toward her mother's bedroom—then spoke in a very quiet, halting voice. "When we were at . . . at a birthday party last year, he roofied me and . . . raped me. I woke up with my pants half off and my underwear ripped." She bit her lip and looked down at her lap.

"Delia, I'm so sorry," Alex said. "Did you call the police?"

She shook her head and gave a little sob, but her eyes were dry. "I couldn't. It was too embarrassing. Besides, he'd just say I wanted it!" Delia bit her lip and turned her head away as she let out a few more sobs. But once again, there were no tears.

The story itself was believable. The delivery was what killed it. It was melodramatic as hell. Susan Lucci had nothing on Delia Nusmith. And of course, it was the last in such a long line of stories. But her claim about Abel didn't have to be true to give someone a motive to go after him. I hated to ruin her date with Alex, but I had to step in. "Delia, did you tell *anyone* else about this?"

She furrowed her brow. "Well, I think I told Tawny. Maybe Anna and . . . I think that's it. I really didn't want anyone to know."

And obviously not her mother. "Did you tell your father or your brother?"

She looked at me like I'd asked whether she'd told the Tooth Fairy. "My father? I haven't seen him in years."

I hadn't gotten the whole answer. "What about your brother?"

She looked momentarily stricken, then dropped her gaze and began to fiddle with her laptop. "I—I didn't want to tell my brother."

I waited for her to look up. "But you did tell him, didn't you?"

Her face reddened. After a moment, she nodded. All at once, she sat up. "Wait! Are you thinking he . . . he killed Abel and . . . ?" She shook her head vigorously. "No! Danny'd never hurt anyone!"

A woman called out from upstairs. "Delia? Are you okay?"

Delia's eyes got huge. "I'm fine, Mom!" She whispered, "What are you going to do?"

I shook my head. "Don't worry. We won't tell."

Not yet.

NINETEEN

I didn't know how solid Dale felt about his Nazi Low Rider suspect. But I did know that if his prints didn't match up, he'd be outta there. That is, unless he confessed—and the likelihood of that was less than zero.

After my evening with Tawny and Rain, I'd told Alex to check out Delia's brother, Danny. When we got back to the car, I asked whether he had Danny's home address.

He nodded. "And work, too. He's a driver for UPS in Burbank." Alex looked at his car clock. "Should be getting off in about an hour. But how are we going to approach him? We can't sell him the story about us helping the police."

True. It was barely good enough for a high school girl. I turned it over in my mind. I needed a hook that would get him talking, and it had to be believable. After a few moments, I had an idea. "Did you dig into his military background at all?"

"Of course. Honorable discharge, but his Facebook buddies from the army call him Wild Man Dan, so we should look into that—"

"Thanks, that's—"

"Also, he graduated from Glendale High with a 2.4, got busted twice in tenth grade for curfew violations, and didn't make the cut in Little League."

"Show-off."

He gave me a self-satisfied smirk and pulled out his cell phone. "Here's the photo I got."

It showed a young man in army fatigues cradling an AK like a baby with a wide grin. Danny was average height, on the slender side, and darker skinned than Delia. I guessed him to be mixed race—judging by his features, half Hispanic. "Can you pull a name from someone in his platoon who lives around here?"

"Sure." Alex pulled out his cell phone. "I assume you're going to make up a story about the guy in his platoon?" I nodded. "Kind of risky, don't you think? If the guy lives local, Danny might know him well enough to bust you."

"You just get me a name—and a photo if you can. I'll take care of the rest. And I'll drive."

I always think better when I'm moving. We switched seats, and I steered us out of Autopia. Fifteen minutes later, we were parked down the block from the UPS warehouse—and I had the beginnings of a story.

"Who do we say we are?" Alex asked.

"Ourselves." Alex gave me a worried look. "He won't make the connection. It hasn't really been publicized that I'm Cassie's lawyer." It would when I appeared in court as Cassie's support person, but so far my involvement had stayed under the radar. And if he recognized me as the lawyer in Dale's case it was all to the good. It'd fit perfectly with my cover story.

By the time we spotted Danny leaving the building, I had fleshed it out enough to sell it. I hoped. He'd put on a few pounds since his army days, but that only made him of average weight. And his hair was a lot longer now. It was thick, black, and straight, and it hung down three inches past his shoulders. Something about that pinged a memory.

Alex and I had parked farther down the block, so we were ahead of Danny. When he was twenty-five feet away, we got out and waved to him with friendly smiles. He slowed down and stared at us, but he kept coming, his expression puzzled. "I'm sorry, I don't think we've ever met."

He didn't sound sorry. His tone was hostile, almost accusing, looking for the scam. This wasn't going to be easy. I kept the smile going. "No, we haven't." I introduced myself and Alex, and we gave him our cards. "We're here because Griffin Lenahan put you on his list of friends to contact." I looked around. "We're hoping you can help him. If you can spare us a few minutes, I'll explain."

Danny's expression was wary, but as he read our cards, it changed to alarm. "Is he in some kind of trouble?"

There was a jittery, angry energy to Danny. His eyes bounced between Alex and me, and he swayed as though he were poised to run at any second. A product of his time in Iraq? Or his natural state? I had no way of knowing.

I nodded. "Is there someplace nearby where we can talk?" I already knew the Santa Fe Café was just around the corner.

He narrowed his eyes as he looked from me to Alex, weighing his answer. I thought for a moment he was going to tell us to go piss up a rope, but he finally nodded. He suggested the Santa Fe Café, and I let him lead the way. It was a tiny place, no more than ten wooden tables, and it had no décor to speak of. I guessed it did a brisk takeout business. A woman behind the cash register told us we'd need to order from her. We ordered Cokes, and she brought us three cans and glasses.

We took them to the last table in the back. Danny obviously wasn't interested in small talk, so I got right down to it. I leaned in and spoke quietly. "Griffin got busted for possession of methamphetamine. He swears the dope wasn't his. Says it belonged to his roommate. But the cops found it in his bedroom. Griffin says he doesn't know how it got there. We're putting together a list of character witnesses to try and convince the DA not to file charges. Did you ever know him to do drugs?"

Danny paused, then looked me in the eye. "This is confidential, right? 'Cause you're his lawyer?" He darted looks around the room.

I nodded. "Absolutely."

His eyes made another lap before meeting my gaze. "To be honest, he was into weed, did a little cocaine. But not meth. At least, not that I ever knew."

"Okay, we can leave out that first part and focus on the 'no meth.' Would you be willing to sign a statement to that effect?" He scanned the place again before he looked at me. Danny nodded, then took a swig of his soft drink. "Griffin's one of the good guys. He was always ready for action. Not like a lot of those pussy slackers I got stuck with over there."

I played dumb. "Over where?"

"Iraq. I did two tours." His expression turned contemptuous. "Would've signed up for a third, but at the end of my second tour, one of the lame-ass fags complained to the sergeant that I was bullying him. The sergeant said he'd have to 'launch an investigation' if I wanted to re-up, so I told him to go fuck himself and got out." Danny took another long gulp of his drink.

We might've just found out why they called him "Wild Man Dan." The anger rolled off him in waves. It wasn't hard to picture him venting that anger on Abel. I gave him a little smile. "I'd say it was their loss."

Danny nodded, still a little hot. "Bet your ass." He took another swallow and emptied the can. I waited to see whether he'd crush it in his hand, but he just set it down and pushed it aside.

"Another round?"

"No, thanks. I'm good."

He seemed a little calmer now. I needed to find out whether Danny had an alibi. "You and Griffin stay in touch?"

Danny nodded. "We have beers every once in a while. Talk about it all."

"By any chance, were you guys hanging out on March second? That'd be the night before he got busted." Actually, it was the night of the murders.

Danny turned so his side was to me and looked at me out of the corner of his eye. "I think I went bowling with some of the guys from work that night."

"And then?"

Danny looked at me, his expression turning hostile. "And then nothing. I went home."

"Anybody waiting for you there?"

Danny glared at me for a long moment. "What's it to you?"

I gave him a sexy smile. "Just wondering."

His face slowly relaxed, and he returned my smile. "Only thing waiting for me were my bills."

I picked up my cell phone and spoke in a coy voice that made me nauseous. "Can I text you my number?" His eyes roamed over my body as he gave me his number. I hit send and smiled again. "There you go." I planned to block his number the moment we left the café.

I had one more line of attack, but I had to make it sound casual. I picked up my purse as though I were getting ready to leave. "You live around here?"

"Yeah, just for the past year or so. Used to live in Glendale."

"Glendale? That's where that family got killed, isn't it? Did you know them?"

Danny's face darkened. "No. But I heard that kid was a piece of shit."

I gave him a puzzled look. "You mean the girl?"

He shook his head, his eyes glittering with malice. "The boy. Abel. A real punk-ass bitch."

"Because?"

Danny stared off. "Let's just put it this way: the world's a better place without that little rat-faced bastard."

I shot Alex a quick look. He patted his left lapel and nodded. He'd recorded it all.

TWENTY

I exhaled for what felt like the first time in fifteen minutes as Alex drove away from the UPS building. "What do you think?"

"I can definitely see him doing it. Is it enough to get him arrested?"

He had the motive, the temperament, and no alibi. But he sure didn't look like any AB gangbanger. "Maybe not. But it's enough to make him a person of interest."

We headed back to the PAB. Dale was in the break room eating a Hot Pocket that smelled like burned cardboard. Luckily, he was alone. When I told him what we'd done, he dropped the half-eaten Hot Pocket on his plate. "What the hell are you doing? You're a lawyer, not a cop. Remember?"

"Hey, I just handed you a prime suspect, and no one in LAPD was even close. You're welcome."

"You really need to back off, Samantha." Dale gave an exasperated sigh and held out his hand. "Give me the recording. I'll get it to Emmons and Templeton."

"How about *I* take this to them, since—you know—*I'm* the one who managed to get it."

He looked me in the eye. "And the one who'll take major-league gas for interfering in an investigation if I don't talk them down off the ledge." He sat back and waved a hand at me. "But go ahead, be my guest. Maybe they'll kiss your ring and name a holiday after you."

I didn't think Emmons was the type to get huffy about how he solved the case, but Rusty Templeton might. I loved the idea of rubbing the cops' noses in the fact that I'd gotten further than they had, but it wasn't worth the risk. I nodded to Alex. "Give it to him." Alex handed over his mini recorder. "I'll expect that back by tomorrow. Are they going to follow up? Or just shove it in a bottom drawer?"

Dale gave me a hard look. "We're not all lazy sacks of shit, Sam. It's not my call, but I'm sure they'll look into this Danny guy."

I didn't like it, but I had to let it go. "I assume no results on the print run for your Nazi Low Rider."

Dale looked worried. "Not yet. But they're riding the print guy hard. We should have them soon."

"Let me know what happens." I turned to go.

Dale stood up. "Sam?"

I looked back at him. "Yeah?"

"Nice work."

I gave him a flat smile. "Yeah, I know."

As we headed back to the car, Alex said, "The only way they won't follow up on Danny is if that Low Rider guy's prints match the crime scene."

I knew that. But in the past couple of days, my gut had been telling me that this wasn't an AB killing, that all this focus on the Nazi Low Riders was just a waste of time. Anyone can wear a blue bandanna. And plenty of young males have some kind of tattoo.

While Alex drove us back to the office—or, rather, inched us toward the office behind miles of red taillights—I called Michelle to fill her in on our escapades and see whether I'd missed anything.

"You got a call from Louis, your co-counsel on that eighteen-count robbery case. He thinks your guy may be willing to plead now. He said you'd understand."

"And I do. That's excellent." I'd asked Louis to get his client to work on mine and make him agree to take the deal. Sometimes this works; most times it doesn't. This was a gift. "Anything else?"

"Deshawn called again. Seriously, what's up with him? His case was done ages ago."

I thought fast. The truth is always the best lie. "A friend of his is in hot water, and he's trying to help, which means he needs me to help." All true. A thousand percent watered down, but true. I ended the call, and when Alex got off the freeway, I asked him to stop at the gas station mini mart near the freeway so I could get a bottle of water.

Also so I could call Deshawn. I hid in the bathroom. "What's up?"

"I can't stay here, man. I'm about to lose my damn mind. There's nothin' going on, nothin' to do."

"You picked the place, remember? Don't you have any friends up there?"

"Hell, no." He muttered something under his breath. "I don't know what I was thinkin' when I told you to put me up here in East Jesus. But you gotta wrap it up and get me outta here."

"I'm working on it, Deshawn. Just give me one more week." Regardless of his ennui, a week was all my credit card could handle. I ended the call with a very strong desire to bang my head against the wall. When we got back, I went into my office and closed the door. And punched the crap out of the pillows on my couch. A hundred thousand dollars. How the hell was I going to find that much money? For a single, desperate moment, I thought about asking Alex to try and hack into some rich guy's bank account. But what if he got caught? I'd never forgive myself.

My cell phone quacked and interrupted my slugfest. It was Dale. "Do I want to admit I got this call?" I was thinking Emmons and Templeton had told Dale to lock me up.

"Definitely not." Dale's voice was so low I had to strain to hear. "It's a no match. We're letting the Nazi go."

I sank back in my seat, feeling vindicated. "They going to see Danny?"

"I sure hope so. Gotta go." He ended the call.

I told Alex to come in.

He must've been able to see the triumph on my face, because he smiled and said, "It's not the Low Rider, I take it."

"No." Something about Danny had pinged in my brain earlier, and now it pinged again. What was it? Alex interrupted my train of thought. "If it wasn't an Aryan Brotherhood guy, do they still need to guard Paula?"

"They probably still will until they have the right guy in custody, just to be on the safe side." I refocused, tried to grab hold of the thought. Then I had it. "Alex, I've gotta make a call, but when I'm done, let's head back to Glendale." I told him where I wanted to go.

Phillip Bryer was happy to see us. "I was just about to have dinner. Lamb stew. My own special recipe. I made a bunch. You're welcome to join me."

It smelled delicious, but I declined. I reminded him what he'd told us about the man he'd seen standing in front of his house the day of the murders. He nodded. "Yeah, and I thought he was looking at the Sonnenbergs' house."

Alex had taken a photo of Danny Nusmith while pretending to answer a text when we were at the Santa Fe Café. He pulled it up now and showed it to Phillip. I held my breath as I watched him study it. When he looked up, his expression was grim. "That's the guy all right."

My pulse jumped. "Are you sure?"

"Very sure."

Now what? I'd probably already pissed off Emmons and Templeton once. It wouldn't go over well if I got caught meddling in the case again. But what were they going to do? They couldn't ignore it just because it came from me. "Do you have any problem telling the police about this?"

Phillip shook his head. "None whatsoever."

I excused myself and stepped outside to call Dale. He answered with dread in his voice. "What now?"

"Shut up and be grateful. I have a witness who saw Danny across the street from the crime scene the afternoon of the murders."

"How close?"

"Directly across the street, and he seemed to be watching the house."

Dale sighed. "You with him now?" I said I was. "Okay, give me his name and address. And stay there. Emmons and Templeton are going to want to find out what you said to the guy. I assume you showed him a photo." I said I had. "They'll want to see it."

"I'm going to let this guy have his dinner in peace. Tell them to call me when they're close."

"Okay, but don't go far." He ended the call.

I went back inside. "The police will be coming by to take your statement pretty soon. We'll be back when they get here. In the meantime, enjoy your dinner. And thank you."

When we got back in the car, Alex said, "We have to wait for the detectives, I take it." I nodded. "That's actually good police procedure—"

I pointed a finger at him. "No, you're not. You're not talking to me about that goddamn book."

Alex was unperturbed. "It's a different one. But okay. What're we going to do for the next hour?"

"For starters, hit a drive-thru. I'm starving."

"There's a Wendy's on Glenoaks Boulevard."

It was no lamb stew, but I was in no position to be picky. I was ready to eat the headrest. "Let's do it."

We'd just parked and unwrapped our burgers when Dale called me back. "Never mind about hanging around. Danny admitted he was there."

"You're kidding. What'd he say?"

"That he was thinking about beating the shit out of Abel for raping his sister, but—"

I finished the statement for him. "But he decided not to, and he's denying the murders."

"Yep. So they arrested him to buy time to run his prints. And they asked me to give you a message. It's two words."

Finally. I said, "Thank you?"

"You got the second word right." He ended the call.

Ungrateful bastards.

TWENTY-ONE

We headed back to the office, and I stretched my legs, glad that Alex was driving. "I know we've been doing a lot of running around, but did you happen to have a chance to get Cassie's cell phone records?" I'd been curious to know who she was talking to and texting so much ever since Debbie had told me about it. I always wanted to know everything that was going on with my clients. This routinely put us at odds, because my clients never wanted me to know anything about what they were up to.

Alex nodded. "I put them on your desk."

I didn't remember seeing them, but the brief time I'd spent in my office had been taken up with beating the snot out of my couch. "Anything interesting?"

"Actually, yeah. Some calls to her besties, Tawny and Rain. But, like, a hundred calls to one Earl Lee Riser."

Early Riser. Shit. "A burner phone?"

Alex was unhappy, too. "Yeah, so I have no clue who that is. And before you ask, yes, I'm working on the cell tower records."

But that'd only give us a general area where the burner phone usually was when it took and placed calls. It wouldn't pin down the calls to a house or an apartment. Now I was more curious than ever. Who was this guy? I supposed I'd have to bite the bullet and ask Cassie. She probably wouldn't tell me, but whatever. It wasn't our highest priority right now.

The high priority was Danny's prints. I was hoping they'd match the latents at the crime scene.

Alex turned in to the parking lot under our building and managed to find a space right next to my car. I was shocked—until I remembered what day it was. I sighed. "Sorry to ruin your Saturday." Not that I hadn't done it before, but still.

"My Saturday night *and* my poker night."

"Poker night?" Somehow, I hadn't pictured Alex as a poker player.

Alex raised an eyebrow. "What? You thought I'd be playing mah-jongg?"

I shrugged. "Or bridge, maybe."

He reached across me and opened my door. "Get out."

I slept in late Sunday morning, which meant I had to run all day to squeeze in my chores. When I walked into the office Monday morning, Michelle was talking into her headset.

"Oh, wait. She just walked in. Hang on." She hit mute and said, "It's Dale, line one. Sounds serious."

I hurried into my office, threw my purse on the couch, and picked up the phone. "Thanks, Michelle, I've got it." She clicked off. "Tell me it's him."

"It's not. It's a no match. We had to cut him loose."

I flopped down in my chair. "Shit! You've gotta be kidding me."

"I wish I was." Dale sighed. "Back to square one. Glad it's not my case."

I leaned back and stared out the window. I'd bet Emmons and Templeton were bouncing off the walls. I particularly enjoyed that mental image of Rusty Templeton.

Ten minutes later, Emmons called. I prepared to play dumb about Danny, but it turned out that wasn't why he'd called. He just wanted to tell me that Paula had improved enough to be brought out of her coma. She wasn't able to do much talking yet, but she was somewhat responsive to the doctors and seemed to understand what was being said to her. The doctors said Cassie could come see her tomorrow morning.

Emmons said he'd called Barbara first, but she couldn't do it. "She suggested maybe you wouldn't mind. I figured Cassie would want to see her as soon as possible."

It'd be nice to be involved in good news for a change. And I could use the car ride to ask Cassie about Earl Lee Riser, our burner phone mystery man. "I'd be glad to. Will you and Rusty be there?"

He sighed. "Yeah. We have to stay close in case she can give us something to go on. We're all out of leads. And the docs don't know how she's going to do. She could recover, or she could go lights-out real fast. So we can't afford to miss our window." He paused. "Uh, Sam, do me a favor? Don't get into it with Rusty, okay?"

I bristled. How did his bitchy 'tude become *my* fault? "You going to give him the same speech? 'Cause last I checked, he was the one who got all up in my shit first."

Emmons gave a ragged sigh that sounded like he wanted to pull out his few remaining hairs. "All I'm asking—"

I was fighting a losing battle. He just wanted peace, and he was pushing on the side most likely to make it. "Fine. I'll do what I can."

I ended the call and arranged with Barbara to pick Cassie up at ten a.m. Then I went out to the reception area and filled Alex and Michelle in on Paula and the fact that Danny was out of the picture. After chatting for a few more minutes, we all went back to work.

An hour later, Alex came to my office. "I just got off the phone with Dale. He wants to come by in fifteen. Will you be here?"

I nodded. "Did he say what he wanted?"

"He's got something on Kevin Hausch."

That reminded me, Alex had been trying to find Julio's sister. "Did you get anything on the sister?"

"I confirmed that she made it to Nogales. But after that, nothing."

Damn. If Alex couldn't find her, she was either dead or abducted by aliens.

Dale showed up ten minutes later. We all convened in my office. He flopped down on the couch, and Alex turned a chair around.

I leaned against my desk. Dale was not happy. "What's wrong?"

Dale's expression was dark. "Hausch worked at San Luis PD in Arizona ten years back."

Why was that bad news? "So?"

"My source says he left on bad terms. The sergeant there thought he let some gangbangers slide on a crack case. Nothing official, so LAPD didn't know about it. And San Luis is just three hundred miles away from Nogales, where Julio's sister disappeared. Not next door, but close enough to the action to make me wonder. My buddies in the gang unit tell me the MS-13 is heavy into human trafficking. Deportees have been getting smuggled off the buses and sold into slave trade—sex and other."

The MS-13 was arguably the deadliest and largest gang operating in the Americas. If Hausch was in bed with them . . . "Are they saying cops are taking bribes to look the other way?"

"They think it's likely, although they don't know of anyone specific. But Hausch has no prior disciplinary record here in LA. And it's possible that sergeant in San Luis just had a hard-on for him. So this could turn out to be a witch hunt. But it should be checked out. The problem is, I can't afford to let my fingerprints show up on any of it."

Because if they did, the department would want to know why, and that would screw Hausch for potentially no reason. Not to mention make Dale look like a backstabbing rat. Just what he needed. But sinking more time into this freebie definitely wasn't something *I* needed. "I really want to help, but this hydra just sprung about fourteen more heads, and I'm already stretched pretty thin."

Dale sat forward and clasped his hands together. "I know, and I never intended to do that to you. So I've got a proposal. The person I need right now is Alex. How about I pay his salary this month?"

I certainly didn't mind. And—just as a bonus—I could bump up Alex's salary. Unfortunately, Alex beat me to the punch—with the truth.

"I'm in," Alex said. "I get four thousand a month."

Dale nodded. "Sold. I need you to see what you can dig up on this smuggling business in the Arizona border towns. Check out cases with immigrant crime victims, and see if you can find any news stories on dirty cops in border town PDs. Especially cops who've been busted for bribes. I'll keep pushing on my end, but I've got to be discreet, and that'll slow things down."

I studied him. I wouldn't have thought that he'd be willing to put himself in this position. "If Hausch is dirty and anyone finds out that you've been snooping around, you're not going to get much love from the department."

Dale set his mouth in a grim line. "But I'll get lots of love from Hausch if it doesn't pan out."

"True." If we shredded any connection between Hausch and Julio Valenzuela, the case against Hausch would wash out.

Dale had a determined look. "Either way, I've got to know. If he is dirty, he's got to go down for it."

I respected that. "Okay. We'll see what Alex comes up with." I told him about taking Cassie to visit Paula.

"Yeah, Rusty told me she's awake. He's not holding out much hope, though. She's in really bad shape."

"I'll let you know how it goes," I said.

They headed for Alex's office to knock around some investigative ideas, and I went back to work.

The next morning, I filled Beulah's tank before heading out to Glendale to avoid any nasty surprises and made it to Barbara's house by nine thirty. Cassie looked a lot better than when I'd last seen her, but as she pulled on her seat belt, I saw that she was so nervous she was practically vibrating. "Are you okay?"

Cassie was staring through the windshield. She swallowed. When she spoke, her mouth was so dry it made a crackling sound. "What if she doesn't recognize me? What if she doesn't . . . make it? The doctors said that once they pull her out of the coma, she might . . ."

Reasonable fears all. "It's natural to be scared. But it looks like she might be okay. The doctors say she's responding, that she understands what's being said to her. She could make a full recovery. So let's try to be positive, okay?"

Cassie didn't answer. And she didn't speak all the way to the hospital. I'd wanted to ask her about this Earl Lee Riser person, but now definitely didn't seem like the time.

Cassie trailed behind me as we walked into the room. Paula was in the ICU, and she was hooked up to so many monitors it looked like they could've launched her to Mars. Her head was bandaged and her face was swollen, but the rest of her looked pretty normal. Templeton and Emmons sat in chairs in opposite corners of the room. That was a perfect analogy if ever I saw one. They looked like they'd been there awhile. Newspapers and empty cardboard coffee cups were on the floor at their feet.

When we walked in, they sat up. Cassie took three tentative steps, then stopped a few feet from Paula's bed and stared at her mother.

Emmons spoke to Cassie. "You can talk to her. The doctors said it'd be good for her to hear a familiar voice."

Cassie didn't acknowledge him. She continued to stare down at Paula. After a long moment, in a soft, trembling voice, she said, "Mom? It's Cassie. Can you hear me?"

Paula's eyelids fluttered. She mumbled something in a hoarse voice. Emmons went to the other side of her bed and leaned down to listen, then shook his head. He straightened up and spoke softly to Cassie. "Can you say something else?"

Cassie took a deep breath, her face pale. But this time her voice was stronger. "Hey, Mom. It's me. Cassie. Can you hear me?"

Paula's eyes fluttered again, then slowly opened to half-mast. She focused on Cassie for a long moment. And then her eyes grew round. Her mouth opened wide, but all that came out was a harsh, rasping grunt. As she continued to stare at Cassie, her whole body began to shake.

Then all the monitors started to shriek at once.

TWENTY-TWO

The entire room froze. As the monitors continued to scream, Cassie began to back away. Emmons leaned over, about to ask Paula a question, but doctors and nurses came pounding in. They pushed us out of the room, and we all wound up in the hallway. Cassie's face had drained of color. She looked like she was about to faint, and her voice came out high and shrill. "What's happening? Why did she act like that?"

We all studied Cassie. Emmons spoke first. "It's possible she has a few wires crossed, Cassie. Sometimes trauma can do that."

But no question about it, Paula's reaction was strange. It was hard to interpret. She'd looked . . . scared. Of Cassie? Or was she just shocked to see that Cassie was alive? I'd asked myself before, but I hadn't really drilled down on it. Could Cassie have done it? Attack a sleeping Abel—I guess so. Her father . . . that was a bit of a stretch. He outweighed Cassie by at least eighty, ninety pounds. But with the element of surprise, I supposed it might be possible . . . likewise for her mother. That only begged the question, why? What was her motive? I could see that the cops were thinking along the same lines.

Templeton fixed Cassie with a hard, suspicious gaze. "Why would she react that way to you, Cassie? Can you explain that?"

My lawyer reflex kicked in. "Don't answer him, Cassie." I turned to Templeton. "My client isn't talking. Knock it off with the questions."

Cassie burst out, "I don't know why she acted like that! I didn't do anything!" She grabbed my arm. "Sam, you've got to believe me!" She started to cry.

I put an arm around her shoulders. "It's okay, Cassie. Detective Emmons is right. Things must've gotten jumbled around in her head. It was a huge trauma."

But even though Emmons might have a good point, even though the reaction of a woman who'd only just gotten out of a coma was a shaky basis for an arrest, it was definitely something that had to be checked out. And I could see the wheels turning in Templeton's head, planning just how he'd do that.

Cassie continued to sob on my shoulder. I caught Templeton's eye. "Can I take her home?"

"You sure the Reebers will want her?" He looked skeptical.

"Talk about a rush to judgment. So she looked upset, big whoop. The woman just got out of a coma. Like Emmons said, her wires are crossed, that's all. I'm sure the Reebers will be fine with keeping her."

Rusty continued to study Cassie. He eventually nodded, though he didn't look convinced. "But I'm sending someone with you. We'll let her stay there while we check this out, but she's not going anywhere."

She was basically under house arrest. Cassie moved like a wooden puppet with a few of its strings cut, her head hanging down, her gait stumbling and unsteady. When we got back into the car, she bent forward and put her head down in her lap. I noticed a squad car fall in behind me as I pulled out of the hospital parking lot.

Cassie sobbed all the way back and didn't speak until I pulled into the Reebers' driveway. She sat up, her face red and wet with tears. "Why do they think I did it? Mom's just . . . messed up, that's all!"

I searched her face. That's definitely what I wanted to believe. "I agree, but we'll just have to let the cops do their job." I couldn't believe those words had just come out of my mouth. Oh, if only they would. "But for now, you'll have to stay home—"

"That's not my home! I don't have a home!"

Unfortunately, she was right about that. I corrected myself. "You'll have to stay in the house until the cops finish checking things out."

Cassie hit her thigh with a fisted hand. "Why can't they find that guy I saw? It's not fair! I didn't do anything!" She put her hands over her face and began to sob.

I could see I wasn't going to be able to calm her down. Not that I blamed her. If she really hadn't done it, to not only lose her family but also be wrongly accused of killing them would shatter anyone's sanity.

But what if she had done it? She'd still be plenty bent at getting caught. Right now, all I had was a lot of questions, but I wouldn't get the answers today. I got out and went to the passenger side of the car.

A tall, muscular female patrol officer trotted over and gestured for me to stand back. She put a restraining hand on Cassie's shoulder and unfastened her seat belt, then wrapped a hand around her arm and pulled her out of the car. Cassie looked like a toddler next to the officer. Her body limp, she stumbled along as the officer walked her to the door.

When Barbara saw the patrol officer holding on to Cassie, she stepped back and put a hand to her face. "What on earth?"

I directed the officer to the living room, and she deposited Cassie on the couch. But she remained standing, her eyes trained on Cassie. I told Barbara what'd happened. "If you don't want her to stay here, they'll have to take her to a juvenile facility." Not juvenile hall—she wasn't under arrest. But they'd have to find a bed for her in one of the county facilities for minors, which wouldn't be pretty.

Barbara's face was pale as she took it all in. But her tone was firm. "I'm sure Paula was just confused. Her reaction could mean anything. I think the police are grasping at straws. I don't believe for one second Cassie would do such a terrible thing. That's not the girl I've come to know."

I nodded and told her I agreed, that I was sure they'd clear her. But really, what did any of us know about Cassie? We'd only met her a short time ago, and I'd long since learned that you can never rule out anyone just because you think you know the person. I wondered whether Barbara realized that if Cassie did commit these murders, she was one dangerous criminal. "If you want Cassie to stay, she can't leave the house. And that patrol officer will be here for the duration, until the cops figure it out."

Barbara's eyes drifted toward the couch and to Cassie, who sagged against it. I didn't envy her this decision. But she set her jaw. "No. I'm not going to let them put her in some county . . . orphanage. She can stay here. I know she didn't kill anyone."

It was a brave thing to do, I thought. And a risky thing to do. "I'll tell the officer. But if it gets too much, if you change your mind for any reason—"

Barbara nodded. "Thank you." But now, her decision made, she was determined. "We'll be fine."

I told the officer that Cassie would be staying, then I told Cassie I had to leave. She looked up at me with a vacant stare and slowly nodded. "Are they going to arrest me?"

What could I say? I had no idea what the cops would uncover. Theoretically, there wouldn't be any big surprises; the crime scene should've been thoroughly raked for evidence by now. But I'd seen that theory disproven too many times. "Let's hope not. I'll stay on top of this and let you know what I find out."

Cassie dropped her head and began to sob again. Barbara sat down next to her and put an arm around her shoulders. Cassie laid her head on Barbara's shoulder and wailed. "Please don't let them take me away!"

Barbara looked like she wanted to cry. But the officer folded her arms and watched it all dispassionately. I hoped for everyone's sake that the cops would figure this out soon. I didn't think either the Reebers or Cassie would be able to deal with the situation for long.

When I got back to my car, I looked at my watch. Beulah's clock had decided time was irrelevant about a year ago. It was only eleven thirty. It felt like the end of the day. But I was glad it was still early. I needed to talk to Michy and Alex about all this.

"What?" Michelle sat back in her chair as though I'd shoved her. "You've got to be kidding me!"

Alex tilted his head as though he didn't think he'd heard right. "Was that the first time Paula's responded to anyone?"

That's what worried me. "No. The doctors told Emmons she'd been somewhat responsive with them. She seemed to know where she was, even said 'Stephen.'"

Michelle absorbed the import of that. "So she's not totally out of it."

Not as out of it as I'd have liked. "No." I'd been pacing back and forth in front of Michelle's desk, thinking about what the cops would do now. "I'll bet they've already gone back to the crime scene." I stopped and tried to imagine what kind of evidence they could possibly find. I just didn't know. I was nervous about Cassie's situation, but there was nothing I could do. "I'm gonna try to bury myself in work for a while."

I could tell Alex didn't know which side of the fence to fall on. He shook his head and sighed. "Yeah, may as well. I've been having a hell of a time trying to figure out how to grab the cell tower records." He saw my worried look. "It'll be okay. I've got a few more tricks left."

I went back into my office and passed the rest of the day working on motions. I have this insane ability to tune out the whole world in times of need, and this was one of them. By the time Alex came to my door, it was almost six thirty p.m.

He was rubbing the back of his neck. "I just remembered. We were supposed to go see Julio again today. Do you still want to?"

I'd forgotten about that, too. We'd wanted to see whether we could get a little more information about his sister's last calls and her shoplifting case. I was about to say no, that I had more work to do here, but I'd been holed up in my office with my head down for hours. I needed to get out. "Sure, may as well."

The only thing wrong with going to see Julio now was that he lived in a rough part of Koreatown, and it'd be almost dark by the time we got there. Alex could probably deal with whatever we ran into, but it wouldn't hurt to give him some backup. I got my gun, stuffed it into my purse, and stopped at Michelle's desk. "Feel free to pack it in anytime. I'll call you from the car if we get anything delicious."

"You'll call me from the car regardless. If I don't hear from you by seven thirty, I'm calling the cops."

"Are ya kidding? They'll hang up and cheer. So please don't. Last thing I want to do is give them a reason to be happy."

Michelle nodded. "Fair enough." She fixed me with a hard look. "But call anyway."

I gave her a mock salute, and Alex and I headed out.

We made it to Julio's place a little after seven thirty. It was a cool night, but there was some cloud cover that kept it from getting really chilly. A few stars peeked out between the clouds, and the moon that hung low in the sky gave off a yellow glow. A car on springs bounced down the street blasting a song with bass so heavy I could feel it in my chest.

Julio's apartment was one in a string of twelve that looked like they'd been converted from one of those fleabag motels. And it'd gone straight downhill from there—no easy feat. Cardboard blocked the front windows in some units; dirty blankets or sheets hung in others. One was covered with tinfoil. That occupant had at least done some thinking. The paint had long since peeled off most of the doors, and what little was left was too faded to leave a clue as to what color they'd ever been. Graffiti covered the cracked stucco walls, and the small parking lot was littered with empty fast-food wrappers, cardboard cups, and beer and soft drink cans. A shopping cart with four or five white bundles stood at the far end. The stench of cheap cooking, old grease, and urine-soaked concrete permeated the air. When we got closer to the shopping cart, I saw that the bundles were used Pampers. Lovely.

I looked around. "Just think. If you lived here, you'd be home already."

Alex's nostrils flared, and he shook his head. "Let's get this over with." He pointed to the tinfoiled window. "I believe that's Julio's place."

Alex knocked on the door. No answer. He knocked again. Still no answer. After the third time, the front door of the apartment to the right opened, and a skinny, barefoot woman with fried-blonde hair, wearing capris and a torn men's T-shirt, came out. A lit cigarette dangled from her cracked lips. "You looking for Julio?"

I noticed her teeth were yellow, and one or two were missing on either side of her mouth. Meth. Had to be. I nodded. "You know when he'll be back?"

She looked me up and down, then gave Alex the once-over. "You want to make this worth my time?"

I raised an eyebrow. "Because your time is so limited?"

She flicked her ashes to the side and narrowed her eyes at me. "Because all our time is limited."

Profound. I nodded at her and thought, *That's what I get for making assumptions.* Glad to pay her, I opened my wallet. It was my lucky day; I had some cash. I held up a twenty. "Okay?" She nodded. I gave it to her. "So when's Julio coming back?"

She took a drag on her cigarette and blew out smoke rings before she answered. "I'd bet never. Some bangers came by looking for him a few days ago. I told him about it. Haven't seen him since."

Bangers. Nothing about this felt good. "You see their tats?"

She gave a little snort. "You could see 'em from space. One had a Christ tattoo with a big 'MS' on it. The others had 'Mara' . . . something on their backs."

"Mara Salvatrucha?" I asked.

She frowned for a moment. "Maybe. I remember some big word after 'Mara.'"

Mara Salvatrucha. If she had it right, Julio had the MS-13 after him. I didn't like the way this was coming together. "You ever see those guys around here before?" She shook her head. "Ever seen any other bangers with those tats in this 'hood?"

She picked a piece of tobacco off her tongue and rolled it between her fingers. "Not that I can recall at the moment, but it's possible. I only remember these guys because of Julio."

I'd have to find out whether this was MS-13 turf. "What'd they say about Julio?"

"Nothing. Just asked where he was, when he'd be back. I told 'em I didn't know. But I could tell it was trouble. That's why I warned him."

I nodded. "You did the right thing."

"Believe it or not, I've done a few of 'em in my time. I didn't always live here."

I definitely did believe her. "Meth?"

She gave me a sad, resigned look. "What else?"

We thanked her. She held up the twenty-dollar bill and thanked us back, then went inside. I looked down the row of shithole apartments. "Should we try and door knock the rest?"

Alex scanned the building. "I think the minuses might outweigh the pluses."

Probably so. The later it got, the more likely it was that we'd get robbed or stabbed. And the odds of us finding anyone as literate—or even as conscious—as our meth junkie were slim.

We went back to the car, and as Alex headed west on Sunset, I watched the stores and restaurants get nicer and newer. It was depressing and relieving at the same time. "It looks bad for Julio's sister." And Hausch was looking dirtier by the second. But it didn't make sense. "I don't get it. If Hausch got his MS-13 besties to take Julio out, then why didn't he just do that to begin with? Why ask for my help?"

Alex stopped at a red light and peered at me. "Who says Hausch called them in?"

I hadn't thought of that. "You think they did this on their own?"

The light turned green, and Alex pulled through the intersection. "I think Hausch wouldn't want those bangers to know he's being investigated. It makes him a weak link."

And I supposed they were capable of making a command decision on their own. "So Julio complained to too many people, and those gangbangers found out about it?"

Alex stopped to let an older woman pushing a shopping cart filled with newspapers and stuffed animals cross the street. "You saw the way Julio was acting. Does he strike you as the type to play it cool?"

Definitely not. And Alex was right. Hausch wouldn't want those bangers to know that IA was looking at him. "Then I hope Julio can outrun them."

Alex and I exchanged a grim look. His chances weren't great.

TWENTY-THREE

The next morning, I was on my way in to work when my cell phone quacked. It was Dale. I was stopped at a red light, and there was a motorcycle cop in the lane next to me, so I let it go to voice mail and waited until I got into my office to listen to the message. It was a good thing I did.

Dale had offered to help Emmons and Templeton in their reinvestigation of the crime scene. He'd been looking at photographs when he spotted a pair of girl's fuzzy pink socks in the hamper. They were muddy. It'd been raining the night of the murders. Those socks meant Cassie had been out in that rain. They'd taken a K-9 officer to the house. Once they took the dog to the backyard, it'd taken her about ten seconds to alert to a spot at the edge of the property. Sure enough, buried in a shallow hole were Abel's wallet and a pair of girl's pajamas, blue with yellow daisies. The pajamas were soaked in blood and just Cassie's size.

I asked Michelle and Alex to come into my office and gave them the news.

"Then she did it. She really did it." Michelle looked like she'd been slammed in the face with a frying pan.

I'd bypassed shock and gone straight to feeling like a fool. When I'd first learned of the murders, the fact that Cassie had survived the attack shot up a little warning flare in my mind. But the sheer brutality of the murders, and the fact that the killer had managed to take down the father . . . I just didn't see a teenage girl doing all that.

And yet, I'd had my doubts. I'd noticed little cracks and fissures in Cassie's behavior. The way she'd talked about her mother, the self-conscious, dramatic mourning for Abel—a guy almost nobody seemed to miss, and with good reason—and of course, in hindsight, Cassie's behavior on the way to the hospital. There'd been other, much smaller clues: odd reactions, an inappropriate smile here, a strange expression there. Bottom line: I'd seen all the ingredients; I'd just refused to see what they made.

So to me, the only shocking thing was my own denial.

Alex—who'd been speechless—now was shaking his head. "So *she* threw that brick through the window." He frowned. "Did they test it for prints?"

"Yeah," I said. I'd asked Dale about that. "They didn't get anything. The rain washed out a lot of evidence." Which was why no one had been fazed by the fact that they hadn't found shoeprints in the backyard where Cassie had claimed to see a man running away. A faked forced entry and ransacking. Not genius, but pretty smart.

Michelle was shaking her head. "I can't get over the fact that she buried her clothes and Abel's wallet but left her socks in the hamper. What a weird thing to get tripped up on."

My irritation with myself made me bitter. "I don't know. I think it's a pretty small mistake, all things considered." Such as the fact that this "perp" was just a fifteen-year-old girl who, presumably, hadn't led a life of crime before these murders.

Michelle caught the bitter note in my voice and gave me an impatient look. "Get over it, Kreskin. The girl fooled everyone. Not just you."

Alex tilted his head at me. "She's got a point. Look at all the cops who missed it."

I wasn't consoled.

Michelle sighed. "I heard on the news that Cassie's uncle finally showed up. Hella timing he's got."

Stephen's brother, Nathan, and his wife hadn't exactly sped into action when they found out about the murders. But they lived in Michigan, and the aunt was getting chemo for stomach cancer. She couldn't travel, and Nathan didn't want to leave her. "Given the circumstances, though, I cut 'em some slack."

"Oh, definitely," Michelle said. "I just meant because, irony. You know?"

"Yeah, no question."

Alex rubbed his chin. "What about Paula? Doesn't she have—"

I shook my head. "No siblings, and her parents passed away years ago. She might have cousins somewhere, but no one's made contact yet."

Michelle fished a bottle of water out of the box behind her. "Better dust off your fancy suits. Because if the press liked this case before . . ."

No doubt about that. A fifteen-year-old girl who was a mass murderer wasn't something you saw every day. That Cassie had done it seemed a foregone conclusion. The cops were running tests on the bloody clothing and wallet, but the pajamas were the same size and style as others they'd found in her dresser, and the fact that she'd buried the clothes in the first place spoke volumes. Beyond that, it explained why no one in the neighborhood had noticed anyone breaking into the house, why the AB suspect lead had never panned out—and on and on.

The only real question left was why. "This one's going to be all about motive—"

Michelle nodded. "And you love that."

I really did. For a whole lot of reasons. Why people do what they do intrigues me in general, but particularly when they kill. Usually, it's personal, though sometimes it's business—or even pleasure. But it can also be about justice. I looked at the scar over Michelle's left eyebrow, a souvenir from the pistol-whipping she'd gotten when she'd been robbed at gunpoint several years ago. The judge had thrown out the case on a technicality, but that hadn't been enough for that scumbag piece of shit. After he'd gotten out of jail, he'd tortured her with anonymous death threats. The cops had agreed it was probably him, but they couldn't do anything about it because Michelle had no proof. She'd been losing weight and losing sleep and was on the verge of a nervous breakdown. I knew I had to do something. And so I had.

Bottom line, relatable or not, every killer has a motive. But proving what that is can be tough for the prosecution. The killer's usually the only one who can explain why he did it. The victim gets no say in the matter. So I can shape my client's story to get maximum appeal with the jury: the victim threatened him, the victim had a reputation for being violent, the victim was going to kill my client's girlfriend/brother/sister/cousin, etc. And it doesn't matter how many times the judge says that the prosecutor doesn't have to prove motive. Juries always want to know—need to know—why he did it.

I had a feeling there'd be plenty of *why* to chew on here.

Michelle asked, "Is Cassie still at Barbara's house?"

I shook my head. "The uni who's been staying with Cassie already brought her in." Which pissed me off, because I'd have preferred to bring her in myself and do what I could to ease the pain for Cassie. "They're going to keep her at Twin Towers so they can give her security."

Michelle looked concerned. "She's awfully young, and she's got no record. Any chance the DA will try her as a juvenile?"

I shook my head. "With two—maybe three—dead bodies? I seriously doubt it." The DA would have to go through the motions, put on a fitness hearing to get her certified up to adult court, and I'd make the pitch to keep her in juvenile. But it was a nonstarter. I looked at my watch. It was one thirty. She should be through booking by now. "I should get going."

Michelle gave me a curious look. "Doesn't it bug you that she played you all this time?"

That never even occurred to me. "Not really. If there's a shot at getting away with it, why not take it? I mean, who wouldn't?"

Michelle studied me for a moment. "Maybe someone with a conscience?"

"That silly old thing?"

Michelle gave a little laugh. I joined her, but I wasn't kidding.

"I've got to use a credit card for gas." I didn't have enough cash to fill up Beulah, but if I used the card, we'd be maxed out again.

"It's okay. The Orozcos' check just cleared."

I got my purse and briefcase and headed for Twin Towers.

When I approached the building, I noticed a few reporters with cameramen hanging around the custody entrance. The press was on it already? That was fast. I found a pretty good parking space for a change and moved toward the entrance. As I neared the crowd of reporters, I asked, "What case are you guys here for?"

A cameraman I recognized from Dale's case nodded to me. "Hey, Sam. The Sonnenberg case. That yours?"

"Yeah, but I'm not talking." Yet. First, I had to figure out what my angle was.

The jail deputy at the attorney window recognized me. "Nice to see you, Sam. The inmate said you were coming."

So Cassie had her wits about her to some extent. An encouraging sign. I passed through the metal detector and headed up to the attorney room, which was just a row of cubicles with partitions between the seats and the usual plexiglass between the lawyers and the inmates. It took longer than usual for them to bring Cassie out. I suspected that was because they were keeping her in a segregated area. Juveniles aren't allowed to mix with the adult population.

Cassie finally appeared, a female deputy on one side and a male deputy on the other. It seemed like overkill to have two escorts for one slender teenage girl with no record. But she had butchered at least two people. Her face was haggard and her eyes were wide with terror. I picked up the phone and gestured for her to do the same. The moment I said, "Hi, Cassie," she burst into tears. Between sobs, she kept repeating, "Don't be mad at me! Please don't be mad at me!"

I waited for the sobs to subside, so she could hear me. "I'm not mad, Cassie."

She looked scared and disbelieving. "Are you sure?"

"Very sure. Have the cops tried to talk to you yet?"

She sniffled and wiped her nose. "No. They said they'd want to, but I told them I wanted my lawyer."

I gave her the thumbs-up. The day after I'd brought her home from the hospital, I'd called to tell her that if she got arrested, the only thing she was allowed to say was, "I want my lawyer." And she'd followed my directions. Which meant she'd already done better than 75 percent of my adult clients—some with rap sheets longer than a school bus, who, for some reason, thought the cops really meant it when they said, "You can trust me. I understand why you shot him—I'd do it, too." I gave her a little smile. "You did the right thing—"

"But maybe I should talk to them." Cassie glanced around her. "Is it safe to talk here?"

I'd often worried about that myself. But I hadn't been bitten by it so far. "It has to be. It's an attorney room. Everything you say here's privileged, just between you and me."

But she whispered anyway. "It's true, I did do it. But I had to! I can explain; let me tell them!"

It took me a second to process the fact that she'd confessed so readily. My typical client denies everything, no matter how many witnesses identify him, no matter how much evidence nails him—even if he's caught on videotape. But Cassie wasn't a career criminal or even a streetwise ghetto kid. And she knew—because I was sure the cops had told her—that the evidence against her was pretty damning. So of course, the "why" of it was the only place she could go. But I sure as hell wasn't going to let her tell it to the cops. I studied her face. "Tell me first."

Cassie took a jagged breath and wiped the tears from her face. "Because . . . they were . . . They were coming into my room at night and . . . touching me and making me do things and . . ." She dissolved into tears again. Her whole body shook with deep, racking sobs that came in bigger and bigger waves. It felt as though floodgates that'd been closed for years had suddenly flown open. "I just couldn't take it anymore."

When the sobs finally slowed down, I asked, "Who is 'they,' Cassie?"

"Both of them. Abel and . . . my dad." She closed her eyes, but tears continued to roll down her cheeks. "And she wouldn't stop them!"

TWENTY-FOUR

I stared at Cassie. She had no way of knowing that she was talking to someone who'd been there, done that.

I shifted into trial mode. I'd need an explanation for why she'd told that "skinhead did it" lie. But I already knew what I'd have her say: that she hadn't wanted to "out" the ugly story if she could avoid it. And that might even be the truth. I'd only recently told Michelle about what Sebastian had done to me, and we'd been friends for more than twenty years.

But the story itself seemed a little over the top to me. Assaulted by her father *and* her brother? I'm not saying it couldn't happen, but it had to be pretty damn rare. And on top of that, her mother refused to do *anything* about it? It didn't fit what I'd heard about Paula. She'd been tagged by most of the people we'd interviewed as ambitious, no question about it. But they'd all considered her to be a decent person. Not perfect, but certainly not the type to ignore claims this serious. In short, Paula was no Celeste.

On the other hand, Paula was a politician. If she'd had higher aspirations—as most pols did—a scandal like that would be ruinous. I supposed it was *possible* she'd try to silence Cassie. I'd have to see what else I could find out about Paula.

As for the father, we'd had some indications that Stephen was a little too friendly with younger women. That girl Heather, who lived across the street, was almost as young as Cassie. And clearly, Abel was no angel, either. But did the stories we'd heard about either of them add up to serial molestation?

I stopped myself. It didn't matter whether I bought it or not. What mattered was whether a jury would buy it. I had to find a way to sell her story after she'd lied all this time. And that meant I needed to push her hard for details that I could corroborate. But I'd have to tread lightly. If I came on too strong, she'd clam up—whether she was telling the truth or not. I waited for Cassie to calm down. "Can you tell me when it started?"

She looked down at the counter. "When I was thirteen."

When her body changed. Pretty typical. That's when it'd happened to me. "How did it start?"

Her voice sounded like it was packed in a tiny box. "Abel would come into my room at night, after everyone went to bed. He'd hold me down with one hand over my mouth, and he'd use the other one to . . . to touch me."

I had to force down my own childhood memories of Sebastian's leering grin. "Did you tell anyone about it?"

Cassie shook her head. "He said no one would believe me, that he'd tell them I was just jealous and trying to get him in trouble." She looked up at me with sad eyes. "I kept thinking he'd stop. And I . . . I wanted him to like me. If I told on him, he'd hate me forever."

All of this was so hideously textbook. And as an adopted kid, her need for acceptance only made her that much more vulnerable. "Did it escalate from there?"

Cassie swallowed and stared down at the counter. "Yes. After a while, he started making me touch him, and then he made me . . . he made me give him blow jobs. And then he . . ." Cassie stopped and caught her breath. "He raped me."

I was gripping the phone so hard my knuckles hurt, but I kept my voice even. "Wasn't he worried about getting you pregnant?"

Cassie looked away. "He didn't do it . . . that way."

My stomach lurched. But if that were true, there might be evidence of trauma. That'd be good corroboration. "When was the last time?"

Cassie glanced up at me for a moment, then looked away again. She spoke in a voice so soft I could barely hear her. "Two weeks before the . . . before he died."

"We'll need to get you checked by a doctor, Cassie." She looked up, alarmed. I held up a hand. "If you can't handle it, then we won't do it. But I'm telling you right now, it'll help a lot if we can back up your story with physical evidence. And the sooner we do the exam, the better, because the longer you wait, the less likely it is that the doctor will find evidence of trauma. So think about it, okay?"

She nodded. Then she sat up and lifted her chin. "I don't need to think about it. I'll do it."

Just her willingness to be examined told me a lot. Maybe she really was telling the truth. "Good."

Cassie's eyes darted around the room again. "There's something else you should know. I was stealing things, like earrings, a chain bracelet, little stuff like that." She looked at me, her expression puzzled. "I don't know why I got into that."

"You mean from stores?" Cassie nodded. "Did you ever get busted?"

She sighed and nodded. "Once, when I stole a necklace from Claire's. They let me go with a warning, but Tommy's sister worked there, and she told him about it. I'm sure Tommy and all those guys will tell the cops about it."

"Tommy. Abel's friend, Tommy Dearfield?" Cassie nodded. They hadn't told me when I interviewed them. I wondered why. They'd been willing to say a lot worse things. In any case, shoplifting was pretty textbook, too. I'd done that. Along with many other lovely behaviors, like stashing a pint of Jack Daniel's in my locker so I could get bombed before lunch. Cassie continued. She seemed to want to tell me everything now. "So then Tommy told Abel about it, and Abel said he'd tell Mom and Dad if I said anything about what he was doing to me."

So Abel had held more than one card to keep her from talking. I braced myself for the answer to my next question. "What happened with your father?"

She sank down in her seat, her chin almost on her chest. "It wasn't as bad with him. He'd just make me take my clothes off and lie on the bed, and then he'd . . ." Cassie swallowed. "He'd touch himself."

Not as bad, but nauseating enough. "Did he ever touch you?"

Cassie dropped her head. Her voice was so low I had to strain to hear her. "Toward the end he started to. But he never . . . uh . . . he never . . . took it any further."

"He never raped you." Cassie nodded. "Did he know about Abel?"

Cassie shook her head. "I don't think so."

A trickle of sweat dripped from my hand, down the phone, and into my sleeve. I wanted to stop, to put the phone down and walk away and never come back. I steeled myself for the next part. "When did you tell your mother about all this?"

Cassie bit her lip, and her brow knitted. "I told her about Abel when he started to make me do the . . . the blow jobs." A sob burst loose, then another, and then her whole body shook with sobs. She did her best to talk through her tears. "It was just so sc-scary. I c-couldn't ever sleep. I was always waiting, listening for his footsteps. And then, when I did finally fall asleep, I'd wake up, and he'd be standing there, staring at me with his pants open and . . ." Cassie took a deep breath.

"So I finally told her. But she wouldn't believe me! She said, 'Abel would never do such a thing!' She said she knew I was going to be trouble right from the start. That I'd always been a problem child!" Cassie began to sob again.

I could feel my stomach clench. She was stomping all over my past. The words were different, but the sentiment was the same. When her tears had subsided, I asked, "Did you ever tell her about your father?"

She stared at me as though I'd asked her whether she'd ever stuck her head in a wood chipper. "How could I? If she wouldn't even believe Abel did it, imagine what she'd have done if I told her about Dad! She'd have put me back in foster care! I couldn't go back there! Not ever!" Cassie paused to catch her breath. After a moment, she added, "Besides, he at least never hurt me." Cassie's cheeks suddenly reddened, and she dipped her head.

Her blush told me it might've even felt good. "It's not your fault, Cassie."

She briefly glanced up at me, then bit her lip and stared at the floor.

We're all animals. Certain spots are meant to give pleasure. And they do, whether we want them to or not. The sad thing is, that only adds to the pain for molestation victims, because it makes them feel complicit. That, at least, was one problem I hadn't had. "What about Tiegan or the counselor you had before her—did you say anything to them?" I doubted it, since they had a duty to report claims like this, so I wasn't surprised when Cassie shook her head. "Why?" Cassie's expression was a mixture of sadness and desperation. "I didn't think they'd believe me. My own mother didn't believe me. Why should they?" Cassie looked away. "And I just felt like . . . like it was all my fault. That there must've been something wrong with me. That's why they . . . they acted like that."

Another textbook example of molestation victim thinking. It was like reading *Molestation Victims for Dummies*. I noticed the guard looking up at the clock. I didn't have much more time.

"Tell me what happened that night."

Cassie's eyes were fixed on the corner of the window, and she began to breathe faster. "Mom and Dad were going to be out all night, and Abel seemed . . . totally off the chain. He came to my room and he . . ." Her breath caught in her throat.

"Did he rape you?"

Cassie swallowed and shook her head. "No, but he . . . he—"

I held up a hand. I didn't need to hear any more gory details now. "That's okay. I get it. What happened after that?"

"He left. But he said he'd be back. I didn't know what he was going to do. I was so scared! I was pacing around and around in my room, thinking about all the things he'd done to me and . . . and what he was going to do to me now!" Her expression was terrified. "I had to do something! I had to stop him! I went to his room and I—I just lost it!" Cassie started to cry, her chest shaking with hiccups.

"Where did you get the knife?" No kitchen knives were missing.

Cassie looked confused. "I, ah . . . I already had it. It was a souvenir. From a trip."

"What did you do with it?"

She leaned her head against the wall, her face slack. She looked exhausted. "I threw it down the storm drain."

Part of the reason for those muddy socks. "And your father? Did he catch you in Abel's room?" Cassie nodded. "Abel was already dead?"

Cassie wiped her face on her sleeve. "Yeah. I didn't even know what I was doing anymore. I was just . . . just going crazy."

"Is that why you tried to kill your mom? Because she saw you, too?"

Cassie nodded again. "And because she wouldn't help me. She just let him . . . and pretended it wasn't happening." She dropped the phone, put her head down on the counter, and sobbed. Her voice had a faraway echo through the dangling phone. "I can't believe I did that! I wish I was dead instead of them!" She started to bang her head on the counter.

I knocked on the window. "Cassie, stop it! Stop it right now!" The guard on my side had looked up. He'd alert her guards any second. Finally, she sat up. I motioned for her to pick up the phone. "You have every reason to be freaking out. I get it. But try to calm down. One day at a time. You're not in this alone. I'm going to help you. Okay?"

Her face and eyes were so swollen I didn't know whether she could even see me, but she nodded. "What happens now?"

"First of all, you're not to talk to anyone. Not the cops, not the inmates, not the guards. No one. Can you promise me?"

She nodded. I explained the next steps and that she'd likely be tried as an adult.

She gaped at me. "But I'm only fifteen. Doesn't that make me a juvenile?"

"Yes, but since you're charged with a double homicide, you're presumed to be unfit for juvenile court. I intend to fight them on it. But you need to be prepared. We're probably not going to win that particular battle."

Cassie stared at me, her expression bleak. "Even though they did all those things to me?" I nodded. I watched as shock spread across her face. "Then what . . . what's going to happen if . . . if I lose?"

Should I tell her she was facing life without the possibility of parole? No. She'd been through too much already. I had to give her some hope. There'd be plenty of time for harsh realities later. "You're not going to lose. The jury might only find you guilty of manslaughter, and if that happened, the judge could give you straight probation. Or the jury might even let you go." The latter was a huge long shot, but I'd seen stranger verdicts.

Cassie sat up and put a hand on the window. "Then I'd get out? It'd be over?"

I didn't want to take this too far. "It's possible."

Tears welled up in her eyes. "I'm so glad I have you."

The gratitude on her face made me a little uncomfortable. "I'm not making any promises, Cassie. And you'll need to work with me to get ready for trial. It won't be easy."

She nodded, her expression solemn. "I'll do whatever you say. I promise."

But I wasn't worried about whether Cassie would do as I said. I was worried about whether the jury would.

TWENTY-FIVE

I was wrung out after that interview. I needed a drink, or seven, and a good, long nap. But I didn't have time for any of that.

Michelle called as I was on my way to the parking lot. "Nathan Sonnenberg called. He wants to meet with you."

I was a little surprised. I definitely wanted to talk to him now, find out whether he had any idea what'd been going on with Cassie. But I hadn't expected him to want to talk to the lawyer who was representing his brother's killer. "Where's he staying?"

"At the Marriott near LAX."

"Ugh. I'll be lucky if I can get there by tomorrow night. Any chance he'll meet me in the office?"

"It's worth a try. Here's the number."

Luckily, Nathan was fine with that. He was civil, though I couldn't say he sounded warm. But given the fact that I was defending the girl who'd killed his brother, how the hell was he supposed to feel about me?

As I drove back to the office, I thought about what I'd say to him and what I could ask him. My defense was going to center on his brother's and his nephew's predatory behavior. I wanted to get some idea of what Nathan would say about Cassie's story, but I couldn't reveal it yet.

I hadn't decided whether to go for early media spin and put Cassie's story out there, or play it close to the vest and aim for shock value when I picked a jury. I had no doubt that this case was going to trial. No prosecutor could offer me anything better than twenty-five to life—and even that was a big stretch. More likely, the only "deal" I'd get would be fifty to life. We'd be better off rolling the dice with the twelve-headed monster.

So I couldn't tell Nathan what Cassie was saying. Even if he promised to keep it quiet. You never know how family members are going to react to ugly stories about their dearly departed. Especially stories they probably never heard before.

When I got back to the office, I told the troops about Cassie's confession.

Alex looked stunned. "Are you kidding me? The father *and* the brother?" I nodded. He seemed as troubled as he was shocked.

Michelle folded her arms, her eyes hard as she stared straight ahead. "It does sound over the top, but I don't have such a hard time buying it. And the mother not wanting to believe it isn't such a stretch for me, either." She avoided looking at me. Alex didn't know about my childhood misery.

I nodded. "Her story's extreme, no argument there. But incest cases usually don't involve blood relatives." That's why stepchildren or foster children were the most common victims. Adopted kids were a distant third, but they were still a much more likely target than kids who'd been born into the family. "And we might have physical evidence to back it up."

Alex looked pained and sad. "I don't want it to be true, because it's so awful. But it does explain why she'd do it. I mean, why else would a young girl snap like that?"

Which was exactly what I'd want my jury to think. "So we have a strategy call to make. Do we put out her story now? Or wait until trial?

If I put out Cassie's story now, I'll be giving the prosecution a whole bunch of time to poke holes in it."

Alex folded an arm around his waist and rubbed his chin, his thinking mode. "But we'll have to give them discovery at some point anyway."

"Right," I said. "I'll be calling shrinks and molestation experts." And even if I told the experts not to write reports—a risky gambit that keeps the experts' conclusions confidential but also looks kind of sleazy—I'd still have to turn over their names, so it wouldn't take a clairvoyant to figure out where I was headed with their testimony. "The prosecution would be able to ramp up fast with counter-experts who'll point out why Cassie's story is BS."

Michelle frowned. "But what if the doctor doesn't find any evidence of trauma?"

I waved a hand. "I'll bury it." I don't have to turn over reports unless I intend to put on the testimony at trial. "I think we go with the media blitz."

The buzzer sounded at the outer door. Nathan was here. Michelle stood up. "Starting now?"

"I doubt it. Not unless he already seems to know. I'll just let him talk and play it by ear."

Relatives—especially those who didn't live close by—seldom knew what was going on behind closed doors. But you never can tell. "Go ahead and buzz him in."

TWENTY-SIX

Nathan walked into the office and stopped, one foot in front of the other. He looked around as though he expected someone to jump out and put a gun to his head. I took in his appearance as I moved toward him. He had close-cropped brown hair, watery hazel eyes, and the kind of pale complexion that comes from long, cold winters holed up in tiny, over-heated brick houses and short, humid, bug-filled summers. I'd asked Alex to check him out. Nathan Adam Sonnenberg lived in Bendon, Michigan, population slightly more than two hundred thousand, where he worked as a salesman at a storm window dealership. Hardly a tiny backwater burg. But he acted like the proverbial country mouse come to visit the big city.

For one of the worst reasons imaginable.

I held out my hand, and we shook as I introduced us all. He bobbed his head up and down as he gave a brief, nervous smile to each of us. His hand felt soft and doughy, a description that fit the rest of him, too. The buttons on his plaid cotton shirt strained around a Pooh Bear tummy. *Tummy* isn't my kind of word, but it fit Nathan. I'd bet the strongest curse he'd ever uttered was "Gosh all Friday!"

I thought it might intimidate him if Alex sat in on the meeting, so when I invited him into my office, I stood back and let him enter first, then held up a hand to let Alex know he shouldn't join us. Alex nodded and headed for his office.

I wanted to keep this casual so Nathan would relax and hopefully give me something I could use—a long shot, I knew, but worth a try. I'd planned on inviting him to sit on the couch, but when I stepped in, I saw that he was already sitting in a chair in front of my desk. Probably for the best. I closed the door and went to sit behind my desk. "Nathan, thank you for coming in. I really appreciate it. And let me say how sorry I am for your wife's illness. How's the chemo going?"

Nathan bobbed his head up and down. "It's going well; thank you for asking. We think she's going to be just fine. Knock on wood." He gave a tremulous smile and knocked on the arm of the chair.

I didn't have the heart to point out that he'd just knocked on fake wood laminate. "And I'm very sorry about your brother and his family. Please accept my condolences." Nathan thanked me again, then swallowed and squared his jaw. I could tell he was determined to keep it together, but his eyes looked a little wet, and he was gripping the arms of the chair as though he expected it to rocket into hyperspace any moment. The sooner we got through this, the better for him. I got down to business. "How well did you know Cassie?"

"Not super well. The wife and I came out to visit them for Christmas once, when they first adopted Cassie. And we came out again for Thanksgiving six years ago."

"Did you stay with the family?" He nodded. "How did you get along with Cassie?"

Nathan shrugged. "To be honest, I didn't have that much contact with her. We don't have any children, and she had her friends. But she seemed like a nice girl." He frowned and shook his head. "I don't understand. How could she do such a thing?" He looked bewildered and overwhelmed.

In that moment, I knew I wasn't going to tell him what Cassie had said. I couldn't keep him from finding out later, but I wouldn't do it to him now. "That's what we're trying to figure out."

"Then there's no chance they got it wrong? That maybe they'll figure out she didn't do it? 'Cause I can't imagine what could've happened to make her do this."

I thought it'd land a little too hard if I said she'd confessed, so I softened it a bit. "At this point, it seems pretty clear that she did do it. But the investigation is ongoing. And part of that investigation will involve figuring out why she did it. Did she ever complain to you about how Paula or Stephen treated her?"

He weighed the question for a moment. "No, never."

"Did Stephen or Paula ever complain to you about Cassie's behavior?"

Nathan rubbed his chin. "I remember one of them—or was it both of them? I'm not sure. But I do remember hearing that Cassie and Abel weren't getting along."

"When was that?"

He looked up at the ceiling. "A year? Two years ago? I think maybe it was Paula, but she told my wife about it, not me. I just remember hearing that Cassie was really upset with Abel, that he was being mean to her."

"Mean to her how? What did he do?"

Nathan wrinkled his brow. As the memory returned, his cheeks flushed. "I think it was that he and his friends were spreading lies about her."

"What kind of lies?"

Nathan glanced at me, then looked down at his lap. "I think it was along the lines of Cassie being kind of . . . easy."

I made a mental note to ask her about that. "What was your impression of Abel?"

Nathan cleared his throat and looked down at his lap, where his hands were laced together. "I don't like to speak ill of him. But I always did think he had a mean streak."

I was finding new reasons to hate that kid at every bend and turn. "Why was that?"

He stared out the window behind me. "It started after Stephen and Paula came to stay with us for a week. Just before they got Cassie."

"So Abel was, what? Six years old?"

"Around there. Back then, there were a few families with young children on the block. We took Abel to their houses and introduced him, thinking it'd be nice for him to have kids his own age to play with. The very next day, the parents of two of the kids said they wouldn't allow their children to play with him. He'd pushed one of the little boys into a pond." Nathan frowned and shook his head. "Luckily, the kid could swim, but still. Abel didn't know that. And he'd been caught using the other kid's computer to look at porn"—he glanced up at me—"if you can believe that. Age six!"

This would be great stuff if I could get him to repeat it on the witness stand. "How on earth did he know how to do that?"

"He just typed the word *sex* into the search bar." He sighed. "I'm sure he didn't know what he was doing. It was probably just a trick he'd heard about from some other kid. But it was pretty embarrassing."

"What did Stephen say about all that? What'd he do?"

Nathan pressed his lips together. "Nothing. Abel denied pushing the kid into the pond. He said the kid was lying, that he fell in by accident. I told Stephen I knew that kid and I'd never known him to make up stories before, but Stephen took Abel's side. And Stephen didn't care about the porn. Said it was just boys being boys, and there was nothing wrong with being curious." He blew out a breath. "I didn't agree, but it wasn't my business."

"Then would you say Stephen was pretty permissive with Abel?"

Nathan gave a reluctant nod. "From what I saw. And he was pretty . . . uh, relaxed when it came to the subject of sex, too. When we were in college, Stephen had a big porn collection." Nathan quickly added, "But he was a really good man. And he really loved his family."

A little too much, if Cassie were to be believed. "So you don't think he'd ever fooled around on Paula?" I couldn't believe I'd just said "fooled around." What was next? Jeepers?

"Stephen? No. Not that I was ever aware of. I mean, he'd look. Sure. You know what they say, 'married not buried.' But I never got the impression he'd strayed."

I had to see whether I could get a little closer to the mark, but this was dangerous territory. If I took it too far, he'd shut down. "Did you ever get the impression he liked to look at younger girls?"

Nathan frowned at me. "Are you talking about that situation at work? With that young woman?"

For starters. "Yeah. So you know about the rumors that he was having an affair with her?"

He nodded. "Stephen told me about it. That was nonsense. The woman was a hard worker; she deserved the promotion." Nathan stopped and gave me a suspicious look. "Why does any of this matter? My brother's dead; what does that have to do with anything?" His expression darkened. "If you're planning on dragging Stephen's name through the mud—"

I held up a hand. "No, no one wants to do that, Nathan." I didn't *want* to, but . . . "I'm sorry. Let me get back on track. I was only asking because before Cassie got arrested, I'd been looking into the possibility that the guy Stephen fired was the killer." That much was true, and I'd told Nathan during our phone call how I'd first gotten involved in the case.

"But you ruled him out?" I nodded. "Have you spoken to Cassie since . . . since she got arrested?"

I really didn't want to go there, so I decided to dodge the question for the moment. "A little. How did Cassie and Paula get along?"

Nathan shrugged. "I only saw them together that one Thanksgiving, when Cassie was about nine, and I didn't see anything unusual. But in the past couple of years, Stephen told me they seemed to be at odds. Paula was having a hard time with her."

I deliberately made a dismissive remark. "Harder than any other teenage girl and her mom?" Sometimes, it makes witnesses push back and give more information.

Nathan squinted. "I'd think a little bit more. I seem to remember Stephen telling me that Paula thought Cassie had . . . problems. That she made things up."

Maybe that was how Paula dusted off Cassie's complaint about the molestation. I probed to see whether I could nail it down. "Did Stephen tell you why she thought that?"

Nathan looked out the window and squinted again. "I believe it had to do with something Cassie said about Abel. But Stephen was pretty vague about it."

I didn't think I could get any more pointed without tipping my hand. And it wasn't worth the risk. Nathan clearly hadn't seen anything happen between Cassie and Abel—and certainly nothing between Cassie and Stephen. All he really knew about her was what he'd heard. But Nathan had given me some great stuff.

I excused myself for a "bathroom break" and went to Alex's office. "Do you have somewhere to be tonight?"

Alex gave me a smirk. "*Chica*, I have somewhere to be *every* night."

I rolled my eyes. "Shut up." But it was true. Mr. Gorgeous never had to be alone if he didn't want to be. It was obnoxious. I asked him to give Nathan a lift back to his hotel and record their conversation—just in case talking to Alex "man-to-man" loosened up Nathan's tongue. I'd had a recorder "hidden" on top of a case file on my desk during my conversation with Nathan. He could've seen it if he'd looked. But I'd known he wouldn't.

When I got back to my office, I thanked Nathan for his time and told him Alex would drive him back to his hotel. He looked so grateful I almost felt bad about having Alex record their conversation. Nathan took my hand and shook it. "I really appreciate that, Ms. Brinkman."

"Call me Sam."

"Sam. I don't really know what to think of this whole terrible tragedy. What happened to Cassie." He stopped and lowered his head. When he looked up again, there were tears in his eyes. "My brother and I weren't the closest of kin. But I loved him, and I never would've wanted him to go like . . . like this. And even though I know it's silly, I guess I'm still hoping that there's been some mistake. That Cassie didn't do it." He wiped his eyes. "I'm not sure I really believe it all yet."

He'd spent all the stoicism he had on our interview. I took his hand in both of mine. "I can't imagine how hard this must be, but you have my deepest sympathy."

And I meant it. After Nathan left, I thought about how much worse this was about to get for him. I didn't want it to happen to such a nice guy. But my obligation was to my client. The story was going to come out.

Whether she was telling the truth or not.

TWENTY-SEVEN

"Well?" Michelle's voice broke into my thoughts. I'd been standing in the reception area, staring at the door through which Nathan had just exited. "Come on, spill," she said. "Did he give you anything?"

"A lot more than I thought I'd get." I briefly hit the highlights.

When I finished, Michelle sat back in her chair. "Wow, it backs up a lot of what Cassie said."

"It might." Nathan had painted a picture of a family dynamic that *could* back up Cassie's story. But not necessarily.

Michelle sighed. "Well, it's a step in the right direction anyway. Have you spoken to Tiegan since Cassie got arrested?"

I'd called her that very night because I'd wanted to suggest that she visit Cassie if she could. And maybe bring Rain and Tawny for a visit now and then. Cassie's friends could only go with an adult, and there was no way their parents would do it. Cassie was going to need all the moral support she could get. "Tiegan's in shock."

Michelle leaned back in her chair and stretched. "It'd be scary if she weren't. Did you ask her about the molestation?"

I'd considered it but decided not to. "If she did know, she'll be in big trouble. She's required by law to report it."

"But if Cassie begged her not to tell—"

"I think that's unlikely. Tiegan would've been risking her whole career. But I'll wait until I can ask her about it in person." That way I could get a read on whether she was telling the truth. "We'll need some really solid expert testimony for trial. Better start making calls right away. We've got to tie up the good ones before we go public with the story." Once the prosecution found out what we were up to, they'd start trolling for experts. I wanted to make sure I recruited the best ones so I could keep them out of the DA's hands.

"I'll put together a list. But I'll need at least a day to round them up."

"You can have two days." I still had a couple more people to talk to before I went public. "I won't break the story till after the arraignment, which should be the day after tomorrow."

Michelle studied my face. "How are you dealing with all this, Sam? It's gotta be hammering just about every one of your buttons."

I heaved a deep sigh and nodded. It wasn't really my way to talk about emotional issues. In fact, I hated it. But I'd do it this once. Because I really needed to just this once, and Michy was the only person in the world I could talk to about it. "It sucks. And sitting through that interview . . ." I paused and stared at the floor as I remembered the sick feeling that'd washed over me, again and again. "It was horrible."

She looked worried. "Maybe it's not such a good idea for you to handle this case, Sam."

My whole body stiffened as a burst of anger shot through me. I exploded. "So I'm supposed to let him ruin *everything*? Now he gets to reach in and screw up my practice, too?" I kicked the trash can and sent it flying. "No fucking way!" I fumed on. "This is *my* life." I jabbed a finger into my chest. "Mine! And he's not going to take it from me!"

Michelle watched me, unfazed. After a moment, she spoke calmly. "Okay, I get it. Fine, then keep the case. But you'd better not try to keep it all locked up in some little corner where it can't get out, because that's not going to work. I'm warning you right now: talk to me, talk to a shrink. Hell, talk to a wall. But deal with it. Or you'll implode when you can least afford it."

I hate when she gets like this. All preachy. And right. So I talked about it—about how awful it'd been, how it'd made me physically ill to hear what Cassie had gone through, how infuriating it'd been to hear that Paula had refused to believe her. Reliving the feelings I'd had during our interview was physically painful, my stomach alternately queasy then twisted in knots. I'd had to sit down, my arms wrapped around my torso. But when I finished, I had to admit, I felt better.

Michelle gave me a little smile and joked lightly, "See? Was that so hard?"

I gave her a bitter smile. But I had no intention of ever talking about this again. There's only so much navel-gazing I can stand. "The big question is whether Cassie's story will sell." I thought for a moment. "Tell you what, why don't you come to the arraignment with me? That way, we can go visit her together afterward. I'll have her tell you her story so you can judge for yourself whether it'll fly. It'll do her good to start practicing." I'd do what I could for her, but at the end of the day, it was all about how well Cassie came across on the witness stand. That was a lot of pressure for a young girl. She'd need to have her story down perfectly, and that meant hours and hours of practice.

Michelle checked the monitor of her computer. "I guess I can take the morning off. I *would* like to see for myself how she does."

"Perfect." I righted the trash can and tossed in the crumpled paper that'd fallen all over the floor. "And thanks for listening, Michy."

"Thanks for talking, Sam." She raised an eyebrow. "And I meant what I said. Don't bottle it up."

"Right." Sure. Whatever.

I was about to go back to my office when my cell phone buzzed with a text message. It was Niko. Damn it! I'd forgotten. I was supposed to meet him tonight at eight p.m. for dinner at the Tower Bar on Sunset. He was already there. I couldn't cancel now. I told Michelle. "Do I look decent enough to go like this?" I was wearing a navy pantsuit and black boots.

Michelle dropped her head into her hands and laughed. "You're so impossible." She scanned my outfit, then took off her shoes—black patent leather heels—and handed them to me. "Wear these, fix your makeup, and you'll be good to go."

The perk of having a best friend who wore the same shoe size could not be overestimated. I gave her my boots, put on her shoes, and told her I'd fix my makeup in the car on the way over. "Besides, it's dark in that place. He won't notice." I texted Niko that I was almost there.

Michelle shook her head as she slipped on my boots. "Incorrect, Grasshopper. He's a martial arts guy—"

"Krav Maga—"

She rolled her eyes. "Whatever. They notice stuff. Stop in the bathroom and do it right. Another five minutes won't matter."

I headed for the door. "Okay, fine."

"And we'll spring for Uber, so you can drink. Just call me after, let me know how it goes. Unless it gets too late." She spoke in a sultry voice. "If you know what I mean."

I shot her a look. "The stoplight three blocks away knows what you mean."

I did a rush makeup job and hurried out to the waiting Uber car, feeling pissy. I didn't want to go out. Once I got into a case, I liked to burrow in and push everything else away.

But by the time I walked into the restaurant area, I realized it was a good thing. Michelle was right. Cassie's case was going to get to me the way no other case had. Not even Dale's. And an overly invested lawyer makes for a lousy lawyer. One who can't see the weaknesses in the case. One who loses credibility with the jury. And then loses the case. A break in routine, where I spent time with a real person who wasn't hip deep in murder and mayhem might be just the balance I needed to keep from falling down the rabbit hole of my childhood nightmare.

Niko had gotten us a table in the corner next to a window that overlooked the city. Quiet and romantic. And as I approached, I caught more than one woman throwing glances his way. I'd have done it, too. Niko had that sexy/dangerous thing going for him.

When he saw me, he stood up and gave me a slow smile. He kissed me on the cheek. "Sam, you look beautiful."

We sat down, and I shook my head. "You don't have to be nice. I came straight from work."

"I know. And you look beautiful."

Michelle had been right. This guy didn't miss much. And he was smooth as silk. Absolutely lethal. We ordered martinis and steaks and talked about everything but the case: his early stint as a stunt double—which was what drew him into Krav Maga and martial arts—my early stint in the public defender's office, his plan to open his own studio in six months, my plan to scale up and hire an associate. I couldn't believe how easy he was to talk to.

The evening flew by so fast, the restaurant emptied out before I noticed it was past midnight. I looked around the room. "I think our waiter might be getting ready to put us on a terrorist watch list."

Niko laughed and motioned for the waiter to bring the check. "I'll make it worth his while."

I picked up my purse. "Let's split it."

Niko winced and put a hand on my arm. "Please, let me get this. I'm not trying to diss your womanhood, I promise. But I'm the one who asked for this date. We can negotiate about next time, okay?"

I had to smile. "Fair enough." And I was glad to hear him say "next time." Then it occurred to me how cool it was to be glad about that. I couldn't remember the last time I'd felt that way.

As we entered the darkened lounge just inside the front door, Niko pulled me aside and gave me a long, lingering kiss that turned my body into liquid. When we stepped apart, I was breathless. I covered with a sexy smile, then quickly turned toward the door so I could inhale.

My Uber car was waiting when we got outside. As Niko opened the door for me, I wished I could take things further, but I had to get an early start in the morning. I called Michelle on the way home to tell her how it went. Also to keep her from giving me shit about why I hadn't called.

She'd been happy to hear it'd gone so well. "Now please, oh please, don't screw this up."

I could've gotten huffy, but why? I knew she was right. I'd found a way to dump every guy who'd even gotten close to a serious relationship—whether it was by neglect or by finding flaws Michelle usually classified as utter horseshit. I sighed. "I guess we'll see how I do."

I'd like to be able to say that I got a great night's sleep. But the nightmare had been hitting me like a pile driver ever since I'd met Cassie. And that night was no exception. I woke up, panting and terrified. It's a bad combination. I rolled out of bed and into the shower, then gulped down a cup of coffee. Still somewhat groggy, I filled my giant-size travel cup—Michelle calls it my "Gallon Glug"—and headed to work.

It was only seven thirty when I got to the office, and I had the place to myself. I used the time to make sure all my other cases were in shape so I could clear the decks for Cassie. I planned to go talk to Tiegan and then pay Cassie a visit. I kept my head down, barely taking a minute to look up when Michelle and Alex got in, other than to get the report from Alex that he hadn't gotten anything of note from Nathan during the ride back to his hotel. Not unexpected, but it'd been worth a try.

At noon, I packed up and headed for Glendale. As I drove, I tried to imagine how Tiegan was feeling. Since she was Cassie's counselor, she had to be wondering how she'd missed the signs that something had obviously been terribly wrong in Cassie's life. She'd certainly never mentioned seeing anything "off" about Cassie. But maybe she had noticed problems and just hadn't said anything to protect Cassie's privacy.

If that were true, I couldn't blame her. There'd been no reason to tell anyone until now.

TWENTY-EIGHT

I found Tiegan sitting alone in her classroom, an untouched lunch bag on the desk in front of her. She was staring out the window. I knocked on the doorjamb. She startled before turning toward me. "Come on in."

She seemed deeply troubled and a little unsteady. I took a seat at one of the desks in the front row. Something I'd never done when I was in school. Not even law school. "It's a terrible shock, I know."

Tiegan shook her head. "I just can't believe it. I can't imagine how she could do such a thing." She gazed at the floor for a moment, then shook her head again. When she looked up at me, she asked, "Have you seen her?"

I nodded. "I need to ask you some questions."

Her expression was pained. "Then it's true? She really did it?"

I thought I might end up going public with it, but I hadn't made the decision yet, so I dodged. "I can't comment on that just yet. What Cassie tells me is confidential. I hope you understand. But could you answer some questions for me?"

Tiegan looked uncertain as she searched my face. "I guess so."

"Did Cassie ever tell you that she'd been molested by anyone in her family?" Teachers and counselors were required by law to report any claims of sexual abuse, but I had to ask.

Tiegan stared at me, then slowly shook her head. "I'd definitely have reported it if she had. The only family-related issue I remember her telling me about was her difficulty getting along with Abel. She never said anything about being molested."

"What did Cassie say about the problems she was having with Abel?"

Tiegan paused and knitted her brow. "Just that he'd tease her, get his friends to gang up on her in school. That kind of thing. Typical sibling tension, especially common when you have an adopted child."

"What did you think of Paula? Did she seem concerned about Cassie?"

Tiegan gave a little shrug. "I only met with her once. She came in to see me. But she seemed . . . annoyed. Like she wanted me to give her a quick fix."

"For what?"

"She said Cassie seemed to be frequently angry lately, that she was picking fights with all of them and wasn't sleeping well. Several times she'd found Cassie awake at two or three in the morning."

I sat up. This could back up Cassie's claim about being afraid to go to sleep. "Doing what?"

Tiegan lifted her hands. "Nothing in particular. Playing with her phone, reading magazines, watching TV."

"What did Paula do about it?"

Tiegan sighed heavily. "At first, she'd make her turn out the lights and go to bed. But that would always lead to a fight, and after Paula turned out the light and went to bed, Cassie would just get up again. Paula couldn't stand guard all night to make sure Cassie didn't get up again, so she gave up."

"When did you have this meeting?"

"Maybe three months ago? Not long after I became Cassie's counselor."

I decided to ask her about what Nathan had said. "Did Paula ever tell you she thought Cassie made up stories?"

Tiegan rubbed her left temple. "No. I don't remember her ever saying that." A sad look crossed her face as she stared out the window. "So Cassie was being molested. I don't get how I missed that. There must've been signs . . ." She trailed off, her voice filled with guilt. "I really failed her. But to kill practically a whole family . . . I don't know . . ."

"Again, I can't tell you what she said—"

She held up a hand. "Don't worry, I won't tell anyone." She folded her hands on the desk. "Is there anything I can do to help?"

"Have you worked with any child molestation experts?"

"Not on any case. Just as part of my training. But there was a woman who was pretty good. I'm sure I can find her name in my old class notebooks."

I heard a bell ring in the hallway and saw that it was one o'clock. Lunch was over. "That would be great. And if there's anything else you can remember about Cassie or her family, that'd be a big help, too." I stood up. "Are you planning to visit Cassie soon? The more contact she has with people who care about her, the better. She's pretty isolated in there."

Tiegan gave a solemn nod. "I'll definitely get there in the next day or so." She reached out and shook my hand. "I'm so glad she's got you, Sam."

The door opened, and a few students slowly shuffled in, heads down, as though they were cattle being led to slaughter. "Thanks, Tiegan. I'll do my best."

I wove through the crowded hallway, trying to hold back the flood of high school memories. I'd been a bitter, angry mess of a kid. Not at all like the sweetheart I am today.

Next stop was downtown at Twin Towers to visit Cassie. When they brought her out, she looked miserable and exhausted. She'd already lost weight—Barbara had said that ever since she'd been on house arrest, she'd practically stopped eating—and her orange jumpsuit hung on her like a tent. It made her look tiny and frail. For the first time in my career, I considered having a client wear that ugly thing in court. She looked so pathetic, the jury would melt on sight. Cassie picked up the phone as though it weighed a ton. The receiver looked huge next to her gaunt face.

I kept my voice light. "How are you doing?"

Her voice was so low and strained I could barely hear it. "I'm so tired. They never turn off the lights. How am I supposed to sleep?"

First-timers always complain about that. Not that I blame them. "I know. It sucks. But you'll get used to it. Everyone treating you okay?"

She slouched down in her chair. "No one ever talks to me! They just give orders. And I'm all by myself all day. It's horrible."

She was losing patience with her situation way too fast. I'd have to talk her down or she'd get on the wrong side of the wrong person. "I'll bring you some books to read and see if you can get a little extra yard time." She thanked me in a flat voice that didn't sound all that grateful. I decided not to have my come-to-Jesus talk with her about her attitude today. It'd probably just set her off. I told her I needed to ask her a few more questions. "Did you tell anyone about Abel and your father?" If I could get someone else to say that she'd complained about the abuse, it'd be huge.

Cassie rubbed the corner of the window with her index finger. "Like who?"

"Like anyone."

She stared down at the counter, then shook her head. "I don't want to get him involved."

"This is no time to be noble, Cassie. You're on trial for your life." I stared into her eyes. She nodded, but I wasn't sure it had registered. "If you get convicted of these murders, you could be sentenced to life without parole." Her face froze, mouth half-open.

"Without . . . parole . . ." After a few shallow breaths, she whispered, "You mean I'll never get out? Ever?" I nodded. "Oh my God!" She stared straight ahead. The phone slipped out of her hands, and she grabbed the sides of her head. She began to sob, and I heard her voice coming through the dangling receiver, tinny and distant, saying, "No, no, no, no. I can't do it! I'll kill myself!"

I held up a hand to stop her and pointed to my receiver. "Pick up the phone and listen. Right now!" Still sobbing, she picked up the receiver with trembling hands and put it to her ear. "Cassie, I know you don't mean that. You're upset, and you have every right to be. But if you let them hear you say that, they'll put you on suicide watch. Believe me, you don't want that. Understood?"

Cassie hiccupped a few times, then nodded. "But I thought you said before that the jury would say I was innocent and I'd get out!"

I gave her a firm look. "'Might.' I said 'might,' Cassie. And I'm not saying it couldn't happen. But you have to understand, it's also possible that you won't. That's why I told you before that you have to work with me. Now, let's try that again. Who did you tell?"

She wiped her face on her sleeve and sniffled. "Waylon knew. I told him."

"Waylon Stubing? Your old boyfriend?"

She swallowed hard. "Yeah. Will you make him come to court?"

Depends on whether he backs you up. "Maybe. We'll see." I'd been thinking he was the mysterious Earl Lee Riser she'd been calling and texting. I was just about to ask her, but then realized that if I did, she'd figure out that I'd been snooping around in her life. This was not the time to upset her. Cassie's arraignment was tomorrow, and I needed her to focus. I'd brace her up about her burner-phone buddy later. I explained what happens at an arraignment and coached her on how to say "not guilty" like she really meant it. Talking about what was next and what to expect seemed to calm her down, and I was relieved to see that even in her ragged state, she was a pretty fast study. "And there'll be a fitness hearing; that's where the judge decides whether you're fit for juvenile court. It's not like a trial. It's just a judge and a prosecutor and a probation officer. The law says the judge has to consider a list of things, and he or she will pretty much rely on what the probation officer says about them."

Cassie leaned toward me and gripped the phone. "Like what things? I've never been busted for anything before. Does that count?"

"Yes. But they'll also look at whether the crime was particularly brutal or violent, and whether it shows criminal sophistication." And on those counts, she'd be toast.

Cassie spoke in a quiet voice, her eyes fixed on the edge of the window. "I know it was bad." After a moment, she looked up with pleading eyes. "But I didn't mean to do it! I just . . . went crazy! Aren't you going to tell them that?"

"Of course I am, Cassie." I told her I'd arranged for her physical examination to take place tomorrow afternoon, after the arraignment. "You still okay with that?"

She grimaced but slowly nodded. "Will it hurt?"

Not that I'd ever heard. But then, I wouldn't know. I didn't represent the victims. "I doubt it." I asked how she was doing, whether she was able to sleep last night.

Cassie bit her lip. "Like I said, I do hate the lights being on all the time." She paused for thought as she traced the edge of the window. "But being alone in that cell feels safe in a weird way. No one can get to me, you know?"

I did. "So you didn't feel safe at the Reebers' house?"

Cassie sighed. "Not really. I didn't have a lock on my door, and I was always nervous that Burt—he's the dad—might . . ."

If he'd been inappropriate with her in any way, I sure hadn't heard about it. "Did he do or say anything . . . weird?"

Cassie's eyes slid away. "No, but . . ." She stopped and sighed. "It made me nervous, knowing he was there, just down the hall."

That sounded a little paranoid—which seemed just about right given what she'd been through. We chatted for a while longer, and then a deputy behind me said visiting hours were over. I told her I'd see her in court for her arraignment tomorrow.

Cassie licked her lips and leaned toward me. "Will they bring me in with the other, uh . . . inmates?"

"No, I think you'll come over in a van. They have to keep you separate."

She exhaled, relieved. "Is Tiegan going to come see me?"

"Absolutely. Barbara, too, I think."

"What about Tawny and Rain? Can they come?"

I told her I was working on it, that she should rest up, and then I left.

As I approached the elevator, I mulled over what I'd learned since Cassie had gotten arrested—from her and from everyone else. It seemed more and more likely that she was telling the truth, that she really had been molested.

Or was I too inclined to believe because of my own past?

I wasn't sure I could trust my gut this time.

TWENTY-NINE

I thought about stopping by the PAB to see whether I could find Emmons and get an early update on the test results for Cassie's shirt and jeans. Then I remembered. I was officially on the other side now. I wouldn't get past the front door.

As I left the jail, my stomach grumbled so loudly, a female deputy raised an eyebrow. As usual, breakfast had consisted of my canteen of coffee. But I wanted to get back to the office. I bought a hot dog and a bag of potato chips from a street vendor's cart and ate on the road. I tried not to think about the possible ingredients of that hot dog—probably part pizza rat.

When I got back to the office, I saw that Alex's door was open. I called out, "Honey, I'm home."

Michelle pulled off her headset. "How'd it go?"

I filled her in on my interviews with Tiegan and Cassie. "It all kind of jibes with Cassie's story."

"Sure sounds like it." Michelle leaned back and peered at me. "But you're not sold yet."

I wasn't sure what I was. "I'd like to hear what the doctor says after her exam."

MARCIA CLARK

Michelle looked skeptical. "But it's been a few weeks by now. Might not be . . . much."

That was true. If the doctor didn't see any trauma, that wouldn't necessarily mean Cassie was lying. Alex came out of his office carrying his new love: an iPad mini. "I've been working on Hausch, and I'm pretty much finished with that list of immigrant crime victims involving border town PDs." He nodded toward my office. "Shall we?"

I nodded. "Michy, if you want to come hear this, I'll turn on my ringer. It should be pretty quiet now."

She gave Alex a sideways glance. "Do I?"

Alex shrugged. "It's not pretty."

Michelle stood up. "I'm in."

I sat behind my desk and woke up my computer so I could take notes. Michelle sprawled out on the couch, and Alex took a seat in front of my desk. He tapped his iPad. "Almost all the cases where immigrants were victims were low-level stuff, bar brawls and theft of one kind or another. Then I came across something that happened eight years ago. A truck driver got stopped just north of the border at the checkpoint in Nogales."

"Wasn't Hausch working in San Luis PD back then?"

"Yeah. I'll get there in a sec. According to the official report, he got detained for inadequate paperwork. Something to do with regulations involving transportation of fruits and vegetables—"

I stopped typing. "Wait. 'Something'? I'd like to know—"

Alex shook his head. "Doesn't matter. The cop who stopped him was Mitchell Sanborn. Hang on to that name—"

"Because he's tied in with Hausch?" I asked.

Alex gave me a pissy look. "Yes. They worked together in San Luis for about a year—"

"A year before this—whatever it is—happened?"

Alex exhaled and glared at me. "Yes. You going to let me tell the story or not?" I waved him on. "The driver said he'd left the paperwork

204

back at the warehouse. Sanborn let the driver leave the truck in an empty lot down the street so he could go get it. Only the driver never came back. The truck sat there for three days in a hundred-and-ten-degree heat. Another trucker passing through Nogales stopped for a lunch break and noticed it. He probably wanted to talk to the driver, get some tips about the truck stops south of the border. Anyway, he noticed a really bad smell coming from the truck. When the cops opened the cargo area, they found twelve illegals." Alex looked up, his expression somber. "They were cooked to death."

I couldn't believe it. "Jeezus. Did Sanborn know they were in there?"

"Good question. He wasn't on duty when they found the bodies. He'd actually been off for the last two days before they were found, and he gave a statement denying any knowledge. There's no indication he ever got disciplined."

But that didn't mean Sanborn didn't know. "Assuming Sanborn did know, why would he stop the truck?"

Alex rubbed his fingers together. "To get more money."

"You assume." Alex nodded. "So how do we prove it? How can we find out whether Sanborn was on the take? And more to the point, how do we know Hausch had anything to do with this?"

"We don't. But he was close by." Alex looked down at his iPad mini. "Hausch moonlighted as private security for a warehouse close to Nogales PD. According to their records, the day that truck driver came through, Hausch was working at the warehouse."

A lot of this was just guesswork. But if it turned out to be right, if Hausch and Sanborn were on the take and knew about those immigrants and just left them to die, they were a couple of the most despicable murderers I'd ever seen. "So how do we find out if Hausch was at the checkpoint? I assume the truck driver's in the wind."

"He is. And I checked the ID he supposedly gave Sanborn. The name doesn't match the date of birth or birthplace. So it's bogus."

It figured. "Is there a ray of light here?"

"There is. I found a discrepancy in the reports. The first report shows there were twelve in the truck. The follow-up only shows ten."

Michelle had been half lying on the couch, but now she sat up. "What happened to the other two?"

There only seemed to be two possibilities. "Was it a mistake? Or did they survive?"

"I'm guessing—and hoping—that they survived," Alex said. "And someone—maybe Sanborn—got hold of the follow-up report and dropped them off the list."

I sat back and folded my arms. "How do we know that?"

"We don't. Not for sure. We just know that Sanborn was on duty the day the follow-up was written."

I thought about that for second. "How come no one else caught the discrepancy?"

Alex tapped his iPad again and read his notes. "The sergeant did. Sanborn put in his follow-up that the first report mistakenly included the names of two witnesses on the victim list."

I frowned. I knew that cops take down the names of everyone near the scene, whether they saw anything or not. "But I thought the truck driver who called it in was the only one around."

Alex gave me a pointed look. "Exactly. And I didn't find any witness statements in the paperwork."

Michelle tilted her head toward the iPad. "But if they didn't see anything, then maybe the cops didn't bother to write it up. Isn't that possible?"

I nodded. "It is, and if so, then I'd think the cop who took the initial report would have something to say about it. Did he have any comments about Sanborn's story?"

Alex sighed and shook his head. "Not that I could find. But still . . . it just doesn't feel right."

I had to agree. This whole thing just didn't pass the smell test. The fact that Sanborn wasn't on the job the day the illegals were

MORAL DEFENSE

found—when the report that listed twelve names was written—stuck
in my craw. And if our suspicions about his being on the take were
right, those two survivors were lucky Sanborn hadn't been there—or
they wouldn't have been survivors for long. "Then you think those two
may have escaped?"

Alex nodded. "Again, it's just a working hypothesis, but yes. And I
think Sanborn took them off the list so no one could track them down."

"Did they get names for any of these guys?"

"They got names for all of them. Whether they're accurate is
another story. Anyway, that's what I'm working on now."

This really might be a big break. "Great job, Alex. But stick with
the Internet for now. If you find those two survivors, we'll need to get
Dale on board."

"I agree. And I'll check with Dale, but I'd bet the MS-13 is all
over this."

It seemed likely. "Which means Sanborn and Hausch are in bed
with them. Or were."

Michelle stood up and gave Alex a stern look. "Then all I can say is,
you better not let them get wind of what you're doing."

I turned back to my computer. "Just a sec, Michy. I'm sending you
the contact information for Cassie's old boyfriend, Waylon Stubing.
Can you get me a meeting ASAP?"

"Yep. What time's the arraignment tomorrow?"

"Eight thirty. Want me to pick you up at home?" We all lived in
West Hollywood within a few miles of one another. Not by design, just
dumb luck.

Michelle made a face. "How about I pick you up?"

I lifted my hands. "Why must you all hate Beulah?"

Alex joined Michelle at the door. "We're not haters. We just like
to breathe air—"

"Instead of toxic fumes," Michelle chimed in.

I crumpled up a piece of paper and threw it at them.

A few minutes later, Michelle buzzed me. "You can see Waylon in an hour if you want. He said he could meet you at Kaldi Coffee."

I didn't like the idea of meeting him in a public place. But I needed to find out whether I finally had a witness who'd say Cassie had complained about the abuse to someone before the murders. "Okay. Tell him I'll see him there."

I'd get him to take a walk or drive to a park or something if I didn't like the setup at the coffee shop.

But as it turned out, Kaldi Coffee was fine. Small, off the beaten path, and empty except for a bored-looking middle-aged woman with frizzy red hair, who seemed to be watching a cartoon show on her iPhone. I got a cup of coffee and took a table as far from the window as I could get.

A few minutes later, Waylon showed up. Tall, slender, with sensitive dark eyes, a wide mouth, and flying eyebrows, he wore a black-and-white wool scarf draped around his neck and a black, pinch-front fedora that looked a little too small. Everything about him screamed Drama Club.

He pulled out the chair across from me. "I hope you haven't been waiting long."

"Nope. I just got here." Wow, manners and charm. Cassie had a lot better taste than I'd had at her age.

I thanked him for meeting with me, then asked when he and Cassie had started dating.

He picked at the edge of his scarf as he spoke. "Around the beginning of the year. We got to talking during an emergency drill, and she said she might want to join Drama." He dropped the scarf and made a sweeping gesture with his hands. "And the rest, as they say, is history."

I didn't think they would say that or anything close to it, but I nodded. "How long did you guys date?"

Waylon sighed and pushed his hat back on his head. "About three months. We broke up the day before Christmas." He gave a sarcastic little smile. "Merry Christmas, huh?"

Just three months, and yet she told him what she'd never told anyone else. "Did you guys ever hang out before you started dating?"

He leaned back in his chair. "We've known each other since junior high, and we'd always been friends. But I can't say we ever really hung out before we started dating, other than at school—lunch and breaks, stuff like that."

"Did she ever tell you she had problems with her family?"

Waylon's forehead wrinkled. "Ever? Try always. That's how we first got to be friends."

"By talking about her family?"

"Both our families. I'm adopted, too."

Of course. That made sense. She knew he'd "get it" the way none of her other friends could. "What did she tell you?"

Waylon slouched farther down in his chair and twisted the end of his scarf. "At first, it was just about the way her mom would always remind her how lucky she was to get picked by such a great family. And about Abel always saying mean shit to her like, her real mom was a crack whore and Cassie was probably going to turn out the same." He had a look of disgust. "I know it's not cool to say bad things about the dead, but Abel was a real douche."

This was not news. "You said at first? Did she tell you different things later on?"

Waylon stared down at the table. "After we started dating, she told me he was making her . . . have sex with him."

That was helpful, but more detail would be better. "Can you be a little more specific? Did she tell you what he made her do?"

His cheeks reddened. "Um, oral and, ah . . . I think anal." I'd left my empty packets of sweetener on the table, and he played with one of them now, twisting it around and around. "I tried to get her to go to the cops, but she wouldn't do it. She said no one would believe her, and her parents would kick her out and she'd wind up in foster care."

"Did she ever complain about her father?"

Waylon frowned. "No. Not to me." He stared at me, his expression troubled. "Did she say he was, ah . . . abusing her, too?"

"I can't discuss anything she told me."

"Oh, right. Sure. Sorry."

I shook my head. "S'okay."

He'd corroborated Abel, and that was good. Very, very good. The fact that he didn't know about Stephen might hurt, but not much. I could argue Cassie was too embarrassed to admit that he'd victimized her, too. So far, it was all adding up: the reason why she'd tell Waylon, the reason why she wouldn't tell anyone else. "I don't want to embarrass you, but can I ask you a personal question about your relationship with Cassie?"

Waylon looked at me intently. "Okay."

"Did you two have sex?"

He flushed again, then shook his head. "We made out and stuff, but we never went all the way."

That figured, given what she'd been going through at home. "Is that why you broke up with her?"

Waylon's gaze slid off to the right. "Cassie was the one who broke up. She *said* she was too messed up to be in a relationship."

I caught the inflection. "You didn't believe her?"

"Not really. I got the feeling there was someone else."

I was a little surprised. "Do you know who?"

Waylon shook his head. "But I don't think it was anyone in school."

"Why not?"

"Because I'd have seen him. Or at least heard about it."

"There wasn't even a rumor?"

Waylon met my eyes. "Nothing."

THIRTY

It was after seven o'clock by the time I left Glendale. I called Michelle to find out whether there was any pressing reason to go back to the office. "Does Alex have anything for me yet?"

"No, so don't bother. I'll be cutting out of here pretty soon myself. Did you get anything out of Waylon?"

"Yeah, a lot. Tell you tomorrow when you pick me up."

I ended the call and thought about how I wanted to handle the press. There wouldn't be any in-court coverage. Cassie was a minor, so they couldn't photograph her. The only face time I'd get would be on the courthouse steps. The question was, did I want any face time right now? I didn't think so. Not yet. I needed to know what the doctor said, and I wanted to get Michelle's take on Cassie. There'd be plenty of time to start the battle wagons rolling after tomorrow.

I'd been doing a lot of nonstop running for the past few days, and by the time I got home, I was shot. I put myself to bed at ten thirty, hoping to get in a few hours of solid sleep before the nightmare slashed my psyche.

I didn't do too badly. It was almost six by the time I woke up. A very good night for me. I pulled out one of my three high-priced suits from Barney's. The suits came courtesy of my stepdad, Jack, the real estate mogul whom my mother had persuaded to put a ring on it—and who happened, just by accident (certainly not her design), to be a great guy. He'd bought them for me during Dale's case after I'd been trashed on cable shows for dressing like a bargain-basement rag doll. Someday, women won't have to put up with it. Someday, people are going to care more about what we say and do than what we look like.

But that day didn't seem to be coming any time soon, so I stepped into my black platform heels, sprayed my hair, checked my makeup, and finished my fourth cup of coffee.

Michelle arrived with my fifth cup at seven thirty. On the way to court, I filled her in on what Waylon had said.

She was impressed. "He's probably the best backup yet."

"He's really good. But we'll see what you think when you meet Cassie."

There were a few reporters outside the courthouse, but nothing like the throngs I'd had to wade through during Dale's case. I waved to Brittany, a Channel Four reporter I'd gotten friendly with back then. She motioned to ask me whether I wanted to comment. I shook my head. And I did the same with the other reporters.

When we got into court, I noticed a few print reporters in the audience. But since there were no cameras, the atmosphere was business as usual—a welcome relief. Even so, the bailiff brought out Cassie first and told me they were going to call our case right away, to get the reporters out of there. I barely had ten seconds to introduce Michelle before the judge came out.

Judge James Groff, a young guy I hadn't seen before, took the bench, and as I stood next to Cassie, I could feel her whole body shaking. The prosecutor, a young blonde woman who looked about twelve years old, said in a Minnie Mouse voice that she was just standing in for the arraignment. When she read the charges, I heard an audible gasp from the audience.

So did the judge. He threw a stern look at the audience, and the courtroom fell silent. I liked him already. When he asked Cassie how she pleaded, I turned to her and whispered, "You can do this."

Cassie gave me a frightened glance, and for a second, I thought she was going to blow it. But then, in a clear, if somewhat soft voice, she said, "Not guilty, Your Honor."

I leaned in and whispered, "Good job."

We set a date for the fitness hearing, and the judge called the next case. As the bailiff led Cassie out, I told her we'd meet her at the jail. She looked back and nodded.

It'd take at least an hour for Cassie to get back to Twin Towers, so Michelle and I grabbed breakfast in the courthouse cafeteria.

As she walked past the steaming trays of food, she made a face. "Is this actually people food?" She pointed to the vat of oatmeal. "What the hell is that? It looks like boiled Styrofoam."

We both opted for the safety of toast and cold cereal. Then we headed over to Twin Towers.

Cassie looked drained when they brought her into the attorney room. I picked up the phone and introduced Michelle again. She glanced at Michelle, then turned back to me, her expression worried. "Did I do okay?"

"You did great." It was time to tell her our game plan. "I'm thinking we might go public with your history of abuse. I'm fairly sure we'll have to take this case to trial, and I want the people who're going to wind up on your jury to know your side of things as soon as possible. You okay with that?" It didn't really matter. The lawyer controls the case and sets the strategy. The only decisions the clients really get to make are whether to plead guilty and whether to take the stand. But it's good to let them feel like they have a say in things. Makes them more cooperative.

Cassie's eyes bounced between Michelle and me. "How are you going to do that?"

"By talking to reporters. First me. And then, maybe you."

Cassie looked panicked. "Me? Why?"

I'd known there was going to be some pushback on that point. "It'll be more effective coming from you. But we don't have to make a final decision about that now. Whether you talk to a reporter or not, I have to start getting you ready to testify. Because you're definitely going to have to take the stand. And getting ready means going over your testimony many, many times."

Cassie had gotten so pale I could see the blue veins in her temples. "Does that mean I have to say all those things in court, in front of everyone?"

"I'm afraid so. But the more we practice, the easier it'll get. I promise. So let's start. Tell us what happened with Abel when you were thirteen."

I took her through the whole story. At first, Cassie's voice shook, and she stumbled over her answers as she darted glances at Michelle. But as we got further along, her voice got steadier. She had to stop a few times when tears got in the way, but that was all to the good. I hoped she'd still be able to do that at trial. Sometimes, coaching can bleed that kind of emotion out of a client. But no way would I coach her to cry on the witness stand.

Crying during testimony is only effective if it's real. Nothing turns off a jury faster than fake tears. And since none of my clients are Strasberg graduates, my advice to them is always, "Try not to cry."

When we'd gone through the whole thing, I said, "That was great, Cassie. Now I'm going to give you some homework. For next time, I want you to try and remember as many details as possible. Especially about the first time Abel or your father came into your room. Try and remember what pajamas you wore, what they wore, what happened that day, where you went, who you saw. Any details you can add to the picture will help."

Cassie stammered, "B-but it happened so long ago, and there were so many nights." She hung her head. "I don't know how I'm supposed to remember all that stuff." She looked up at me, her mouth turned down. "And I don't want to."

"I don't blame you. And I'm not asking you to remember everything. But the more specific you can be, the more the jury will believe you."

Cassie closed her eyes and sighed. "I'll try."

I looked at her with sympathy. "I wish there were another way."

Cassie ran a hand through her short hair. "They said the doctor's going to do the exam at three o'clock. Is it a woman?"

"Yes." Dr. Naomi Hawkins was a sexual assault expert. I'd never worked with her myself, but I'd seen her testify in court, and she was fantastic. Had the jury eating out of her hand in the first five minutes. "I think you'll like her."

We talked for a little while longer, and I asked about her living conditions, the food, the guards, and her new schedule—I'd managed to talk them into letting her get some exercise in the yard. She was miserable, of course, but she was basically doing okay, all things considered.

I didn't ask Michelle what she thought until we were in the car. She searched my face before answering. "Let me put it this way: if I didn't know she'd killed them, I'd have no reason to doubt her."

An interesting way of putting it. "Don't forget, she hid her bloody pajamas and lied about the skinhead guy."

"That's not great." She stared out the window and fell silent for a moment. "Obviously, she wanted to get away with it if she could. But I'd buy that she lied because she didn't want to have to tell anyone what was going on. Besides, what other reason *could* there be for her to kill them—especially that way?"

That's what I intended to tell the jury. "I just don't want to get sucked into believing her because of my own . . . issues."

Michelle started the car and pulled out of the parking lot. "I get it, and that's smart. But stop second-guessing yourself. You're not going to turn into a pushover just because of your history. And even if she is lying, if she's good enough to fool you—*and* me—then she's definitely good enough to fool a jury."

And that was the whole point. Wasn't it? "But if she's gaming us . . ."

Michelle glanced at me as she turned onto Temple Street. "Look, I don't like the idea of a kid lying about getting molested, either. It hurts the ones who really were. But if she can sell it, what do you care?"

"I *don't* care. I could give a shit if the kid is lying. All my clients lie to me. I just don't want to get caught flat-footed."

We were stopped at the traffic light. Michelle gave me a piercing look. "Are you sure? Because I think it's more than that."

Spare me. The light turned green, and she pulled through the intersection. "Whatever. How do you think she'll do if I put her with a reporter?"

Michelle glanced at me. After a beat, she replied, "Give her one or two more sessions, and she'll do fine. I noticed she stumbled a little about the dad. She said he didn't touch her at all when it first started, but then later she said he'd always touched her. Get her to smooth out details like that, and you'll be good to go."

We watched a very pregnant young woman in a short, tight blouse and low-slung maxi-skirt that left most of her belly exposed navigate the crosswalk in front of us. She was pushing a stroller with one hand and hanging on to a toddler, who was jumping on both feet, with the other. "That just seems like too many kids."

Michelle gave a little laugh. "And how come she's not cold?"

"Must be a pregnant thing." I mentally reviewed Cassie's hiccup about her father. "I'll smooth out the big stuff. But I don't want Cassie to get too slick." Truthful witnesses never tell the story exactly the same way every time. Little things always change. "And I think it'd be easier on Cassie if we bring in a female reporter. The jail won't let a camera in, so it's got to be print."

Michelle tapped the steering wheel with her index finger. "I'd bet Trevor has at least one woman working for him by now."

That was a great idea. "Can you find out? If he's got someone good, that'd be the perfect solution." I'd met Trevor Skotler during Dale's case. He was smart and tough, and he knew how to play the "I'll scratch your back" game better than most. Back then, his dot-com 'zine, Buzzworthy, was just a one-man operation. But since then, he'd broken several juicy stories, a couple of them big enough to make HuffPo and the Daily Beast consider buying him out.

I thought about my next move. "Did you tie up all of our shrinkers?"

Michelle steered onto the freeway. "Yeah, and I set up interviews with your top three for tomorrow."

"Perfect." I wasn't going to use more than two. Shrinks inevitably find something to disagree about, and even if it's minor, that can make the jury decide to toss it all out. In a case like this, that would be devastating. So I had to screen them carefully.

My cell phone quacked. That duck ringtone was starting to bug me. I checked the screen. It was Alex. "Yeah, what's up?"

"I found them. The survivors from that truck."

THIRTY-ONE

I wouldn't let Alex tell me any more than that on the cell phone. Dale's paranoia had gotten to me. It might be silly, but why take chances?

I told Michelle what he'd said. She slapped the steering wheel. "No one but Alex."

"He is magical." And it was a good thing he was on our side. I couldn't even imagine the devastation and ruin he could inflict on an enemy.

I found his door closed when we got to the office, so I knocked and said, "Julian Assange called. He said to stop hacking his e-mail."

Alex came out. "Well, that's better than your others."

We all convened around the coffee table in my office. "What've you got?" I didn't ask him *how* he got it. I probably wouldn't understand a word he said.

Alex tapped a key on his iPad mini. "Turns out the survivors are brothers. They *were* Louie and Hugo Trujillo. Now they're Santiago and Patricio Gomez. Born in Honduras. Probably fled because of the gangs. Somehow, they wound up in San Bernardino." He sat back. "Dale helped me track them down."

That they were even alive was amazing. "Any idea how they got out of Nogales?"

"Not really. Dale's theory is that the cops on duty that day would've taken them to the hospital, and they escaped from there."

Michelle was incredulous. "And no one in the hospital sounded the alarm?"

Alex's expression was bitter but resigned. "About a couple of broke illegals? A security guard probably looked under the beds for a few minutes and called it a blessing."

If they had escaped from the hospital, those were some tough dudes. They had to have been near death. "Do you have an exact address?"

Alex nodded. "Dale and I are going down there as soon as he can get off work."

"I'm going with you." I wanted to see these brothers and hear their story for myself.

Alex looked worried. "You sure? It's a tough 'hood."

I stared at him. "Give me a break. Worse than Julio's place?"

He gave a little smile. "That one *is* hard to beat." He sighed. "But Dale won't like it."

"Since when have I ever cared about that?"

Michelle nodded at him. "She's got a point there."

Alex was right, of course. Dale didn't like it. He tried to talk me out of it. "We'll video the interview; you'll be able to see everything. If you still need a face-to-face, we'll bring them up here."

I shook my head. I'd given this some thought. "I might be your only shot at getting them to talk. You look like a cop"—I jerked my head toward Alex—"and he looks like he could be your partner." Alex shot me a dagger look. "Your very hot, much *younger* partner." I glanced at Alex. "Better?" He gave a reluctant nod. "Anyway, I'm guessing they might—just *might*—not be fans of the cops."

Michelle leaned toward me and spoke out of the side of her mouth. "There are female cops, you know."

I turned to stare at her. "Really? Must you?"

She shrugged. "Just sayin'."

I prevailed. We were on the road by three o'clock, but that still put us in rush-hour traffic when we hit Pomona. It was after seven by the time we rolled into San Bernardino, and night had fallen. The temperature drops fast in the semidesert, and it was cold enough to make all of us button up.

The neighborhood looked like it had been on the outer edges of an industrial section at some point in the past. The street the brothers lived on was just beyond some abandoned warehouses and other buildings— now crumbling and graffitied, with busted-out windows that looked like giant teeth—that seemed big enough to have housed assembly lines. There was an eerie, postapocalyptic stillness to it all. I took in the grass growing between broken-out walls, a lone sneaker under a fallen rain gutter, the grounds around the buildings that were now just big patches of dirt and weeds. And strewn throughout the neighborhood was the random litter of a place where the residents existed, rather than lived: a shredded truck tire here, a rusty bicycle missing the seat there, a rotting piece of foam rubber, the remains of a couch pillow, fast-food wrappers floating in the breeze. It looked like the end of life as we know it.

The Gomez brothers' place fit right in. It was a small wood-framed shack with a boarded-up window to the left of a splintered, battered door. There was a detached garage behind it that looked like it would collapse in a strong wind. The rest of the houses on the block were similar: tiny, cheaply and haphazardly built, and on the verge of ruin.

We parked a little distance down the street, behind an old pickup truck that'd been stripped of its wheels. I saw a piece of a blanket hanging from the rear window of the cab. Someone used to live in that truck—maybe still did. There were no streetlights—in fact, no lights on anywhere that I could see. "This place looks abandoned. Are you sure this is right?"

Dale scanned the area. "I'm sure it *was* right."

Alex pointed to my purse. "You brought your gun?" I nodded. "I'll go check out the place. You guys cover me."

Dale just stared at him. "Are you kidding? Stand down. I'm going." He started to open the door.

Alex, who was in the backseat, grabbed his shoulder. He leaned forward and pointed to his face. "Look at me, *güero*. Who do you think blends better?" He'd dressed way down for the occasion, in old jeans and a ratty-looking brown sweatshirt. And of course, he was Latino. Someone who might be a friend or relative of the Gomezes'.

Dale didn't like it, but he couldn't argue with the logic. Alex got out, and Dale and I crouched behind the pickup truck, our guns in hand. We watched as Alex knocked on the front door, got no answer, then tried to peer through the sides of the boarded-up window. He shook his head and moved toward the garage. After circling all the way around it, he came back, and we all got into the car.

He pointed to the left side of the garage. "There's a door near the back. No windows. But I think someone lives there because the door-knob works, and it isn't dusty. The house might be occupied, but it doesn't sound like anyone's there right now."

Dale looked impressed. "You noticed the doorknob wasn't dusty?" He nodded at Alex. "Not bad."

Alex dipped his head. "Thanks. So now what?"

Dale sighed and sank down in his seat. "We wait."

Knowing a stakeout was a distinct possibility, we'd brought provisions. But I was afraid to drink water. Indoor plumbing is a nonnegotiable item for me. I nibbled on a turkey and Swiss sandwich and washed it down with tiny sips.

We talked about what we might or might not find here. And what to do about it if the brothers wouldn't talk. The answer: not a whole hell of a lot. Even though we could probably prove they'd escaped from the death truck, if they wouldn't—or couldn't—tell us whether dirty cops were involved, there'd be no point in bringing them in. That'd just get them deported and do nothing for our investigation. We all agreed they didn't deserve that. They'd been through enough hell.

In the meantime, the only person I saw on the street was a homeless man who was pushing a shopping cart with his black dog on a long leash tethered to the handle. I was glad to see that the dog looked well fed. They entered a shack at the end of the block.

After two hours, I was starting to think this operation was a bust. But finally, at a quarter to ten, a short, slight Hispanic man in battered combat boots with no laces and a long, army-green wool coat drove up in an ancient Pinto and parked in front of the Gomezes' house. He moved past the house and headed to the side door of the garage. He pulled a key out of his pocket, unlocked the door, and stepped inside.

Dale sat up. "That might be our guy." He held up the photos Alex had found on the Internet. But they were just head shots, taken at a family gathering and posted on a relative's Facebook page, so it was hard to get an idea of size or height.

Alex grabbed the door handle. "I'll go. You guys can—"

Dale shot him a look. "No. I'm going with you. Sam, you stay here."

I shook my head. "Fuck that. I'm going, too. This guy's not going to be stupid enough to think he can take on both of you."

Alex looked at Dale. "She's probably right about that."

Dale shook his head at me and sighed. "Fine. But stay back."

"Fine." I held up my gun. "But I am locked and loaded."

Dale glared at me. "Yeah, not exactly comforting, since you'll be behind me. Keep that thing down unless I say otherwise." He muttered, "This is the last time we do this shit together."

I glared back at him. But I let them get out first and kept the gun down at my side.

We quickly scanned the area to make sure no one else was coming, then headed for the garage. I stayed a few paces behind and stopped about ten feet from the door. Alex knocked and said something in Spanish. A few seconds later, the man came to the door. With his coat off, I could see he was even smaller than he'd looked. Alex and Dale were easily a foot taller. And he didn't seem inclined to put up a fight. He stood back and held up his hands. He told them in Spanish to take whatever they wanted.

That wouldn't be much of a haul. Looking over his shoulder, I could see that the room was still just a garage. The only nod to residency was a cot and a table that consisted of a slab of wood balanced on cardboard boxes.

I could also see very clearly that this guy was not one of the Gomez brothers.

Alex explained that we weren't there to rob him, that we weren't cops, and that we were just looking for Santiago and Patricio Gomez. Dale showed him the photos. I watched his face carefully.

He glanced at the photos and shook his head. *"No, no los conozco."*

Alex pressed him. *"Estas seguro?"*

The man nodded vigorously. *"Sí, sí. Estoy seguro."*

He was sure.

THIRTY-TWO

"Bullshit." I folded my arms and stared at the garage through the front passenger-side window of our car. "I saw his reaction when you pulled out those photos." His eyes had widened—for just a split second, but it was long enough to show he was lying.

Dale was watching the garage, too. "I agree. But I'm not so sure it helped to tell him we weren't cops."

Alex sighed. "I figured I didn't need to tell him that we weren't Mara Salvatrucha."

True, none of us had MS-13 tats, but tats can be hidden. And this guy clearly wasn't willing to take any chances. It was hard to blame him. "So what now?"

Dale drummed his fingers on the steering wheel and stared at the garage. "We keep waiting."

We all slunk down in our seats. No one was in the mood to talk. If this didn't pan out, it was game over. We'd be at a dead end. After another half hour of nothingness, I was bored, tired, and depressed. My eyes were closing, and I was just about to drift off when Alex hissed, "He's coming out."

I jerked awake to see the man leave the garage, lock the door behind him, and head down the street. When he was fifty feet away, Dale opened his door. "I bet he's going to warn the Gomez brothers. I'm gonna follow him. I'll call you guys and leave the line open so you can hear what's going on."

I opened my door. "I'm going with you."

He gave me a stern look. "No, you're not. Stay here."

I waited a few seconds, then got out. Dale threw an angry look at me over his shoulder, but he kept going. The darkness was so thick I could barely see him, though he was just twenty feet away. And we had to tread carefully so the man wouldn't hear us. I could feel my stomach muscles clenching as I navigated down the cracked, uneven sidewalk. Dale periodically stopped and signaled for me to wait and let the guy get farther ahead of us. This was probably the worst tailing I'd ever seen. But our suspect hadn't made us, so it was good enough.

After ten minutes of squinting in the inky darkness and tiptoeing across cratered, litter-strewn concrete, I was sweating under all my layers of clothing.

We wound up at a huge warehouse. Unlike the buildings behind us, this one was alive and humming with activity. There were big rigs in the parking lot and workers moving around on the loading docks at the back. A faded sign above the docks said this was the SONORA FRUIT PACKING COMPANY. Our man headed around the side of the building. We followed at a distance and saw him stop outside what looked like an employee entrance. Dale pointed to the stacks of wooden crates on our left. We strolled over, trying not to draw attention, and ducked behind them.

I craned my neck to one side and then the other to get a view of the entrance. I finally found a space between the crates that I could see through if I stood on tiptoe. After a few minutes, a worker came out holding an unlit cigarette. Our man spoke to him, and the worker looked at his watch, then said something in reply. We were too far away to hear what they were saying. I whispered to Dale. "Think our guy's asking when the Gomez brothers are getting off?"

"Maybe." Dale took his phone out of his pocket. "Alex, you there? I think we've got him." He gave Alex directions to the fruit-packing plant, then told him, "I don't see any security. You can probably get close. We're just past the loading docks." Dale described our hiding spot.

My calves were starting to ache from standing on tiptoe for so long. I lowered my heels to give them a rest. I was freezing in my sweat-soaked T-shirt, now that we were standing still. I pulled up the collar on my coat, wrapped my arms around my body, and swayed to try and warm up. Seconds later, Dale whispered, "I think we've got something."

I popped back up to look. Our garage guy was standing to the left of the entrance with another man and speaking with some urgency. The other man scanned the area, and as his head swiveled in our direction, I saw that he looked like one of the Gomez brothers. And his expression was panicked. They took off, moving at a fast clip but not running.

Dale pulled out his phone. "Alex?" He shook his head. "He must be driving. Shit. We're gonna lose him."

"The hell we are." I tucked my hair into my coat and shoved my hands into my pockets, hoping to look nondescript enough to blend in, then started after them.

Behind me, I heard Dale mutter, "You're gonna get us killed." But he moved around to get ahead of me, and we walked as fast as we dared. Gomez—at least I assumed he was—and his roomie seemed to be headed for the street at the front of the building. Dale and I did our best to stay back, and we stopped behind every car or truck we passed in case they looked back. But we had to be cool about it, or the other workers would notice. Then we'd have a whole new set of problems.

When they reached the street, we were just fifty feet behind them. Dale whispered into his cell phone. "Alex? You there?" I held my breath as I waited to hear whether he answered. And exhaled as Dale began to tell him where we were. "Yeah. So just pull up next to them, and I'll push in from my side." But as we reached the corner, Gomez and his buddy broke into a run and turned right. I started to give chase, but Dale held me back. "Wait. Let's see what they do."

We moved to the corner and saw that they were already halfway down the street. We followed at a slower pace until we saw them cross to the other side. There was a rusted old storage pod on the curb to our left. We hid behind it and watched as they ran to an old, badly beat-up white Datsun that was missing its back bumper. I hissed to Dale, "Shit! Where's Alex?"

Then I heard Alex's voice coming through Dale's cell phone. Dale put it to his ear and listened, then said, "Perfect, now turn right." He described our position and the junker they'd just gotten into. Gomez started the car. It kicked over with a slow, reluctant whine. I willed it to choke and die, but no such luck. He gave it more gas, and the engine coughed to life. Gomez gunned it. The car jumped away from the curb, tires squealing. A loose pipe under the carriage threw sparks as it scraped along the road. Compared with that heap, Beulah was a goddess.

Seconds later, Alex's black Toyota Camry rounded the corner and pulled up next to us. Gomez had reached the end of the block. He made a fast right, and I heard the old car give a harsh roar as he took the turn. We jumped in, and Alex stomped on the gas; we flew down the block.

"Try to hang back," Dale said. "I don't think he's going far. Let's see where he's headed."

Alex eased off the pedal, and we caught a glimpse of their taillights as they hung a left at the next corner. I hoped they'd go back to the house we'd been staking. If they were heading to some friend's house, we'd have to pull the plug. We couldn't risk walking up to an unknown place where we might be outnumbered—and outgunned.

As Alex rounded the next corner, he turned off his headlights. The white Datsun had slowed, which quieted the engine but did nothing to calm the screeching pipe that dragged underneath. Alex fell back farther. The Datsun made another left. We were in luck. "It looks like they're heading back to the house."

Alex nodded. "Seems so."

"And I bet I know why," Dale said.

I saw the ghost warehouses up ahead. If they made a right at the next corner, we'd be back at Gomezes' place. Sure enough, they turned right. Alex stopped just short of the corner. Dale got out and looked down the street to make sure. He raised a thumb, then got back inside. "My guess is he's about to pack up and clear out. Leave the car here."

We all got out and found a hiding place at the side of the house next door—more accurately, a shack that was little more than a lean-to—and waited. After a few minutes, Gomez emerged from the house carrying an army duffel bag in his hand and a toaster oven under his arm. The other guy was nowhere in sight.

Dale whispered to Alex. "On my three. One, two, three!" They shot out into the street, and I followed. Gomez stopped dead in his tracks when he saw them, then dropped the duffel bag and oven and tore off down the street.

We all pounded after him, Dale in the lead. But as we ran down the pitch-black street, I started to worry that Gomez might have friends around here. Friends who wouldn't mind carving up some strangers just for the fun of it. Gomez came to a chain-link fence. I hoped it'd stop him. But he flung himself up and over it with amazing agility.

Alex had passed Dale. He took the fence at a running leap and flew over it. Dale wasn't far behind, but by the time he got over the fence, Alex was way ahead and gaining on Gomez, running across an empty, weed-covered field. I was about to climb the fence when I saw that it ended just ten feet to my right. I'd have laughed if I weren't so winded. I ran around the fence and fell in behind Dale. The street at the far end of the field, where I saw more housing similar to the Gomezes', was just fifty yards from Alex now. If Gomez had friends in those houses, we were in big trouble.

I tried to catch up and warn Alex, but he was too far ahead. When they'd reached the last ten yards before the street, I yelled to Dale, my voice hoarse and winded, "Get them before they hit the street!"

Dale raised a hand to show he'd heard me and barreled toward them. I kept running, but the sharp pain in my side was slowing me down. Gomez hit the street and yelled, *"Ayudame!"*

Help me! His voice echoed down the block. Someone was bound to come out any second. Alex made a flying jump and threw himself on Gomez's back. They went down. At that same moment, the front door of one of the houses opened and a burly man in a tank shirt stepped out. I pulled out my gun and stopped, about to take aim when Dale finally reached them. He yanked Gomez away from Alex and held on to him.

Alex called out, *"No hay problema! El es mi hermano! Estamos jugandos!"*

I didn't know whether I'd have bought the claim that they were just brothers, playing around. But apparently, the man in the doorway did. He waved them off and went back inside. I bent over, hands on my knees, and tried to catch my breath. After a few moments, I trotted over to the group.

When Gomez saw me, his expression changed from terror to confusion. I didn't look like either a cop or a gangbanger. His eyes shifted among the three of us, then he asked Alex, *"Que quieres?"*

He'd stopped struggling, but Dale hung on to his arm while Alex explained who we were—and weren't—and what we wanted. Gomez looked at each of us carefully for a long moment. Finally, he nodded and agreed to talk. But he was nervous about having left everything he owned out on the street, so we headed back to his house. Luckily, the duffel bag and toaster oven were still there. Gomez locked them in his car, then invited us in to talk.

The house consisted of one room with a sink against the wall—probably the only one in the place. It was so cold inside, I could practically see my breath. The air smelled of onions and beans. The source of the latter was a banged-up pot on a hot plate. Two plastic plates, a bowl, and some plastic cutlery lay on a towel on the small counter next to it. There was a door at the far end of the room that I assumed led to a bathroom—though I wouldn't swear to it. The only seating available was a couch that'd been ripped and torn in so many places it was hard to find a patch of fabric big enough to sit on. Alex and Gomez sat on opposite ends—which still put them within about a foot of each other—and Dale perched on the arm. I remained standing. The stitch in my side was gone, but my chest still felt raw from all that racing around in the cold night air, and the frigid temperature in that room wasn't helping matters. I shoved my hands into my coat pockets and shifted from one foot to another to generate some body heat.

Alex did the translating. We confirmed that he was indeed one of the Gomez brothers—Santiago Gomez. I speak some Spanish myself, but I'm not good enough to keep up when people are speaking as fast as Alex and Santiago were, so I gave up and waited for the translation.

After a few moments, Alex held up a hand and told us what he'd said. "He remembers that when they stopped in Nogales, a police officer spoke to the truck driver." He turned back to Santiago, who continued with his story. Alex translated again. "He and his brother were sitting next to the partition between the driver and the back of the truck. There was a little window that was usually closed, but the driver had opened it just before they got to the checkpoint to tell them all to shut up, and he hadn't closed it all the way."

I asked, "So he was able to see who the driver was talking to?"

Santiago answered. *"Sí."*

I pulled out photos of Hausch and Sanborn. "Was it one of these men?"

He stared at them for a long moment, then, with a shaking finger, he pointed to Hausch. *"Sí. Es el policía."*

Alex asked him if he was sure. He gave Alex a hard look. *"Sí, estoy seguro."*

"Do you remember what they said?" I asked.

I'd stretched past Santiago's English vocabulary. He looked at Alex, who translated for him.

His face hardened with anger. *"Pues, sí. Como podría olvidarlo?"*

Yes. How could I forget? He stopped to calm himself for a moment, then he continued in heavily accented English. "He say, 'Where the money is?' Driver say, 'I pay you already.' *Policía* say, '*El precio* . . . price . . . go up.' Driver . . .'" Santiago made a walking motion with his fingers and gave a little whistle.

I thought I understood, but I wanted to nail it down. "The driver left? *El se fue?*"

Santiago nodded. *"Sí."*

It was a simple but harrowing story. Hausch was a dirty cop who took bribes to let someone—possibly the MS-13—deal in human trafficking. When the driver hadn't paid up, Hausch had walked away and left the truck—and the men trapped inside it—to bake in the fierce desert sun. That probably hadn't been the plan. Hausch had likely expected the driver to come back and pay up. Not that it mattered. Santiago's testimony would shred him. Hausch was going down, and I couldn't wait to see it happen. "Can you ask him how he got away from Nogales?"

Alex did, then translated his answer. "He and his brother escaped from the hospital during the night."

I glanced at Dale. "Right again."

Dale gave me a flat look. "I have done this before." He turned to Alex. "Can you ask him where his brother is?"

When Alex translated the question, Santiago teared up and had to pause to collect himself. Then he gave a lengthy answer.

Alex grew increasingly troubled as he spoke, and by the time Santiago finished, Alex was really upset. He took a deep breath and swallowed hard. "Santiago and his brother made it to Pomona, where they had relatives. But after a couple of months, the relatives heard that the MS-13 were looking for them. They packed up that night. Santiago wanted to leave right away, but his brother had to say good-bye to a woman he'd been dating. They ambushed him on the way home and stabbed him to death."

Those fucking monsters. "Please tell him how sorry we are."

Alex told him that, plus a few more things I didn't catch that were probably a lot more poetic. While Alex spoke to Santiago, I thought about how to persuade him to come up to LA to testify. "Can you ask him if he'd like to relocate to LA?"

Alex inclined his head toward me. "You think you can find him a job?"

I shrugged. "I'm sure I can find him something. And he's going to need to be in LA to testify. So why not move?" I looked around the room. "It's not as though he's living large down here."

Alex spoke to him in Spanish again. Santiago seemed to like the idea. He nodded and said, *"Sí"* a few times. He said something else to Alex, then he stood up and headed to the door.

Alex turned back to us. "He seems to like the idea of moving to LA."

I turned and watched him walk out the door. "Then where's he going?"

"He just wants to bring in his stuff. He was getting nervous that someone might break into his car."

I didn't blame him. Until I heard the engine of the old Datsun cough and kick over. I jumped up and ran to the door.

Just in time to see the car speed down the street, sparks flying behind it.

I looked at Dale. "You really have done this before."

He stared at me, exasperated. "Shut up."

THIRTY-THREE

We searched the room for any clue as to where he might've run, but either he didn't keep addresses around or he'd already packed everything up. We had to admit defeat.

Alex and I were pissed off, but Dale looked like he was ready to kill someone. As he paced around the tiny space, his face got redder and redder. I was a pacer, too. Another one of those little habits we shared.

Dale finally stopped and looked at us, his hands on his hips. "We found him once; we can find him again. And this time, we drag him into court with a subpoena."

I hated to rain on his parade, but that was hopeless. "And then he lies his ass off—"

Dale fired back. "And then we all testify to what he told us."

He hadn't played this out. "You sure you want to do that? It won't exactly endear you to the department, and wasn't that the whole point of taking on Hausch's case?"

"Screw that. He's a murderer. Jeezus! Ten dead—eleven if you count Santiago's brother. And he's obviously in bed with the MS-13." Dale started pacing again. "He probably did have something to do with disappearing Julio's sister—and God knows how many others!"

I nodded. "No argument."

Dale set his jaw. "Hausch has got to go down, Sam."

I thought it was cool that he was willing to screw his chances of getting into RHD to do the right thing. Except it wasn't worth it. "Let me tell you how this plays out in court. Santiago swears he never fingered Hausch. We say he did—and that he actually heard Hausch ask for more money. Hausch's lawyer then jumps up our collective asses about how we tainted Santiago's ID by only showing him photos of Sanborn and Hausch. He says, 'Talk about a suggestive lineup. Those guys look so different you may as well have shown him photos of Hausch and a refrigerator.' Plus, don't forget, Santiago only saw him through a crack in a small window." Dale started to argue, but I held up a hand. "Wait, we're not done. Next, the lawyer goes after what Santiago supposedly heard. 'How the hell would *he* know what they said? He can barely say his own name in English.' The judge, who doesn't like the idea of nailing a cop anyway, says, 'Case dismissed.' Hausch walks, you look like a backstabbing piece of shit, and you'll wind up *wishing* you were in Cold Cases when you see the sinkhole they shove you into."

Dale raked a hand through his hair, his face dark as thunder. "I can't just let this go."

I stared at the floor, thinking. "I didn't say we had to let it go. But if you shoot at the king, you'd better kill the king. We need other witnesses. Find that other cop, Sanborn. Maybe we can twist him hard enough to scare him into testifying against Hausch. And try to find out who else went missing like Julio's sister did. If we can find even one of them who'll finger Hausch, we'll have enough to move on him."

Alex pulled the car keys out of his pocket. His expression was bleak. "I don't like our chances on either front."

Neither did I, but it was a shock to see Alex, the ever-confident can-do guy look so defeated. "Maybe we can't get Hausch. But it's worth a try. And you never know. Sometimes justice moves in mysterious ways."

It was a quiet ride home. No one was in a great mood, and really, what was there to say? For all intents and purposes, we were back to square one.

When I got home, I took a long, hot, soapy shower and poured myself a stiff shot of Patrón Silver. Tomorrow, I'd get the results of Cassie's doctor's exam and meet with the shrinker experts. Then it'd be time to put my media blitz into action.

I'd had my usual bad night, but—unusual for me—I fell back asleep. When I finally woke up, it was after eight. Shit! I jumped out of bed. Dr. Hawkins was going to call at nine, and if I missed her, it'd be hell trying to get ahold of her again. She was one of the few sexual assault experts who still had a clinical practice.

I threw on slacks and a sweater, gulped down two cups of coffee while I did a minimal makeup job, and raced to the office. Well, *raced* might be a strong word—Beulah doesn't do race. But I managed to get to the office at one minute before nine. Michelle, angel of mercy that she was, had brought in coffee and bagels. She handed me one of each and a little container of cream cheese. "Dr. Hawkins is on line one. Go."

I hurried into my office and picked up the phone as I set out my breakfast. "Jeez, Naomi, when you say nine o'clock, you really mean it."

She gave a little laugh. "It's a Virgo thing."

Or not. I'd had a friend in law school who was a Virgo. She was late so often I accused her of not being able to read a digital clock. "So how'd it go?"

"No vaginal trauma. No external bruising around the genital or breast area."

"Is that bad? From what Cassie said, it didn't sound like there'd be—"

"No, that's not a problem at all. It's consistent with what she reported. And I did find evidence of anal trauma, which is also consistent with what she reported. But . . . are you sure the last assault was three weeks ago?"

"That's what she said. Why?"

"Because there was some slight evidence of trauma, but it looked relatively fresh. As a general rule, injuries in the perianal area heal very quickly, within hours. And other signs of abuse, such as anal laxity, usually disappear after seven to ten days. Even if Cassie'd had scar tissue, it'd be gone by now."

That worried me. "Is it possible Cassie injured herself so you'd find trauma?"

"Of course. It's also possible she didn't, and I'm misinterpreting what I saw. It was fairly subtle. And you should know that there's a margin of error when it comes to interpreting certain signs. Other doctors might not even classify the irregularities I found as trauma."

But I had to know how this would play in court. "What would you say about the possibility that she injured herself?"

"That even if she did, that doesn't necessarily mean she's lying. It may just mean she's desperate for us to believe her. I assume she knows how much it would help her case if I said I found evidence of trauma."

She did—in part, because I'd told her. "So bottom line, what would you be able to say to the jury about your findings?"

"Basically that they don't conflict with what she's reported."

"But they don't necessarily support her story, either."

Naomi sighed. "Yes, in layman's terms, I'd say it's a wash."

I ended the call feeling conflicted. The jury would want to hear from a medical doctor. But the possibility that Cassie had deliberately injured herself—even though there was an innocent explanation—worried me. I'd have to wait and hear what the shrinkers had to say about that before deciding whether to use Naomi.

Which would be soon. Dr. Michael Edelman, the first of the three shrinkers, was due in forty-five minutes. I used the time to write up a sentencing memo on an arson case. The idiot had set fire to a chair in an abandoned office building near Skid Row. The cops caught him dancing around it and singing, "Happy birthday to me." And he kept singing in the patrol car, all the way to jail. The cops had it on video. Big shock: the dipshit had been high on Molly, AKA Ecstasy. I was trying to persuade the judge to give him low term, but the prosecutor had been acting all chesty about how the "potential consequences of his actions were devastating." Yeah, okay, but the actual consequences were a charred piece of junk furniture, a pile of ashes, and a tortured version of "Happy Birthday."

Dr. Edelman showed up ten minutes late, which I didn't mind because it gave me the chance to finish my memo. He had that young/old look going for him. Salt-and-pepper hair and a tailored dress shirt and slacks that showed a fit build. He told me to call him Michael and gave me a crinkle-eyed smile. The women on the jury would eat him up.

He confirmed Naomi's positive spin on the possibility of Cassie having injured herself. "Matter of fact, I've seen a lot worse. One of my patients actually did it with the handle of a screwdriver."

"How do you know she did it on purpose?"

"He. Because he admitted it. His abuser was the director of the summer camp where my patient had worked. He claimed my patient was the one who'd made a pass and that he'd rejected it."

"So the director claimed your patient lied because he was pissed off." Michael nodded. "How did you confirm your patient was telling the truth?"

"Everything about him and his story seemed authentic, but there were also fresh complaint witnesses. He told his sister and a friend about it. And yes, the jury did convict the director."

If Cassie's ex-boyfriend, Waylon, held up, I'd have a fresh complaint witness, too. I briefly described Cassie's story. "What do you think?

Does it strike you as incredible that she'd have been assaulted by both her brother and her father?"

"We both know it *could* be true. Sadly, there are so many cases of molestation that are bizarre. And Cassie wouldn't be the first I've seen who was assaulted by more than one member of the family. Most of those cases involve foster children, but that doesn't mean it couldn't happen to others—even blood relatives. The other possibility is that her story could just be partially true. It seems pretty clear that the brother was the primary assailant. So it's possible she put the father into the mix to shore up her credibility, not realizing that it might actually have the opposite effect. But then again . . ." Michael steepled his hands in front of his face and thought for a moment. "It's a tough thing to admit. Much worse than a brother. A father is supposed to protect a child. Children want and need to believe in him as their hero, and they don't let go of that need even when they really should. So it's pretty rare to see a child make up that kind of lie. My guess would be her father did *something* to her."

"You mean, even if he didn't touch her?"

"Right. If he's putting out a sexual vibe with her, looking at her like a woman instead of his daughter, making sexual comments about her— all of that can be very damaging. In any case, whatever the specifics, it's hard to believe there wasn't something very wrong in that family."

I liked him. And not just because he echoed the very theme I intended to pound into my jury: that something had gone very wrong in that family. He had a warm, down-to-earth way about him. Not condescending or imperious or overly ingratiating like some of the other forensic shrinkers I'd seen. I put Michael Edelman down as a solid "possible."

The other two experts said roughly the same thing. And one, Dr. Amy Rappaport, was an adopted child who'd been molested by her father. She was a less solid "possible." Her personal experience would give the prosecutor a lot of ammunition to claim bias. But her confirmation of the likely authenticity of Cassie's story was reassuring to me on a personal level.

After the last expert left, I went out and told Michelle what they'd said. "Think we've got enough to go to the press?"

Michelle adjusted her Scünci—gray and pink stripes today—and sat back. "Sure sounds like it. And I talked to Trevor. He said he's got just the reporter for you." She glanced at the notepad next to the phone. "Sheryl Hallberg. Been with him for a few months. He says she's great. Do we trust him?"

"We do about that. Okay, set it up for this afternoon if you can." I didn't want to give Cassie too much advance notice of the interview. It'd just give her time to get worked up into a freaked-out mess—or worse, think up ways to embellish her story.

I went back to my office. Ten minutes later, Michelle walked in. "You're all set. She'll meet you at the jail at four thirty."

I looked up, surprised. "That was fast."

Michelle seemed unimpressed. "It's a great story. And how often do reporters get to talk to a defendant?"

When she put it that way . . . "I hope this isn't a mistake."

If it were, it'd be a big one. Possibly the biggest professional mistake I'd ever made.

THIRTY-FOUR

"Hey, Sheryl, thanks for coming on such short notice." I smiled and put out my hand as I glanced around to make sure none of the jail deputies were watching us. We were standing in the lobby at Twin Towers, and I needed to keep the introductions low-key.

Sheryl had long, oily-looking dark hair that lay flat against her head. She wore no makeup, and her dark eyes bulged under thin eyebrows. And she had that reporter cosplay thing going on: faded "boyfriend" jeans—that really were men's jeans—a gray pullover sweater, and an army-green cargo jacket with bulging pockets. She looked me over with a superior air as she shook my hand. "Thanks for giving me the interview."

But her tone said I was the one who should be thankful, that she was the genius, girl-wonder reporter, and that I was the lucky beneficiary of her boundless talent. I nodded toward the jail deputy behind the desk. "Remember, you're my assistant." I hadn't been sure how the jail deputies would feel about a reporter coming in, so I'd decided not to take a chance.

"Yeah, got it."

I really didn't dig her vibe, but I needed her on my side. So I did my best to charm her as we made our way to the attorney room. She didn't make it easy. When I congratulated her on getting the gig at Buzzworthy, she thanked me in a tone that said she thought it was beneath her. When I asked where she'd worked before Buzzworthy, she dusted me off with "lots of places." I wondered whether Trevor had deliberately screwed me over by sending me a jerk. I wanted to kill the interview right then and there. But that would make Sheryl "I am womyn" an enemy for life. All I could do was hope she'd warm up when she sat down with Cassie.

I'd warned Cassie when I'd first brought up the idea of telling her story to a reporter that the reporter might try to provoke her. "Whatever she does, don't let her get to you. If you feel yourself getting angry, take a deep breath and wait a few seconds. I'll jump in to pull her back. Okay?" Cassie had nodded, but she'd—very understandably—looked terrified.

And now, when the guard brought her out, she didn't look any better. She was mouth-breathing, and her eyes were wide and staring. I gave her a reassuring smile and squeezed a chair in next to me for Sheryl—which gave me the lovely opportunity to discover that Sheryl's disdain for all things feminine included deodorant.

Sheryl started out with routine background questions about Cassie's childhood. Cassie spoke in short, halting sentences and looked everywhere but at the reporter. I was getting more nervous by the second. If things didn't loosen up soon, this could turn out to be a real debacle. I tried to act relaxed, but inside my guts were twisting, and I found myself holding my breath with every question.

But when Sheryl asked about the closed adoption and Cassie's desire to find her birth mother, they seemed to find their groove. Sheryl began to nod, and the clinical tone she'd begun with shifted to conversational and then got downright sympathetic. I finally let myself exhale.

"So tell me about the abuse, Cassie." Sheryl made a show of putting down her pencil and looking into Cassie's eyes.

Cassie teared up. "It started when I was thirteen."

She made it all the way through her story. Sheryl stopped her only a few times for clarification. It went about as well as I could've hoped.

With just one exception: she'd said nothing about her father. Nothing. Was it because Cassie was too embarrassed to admit it? Or had she made up the story about Stephen and feared that the reporter would catch her in the lie? When Sheryl left, I congratulated Cassie. "You did great, Cassie. Really. I'm proud of you."

Cassie gave a little smile and leaned back in her chair, looking tired but relieved. "Thanks. She was pretty nice, actually."

We'd see about that when the story came out. I'd had more than one supposedly warm, friendly interview result in a nasty hit piece. "I'm just curious—how come you didn't tell her about your father?"

Cassie's eyes slid away. "I just . . . didn't want to."

"Didn't want to . . . why? You told me about it."

She picked at a thread on the knee of her jumpsuit. "You said that was confidential." She glanced up at me briefly. "Just between us."

"It was. But why didn't you want to tell Sheryl?"

She looked away and turned to the side, so the phone receiver was between us.

"Cassie, was it because it didn't happen? Or because you're embarrassed?"

She spoke without looking at me. "I just didn't want to, that's all."

I wasn't sure what to do with that nonanswer. But now, it no longer mattered whether it was true or not. "I need you to realize what you just did. That was your first public statement. If you decide to tell anyone else that Stephen molested you, it'll raise questions about your honesty."

Cassie didn't like what she was hearing. She turned back to me and frowned. "Why? Just because I didn't say it this time? Maybe I just didn't feel like it!"

"And you can certainly say that if you want to talk about your father at some later point. But I'm warning you, it's risky. People might not believe you. So we'll need to think very carefully about whether you ever talk about your father again."

Cassie's face was anguished. "Why didn't you tell me that before?"

"I did. I told you that whatever you said to Sheryl would be the story we had to stick with."

She stared at me. "But you said it was okay if I didn't tell it exactly the same way every time."

"About little things, Cassie. Details. Your father assaulting you is not a detail." Cassie slouched in her chair again. She went back to picking at a thread on her jumpsuit. I wondered what was going on in her head. More than that, I wondered whether I'd ever know the whole truth about what'd happened to her. I sighed as I watched her through the glass.

The guard warned me that visiting time was almost up.

I had one more question. This probably wasn't the greatest time for it, but I couldn't afford to put it off. "Let's talk about something else, okay?"

Cassie's voice was barely above a whisper. "Whatever."

"Can you tell me why you broke up with Waylon?"

She gave me a puzzled look. "Why are you asking me that?"

I wasn't going to play these cat-and-mouse games with her. "Cassie, you need to trust me. I don't ask questions 'just 'cause.' Why did you break up with him?"

A defiant look crossed her face, but it passed, and she answered in a tone that was offhand. "I knew him since junior high. We were really more like friends than girlfriend and boyfriend. I guess I was just over it."

Was her nonchalance an act? I couldn't tell. "That's funny. Waylon had the impression you broke up because you were seeing someone else."

Cassie sat up. "What? No, I wasn't."

I saw a touch of alarm. "Was it someone in school?"

Her face closed. "I wasn't seeing anyone else. He's wrong."

The guard announced that visiting hours were up. I didn't believe Cassie, but she obviously wasn't going to tell me. I wondered whether there was someone who could. "Has Tiegan been visiting you?"

Cassie looked at me as though she were trying to figure out my angle. "Yeah. She's been here a couple of times. Why?"

I gave her a friendly smile. "Just making sure you have people to talk to."

The guard on her side came in to get her. She peered at me for a moment, then stood up and walked out.

I called Tiegan from the car and asked her whether she could try and find out who Cassie had been seeing after she broke up with Waylon.

Tiegan wasn't optimistic about her chances. "She never talked to me about Waylon, so I'd guess the odds of my getting her to talk about who else she might've been seeing are pretty lousy. But I'll try. I just don't get why she won't tell you."

"Me neither. And maybe it doesn't matter. But secrets have a way of biting you on the ass when you go to trial. So I want to be able to check this guy out."

She said she'd do her best. If Tiegan couldn't pry it out of her, I'd have to find another way, because I was beginning to think that this mystery boyfriend might be more than just a personal wrinkle in Cassie's life.

Assuming Cassie had been seeing someone, it would've been in the months just before the murders, and that raised some serious questions: What if she'd told him about the molestation? And if she had, was it possible that he was the killer? What if Cassie was covering for him, painting herself as some romantic martyr?

I posed the questions to Michelle when I got back to the office. "But it seems crazy that she'd cover for the guy."

Michelle looked noncommittal. "I don't know. Teenage love can be a crazy thing. I'll say this much, if she is covering for him, she's bound to crack—and soon."

I remembered the utter shock on her face when I told her she'd probably be tried as an adult. "Yeah, definitely. But even if he's not involved, he might be another fresh complaint witness." And I needed all I could get.

Michelle seemed puzzled. "Are you sure this guy exists? We still haven't ruled out the possibility that Waylon is the guy with the burner phone. Maybe his folks didn't want to pay for a regular cell phone plan. Burners are cheaper, you know. Besides, if there is some other guy, I don't know why she'd want to hide him."

I didn't, either. So maybe I was wrong. Maybe there was no mystery boyfriend. But I had this gut feeling . . . Michelle pulled me out of my reverie.

"How'd the interview go?"

I gave her the rundown and told her about Cassie leaving her father out of it. "What do you think? Was she lying about Stephen all along? Or is she too ashamed to put it out there?"

Michelle tilted her head to one side, then the other. "I vote for the latter. How much of a victim does she want to be? Abel's bad enough."

Totally possible. Or not. Everything about this case was like that. This. Or that. Yes. Or no. It was making my head ache. "Well, either way, it's about to go public, and that means reporters are going to go after Paula and Nathan to get their reactions."

"Speaking of which, how's Paula doing?"

"I think we're about to find out."

The very next day, in fact. The Buzzworthy interview came out that morning, and by noon, it'd gone viral. Along with Paula's responses.

Paula, it turned out, had improved somewhat, but she was still in ICU and her prognosis was unclear.

She was, however, well enough to give a brief statement to the press through her doctor, who read it for the camera. "Cassie is a murderer. She is not a victim. She never told me she had been assaulted. Everything she said is a lie. It's just an excuse to get away with murder." It was playing all over the Internet and on every broadcast and cable TV news show.

But either Nathan refused to talk or no one asked him, because I saw no statements from him anywhere. He might've been afraid to make glowing remarks about Abel after what he'd told me. Or he just might not relish the idea of being in the spotlight. Especially this one.

Paula's denial, Nathan's absence—neither was a huge surprise. That came the following Monday.

I was on the phone when Michelle appeared in the doorway looking like she'd just heard Brad Pitt was a woman. I held the phone against my shoulder. "What?"

"Turn on your TV. Channel Four."

I ended the call and turned on the little TV on top of my bookcase. A gray-haired woman in a black wool blazer who looked familiar was standing at a podium stacked with press microphones. Three women stood behind her. ". . . and it's a tragic example of the devastating impact sexual assault has on children, particularly within the family. Though we of course do not condone what she did, we stand by Cassie Sonnenberg."

She stepped aside, and a man strode up to the podium. "As vice president of Stop Assaults on Children, I just want to second what Nancy said and to add that no child acts out so violently for no reason. We must face the fact that tragedies like this do not occur in a healthy household with vigilant parents."

Reporters shouted out questions I couldn't hear, but they declined to answer and left the podium.

Michelle had a little smile of disbelief. "I've gotta admit, I did not see this coming. You?"

"Yes, I predicted every word," I'd spoken with sarcasm. "Hell no, I didn't see this coming. But I love it. What are you seeing on the Internet?" In a high-profile case, you have to keep in touch with the zeitgeist.

Michelle held out a hand and tilted it from side to side. "It's mixed. Some are totally on Cassie's side. Others think there had to be *something* weird going on in that house, but they're on the fence. But there's also a contingent that says she's a monster, and the molestation is a bullshit story Cassie made up to get away with murder. Some even blame you for feeding her that story."

I gave a short laugh. "I'd have made up a much better lie than that. Any reaction to Paula?"

Michelle's face tightened. "That's where most of the anti-Cassie votes are coming from. They totally believe Paula."

That figured. "What does the pro-Cassie team say about Paula?"

Michelle glanced at her monitor. "Pretty much what you'd expect: that Paula's lying to cover her own ass for not helping Cassie."

"Okay, we'll see which way the wind is blowing when we get closer to trial."

We probably wouldn't get to trial for at least another six months, and when it comes to public opinion, even one month can make a big difference. Especially if groups like Stop Assaults on Children kept the campaign going.

Michelle nodded toward the TV. "I guess we just became a cause."

If so, Cassie was about to be the poster child for young sexual assault victims.

And now there was no changing her story. Stephen was out of the picture.

THIRTY-FIVE

I looked at my watch. Almost noon. The fitness hearing, when the judge would decide whether Cassie should be tried as a minor or an adult, was scheduled for one thirty. I packed up my briefcase, told Michelle I'd call in after it was done, and headed out. This time I hadn't had to dress for success. The hearing was held in juvenile court, which meant no press, no audience—just the necessary court personnel and the prosecutor who'd be handling the case.

That prosecutor turned out to be Gideon Sitkoff—not so affectionately known as Gidiot Shitcough—a pompous ass whose only real talent was buying thousand-dollar suits on Daddy's dime. He had a small, rectangular head—the effect amplified by his short haircut and long sideburns—a short, wide torso, and long, skinny legs. As always, he was a picture of sartorial splendor in a black pinstriped Hugo Boss suit and pearl-gray dress shirt. But his belt looked like it was three inches below his armpits. Further proof that big money has nothing to do with good taste.

The fact that the DA's office was letting him handle a case this big said nothing good about their managerial judgment. But I planned to hold my nose and give thanks to the trial gods that I got him. If ever a prosecutor could lose a case like this, it'd be him. I'd never seen anyone so perfectly in tune with all the ways to piss off a jury. In one case, he'd used a water bottle to demonstrate how a defendant hit the victim with a baseball bat but didn't think to make sure the cap was screwed on tight. He sprayed the entire front row of jurors. And in another case, when a juror in the upper row said she couldn't hear the witness, he suggested she turn up her hearing aid. She didn't have a hearing aid—the juror next to her did. Another prosecutor would've apologized for the mistake. Not Gidiot. He suggested that perhaps she needed one.

So really, although he was annoying as hell, he was a gift.

The fitness hearing can take one hour or one week, depending on whether the defense wants to put up a fight. I wanted to put up a fight, but in this case, that'd mean putting Cassie on the stand—a very bad thing because it'd give Shitcough a preview of her testimony. Since the brutality of these murders and the fact that Cassie had done a somewhat sophisticated job of covering up her role in them made it virtually a foregone conclusion that she'd be found unfit for juvenile court, the wiser move was to hold our fire until trial. So the probation officer gave his spiel, I gave my spiel, and it was over in about an hour. Cassie was certified up to adult court.

When the bailiff took Cassie away, I went over to Gideon. I needed to know whether he was going to do a preliminary hearing or take the case to the grand jury. A preliminary hearing would entail a public, though brief, showing of probable cause. The grand jury convened in secret. Since I'd already gone to the press with my defense, and there wasn't much I could do to dent the DA's case—it was just physical evidence and Paula's statement—I didn't need the chance to win over hearts and minds in a public hearing. "You going for a prelim or grand jury?"

He leaned back, nostrils flared, as though I were carrying the black plague. Gideon was one of those prosecutors who thinks all defense lawyers are pond scum—but he took it to an extreme. "Why? Are you worried about how your murderous devil spawn will fare on camera?"

I sighed. "I just want to know whether I need to prepare for a prelim."

"As of now, I'm planning on taking the case to the grand jury. I'll let you know if that changes." I held out my hand. He stared at it. "What?"

I was tempted to rub my hand all over his face. He'd probably faint. "My discovery. Where is it?"

"My assistant's e-mailing it to you this afternoon."

"*Gracias.*" I headed for the door, then turned back and blew him a kiss. He turned away so fast he almost fell.

The freeway was wide open for some mysterious reason. I got back to the office by three o'clock and found the discovery already waiting for me in Michelle's inbox. Alex and Michelle joined me to look it over. "Seems like this is everything they've got to date." We had crime-scene video footage and still shots, Cassie's cell phone records, school records, medical records, Abel's cell phone records, and Paula's official statements accusing Cassie of the murders and denying that Cassie had made any prior claims of molestation. I scanned Paula's statement. It was brief but certain. She'd been attacked from behind, so she hadn't been able to see Cassie in the act. But after she'd gone down, she'd seen Cassie's feet, recognized her socks and the pajama bottoms. Then she'd passed out. It was just a brief look, but Paula was adamant. That was Cassie. And of course, now we knew Paula was right.

We scanned the video first. It was a bloodbath of a crime scene, one of the ugliest I'd ever seen. The camera first took in the busted-out window and the curtains that'd been pushed aside and soaked in the rain. Then, it moved down to the bed just below, where Abel lay on his back, his dead, milky eyes fixed on the ceiling, throat slashed from ear to ear like a huge, macabre smile. His chest was covered in blood. One arm was flung out, and the back of his hand rested on the nightstand, exposing a palm covered in blood. A lamp that'd probably been on that nightstand lay on the floor. The video camera moved in close to show the blood smears on the shade. I pointed. "Looks like he knocked it down after she stabbed him."

Michelle asked, "And they think she killed him first?" I nodded. Michelle flicked a finger at the monitor. "Keep going."

I hit play. The camera panned around the room to show the ransacking, the dresser drawers that'd been pulled out and rifled through, the nightstand drawer that was on the ground. It then moved across the floor to where Stephen lay facedown in a pool of blood, his head turned to the side. There was blood all over the back of his head and neck. A gloved hand pointed out the source: deep gashes at the base of his skull, in the middle of his neck, and three more in his back. The camera moved up to his face. His eyes were vacant but wide open. The same gloved hand pointed to the side of his neck, where there was another penetrating stab wound—the source of the blood pooled underneath him.

"Looks to me like she got him from behind at first." Alex pointed to the frontal neck wound. "So she turned him over to finish him off?"

I paused the video. "Or she did it when he turned around." I stared at the monitor. Stephen had been stabbed quite a few times. Rage? Or just an effort to make sure he was dead? According to Cassie, she'd just panicked, gone "crazy." I'd probably never know for sure. I hit play again.

The paramedics had already taken Paula away when the video was shot. Only the blouse they'd cut off her body remained—that and the bloodstain on the carpet where she'd been found. "I'm sure they took still shots before they moved her. We'll need to check out the DVD."

Michelle pushed away from my desk. "I'll pass. I can't look at that anymore. How come she didn't slice up Paula like the others?"

I stopped the video. I'd watch the rest later. "I'd guess because Paula went down fast and seemed to be dead." But I could also argue that Paula was just a secondary target. That the main focus of Cassie's rage was her abusers.

As I'd watched the video, I'd imagined Cassie wielding the knife, slashing Abel, stabbing her father, then her mother. When I first heard about the murders, it seemed obvious that the killer had to be a man—a strong one. But now, with the benefit of the video and the knowledge that the killings had gone down one at a time and that each victim had been taken by surprise, I saw how it was physically possible for Cassie to do it. Unfortunately, so would the jury.

And the gruesomeness of the crime scene would make any jury want to hang her from the nearest tree. I'd have to find a way to push those images out of their heads and get the jury to focus on the little girl who'd been abused. And it'd be Cassie's job to make them love that little girl. One good thing about the hideousness of the scene: it might help convince the jury that this had to be one very messed-up family to have produced a child who could do something like that.

We moved on to the police reports and witness statements—such as they were: primarily neighbors who spoke glowingly of the Sonnenbergs but didn't see or hear anything. The only new addition was statements from a few students in Cassie's school who said they thought Cassie was a liar.

Alex frowned at the monitor. "Is that stuff even admissible in court?"

"Can be. It depends. But we've got plenty of friends to knock that down. What I don't see is a statement from Nathan."

Michelle toyed with the little jade "money tree" she'd bought for me in Chinatown. "I wonder if it's because he believes Abel molested her. He gave you one hell of a statement."

He sure had. "And if I can get him to say even half of it on the witness stand, it'll play really well for us." I'd just had another thought. "You know, it's probably a good thing Cassie left Stephen out of her story. I think if she'd talked about him, Nathan would've had to fight back."

But what I'd really wanted to see were the records that showed the cell towers accessed by Cassie's cell phone and the burner listed under the fake name Earl Lee Riser. And I needed to find out who he was. I hadn't had a good opportunity to get into it with her yet, but I made a mental note to do it at our next meeting. No more nice guy; I needed answers. I scrolled through the cell phone materials. "I don't see the cell tower records. I can't believe they don't have them yet. Alex, any progress on your end?"

"I'm working on it. But cell tower records are a little tougher than phone records."

That reminded me of Alex's other work: Hausch. I'd been so wrapped up in Cassie's case, I'd forgotten to check in with Alex about it. "By the way, anything new on Hausch?" Hausch had called me for an update the day before, but I'd been too busy to take the call.

Alex sighed. "It's not easy. Let's just say it's a work in progress."

I scrolled through the cell phone bills, then saw that they'd pulled actual texts off Cassie's phone. I pointed them out to Alex and Michelle. We hadn't seen these yet. I'd been thinking the burner phone Cassie'd been calling belonged to her mystery boyfriend, but the texts didn't seem all that romantic. They were just quick notes, like, *"When can I come over?"* and *"When are you getting home?"* But then I found one that intrigued me. *"I'm sorry. I promise I won't text you so much anymore."* I pointed to it. "Sounds like Earl told her to cool it."

"So is he just telling her to knock it off because she's bugging him?" Michelle leaned forward, her chin in her hand. "Or because he's afraid to have someone see Cassie's texts?"

I scanned the pages of calls listed for the last month before the murders. "Hard to tell. If it's the latter, it makes it seem like he's an older guy—maybe a lot older. But there're about a hundred calls to and from that burner phone in just one month. It's a pretty tight relationship, no matter who this guy is." I flipped to Abel's cell phone records—and zeroed in on the last call. It showed that a call had been placed to the burner at 1:04 a.m. on the night of the murders. I highlighted it on my monitor. "Check that out. That was, what? Maybe ten, fifteen minutes before Cassie called the cops?"

Alex pulled out his iPad mini and tapped the screen a few times. "My notes say she called the cops at 1:26 a.m."

"From Abel's phone? Or hers?" I asked.

Alex looked down at his iPad again. "Abel's phone."

I made a mental note to ask her why she'd used his phone instead of her own.

Michelle sneezed and grabbed a Kleenex out of the box on my desk. "Looks to me like she stabbed everyone, then freaked out and called her boyfriend."

That sounded right. "And maybe he gave her the idea to frame some Aryan Brotherhood guy." I'd always thought it was a weird story for Cassie to make up. A little too sophisticated. "But if she's calling him at a time like that, telling him what she did, don't you think she'd have told him about the molestation?" If so, he'd be an even more critical witness than Waylon, because he'd also be able to give us her state of mind on the night of the murders. "I've got to find out who this guy is."

Michelle sneezed again.

Alex said, "Bless you."

I glared at her. "If you get me sick, I swear . . ."

"I'm not sick. It's just all the dust in your office." She made a face at me. I made one back. "Tiegan couldn't get her to name the guy, I take it?"

I'd just asked Tiegan about that yesterday. "Not so far." I checked my computer for the time. It was four o'clock. Visiting hours ended at six. "I think I'll go take a crack at Cassie myself."

And I did. I leaned across the counter and locked eyes with her through the window. "Look, Cassie. I've got your text messages, and I know you called him the night of the murders. You guys are obviously close. I'm betting you told him about the molestation. That makes him a critical witness. Do you understand me?" I'd intended to ask her why she'd used Abel's phone that night, but now I decided to hold off. There were much bigger issues on the table.

Cassie held my gaze for a moment, then looked away. "He's not a boyfriend. He was just someone I could talk to. But I never told him about . . . anything."

"Then what'd you tell him the night of the murders?"

She hunched over and played with the phone cord. "Nothing. It hadn't even happened yet. I was just freaking out, and I needed to hear his voice."

"At one o'clock in the morning? You'd never called him that late before."

Cassie shot back, "I told you, Abel was acting crazy and I was alone with him! I was freaked out!"

I kept after her. "I don't know why you're shielding this guy, but I'm strongly advising you to knock it off. This is your life, Cassie."

She clutched the phone and stared down at the counter. Her voice was low, but it trembled. "He won't help me, Sam. And I don't want him to." Cassie looked up at me, her expression fierce. "I don't want him dragged into this. He has nothing to do with any of it. So let it go!" She was breathing hard.

The stubbornness I saw in her face made it clear I wasn't going to change her mind today. I wondered what the story was with this guy.

It was time for a come-to-Jesus talk. "Cassie, you don't have time to be a kid anymore. If we lose this case, you'll spend the rest of your life in prison. I'm the only one who can keep that from happening, but I can't do it all on my own. I need you to help me." Cassie was chewing on her thumb, and she wouldn't meet my eyes. "So think very carefully about this. Because keeping me in the dark is the very worst thing you can do."

I called the guard and said we were done. Cassie never looked up, even when the jail deputy took her out.

I ran into Tiegan in the lobby. "Hey, nice to see you. I think Cassie could use a friendly face about now."

Tiegan's smile faded into a look of concern. "What happened? Bad news on the case?"

"Not really. I just had to straighten her out about being honest with me."

Tiegan looked surprised. "She's been lying to you?"

"More like holding out on me. She still won't tell me who that boyfriend is. It'd be great if you could give it another shot."

Tiegan sighed. "I'll do what I can, but she's a stubborn little thing. By the way, did you get any more information on that burner phone?"

"We got Cassie's text messages." I shrugged. "The texts weren't super romantic, but there were enough of them to make it pretty clear it belonged to our mystery man. So anything you can do . . ."

"I'll keep trying." Tiegan put a hand on my arm. "Thank you for working so hard, Sam. I know Cassie appreciates it, even though she may not show it."

I told her it was my pleasure and wished her good luck. I walked out to the parking lot.

I didn't know why Cassie was stonewalling me about the boyfriend. It made no sense.

But I couldn't wait around for her to wake up and smell the prison coffee. I had to figure out a way to find this guy.

THIRTY-SIX

When I got back to the office, Michelle said Alex needed to talk to me. I dropped my briefcase and purse in my office and was about to go see him when he showed up in my doorway. I took in his dark expression. "What's wrong?"

He sank down onto the couch, his hands on his knees, chest concave, totally deflated. "Dale just called. Sanborn's dead."

I closed my eyes. "Shit." Getting Sanborn to turn had been our best hope of nailing Hausch.

I flopped down on the other end of the couch. "Did Dale tell you how and when Sanborn died?" I wondered whether the MS-13 had decided he was dispensable.

"Drunk driving accident about two months ago. He got shit-faced and drove into a pylon. There's no indication of foul play."

And if Sanborn had pissed off the MS-13, they wouldn't have bothered to cover it up by making it look like an accident. They preferred to send messages. I had another idea. "Maybe Dale can get some of the other cops at Nogales PD to talk?" We already knew that there was nothing official in either Sanborn's or Hausch's file showing a connection to the MS-13, but like in any office, there were bound to be rumors and gossip. Some of it might prove to be a real lead.

But Alex was shaking his head. "Dale thought of that. He actually went to Nogales and got one of the cops to talk. She did remember Sanborn hanging around with Hausch now and then, but she actually laughed when Dale asked whether Sanborn might have gotten a little too friendly with the MS-13. She said Sanborn never handled a case heavy enough to put him in contact with the gang, called him a 'lazy pussy.'"

"Doesn't mean he wasn't in bed with them. Did she know anything about Hausch?" Alex shook his head. Damn. The Sanborn angle was vapor. Now the only way we'd get Hausch was if Alex turned up Julio's sister or someone else who'd been trafficked and escaped—and was willing to testify against Hausch. I almost didn't want to do it, but I had to ask the question. "Any luck with your search?"

Alex shook his head. "I'm not giving up yet, but it's not looking good."

We were hosed. We sat in glum silence for a moment, then Alex got up and went back to his office. Alone with my frustrated, miserable thoughts, my other problem came rushing back to mind. Deshawn. He'd left me another message saying that he couldn't spend another "damn minute" in that "fuckin' dump of a motel" and that "boring-ass town." The good news was, he was still alive. The bad news was, if he lost all patience and came back down to LA, he wouldn't be for long. And I still had no clue how I was going to bail him out.

Depressed, I threw myself into my other cases, then went over the reports on Cassie's case again to make sure there was nothing I'd missed. At seven thirty, Michelle stopped by to say she was leaving. I barely looked up to say good night. When Alex came to my door at nine o'clock and said I should pack it in, I waved him off.

When I was starting to see double and couldn't come up with coherent sentences anymore, I looked at the clock and saw that it was past midnight. Time to get my sorry ass home. My emotions were in a mad kind of swirl when I got into my car. The frustration at losing our last shot at Hausch, the fear for Deshawn's safety, and the awful memories being dredged up by Cassie's case all blended together and spun in a frenzied circle.

I don't know how it happened—I must've been driving on autopilot—but somehow, I wound up in Bel Air, parked outside the wrought-iron gates in front of the mansion where I'd been put through hell when I was thirteen. I stared at the upper-floor windows that peeked through the majestic oak trees circling the property. All the bedrooms were on that upper floor, but I couldn't see my room—or as I'd called it back then, my torture chamber—from the street. Sebastian had given me a room at the back of the house, where I'd have no chance of being heard if I screamed out the window.

I don't know how long I sat there staring, reliving those horrible nights when I wished I were dead and thinking of the day when I'd get the chance to make him pay. I only know that I caught a sudden movement out of the corner of my eye, just inches from the driver's-side window. I yelped, sure it was Sebastian. My heart pounding like a jackhammer, I glanced out my window as I fumbled for the ignition key.

But it wasn't Sebastian. It was Dale. I stared at him, frozen for a long moment, as he motioned for me to open my window. How had he known I was here? I rolled down the window, and he bent down and looked at me, his expression worried. I asked, "How?"

Dale watched me closely as he answered. "A friend in dispatch heard the patrol unit call in your license plate as a suspicious vehicle and gave me the heads up."

A numbness washed over me. I turned and stared through the windshield.

Dale spoke quietly. "Sam, you can't stay here. The patrol unit's gonna be back any minute. What are you doing?"

I had no rational answer to that question. "I don't know." I continued to stare through my windshield.

"If the patrol unit comes back and finds you here, it'll be trouble." Dale paused, then continued. "Sam, he's done enough damage. Don't give him this, too."

All of a sudden, I was very, very tired. I leaned forward and lay my head on the steering wheel. My voice was ragged as I answered. "Sometimes I can't stand it. I just . . . can't."

Dale's voice was hoarse. "Let me handle this, Sam. I promise, I'll find a way. He's not gonna get away with it forever. But please, don't let them find you here."

I sat up, the numbness now gone. Dale was right; I needed to get out of there. I started my car and tried to smile, but my lips trembled and fell. "Thanks, Dale."

Sadness mixed with anger in his face, but his voice was soft. *"De nada."* He glanced up and down the street. "You'd better get going."

He patted the roof and stepped back, and I pulled away.

THIRTY-SEVEN

I woke up late the next morning. It'd taken me a while to get to sleep. I tried to figure out what had made me go to Sebastian's house, but I couldn't. It was crazy. And I appreciated Dale's saving me from the humiliation of getting caught there. But I wasn't going to let him take care of my Sebastian problem. I'd been dreaming of the day when I could make that monster suffer for what he'd done to me, and I wasn't about to let anyone rob me of the satisfaction. Now more than ever, the thought of all the other little girls he might've gotten his hands on—might still be getting his hands on—was eating at me. If I could stop him from destroying even one girl's life, I was damn well gonna do it. I didn't know how or when. It wasn't easy to get close to someone like Sebastian. But I'd find a way.

I wasn't in denial about the fact that Cassie's case was weighing on me. But other than last night, I was handling it. I was fine.

I didn't get to the office until after ten, and Alex was waiting for me when I walked in, with his iPad and a sheaf of papers.

I stifled a yawn. I hadn't had nearly enough coffee. "What's all that?"

"Cell tower records for Cassie's calls." He held up the papers. "To that burner."

Alex had been trying to get them for a while, and the DA still didn't have them. "How'd you do it?"

He lifted an eyebrow. "You really want to know?"

Of course not. I nodded toward my office. "Tell me what we've got."

He sat on the couch and tapped his iPad. "The burner seemed to be either near the school or in Atwater."

"Atwater? Where's that?"

"Between Griffith Park and Glendale. About fifteen minutes from Cassie's house."

"Near the school. Would a kid who lives in Atwater go to Cassie's school?"

"No. I checked that out. He'd go to John Marshall in Los Feliz. So I'd guess that when the burner was around Cassie's school, they were hanging out."

This was a lot less helpful than I'd thought it would be. "Great." My voice was sarcastic. "We're almost there. How many people live in Atwater? A million?"

"Around fifteen thousand. Largely Hispanic."

"Beautiful. That nails it right down. All we have to do is ask whether anyone saw Cassie hanging around with a Hispanic guy. She couldn't possibly know more than one."

Alex sighed and spread his hands. "The records are what they are." He gathered the pages and his iPad and stood up. "They're not a game ender right now, but I bet they'll come in handy when we know more."

"Should that day ever come." Which seemed unlikely. "But thanks, Alex. You did great. Any luck with the missing deportees?"

A stubborn look crossed his face. "Not yet. But I'm working through the list. Someone will talk."

I wasn't so sure, but I'd rained on his parade enough for one day. I worked until noon, then packed up and got ready for court. I had my eighteen-count robbery case set for the afternoon calendar. I stopped at Michelle's desk. "Okay, wish me luck."

She raised an arm. "May the guilty plea force be with you."

I tried not to feel confident as I walked into court. The gods of guilty pleas punish you for being too cocky. But they didn't punish me today. We took the plea, my client looked as happy as anyone facing twenty years in prison can look, and I got back on the road.

Traffic was so bad I was sure there had to be a ten-car pileup somewhere. But other than a guy who'd pulled to the shoulder to fix a flat and a cop who was writing some poor schlub a ticket—which for some reason makes everyone stop and look, as though it were some rare, exotic event—there was no reason. Just too many people.

By the time I got off the freeway, it was almost five o'clock, and I saw that Beulah was starving. She was not the sort you could push to the very last drop. It took at least a gallon for her to coast three feet. I stopped at a gas station near my office, put the nozzle in her tank, and watched as the price meter flew through my bank account.

I'd just reholstered the nozzle and screwed in Beulah's gas cap when a familiar voice called out, "Sam? That you?"

I turned and saw Deshawn hunkered down over the steering wheel of a late-model red Mercedes. This was exactly what I'd been afraid of when I got his last message. He'd bailed on Oxnard and come back to town. And where on earth did he keep getting these cars? I knew this couldn't be good news—*I* was supposed to deliver that. I walked over to him. "What're you doing here?" He was wearing huge dark sunglasses and a watch cap pulled down to his eyebrows.

He scanned the area around us with a furtive look. "I couldn't take it anymore. I was goin' nuts up there." He saw my incredulous look.

"Chillax. I got homies down here can keep me safe for a bit. 'Sides, this way you don' gotta pay for the hotel."

I glanced around. "Are you *trying* to get yourself killed?"

"We gotta talk." He pointed to the parking spaces near the air pump. "Put your car over there and get in."

Deshawn followed as I backed Beulah into a parking space. When I got into the Mercedes, he gestured for me to sit lower. I slid down a few inches.

He shook his head. "No, I mean get down. Get your head out da way."

"Out of the way of what?" I slid down till the top of my head was barely visible above the window. I raised an eyebrow—not easy to do with my chin in my chest. "Isn't this a little much?"

"No." Deshawn hugged the steering wheel as he pulled out of the gas station. He drove to a quiet street a few blocks away and pulled to the curb, but he left the engine running.

"Can I sit up now?" I was curled up like a comma, not the most comfortable position.

Deshawn looked out the window, swiveling his head from left to right. Finally, he nodded. "Just keep your eyes open. It ain't safe."

We were in a fairly decent residential neighborhood in West Hollywood. Hardly what you'd call the mean streets of Juarez. I sat up and rolled my shoulders to get the kinks out. "No one's going to try and take you down here."

He took off his sunglasses. His eyes darted everywhere as they circled all around us. "'Member I told you about the guy who fronted the dope to my play cousin?" I nodded. "'Member I told you how my play cousin ain't ezactly Braveheart?"

Uh-oh. I knew where this was going. "Your play cousin dumped you out?"

"Like I was last night's ho."

So now Scarface knew the dope landed with Deshawn, and he was coming after him. "Did your cousin tell him where you live?"

Deshawn looked at me like I was a half-wit. "'Course he told him."

"Where are you staying?"

"You don't need to know." Deshawn scanned the area again. When his eyes circled back to me, I could see he was panicked. "I got to have the money right now, Sam. This dude don't play. He catches up with me, I'll be lucky if all he do is kill me."

I could feel my scalp sweating. "I don't have the money yet."

"Then get me the dope. You gotta do something, and you gotta do it now. I can't wait no more. You can't do the money, do the dope. That'll work. If it's good."

I'd never be able to manage that. "No way I'll ever get my hands on that kind of pure." Deshawn looked like he wanted to jump out of his skin. "Can you just buy a little more time? I'll get you the money. I swear." The idea of having Alex hack into someone's bank account was starting to seem like the perfect—well, to be precise, the *only*—solution.

Deshawn started to answer, but something in the rearview mirror caught his attention. "Oh, hell no." He slid low in his seat. "Get down!"

I got back into my curled-up position and hung on to the sides of my seat as Deshawn stomped on the gas. My head flew back as the car leaped out into the street. "Jeez!" I was about to say "Paranoid much?" when I heard a car roar up behind us. Shit! I slid farther down, my ass almost on the passenger-side floor. As Deshawn neared the intersection, I heard something hit the rear window, a crackling sound. I twisted around to see what it was. Three neat little spiderwebs. "You've gotta be kidding! They're fucking shooting at us?"

Deshawn hung a left on two wheels and gunned it down the street. "Didja think I been lyin' to you about this shit?!"

I'd never thought he was lying. I just never expected them to be crazy enough to try and take us out in the middle of a residential neighborhood in broad daylight. Then it occurred to me that I'd only heard a spitting sound when the bullets hit the glass. Must be using a silencer. But why hadn't the bullets penetrated the window? "Is this thing bulletproof?"

"Not if they got AKs."

AKs??? I tried to get a look at the car in the side-view mirror. It was a white Honda Civic. Not exactly the death mobile I'd expected. But it was smart. They could hide in plain sight, blend in with traffic. Unlike the neon sign Deshawn was driving that practically screamed "Shoot me!" Deshawn hung a fast right that threw me against the door. I tried to grab on to the seat, but my palms were so sweaty they slid right off. My heart hammered against my rib cage. "Go to the sheriff's station!"

He was hunched down, his eyes barely above the steering wheel. His voice was tense and low. "And then what? We can't stay there. He just wait till we got to go. And then I look like a snitch. Be in even worse trouble." We reached another intersection, where the car ahead of us was waiting to make a left. Deshawn was barreling so fast there was no way he could brake in time.

I stretched my hands toward the windshield and screamed, "Look out!" At the very last second, he swerved around the car, the passenger-side tires jumping up and over the sidewalk. But just as we leaped into the intersection, I saw that a car coming from the other direction was about to turn left in front of us. I screamed again. "Deshawn, look out!"

He swerved to the right, missing it by inches, as the driver leaned on his horn. I sank down to the floor as a wave of nausea left me in a cold sweat. I racked my brain, trying to think where we could go. We hit a bump in the road so hard we caught air, and my head banged into the glove compartment as we landed. It hurt like hell, but it made me forget about throwing up. I reached into my purse and pulled out my cell phone.

Deshawn saw me out of the corner of his eye. "What you doin'? I know you ain't callin' the cops."

"Why not? I'll just say someone's firing shots on the road."

Deshawn blew out an exasperated breath. "You'll get us busted, too! You think the cops not gonna look at the car they're chasin'? Put that shit away!"

He had a point. The minute the cops spotted the other car, they'd spot us, too—and wonder why we were getting shot at. Then they'd run Deshawn's record. I slid my cell phone back into my purse.

Crack, crack! Two more shots! One hit the driver's-side mirror. Shit! If there was no place to hide, we'd have to outrun them. But actually, in Deshawn's ride, we might be able to. I had an idea. "Go left at the next intersection and head for La Cienega."

Deshawn floored it and took the turn so fast we fishtailed. I fell into the passenger-side door, bumping my head again. If I got out of this alive, I'd probably have brain damage. As Deshawn neared La Cienega, I heard the *ping* of something hitting metal on my side. A second later, there were three more. *Ping, ping, ping.* Shit! "Are they aiming for the gas tank?!"

Deshawn croaked, "Goddamn!" I could see sweat rolling down the side of his face. The light was red at the intersection, but Deshawn blew through it and turned right onto La Cienega, the tires screeching. Horns blared behind us. "Where we goin'?"

I was bracing myself with one hand against the passenger door and the other one on the console. "The freeway. We'll outrun them."

Deshawn was breathing hard as he tried to weave through traffic. I craned my neck to look into my side-view mirror. The white Honda was still on our tail. The good news was, the asshole couldn't shoot at us in traffic. The bad news was, I'd forgotten that the on-ramp we were headed for curved up and over the freeway. If he got close enough, he'd be able to ram into us and push us over the side.

But there was no turning back now. The traffic had lightened up, and as we neared the off-ramp, we hit a stretch of open road. My stomach had started to seesaw again, and I felt hot bile burn in my throat. *Ping, ping, ping!* Three more shots hit the passenger side of the car. I scrunched all the way down on the floor, put my head between my knees, and wrapped my arms over my head. This was not going to end well.

I heard more horns blare and looked up to see that Deshawn had blown through the light at the bottom of the on-ramp. The Mercedes began to climb up the elevated road. This was it. I looked in my side mirror, hoping we'd put some distance between the Honda and us. No such luck. It was pulling up to our rear bumper.

Deshawn floored it, but it was just a two-lane ramp, and there were cars in front and to the left of us. There was nowhere to go. The Honda was right behind us and trying to edge to our left. Up ahead, I saw that the guardrail on our right was damaged, the metal bent down almost level with the road. One hard shove and we'd plummet over the side. I looked back and saw that the car on our left was falling back, giving the Honda room. "Deshawn! Pull to the left!"

But before he could maneuver, the Honda had moved in. I saw the driver's head turn toward us as he jerked the steering wheel to the right and slammed into us. I screamed as the Mercedes lurched to the right. The tires started to slide off the road, and I stared down at the traffic below. The car teetered there for a second, and I steeled myself for the final shove that would send us flying.

But Deshawn yanked the steering wheel to the left and slammed into the Honda. It swerved away and scraped against the low wall. Deshawn fell back and then gunned the engine and rammed straight into the passenger side of the Honda. I'd never heard a more satisfying sound than the crunch of that driver's-side door against the concrete. As car horns blasted all around us, Deshawn floored it onto the freeway. I leaned back and gulped air, and after a few seconds I managed to push myself up off the floor and get back on the seat. My shirt was drenched in sweat, and I was shaking all over.

Deshawn didn't look much better. His voice was shaky as he said, "We gotta ditch this ride, like, *now*." But his hands were steady as he steered through the traffic.

I was still trying to catch my breath as I pulled out my cell phone. "Not a problem. I got this." It was pretty amazing what Deshawn had just pulled off. That made me realize that I only knew about the times he got caught. I'd never stopped to think about how much *more* he'd probably done.

Today's Olympic-level performance showed it was one hell of a lot. Not for the first time, I acknowledged that Deshawn had more than enough brains and talent to make it in the straight world—if only he'd wanted to.

THIRTY-EIGHT

Deshawn ditched the Mercedes on a tiny side street where there were no parking restrictions, and we walked to the dive bar I'd spotted a few blocks away. I ordered a double shot of Glenlivet. Deshawn ordered a triple shot of Jägermeister. We took our drinks to a booth at the back, where it was so dark I could barely make out the whites of his eyes.

Just looking at his drink made my stomach lurch. "How can you drink that shit?"

He stared at me like I'd said Mickey Mouse was a sewer rat. "You ever tried it?"

I shook my head. "Can't get past the smell."

We polished off our drinks in one swallow. Deshawn leaned his head back and closed his eyes. After a moment, he blew out a breath. "That was intense, man."

Deshawn: the master of understatement. "Ya think?" I was still light-headed. "Awesome driving back there."

He nodded. "Amazing what you can do when you 'bout to die."

"They're not going to get their dope or their money if you're dead."

"I was jus' kidding. I don' think they tryin' to kill me—least not yet. They tryin' to snatch me. Make me tell 'em what happened to the ~~dope.~~" ~~He gave me a meaningful look.~~

I didn't need the added incentive. I already felt bad enough for putting him in this position. "I'll get you the money. You sure you're safe with your homies?"

"For a little bit. Won't last long, though. Somebody'll tell somebody something. People always be runnin' their mouths."

I had to figure this out, and fast. But right now, I just wanted to enjoy the fact that we were still breathing. By the time Alex showed up, we'd polished off another round and were feeling much better than we should. I'd told Alex that I'd gone to see one of Deshawn's buddies who was a potential new client and that we'd gotten into an accident. That explained the nasty bumps on my head, which hurt like crazy now that I had the luxury of being able to think about pain.

Alex dropped Deshawn at a friend's house—not the place he was really staying; he'd made it clear at the bar: "Not like I don't trust you or nothin', but I can't take no chances. They catch up with you . . ." I got the hint.

When Alex took me to my car, he looked at my forehead—which I could tell was visibly swollen. "Let me drop you at home. I'll pick you up tomorrow morning. You can get your car then."

I agreed, though I didn't realize just how right he was until I got home and saw my bed. I fell on top of the covers and didn't move again until sometime after midnight—when I finally woke up, undressed, and got under the covers.

The next morning, I found a couple of nasty bumps on my forehead and cheekbone. I did the best makeup job I could and hoped no one would notice.

Alex picked me up bright and early at seven thirty, and we bought coffee and bagels on the way to my car.

When I walked into the office, Michelle stared at me. "What happened to your forehead? And your face?"

I told her the same story I'd given Alex about getting in an accident on the way to meeting a potential new client.

She had a look of concern. "Is Deshawn okay?"

Define *okay*. I gave her a smile. "He's good."

I took an egg bagel and one of the coffees into my office and sat down at the computer. But I didn't open a case file. I thought about how to get the money for Deshawn.

When I went out to get a refill on my coffee, Alex came out of his office looking glum. "I give up."

Michelle and I stared at him. I put a hand to his forehead. "Are you okay?" I'd never heard him say anything like that before. Ever.

"I can't get anyone to talk to me. Doesn't matter what I promise, what language I use, how sympathetic I am. These people don't care. They don't know; they don't remember; they're sorry."

I summed it up. "The families of the missing deportees. They're scared." Alex nodded. "We knew it was a long shot, Alex. If you couldn't make them talk, no one could. How many did you reach?"

"More than a hundred and fifty." He sighed. "I'll show you. It's unbelievable. I thought for sure *someone* . . ." He shook his head and went back to his office. He came back out a few seconds later with two sheets of paper and handed them to me. "Check it out."

I took the pages and my coffee into my office and started to scan through the list of missing deportees. On the second page, I saw a name that made me stop and put down my cup. I highlighted it with a yellow marker and called out to Alex. When he came in, I handed him the pages and pointed to the name I'd highlighted. "I want you to check that name for me. Get all the information you can find on her."

"Sure. But I never got an answer when I tried her parents. Want me to try the rest of the family?"

"No. Do not make any phone calls to anyone. Just see what you can get on the Interweb. Got it?"

Alex gave me a sober nod. "Got it. Research only. No contact." He went back to his office.

I'd just pulled up the trial brief I'd been working on when Michelle buzzed me. "We got some more discovery on Cassie's case. Check your e-mail."

I did. "Looks like a sound recording and a transcript. Probably a witness interview."

"Mind if I listen?"

"Be my guest." I downloaded the attachments. Michelle came in and stood behind me. I hit play. My office filled with the familiar robot-sounding male voice, warning that the call was being recorded and monitored. A jail call. There was only one reason the DA would be sending it to me. "This must be Cassie." And if so, it was bad news.

A voice I recognized as Waylon Stubing's said, "Hey, Cassie. How're you doing?"

Cassie's voice was bitter and anxious. "It's horrible in here. I'm scared all the time."

"Yeah, I hope your lawyer can get you out of this." Waylon sounded halting, stilted.

He clearly didn't have much experience talking to prisoners. Or killers.

"I need your help with something." Cassie's voice was low.

There was a long pause. "Uh . . . okay. But what can *I* do?"

"You need to tell my lawyer." Cassie's voice was so low I had to turn the volume all the way up. "Tell her about Abel molesting me. Anal and oral stuff. Tell her I made you keep it a secret—"

Waylon sputtered a little. "B-but you—"

Someone was yelling in the background. It sounded like a guard was giving orders.

Cassie spoke again, her voice rushed. "I gotta go."

The line disconnected, and a dial tone blasted through the room. I hit stop. "Shit, shit, shit!" I pounded my fist on the desk.

Michelle put her head in her hands. "Oh my friggin' God."

Cassie had just tanked her case.

"Do you realize what you did?" I gripped the phone and stared through the window at Cassie. I'd run straight downtown to find out what the hell Cassie had been thinking and whether there was any way to repair the damage.

All the way to Twin Towers, I kept telling myself not to lose it with her, that she was just a kid. And in fairness, I'd had adult clients who'd said even dumber things on jail calls. You'd think the recording that plays every five minutes, warning them that the calls were being monitored, would clue them in to the fact that everything they were saying was *being monitored*. But no. Time and time again, the dipshits blab about "disappearing witnesses" and "dumping the evidence" and turn a perfectly defensible case into a slam-dunk no-brainer for the DA.

Cassie looked at me with teary, sorrowful eyes. "I wasn't asking him to lie for me! I'd made him promise not to tell before."

"But it was already public knowledge. You did an interview with a reporter, remember? It's not a secret to anyone anymore. How could he not know it was okay?"

"I had to make sure!" Cassie wailed. "What if he pretended not to know? You would've thought I lied about telling him."

I supposed it was the excuse I'd have to run with, though I still didn't like it. In any case, like it or not, I had my answer. I searched for an upbeat subject to calm things down. "Has Tiegan been in to see you today?"

Cassie's face cleared like clouds that parted for the sun. "Not yet. But she said she'd be back this afternoon. Tiegan's really been there for me. She's the best thing that's ever happened to me. Except for you."

That was a little—no, a *lot*—more gush than I'd expected. But okay. "I'm very glad she's been there for you."

Now that she was softened up, I decided to take another run at Mr. Burner Phone. "We need to talk about this guy you were calling, Cassie. We know he lives in Atwater, and we know you called him that night. If he was with you, if he had something to do with . . . what went down, you have to tell me. It's very admirable that you've been shielding him. But you need to face the fact that you could spend the rest of your life in prison. That call to Waylon looks bad. Really bad. It's going to be an uphill battle now for me to get the jury to go for manslaughter. And even if I do, the judge could give you more than ten years in prison." Cassie looked away and scratched at a spot on the wall next to the phone. "Cassie, look at me." I waited for her to meet my eyes. "This guy's not going to wait ten years for you. Trust me."

Cassie teared up, but she set her jaw. "I'm not letting you drag him into this! He's got nothing to do with it."

I leaned in close and looked directly into her eyes. "You need to let me be the judge of that, Cassie. If you're right, I'll be happy to leave him out of it. But you have to let me talk to him and find out. There could be ways he can help you that you don't know of."

But she pressed her lips together and shook her head. I knew she was lying. This guy was important. I wanted to reach through the glass, shove my hand down her throat, and yank the name out of her. But short of that, there was nothing I could do.

I just had to wait for her to crack.

THIRTY-NINE

Frustrated by Cassie's maddening—and puzzlingly self-defeating—refusal to give up Mr. Burner Phone, I needed to find a way to relax and let go, or I'd lose it and ram my car into a wall. So on the way back to the office, I tuned in to a jazz station and let my mind float.

As "Night Dreamer" played on the radio, thoughts of other cases began to weave through my mind in no particular order. And somehow, without my even being aware of what I was doing, I came up with a plan. One that could help me kill two birds with one stone. It wasn't a great plan, maybe not even a good plan, but it was all I had. A lot would depend on my delivery. And if it didn't pan out, I'd have a very dangerous enemy for life. But I already had so many of those, what was one more? Let him take a number.

I called Kevin Hausch and told him I had some good news. "I'm close to downtown. If you can get away, I can meet you this afternoon. How about the Blue Cow on Grand?"

It was as public as you could get—all windows, on a main drag, and close to the Dorothy Chandler Pavilion. Hausch said he could make it in half an hour. Perfect.

Hausch was already there when I arrived. I was glad to see that he'd taken a table next to the windows that faced Grand Avenue—nice and public. I noticed he'd put on a little weight in the short time since I'd last seen him. The buttons on his shirt strained a little harder around the belly, and his jowls seemed to hang a little lower. Apparently being a mass murderer and a stooge for the MS-13 could weigh on a person.

He'd ordered coffee, and I saw that a few empty sugar packets on the table in front of him had been folded into little accordions. That, and his grim, no-smile, no-handshake greeting told me something was very wrong in his world. For someone who'd just been promised good news, he sure didn't look happy. I sat down, and the waiter came over with a menu. I ordered coffee and asked Hausch, "You hungry?" He shook his head. When I told the waiter we didn't need the menu, he didn't look happy, either. I wanted to take a minute to do a temperature check, so I asked, "How've you been?"

Hausch shrugged. He turned his little square coaster of a napkin around and around, as though he were working a two-dimensional Rubik's Cube. "I've been better. That jerk Julio went missing. Witnesses said he got dragged into a car by MS-13 bangers."

One theory confirmed. Sadly. "How's that bad for you?"

Hausch pushed the napkin aside and stared out the window. "Because he's been claiming all along that I was connected to MS-13. When IA heard they'd snatched him, they decided to dig into it. So if you've got some good news for me, now would be a great time to hear it."

This was the first I'd heard that Julio had linked Hausch to the MS-13. But I'd gotten all the paperwork from Hausch, so I wasn't surprised he'd held back what he didn't want me to know. And this new development gave me even more reason to believe my plan would work.

I looked directly into his eyes and took my shot. "Actually, come to think of it, this might be good news for both of us." I asked whether he remembered the story about the ten illegals who'd died from heat stroke in the back of a semitruck. "Remember how there were two survivors who'd disappeared?"

I studied his face, his body language. An innocent man would say, "What the hell does that have to do with me?" Or, "Yeah, I remember that. I was working near the border myself back then; we all heard about it. But I don't remember anything about there being any survivors. Where'd you get that from?" Because no one had ever acknowledged that any of the men in that truck had survived. But Hausch said nothing. He'd come to a complete stop. No more folding empty sugar packets, no more fiddling with his spoon, and no more playing with his napkin. Hausch put his hands on his knees and glared at me under his heavy brows, like a bull about to charge. The air around him buzzed with a dark, violent energy.

I pretended not to notice and continued in a light tone, a half smile on my lips. "So I decided to see if I could find those survivors. And damned if I didn't get lucky and find one. Well, in a way both of them, but the other one's dead. Killed by the MS-13, as a matter of fact." I paused for effect, then continued. "Did you know they were brothers?" No answer. "Anyway, Louie Trujillo—FYI, not the name he's using anymore—says a cop told the truck driver that the price for smuggling illegals had just gone up. And when I asked him who the cop was, you'll never guess who he identified?" I dropped the half smile and gave him a cold stare. "Now here's *your* good news. I'm not a cop, and I don't care about getting you busted. What I do care about is getting paid. But I know you're not rolling with the fat stacks, so I'll be reasonable. A hundred and fifty grand. Pretty cheap when you consider you're buying your way out of ten life sentences."

Hausch drilled me with a death glare for a long moment. When he finally spoke, his voice was contemptuous and threatening. "That asshole's lying. I had nothing to do with it. So you can go pound sand, lady. I'm not paying you jack shit. Besides, who're they gonna believe? Some dumb taco bender? Or a veteran police officer?"

I glared right back at him. "Slight correction: a veteran officer who's already being investigated for possible ties to the MS-13."

Hausch narrowed his eyes. "Does your daddy know what you're up to?" He'd said it with a sneer, but I saw fear lying just beneath the bravado.

I gave him a steady look. "No one knows what I'm up to. But if you're thinking about making a move on me—and I sincerely hope you're not that stupid, because that would be depressing—I've got packages that'll automatically go out to all the right places if I don't show up for a certain call." I let him absorb that for a moment. "Anyway, you want to roll the dice? Be my guest. Just remember, they don't fall your way, you'll die in prison." I pulled out a slip of paper with a typed phone number. "I'll give you forty-eight hours to decide what you want to do." I looked at my watch. "It's three thirty-four right now. That means two days from now, at three thirty-five, I'll be sitting down with IA." I threw a ten-dollar bill on the table and stood up. I pointed to his bulging gut. "And lay off the pasta. You're not getting any younger."

I walked out, the scalp on the back of my head tingling as I imagined his eyes shooting laser death rays behind me. When I got to my car, I called Dale and told him what I'd done.

He was a little less than pleased. "Are you out of your fucking mind?! He'll sic the MS-13 on you—if he doesn't get you himself!"

I had to make him see this was a win-win. "Hold on. Listen, if he pays, you bust him. If he makes a move on me, you bust him. If MS-13 makes a move on me, you get to bust them *and* him. There're so many ways this goes right."

Dale didn't say anything, but I could hear him breathing. "Pack up right now. You gotta get out. You're staying with me!"

"Thanks, but I think I'll just go stay in a hotel for a few days. Lots of people around—"

"Tupac got killed in a hotel lobby."

"In Vegas. Anyone could get to anyone in that place. I'll do the Four Seasons. The MS-13 won't be doing any drive-bys in Beverly Hills."

Dale's voice was exasperated. "How the hell do you know?"

I didn't. It just felt like my odds were better there. "And if you want to get a room near mine, that's fine."

Dale was silent for a moment, but I could feel his frustration through the phone. "Where are you now?" I told him I was heading back to the office. "Okay, I'll meet you there. We'll take Alex and go to your apartment so you can pick up what you need for the next few days. And drive slowly. I want to get to your office before you do." He ended the call.

Drive slowly. Like I had a choice. But I'd known that would be his reaction. In fact, I'd been counting on it.

Of course, Dale did get to the office before me, and when I walked in, I noticed the subtle signs that told me he *might* have already told Michelle and Alex what I'd done.

Michelle stood up, hands on her hips and fire in her eyes. "What the *hell* were you thinking? What is wrong with you?"

Alex was a little more conciliatory. "It was a cool move, Sam, but seriously, what happens if he doesn't take the bait? You're the one who said we don't have enough to get charges filed. And he doesn't have to do anything right now. Once you go to IA and tank Hausch, one of those bangers can come after you any time."

I had an answer. "Once I tank Hausch, they have no reason to mess with me. It'll be over."

Michelle was still glaring at me. "Yeah, 'cause they're all such rational thinkers." She jerked her head toward Alex and drilled me with a look of fury. "And what are you going to do if IA doesn't buy your story and Hausch gets off? You can't stay in that damn hotel forever!"

Dale was leaning against the wall, arms folded, radiating a cold anger.

I stared them down. "I won't need to. That asshole is going to drop a sack of cash in my lap, and I'll be recording him."

Michelle threw up her hands. "You're hopeless—just friggin' hopeless." She flopped back down in her chair and hit a key on her computer. "I just sent you your phone messages. Oh, and your other exercise of great judgment—the Orozcos—want to come see you."

Their timing was awesome. "When?"

Michelle gave me a weary look. "When they always do: now."

"Tell them they can come in at five o'clock. We should all be back by then."

Michelle glanced from Dale to Alex. "Wait, you're *both* helping her move into the hotel now?" They nodded. She fixed me with a steely glare. "Then you get back here way before five. I'm not gonna be alone with those hyenas."

Forty-five minutes later, I walked into my room at the Four Seasons.

I got the most basic room they had, and though it was small, it was still plush. The color theme was gold and beige, a large flat-screen hung on the wall opposite the grand-looking king-size bed, and I had a balcony that gave me a view of the city. If these were my last few days on the planet, at least I'd get to enjoy them in style.

Dale got a room across the hall from me and I checked it out. It was just like mine but without the view. That didn't seem to bother him. He took in the amenities. "I should remember this place. Be nice to end a date here."

I covered my ears. "Can you please keep that to yourself? *Dad?*"

Dale sighed. "Sorry."

I headed back to my room. It was almost four thirty. I had to get moving. The Orozcos had no reason to harm Michelle, but logic and reason played such a small part in their lives. I hung up the clothes I'd need for court and left the rest for later.

I hurried back to the office and had barely dropped my purse behind my desk when the outer door buzzer sounded. Michelle called me on the intercom. I made sure my gun was within easy reach in the top left drawer, then picked up the phone. "Ready."

I heard Michelle buzz them in and say, "She's waiting for you in her office."

I stood up. Ernesto appeared in my doorway and nodded. "Ms. Brinkman." He took me in with flat eyes that I knew wouldn't even blink if someone gutted me like a deer right in front of him. Over his shoulder, his son, Arturo, didn't even bother to nod. He fixed me with his usual malevolent stare.

I gestured to the chairs in front of my desk and told the lie of a lifetime. "Gentlemen, it's a pleasure to see you. I have news."

FORTY

Dale followed me to court the next day and sat through my first three cases—all of them boring pretrial appearances. By the time the judge announced the afternoon recess, Dale was ready to blow his brains out.

My last appearance of the day—a probation violation hearing on a meth possession case—took a little longer than expected. At our last hearing, I'd almost persuaded the judge to reinstate Gracee Unger's probation. But today, Gracee—in her infinite wisdom—showed up in court high as a kite, her eyes spinning around in her head like pinwheels.

I gave it my best shot, but the judge wouldn't even let the DA respond to my plea to give her probation. He looked from my client to me. "Seriously, Ms. Brinkman? Even I can tell she's speeding, and I'm a naïf when it comes to drugs. Probation is revoked. Defendant's remanded into custody."

As the bailiff approached to take her away, Gracee quickly leaned in and whispered, "Tell my mom to dump the stash."

Her mom. Why was I not surprised? "Will do."

Dale picked me up in front of the courthouse, and when he dropped me at Twin Towers, he said, "I'm driving you to your car, so text me when you're done."

I sighed, but Dale's expression told me there was no point arguing. I amended my earlier thought that this would get old: it was already old.

When I walked into the lobby, I bumped into Tiegan, who was on her way out. She looked worried. "Hey, Sam. Cassie told me about that phone call with Waylon. How badly is it going to hurt her?"

I didn't see the point in being brutally honest. Spilled milk and all that. It was what it was. "It's hard to tell, but it sure doesn't help."

Tiegan sighed. "Cassie says she just wanted him to know it was okay to tell people. Do you think it's true?"

"I really don't know. But what matters is what the jury thinks, and that's going to depend on how they come across when they testify. We'll just have to wait and see. How was Cassie?"

"Pretty good, I thought, all things considered. She seems pretty optimistic." Tiegan seemed relieved to be able to say that. "Well, if you need me for anything . . ."

"Thanks. I'll let you know."

But when I saw Cassie, she didn't look like she was "pretty good" at all. Everything about her sagged—her shoulders, her eyes, her mouth. She was slumped in her chair, and she picked up the phone as though it weighed fifty pounds.

I put the phone to my ear. "What's wrong, Cassie?"

She stared down at the floor. A long moment passed before she answered. "Nothing."

I peered at her, wishing for the thousandth time that I could see into her head. "I can't help you if you won't talk to me. Is this about your phone call with Waylon? Are you worried about that?"

Cassie shrugged. "Yeah, I guess."

No, that wasn't it. "Is anyone giving you a hard time in here?" Cassie slowly shook her head.

I took a few more runs at it, but finally, I had to give up. Obviously, something was bothering her. But it was just as obvious that she wasn't about to share it. I told her I'd be back tomorrow or the next day. "If you decide you want to talk sooner, just call me. But don't—"

"Yeah, I know. Don't say anything about it on the phone."

"Right." At least the disaster with Waylon had taught her a lesson.

Dale drove me to my car. "That was fast."

I told him about our visit.

Dale was unfazed. "Don't you think she should be depressed? She might spend the rest of her life in prison. And she's only fifteen."

"True." But I didn't believe Cassie was focused on anything that realistic. Because like Dale said, she was only fifteen. No, it was something else. Something much more immediate.

Dale pulled up next to Beulah. "I assume you haven't heard anything from Hausch?"

"Not yet. But he'll call. He's got until tomorrow afternoon." But I didn't think he'd push it to the last minute—whether he intended to kill me or pay me. "The second I hear from him, I'll—"

"Yeah, you'd better, and I'm not kidding, Sam. The second you hear from him." Dale looked me in the eye. "I'll need time to get set up."

We'd planned for me to meet Hausch in a public place—we were considering a couple of different shopping malls—and I'd have my recorder running in my pocket. I'd also leave my phone line open so Dale could monitor what was going on. He'd tapped a couple of friends, too, saying he needed help with a "personal security situation." I didn't know exactly what kind of story he'd told them, but that was his call. Dale's plan was for me to meet with Hausch and record the conversation. If Hausch tried to buy me off, I'd give the signal, and Dale and company would move in and arrest him.

But I had a plan of my own.

I didn't waste any time when I got back to the office. I woke up my computer and went to work on my time sheets. Ordinarily, I avoid that chore until Michelle puts a leash around my neck. But the bill I was racking up at the Four Seasons was a great motivator. I'd just finished and was about to pull up the trial brief I'd been slaving over when I got a call on the burner phone I'd bought the day before. My heart started to pound. This was it. I took a deep breath, blew it out, and answered in a strong voice. "Yeah?"

His voice was harsh. "Meet me in Echo Park by the pedal boats in one hour."

Echo Park, where gangbangers roamed freely and there was a lake perfectly situated for a body dump. "You're kidding, right?"

He spoke fast. "Come up with a better suggestion."

"The Glendale Galleria, in front of the UNIQLO. One hour."

If he refused, it'd be game over.

Hausch expelled a long, hot-sounding breath. "If I see anyone else, it's off."

"Likewise."

The line went dead. I had no time to lose. I made the call, changed into jeans and a sweatshirt, and headed out.

FORTY-ONE

I scanned the area in front of UNIQLO. Hausch wasn't there yet. The bench to the right of the entrance was up against a wall. I liked that. But there was a jewelry kiosk ten feet in front of it being worked by two bored, young salesgirls who stared out at the passing crowds. I didn't like that. The fewer people who noticed Hausch and me, the better. I opted for the bench anyway. Sitting would give us a lower profile, and I had the security of the wall at my back.

But sitting also made me feel vulnerable. I tried to act casual as I looked around at the shoppers, checking for my backup. The problem was, I didn't know what they looked like, and if they were any good I wouldn't be able to pick them out.

I gave up on that and searched for signs of trouble, like the wrong kind of tats. The kind sported by the MS-13. The best defense is always self-defense. But as I zeroed in on the crowds, I realized I faced an overwhelming task. The tattoo craze was of epic proportion. Everyone—boys, girls, teens and older, people in their forties and fifties—had some kind of tattoo. Rainbows, hearts (so common it couldn't possibly count as personal expression anymore), palm trees, eagles. It was a population of walking comic books. Me, I couldn't stand the idea. Too much commitment.

But overwhelming as it was, I couldn't stop trying to scope out every exposed arm, leg, chest, and head. And in my hyperaware state, all the sights, sounds, and smells screamed at me. The candy-apple-red banners strung from the ceiling announcing a sale on Blu-Ray players at Electric City; the cobalt-blue blouse of the Asian mother who was carrying a baby in a front pack; the canned pop music playing an old Backstreet Boys song, "Quit Playing Games (With My Heart)"; the thrum of what felt like a thousand people talking, babies wailing, and the smell of an amalgam of colognes and cinnamon buns and hot dogs.

As I peered closely at the people moving around me, the effort of sussing out every tat I saw was making me dizzy. A chunky man in sagging jeans and a white tank top stopped at the kiosk in front of me. I thought I noticed a Jesus Christ tattoo on his arm—a favorite of the MS-13—and my heart gave a loud thump. But the words under the bearded figure turned out to be RAYMONDO R.I.P. My head swam with relief.

A young girl clung to a bald guy's arm that was inked with a spider-web. That was definitely a gang tat. My heart gave another hard thump. I studied him carefully as they approached, trying to see whether he glanced my way. Sweat trickled down into my bra. But they walked past without a hint of interest in me.

As the minutes ticked by, I was feeling more and more light-headed. I had to force myself to breathe so I wouldn't faint.

I checked my watch. Hausch was ten minutes late. Was he bailing on me? Or was he getting his people into position? The lunacy of my plan was suddenly—and very painfully—clear. Dale had been right: there were so many ways this could go so very wrong. I should pull the plug; this was too insane even for me. I stood up.

And at that moment, Hausch came lumbering toward me with his bearlike gait. He was wearing a black parka and khakis. My eyes bounced everywhere as I checked the area around him. He seemed to be alone. My head was buzzing with the struggle to see and hear everything at once. I expected him to be carrying some kind of bag, but there was nothing in his hands. A serious I'm-about-to-die feeling of dread spread through me. Then a completely different reason for fear occurred to me: Could this be a reverse sting? Had he reported me for blackmailing him?

I thought fast. I could say that *I'd* planned to sting *him*. That I'd never planned to keep the money. Or I could just say that he was lying. That I was here to tell him that I couldn't represent him anymore because I felt he was involved in criminal activity, i.e. the disappearance of Julio. Something like that.

When Hausch got within ten feet, I motioned to the bench. I sat back down and felt the bench sag under his weight as he joined me. I kept my eyes on his hands. "And?"

He said in a flat voice, "Nice to see you."

Was he making this look good in case someone was watching? Or was he buying time to get his bangers into position? "Likewise." I felt another rivulet of sweat drip down my chest.

His right hand slid inside his parka. I stiffened. He wouldn't shoot me here; he'd never get away with it. Should I run? Scream? But a second later, his hand came out. It was holding a gift-wrapped box, about ten by five inches. He handed it to me and forced a smile that looked like a death rictus. "This is a onetime thing."

Relieved to some degree, I took the box, thinking it seemed awfully small. "If it's all there."

"It's all there." He gave me a murderous look. "And if I ever see you again, you'd better run."

Hausch stood up and headed for the exit on the right. I pulled out my cell phone and made the call. "The Glendale Boulevard exit."

Only now did I spot my backup, as they headed out behind him.

I waited for a few moments to see whether anyone was following them or watching me. When I was as sure as I could be, I got up and headed for the exit on the left. As I scanned the crowds for any sign of trouble, the skin in the middle of my back itched with the fear that a knife or bullet was about to plunge into it.

When I made it to my car, I finally let myself exhale.

But I kept my eyes on the rearview all the way back to the hotel, and I practically ran to the elevator. The moment I got to my room, I took off my jacket, turned off my recorder, went to the bathroom, and threw up.

One hot shower and a triple shot of Don Julio later, I checked out my "present." Sure enough, it was all there. Who knew one hundred and fifty thousand dollars could look so small?

But I was too keyed up to sleep. I'd spent the past two hours thinking every passing second would be my last. So I poured myself another drink, turned on the television, and found a rerun of *Kill Bill*. I fell asleep to the whistling theme song and Uma Thurman's high-booted strut.

Sometime in the night, I must've woken up and turned off the television, because when my cell phone quacked, the room was quiet and dark. I squinted at the screen. I didn't recognize the number, so I let the call go to voice mail. It had to be three in the morning. It wasn't. It was seven thirty. Those blackout drapes really did their job. I decided to take another shower to clear my head. When I got out, I saw that the caller had been Dale.

I listened to his message as I got dressed and put on makeup. He said it was safe to check out and go home. I wouldn't have minded another night in that room. I gave it one last longing gaze before packing up all my gear—including the money. Then I listened to my other message. What I heard made me fly out the door.

When I got to the infirmary at Twin Towers, a nurse showed me to Cassie's bed. Her bandaged wrists lay on top of the covers, and an IV was pumping some kind of fluid into her arm. I thought she was sleeping, but when I reached her bedside, her eyes half opened. "Hey, Sam." Her voice was weak.

The nurse who told me she'd managed to break her plastic fork and use the jagged edge to cut her wrists said it was an "amateur effort." The cut was horizontal, so the bleeding was relatively slow. Still, I wouldn't call it nothing. She'd lost enough blood to justify a couple of days in the infirmary. Was this my fault? Should I have seen it coming after she'd been so depressed the last time? But she'd never done anything like it before, and she certainly hadn't said anything that even hinted she was this depressed. "Why, Cassie? What happened?"

Her voice was hoarse. "I just felt so . . . hopeless. I don't want to live like this . . . here."

I stared at her. Something was really off. I pressed her as much as I could, given the circumstances, but she wouldn't budge. I needed to enlist some help. "Have you seen Barbara lately?"

Cassie stared at the foot of the bed. "A few days ago."

"How'd that go?"

"Fine." Cassie's mouth turned up in a tiny, one-second smile. "She's so nice."

"You won't be able to have visitors until you get out of the infirmary. But I'm sure she and Tiegan will want to see you as soon as they can."

Tears welled up in Cassie's eyes. "Tiegan won't come."

What? Since when? "Why do you say that, Cassie? What happened?"

Cassie turned her head away. "I just know she won't."

I tried to press her for an answer, but I got nowhere, and after a few minutes, the nurse said my time was up. I told Cassie I'd see her tomorrow and left.

But I intended to find out what the hell was going on right now. I drove straight to the high school and waited in the hallway for Tiegan's class to end. When the bell rang, I stood back and let the tidal wave of teenagers pour out, then went inside and told her what had happened.

I sat on a desk in the front row. "She says you won't want to visit her. What's going on?"

Tiegan stared at me, speechless, her expression stunned and confused. "Nothing happened. I have no idea why she'd say such a thing."

It didn't look like an act, but she had to have some clue. "I saw Cassie after you visited her yesterday. She seemed more depressed than I'd ever seen her. Did something happen during your visit to upset her?"

Tiegan really did look freaked out. "N-no. Not at all. We just talked about the usual things. They're letting me give her homework and books to read. We talked about how that was going, how she's doing in the . . . the facility." Her eyes dropped back down to her desk, and she shook her head. "I don't get it."

"And you don't know why she'd try to kill herself? She didn't say anything to you?"

Tiegan looked utterly clueless. "No. Not at all."

I didn't know what to make of it. All I knew was that someone was lying.

FORTY-TWO

"Jesus H. Christ." Michelle pushed back from her desk. "Are you kidding me? What on earth is going on?"

Alex had pulled the old secretary's chair to the side of Michelle's desk. "I don't get it. I thought you said that last time, Cassie was gushing about Tiegan being her rock and her savior."

"She was. But I guess something must've happened to change that."

"Though Tiegan says it didn't." Michelle looked exasperated. "This is so . . . weird. So now what?"

I stared at the floor and thought about my conversation with Tiegan. "Alex, dig up everything you can find on Tiegan. Where she comes from, where she's been, who she's worked for, who she's been with—the whole ball of wax." My cell phone quacked in the pocket of my coat. I checked the screen. "I need to take this." I moved toward my office.

Michelle had an irritated expression. "You can change that ringtone any time."

I nodded. I really did need to change that stupid thing. I stepped into my office and answered the call. One minute later, I walked back out, briefcase in hand. I saw that Alex's door was closed. He'd already jumped on it. I'd probably have everything, including where Tiegan was when she lost her first baby tooth, by tonight. I didn't even want to remember how I'd bumped along before I had him.

Michelle took in my briefcase and gave me a puzzled look. "Did I miss something? I don't have any appearances on the calendar for you today."

I shook my head. "It's just an informal meeting with the DA in Beverly Hills on that DUI."

Michelle smiled. "Still trying to beat her into submission?"

"It's gonna happen. I should be back sometime after lunch."

It would've been much sooner, but I actually had more than one meeting, and my first one wasn't with the DA. And it wasn't in Beverly Hills. It was in Culver City. Not that far as the crow flies, but about an hour away as the car crawls. Crosstown traffic is such a bitch.

Luckily, the parking at the Fox Hills Mall wasn't terrible. But getting into the mall wasn't the problem. The problem was getting out. It was a brisk day, and the wind that'd kicked up felt like a cold knife as it sliced through my open coat. I pulled it closed and hurried inside.

I found the Hot Dog on a Stick eatery, ordered a lemonade, and took a table against the wall. The employees had to wear clown-style red, blue, and yellow shirts, shorts, and beanies. It might have been the most humiliating uniform I'd ever seen.

Ten minutes later, Deshawn hurried in, head down, shoulders hunched. He may as well have worn a sign saying I'M TRYING TO HIDE FROM SOMEONE! It was pretty chilly in the mall, but I noticed a film of sweat on his forehead. He sat down at the table next to me. "You got it all?" His eyes darted back and forth as he scanned the crowds passing by the hot-dog stand.

I nodded. "Plus a little more. I figure you'll owe for the damage to that Mercedes." I took the gift box out of my briefcase and handed it to him. "Happy birthday."

He slipped it into the pocket of his puffer coat without looking at me. "Thanks." Deshawn slid halfway off his chair, then paused and glanced at me. "How'd you do it?"

"Magic." I kept my eyes focused straight ahead on the shoppers passing by. "Call me and leave the line open. I'll watch your back."

Deshawn pulled out his phone, tapped in the number I'd given him, took one more fast scan of the crowds, and hurried out. I watched for any signs that he was being followed, but I didn't see any. I moved to the entrance and pretended to take one last sip of my lemonade as I paused at the trash can. I spotted Deshawn pushing through the outer exit doors. There was no one behind him as far as I could tell.

I gave it another few minutes, then headed out in the opposite direction. I pulled my collar up to hide as much of my face as possible, glad it was cold enough to make that look natural, and hoped Deshawn's nemesis hadn't gotten a good look at me during the car chase. I moved as fast as I could without appearing as though I were running for my life. The cold wind tossed my hair around, exposing my face, so I kept my head down.

My hands were freezing, but I didn't want to put them in my pockets. I needed them to be free. I scanned the parking lot constantly as I neared the car. A young male was pacing next to a blue Jetta as he talked on his cell phone. His shaved head was covered in multicolored tats. I slowed and watched him, my heart pounding. He looked around the parking lot as he spoke, but he didn't seem to be interested in me.

I picked up my pace, but when I got within twenty feet of Beulah, I spotted a man in the driver's seat of a silver Audi that was parked behind me. I tried to get a better look, to see whether he was watching me, but his windows were tinted. Should I run? If he wasn't after me, I'd only be tipping off the guy who really was. And if the guy in the Audi was waiting for me, I was already toast. I couldn't outrun a car. The only thing I could do was keep moving and hope it wasn't him. Even if I made it to my car, outrunning him in Beulah would be an exercise in futility.

When I reached my car, I quickly shoved the key at the lock, but my hand was shaking so badly I missed. At that moment, I caught a movement out of the corner of my eye. I shifted my gaze without turning my head. The man in the Audi was moving—he was getting out.

Shit! I could hear my heart pounding in my ears. Screw the key. I hit the remote and grabbed at the door handle. My sweaty palm slid off, and the handle bounced back. My throat closed as I grabbed the handle again. This time I gripped it and yanked with all my might. The door flew open, and I jumped in. I jammed the key into the ignition and begged Beulah not to fuck with me. In a rare display of cooperation, the engine kicked over. I threw her into gear and punched the gas. The car leaped forward with a loud squeal as I burned rubber and headed for the exit.

I hazarded one quick glance in the rearview mirror. The man in the Audi was walking toward the entrance to the mall, head down against the wind. Not the least bit concerned with me. I slowed down at the exit and took a long look in all my mirrors. There was no one behind me.

I put my head down on the steering wheel and took deep breaths. My pulse had just begun to approach normal when a horn blasted. It sounded like it was in my backseat. I jerked up and saw a woman shaking her fist at me in the rearview mirror. I waved to her and pulled out into traffic.

I headed for my meeting with the Beverly Hills DA. It took an hour of alternate wheedling and needling, but by the end, I had the distinct feeling she was ready to cave.

As I left the courthouse, I got a text from Deshawn. An emoji smiley face and a thumbs-up. All good. It was over. I was so relieved I felt as if a fifty-pound weight had been lifted off my shoulders.

All in all, it'd been a pretty productive day.

I was trying to decide whether to go back to the office or treat myself to an early day when I noticed I had a voice mail from Dale. He wanted to meet me for dinner at seven thirty, Morton's Steakhouse on La Cienega.

I never turn down a good steak dinner, and besides, I was in the mood to celebrate. And it was Friday; I didn't have to worry about getting to court in the morning. I texted him to say yes, then checked in with Michelle. She said nothing was going on and gave me the green light to call it a day.

I went home and treated myself to a long, hot bath, then got ready for dinner. Just having the time to do those things was a delicious luxury. I walked into Morton's feeling more relaxed than I had in months.

I could tell something was bugging Dale from the moment I sat down. Over our crab leg appetizers, he asked me how I was doing with a pointedly intense stare. But when I told him I was doing great, he let it go. I actually knew what was on his mind, but I wanted to let him bring it up.

We'd finished dinner—prime rib eye on the bone, baked potatoes, and asparagus—and were sipping the last of our wine when he finally got to it.

Dale watched as the waiter took away our plates, then leaned forward, his arms folded on the table in front of him. "When I called you this morning to tell you that we could check out, I didn't have time to explain what'd happened."

I took a sip of wine. "Yeah, I wouldn't have minded another night there, but whatever."

Dale tilted his head a little and gazed at me. "Seems Hausch was killed in a drive-by last night."

I raised my eyebrows. "Really?" Dale nodded. "Well, lucky us. I can't pretend that's bad news." I shrugged. "But I guess it was bound to happen. Playing with bangers is a dangerous business."

Dale peered at me. "Yeah, well, there are a couple of strange things about it, though. It happened near his house in Simi Valley. Not exactly gang turf."

Simi Valley is, and pretty much always was, your quintessential "sleepy bedroom town," where lots of cops lived. "Why are they saying it's a gang drive-by?"

"The witnesses—two of whom were off-duty cops—said they were throwing gang signs out the car window."

I flicked at a bread crumb. "Did they happen to recognize the signs?"

"They're working on it." Dale fixed me with an intense stare. "And one of the shooters yelled, "*Para mi prima!*' For my cousin."

I nodded slowly. "Given what Hausch was into, I'd say the only surprising thing is that it took this long."

Dale continued to stare at me. "But don't you think it's an interesting coincidence that Hausch got offed just when we found out what he's been up to?" Dale sat back, but his stare was unwavering. "I do."

I returned his gaze. "I don't. Hausch said IA was bearing down on him. Maybe his little gangbanger buddies found out and decided he was too big a risk." I glanced at the dessert menu. "Besides, it all worked out okay, didn't it?" I gave him a little smile and pushed the dessert menu toward him. "Want to share the Hot Chocolate Cake? I hear it's fantastic."

FORTY-THREE

It was a relatively uneventful weekend, which gave me a chance to finish my chores and have an easy, relaxed Sunday. I'd planned to go visit Cassie on Monday, but Alex texted me late Sunday night and said he had information about Tiegan I might want to follow up on. So the next morning, I headed to the office. I got in at seven thirty, hoping to get some work done before anyone was around.

But when I pulled into the parking lot, I saw Alex's black Camry. So I dropped my purse and briefcase on my couch and went to his office. As I raised my hand to knock, his voice came through the door. "If you tell me you're from *RuPaul's Drag Race* one more time, I'm quitting."

"Fine. I'll be in my office."

A few minutes later, Alex came in with his iPad. "Your friend Tiegan has an interesting past. She taught at Mission Viejo High School for two years, then moved to Pasadena High for one year, and then she wound up at Glendale High. That's three schools in four years."

A lot of moving around. Not usually something teachers like to do. As a general rule, they gain tenure by staying in one place. "Any complaints about her?"

"Not that I could find. But maybe they just didn't document them. You never know. What's also interesting? She lives in Atwater Village."

I sat up. That's where the burner phone seemed to live. "You're saying Tiegan owns the burner phone? *She's* Earl Lee Riser?"

Alex lifted his hands, then dropped them. "It's possible. I mean, a lot of people live in Atwater. But not all of them are friends with Cassie. And some of the calls between Cassie and that burner were near the school, so . . ."

I didn't like any of this. "But if that's true, then why didn't Tiegan tell us?"

Alex raised an eyebrow—and no one could do it more dramatically. That fishhook soared. "An excellent question."

One I planned to ask her very soon. But not before I did some digging on my own. "Let's go see that principal in Pasadena." I wanted to find out why Tiegan had left after just one year.

Michelle came in just as we were about to leave. I told her what we were up to.

"Interesting," she said. "Oh, before you go, did you hear that Hausch got nailed in a drive-by the other night? Guess that's why Dale said you could stand down."

"He told me about it last night over dinner." I started for the door, then stopped. "Have there been any other media appearances by those child advocate groups?"

"That woman, the one we saw on TV, did an interview for the Daily Beast. And the Internet buzz seems to be leaning more in her favor." Michelle frowned. "I'm surprised your DA didn't leak to the press about Cassie's phone call to Waylon."

I was, too. "I have a feeling someone smart got to him." No way Gidiot would've had the brains to realize that you save that kind of dynamite for trial. If he'd put it out now, I'd have responded with Cassie's explanation, and then everyone would have time to kick it all around. By the time we got to trial, it'd be old, watered-down news. "We probably won't be back. But I'll call you with updates."

We took Alex's car because he's addicted to the security of knowing he'll get to where he's going. No sense of adventure.

Pasadena is one of the older cities in LA County, and, unlike so many other parts of the county, they did their best to maintain the original appearance of the buildings, with their intricate stonework and detailed architecture—especially on the main drag, Colorado Avenue. It lent the place charm—a rare commodity in Southern California.

Pasadena High wasn't such an architectural wonder, just a plain, boxy, two-story building. But it sat at the base of the San Gabriel Mountains, and the grounds were as green and manicured as a golf course. Like a great deal of Pasadena, it had an orderly, everything-in-its-place, tidy feel.

Principal Tyrone Watkins was young, welcoming, and awfully hip for a principal. I don't remember ever having a principal like that. When we apologized for being late, he said, "It's cool." And when we told him our business concerned a former teacher, he said, "No worries." He even said to call him Tyrone.

I told him we'd understand if there were anything he couldn't legally share with us.

He nodded. "But then you'll just serve me with a subpoena. So let's see if we can avoid the hassle. Fire away."

I really liked this guy. "You had a teacher named Tiegan Donner a few years back. Were you here then?"

He smiled. "I remember her. She was great."

I hadn't expected to hear that about a teacher who'd left after just one year. "Did you have any complaints about her or anything? She wasn't here very long."

He nodded. "Yeah, that was a loss. She said she needed to relocate for personal reasons. But I never had any complaints about her. We were all pretty surprised when she left, but . . ." He turned his palms up. "Things take place."

"Did she say what the personal reasons were?"

He shook his head. "I assumed it was a family issue. But when I asked about that, she said her family lived in Ohio." Tyrone frowned. "Or was it Missouri? One of those states in the middle."

In short, Pasadena was a bust. Alex and I regrouped in the car. I pulled up Google Maps on my phone. "Want to try Mission Viejo?"

Alex looked at my phone. "It's about an hour and a half away, but I'm game."

I had a feeling we might be on one gigantic turd hunt. But in for a penny . . .

Mission Viejo is further south, not far from San Diego. The high school was made up of a series of red-roofed, one-story buildings that had a Spanish feel, and it was huge. I figured they must have a serious athletic program because the school sported an Olympic-size swimming pool, a well-cared-for track, and two football fields.

Our principal this time was a woman, Charlene Mayfield. She reminded me of the girls' basketball coach at my high school: thick, short grayish-blondish hair; leathery brown skin; and a muscular body. She talked like a drill sergeant. Not hostile, just very direct, in short, staccato sentences. Charlene didn't immediately remember Tiegan. It'd been about three years. Apparently, Tiegan had taken some time off before moving to Pasadena High.

Charlene pulled up a file on her computer, and then the light dawned. "Oh, yeah. Weird deal there."

Had we finally gotten lucky? I leaned in. "A complaint?"

"No. Well, not by someone else. By her. She said a student was stalking her."

Weird deal, indeed. "Were the police involved?"

Charlene gave a short, emphatic shake of the head. "She wouldn't have it. Said she didn't want to cause trouble for the guy. He was just a kid, and she felt sorry for him."

Awfully kind of Tiegan. But odd. "So she left?"

Charlene gave a curt nod. "I wasn't happy about it. If the kid's got a problem, better to handle it now than let him get in real hot water when he's an adult."

"And you told her that?"

Charlene humphed. "'Course I did. But she promised she'd talk to the parents privately. Let 'em know so they could get him help."

It'd be nice to have a chat with that guy. "Did you ever find out who he was?"

"I tried." Charlene's expression was mildly disgusted. "Mainly I talked to the other teachers. But no one remembered seeing a boy hanging around Tiegan's classroom—or hanging around Tiegan, period." Charlene sat back and folded her arms—not easy to do over her ample chest. "I didn't believe them. Someone had to have seen something. I tried to tell them they weren't doing the kid any favors." Charlene blew out a breath. "Didn't matter. They gave me diddly-squat."

"What about the students? Did you try talking to them?"

She looked at me incredulously. "You're kidding, right? We've got three thousand kids, and this boy wasn't necessarily in any of Tiegan's classes." She gave me a frank look. "And do you really think a kid is going to tell me anything?"

Not for one hot second. We thanked Charlene and headed back to LA.

I leaned my seat back and watched the palm trees sway in the breeze. "What are we missing, Alex?"

"I'll be damned if I know. So who do we talk to now?"

There were really only two choices. "Tiegan or Cassie. But I'd guess Cassie's the weaker link."

Alex didn't look optimistic. "Then we hit up Cassie?"

I nodded. "And hope for the best."

FORTY-FOUR

When Alex pulled into the parking lot at Twin Towers, I decided it'd be best if it was just Cassie and me. "I hate to do this to you, Alex, but—"

He held up a hand. "Totally get it." Alex parked close to the entrance, then pulled out his iPad. "I told Dale I'd give him a hand with the Orozco investigation. I've got a line on the driver of the custody bus. He might have a cousin who's a Southside Creeper."

"Great." I got out and headed for the jail, wishing that just for once, Alex weren't so damn good at the gig.

A custody bus driver would be in a perfect position to get Ricardo put into the Southside tank. The only problem was, I knew he hadn't done it. If Alex's lead panned out, and the driver was connected to the Creepers, I'd have to dream up a reason why I knew it wasn't him. I wasn't about to get an innocent guy killed just to make the Orozcos go away. Unless he turned out to be a total scumbag who deserved it. But I doubted I'd get that lucky.

The guards said it'd be fifteen minutes or more before they could get Cassie up to the attorney room. That was fine by me. I needed time to think. Tiegan had to be Earl Lee Riser, the owner of the burner phone. But how was I going to get Cassie to confirm it? I tossed some ideas around in my head, but when they finally brought her up, I still had no inspiration. So I went straight at it.

I sat down and picked up the phone. I noticed the bandages on her wrists had been replaced with single gauze pads held on with lots of surgical tape. "I was surprised they let you out of the infirmary so soon. You must be doing pretty well." Not true. I wasn't surprised. She hadn't been that badly injured, and the doctors move inmates out of the infirmary the moment they can stand up.

Cassie shrugged; she looked listless. "I guess."

I wondered if the apathetic look was chemically induced. "Are you taking your meds?"

She made a face. "They make me sick. And tired. And I don't feel any better. Just kind of flat and . . . slow."

I'd heard that from clients before. I think they must give inmates elephant tranquilizers instead of antidepressants. "I can ask to adjust your meds, but after your . . . incident, I think it'll be a while before they let you stop altogether."

Cassie slouched in her chair and stared down at the counter. "Barbara said she's about to start a new job, so she won't be able to come see me very much." Cassie wrapped her free arm around her waist, which looked even smaller than it had before. She'd never looked so forlorn.

"I'm sorry to hear that." Especially if it was true that Tiegan wouldn't come anymore. It made me feel a little guilty about squeezing her for information. Not enough to not do it, though. "Cassie, we got the cell tower records for the calls on your phone. We know the burner phone was usually in Atwater. And Tiegan lives in Atwater. So you may as well talk to me about it. There's no reason to pretend anymore." It was a half bluff. I hadn't said anything that wasn't true. I'd just left the door open and hoped she'd walk through it.

She dropped her eyes to the bottom of the window and bit her lip. "So Tiegan . . . she—she told you?" Cassie glanced at me. I held her gaze and nodded. Cassie hunched over and dissolved into tears.

What the hell was going on? I waited for her to calm down, then spoke in a quiet voice. "Let me hear your side of it." Whatever "it" was.

Cassie swiped away the tears with the back of her hand. "Tiegan told me she deleted my texts and got rid of the phone. But I really didn't say anything . . . bad. She just didn't like me to text her so much."

So I was right. Tiegan was the owner of the burner phone. And all this time, she'd been telling me she had no clue who owned it. I felt like a bowling ball had landed in the pit of my stomach. Something was very wrong here. "Why not?"

Cassie sniffed hard and wiped her nose again. "In case anyone saw. She was a little paranoid about it. But I don't blame her; it was kind of dangerous. She could lose her job."

I put on an understanding expression and nodded. But inside, my brain was screaming. If my guess was right, I finally had the answer to so many questions—one that I'd never have seen coming in a million years. I rolled the dice again. "When did it start?"

Cassie's chin trembled, and she bit back another wave of tears. "A month after she got assigned to be my counselor." She looked at me, her expression anxious. "I just want you to know . . . I—I'd never done anything like that before." Her eyes drifted away. "I never thought I was . . . like that." Cassie tilted her head to one side and fell silent for a moment. "I thought about that a lot at first. Would I have ever done it if Tiegan hadn't . . ." A long moment passed as Cassie stared at the bottom of the window. When she finally looked up, tears had filled her eyes again. "But I'm not sorry. I'm not. She made me happy; she cared about me, made me feel like I was someone special. She *wanted* me."

As I'd guessed, Tiegan and Cassie had been . . . I couldn't bring myself to call them lovers. Lovers are equals, two adults. Or even two teenagers. Not a woman in her late twenties and a fifteen-year-old girl. But clearly, they'd been involved.

And I'd been played. So played. I remembered how many times Tiegan told me she'd tried to get Cassie to give up the name of the guy who owned the burner phone. How she'd said she'd try to find out who Cassie's "boyfriend" was.

My buddy Tiegan was quite the piece of work. "Is Tiegan the reason you broke up with Waylon?" Cassie nodded. "Did she tell you to?"

Cassie exhaled; her breath came through the receiver like a loud wind. "N-not really. I just knew she wouldn't like it if I kept seeing him once we . . . ah . . . started . . ." Cassie cleared her throat and bent her head. "Started hanging out together."

A vulnerable kid preyed upon by an adult in power. And Cassie, an adopted child, a sexually abused child, was about as vulnerable as it gets. I wished the story weren't so familiar. "Did you feel like you had to keep seeing her, Cassie?"

Cassie's face screwed up, tears now spilling over, as she shook her head. "I was happy. We were going to move in together. Everything was going to be so perfect."

Move in together? I didn't know how they thought they'd pull that off without Tiegan winding up in the back of a patrol car. "Was Tiegan onboard with that plan?"

Cassie squeezed her eyes shut and nodded. "We were going to move, go someplace where no one knew us." A hiccup passed through her chest as she bit back sobs. "And then I screwed everything up."

I felt like I was stumbling, blindfolded, through a maze. "How did you do that?"

Cassie wiped her face with her sleeve, the phone clutched to her ear, her free arm now wrapped so tightly around her small frame, it gripped the opposite side of the chair. "I couldn't take it anymore! I had to get away, so I told her about . . . all of it. About Abel and my father and . . . all of it. I thought if she knew, she'd take me away, and we could live together!"

"When? When did you tell her?"

Cassie began to tremble. "That day. After school."

A dawning awareness spread through me as the import of what she was saying sank in. "The day of the murders?"

She looked at me, her face filled with sadness. "Yes. If I hadn't told her, she wouldn't have . . ." Cassie dropped her head. "It's my fault, all of it."

FORTY-FIVE

The new scenario was solidifying in my mind, but I didn't want to put any ideas in her head. I wanted to let Cassie tell it on her own. I'd figure out how to package it later. "What exactly did Tiegan do when you told her what'd been going on?"

Cassie stared at a point over my left shoulder. "She totally lost it." Her voice was low and tight. "I never saw her like that. Ever. She was always so sweet, so gentle. But when I told her, she just went berserk!"

"Where were you? At school?"

She nodded. "It was late, though. I went to see her after her counseling sessions were done. There was no one around." Cassie's gaze shifted to the right as she relived it all. "Tiegan's face got so red. She started pacing all around the room, calling them all kinds of names, saying they were animals and they should be put down."

"And you're sure no one heard all this?" I was building the case in my mind. Other witnesses to this scene would really help.

Cassie thought for a moment, then shook her head. "I don't think so. I didn't see anyone around when I left."

"Did Tiegan make any threats? Say that she was going to do anything?"

"At first she just said she was going to report them. But I told her she couldn't. That they'd send me away, put me in foster care, and . . ." Her chin trembled. "And then I'd never see her again!"

"So she agreed not to do that?"

Cassie nodded slowly. "And then she said she'd . . . take care of it."

"How was Tiegan acting at that point? Was she yelling? Screaming?"

Cassie's face wrinkled; she seemed confused. "No, not at all. After she had that meltdown, she got real quiet. She seemed okay. She said she was glad I told her. She said it must've been really hard for me to keep all that inside. I told her I was glad, too, that it felt so much better to be able to talk to her about it. Then we talked about how she'd help me get out of that place. How we'd move far away, and she could work at another school and we could be together."

"So she'd calmed down by the time you left?" Cassie nodded. "And after that, what happened?"

"I went home, did my homework, watched some television. Mom and Dad left. They were going to spend the night at a hotel to celebrate their anniversary, so I didn't have to help with dinner." She leaned against the wall, her expression pained, wistful. "I remember I was so happy when I went to bed that night. I was finally going to get out of there and be with Tiegan."

I braced myself for what I was about to hear. "What happened that night?"

Cassie ran a hand through her hair; her eyes were fixed on the wall behind me, but she was focused inward. "I heard knocking on my window. It was late. I'd been asleep for a little while. I woke up and saw Tiegan standing there. It was like one of those scary movies. It'd been raining, and her hair was all wet and straggly and she looked . . . weird, like calm and crazy at the same time."

"Did you let her in?" Cassie nodded. I pictured the crime scene. "How?"

"I took the screen off my window."

I remembered the windows in that house were low. "Was she wearing gloves?" Cassie frowned for a moment, then she shook her head. No gloves. There was hope. "What happened next?"

"She seemed like, almost like she was in a trance. I was afraid of her. She asked me where Abel's room was. I said, 'What are you going to do?' But she wouldn't tell me. She just grabbed my arm and said, 'Tell me!'—like, really intense."

"And did you?"

Cassie sat up now, and I could feel her anxiety. "I was afraid not to! So, yeah. I told her. She told me to stay in my room. But I was afraid Abel would hurt her."

"So you followed her?"

Cassie nodded. I could see her breathing getting faster. "But I stopped at the doorway." Now her words came out in a rush. "She had a knife, and she just whipped it across his throat and then he woke up, and blood was everywhere and . . ." Cassie put a hand over her eyes. Her voice was thin, almost strangled. "It was horrible! I couldn't look!"

"What did you do?"

Cassie was gripping the phone so tightly I saw her forearm begin to shake. "I don't know. I think I just stood there. Then I heard the front door open. I didn't know what to do; I didn't want them to see me in there, so I hid in the corner."

"Inside Abel's room?"

"Yeah." Cassie's breath was getting faster and shallower now. Her words tumbled over one another as though they were one long sentence. I had to strain to understand her. "And I told Tiegan to look out, someone's coming. But then I heard my dad's voice. I told her to run, get out of there! I went over to Abel's window to pull out the screen, but she'd gone to the side of the doorway, and when Stephen reached for the light switch, she stabbed him right in the throat, and I heard him scream. I told her to stop! But she wouldn't!" Cassie's face was white. Her nostrils flared, her eyes were wide, and they moved back and forth as she spoke. "He fell down and she—she stabbed him over and over!" She put her hand to her chest, which was heaving now.

"And then your mother came in?"

Cassie nodded. "She stabbed her . . . just like Stephen." Cassie covered her mouth and half sobbed, half screamed. "I told her, 'Stop!' But she wouldn't. She wouldn't listen." She dropped her head and cried.

A part of my mind was assessing what she'd said, comparing it to the crime scene and the evidence. From what I could remember, it was matching up pretty well. "What happened after that?"

"I—I went to them. Tried to help them. I took off my pajama top and held it on my dad's throat to try and stop the bleeding, but it was too late. Then I went to Paula . . . but I thought it was too late, that she was gone."

I noticed she'd used her parents' names. She'd never done that before. "What was Tiegan doing?"

"Nothing. She was just standing there, staring at them, with the knife in her hand. She seemed sort of out of it, like she couldn't believe what she'd done."

She wasn't *that* out of it. "But she took off. And left you in one terrible situation."

Cassie started to speak, then stopped. She nodded. "That was my idea. If they found out she did it, she'd be in prison forever. But I'm a juvenile. I thought they couldn't lock me up for that long."

I remembered her shock when I'd told her how wrong she'd been. "So what happened when Tiegan left?"

"She said to give her ten minutes and call her just before I called the cops."

I remembered the call made to the burner phone that night. "What phone did you use to call her?"

She frowned, then shook her head. "I don't remember. I just know I did it. I called her and then the cops right after. She told me what to say."

"That an Aryan Brotherhood guy did it?"

"Yeah." Cassie slumped back in her chair, depleted.

I had to push away the shocker of her relationship with Tiegan for a moment to let her version of the murders sink in. First of all, Tiegan's motive. Did it make sense that she'd lose it like that and decide to take out the whole family? Well, actually, she hadn't targeted the whole family. She'd gone after Abel. The father and mother were collateral damage—wrong place, wrong time. I supposed targeting Abel made sense. Cassie had always downplayed the father's role. I didn't find it hard to believe she'd done the same when she told Tiegan what'd been going on. And if Tiegan was messed up enough to seduce a teenage girl, I supposed it was possible she'd go over the edge when she heard what that girl had been going through.

At any rate, I thought I might be able to sell it to a jury.

Otherwise, at first blush, I thought her story hung together pretty well—with one exception. "Why did you bury your pajamas in the backyard?"

Cassie stared at me numbly for a moment. "I don't really know. I just thought it'd look bad to have blood on me, that the cops would never believe I was just trying to help them."

Maybe, maybe not. I'd let it go for now. "And Abel's wallet—you wanted to make it look like a burglary?" Cassie nodded. "What happened to the knife?"

"Tiegan took it. She said she'd get rid of it." Cassie leaned her head against the wall again. She looked like she'd just run through nine miles of quicksand.

I'd go over this story with her a thousand more times to get it all straight, but for now, I could see she'd had enough. There was just one other, non-murder-related question, though. "Do you know if Tiegan had been with other girls?"

Cassie's body was limp, her free hand laying palm up in her lap. "No. But she did tell me about a girl who'd been stalking her. A junior. It wasn't around here, though."

"Was it at Mission Viejo High?"

Cassie frowned. "Yeah, I think so." A curious expression flitted across her face. I could see she'd wondered how I knew, but she just didn't have the bandwidth to get into it at the moment. Her features sagged, and she leaned her head against the wall. "I'm sorry I lied to you." But a second later, she sat up, a worried look on her face. "You can't tell anyone, right? You said everything I told you was confidential."

Her devotion to Tiegan, given what her life had been, was understandable. But if this story was true—or, more to the point, sellable—there was no way I was going to let her misplaced loyalty doom her to a life of wasted martyrdom. "It is. But you can't take the fall for this, Cassie—"

She sat forward with effort, her expression tortured. "It's all my fault, don't you get that? If I hadn't told her—"

The guard announced that visiting hours were over.

Cassie gave me a wary look. "What are you going to do?"

I had an idea, but I wasn't about to share it. "I'm going to give you some time to think about this. I get that Tiegan was good to you, that she was there for you when it felt like no one else was. And I get that you feel like covering for her is the right thing to do—now. But I promise you, six months, a year from now, after you're convicted, you'll realize it wasn't. And you'll spend the rest of your life regretting it in a six-by-eight-foot cage. So when you go back to your cell, I want you to look around at those walls and think: 'I'm going to get old and die here.' And think about all the things you'll never get to do. No hanging out with Tawny and Rain, no shopping, no college, no acting school, no boyfriends." I didn't say "no girlfriends." I knew she'd be able to find plenty of those in prison. I looked directly into her eyes. "No life."

As the guard took her away, I wondered whether anything I'd said had landed. Not that it mattered.

I was going to make this come out right, regardless.

FORTY-SIX

Alex stared at me for a long moment. "I'm glad you told me not to start the car." His mouth had fallen open as I told him about my conversation with Cassie. Now he shook his head and stared at Twin Towers through the windshield. "An affair with a female teacher? I never would've guessed."

But he didn't look terribly rocked by it. "She took advantage of a messed-up kid, Alex."

He held up his hands. "I'm not saying she didn't."

I drew a circle around him in the air. "Not really feeling the outrage."

Alex was puzzled at first, but then he nodded, looking chastened. "You're right. It's a double standard, I guess. It does feel a little less . . . horrible. Tiegan's a woman. And she's really pretty." He sighed to himself. "And small."

I nodded. "I know. It feels different because the physical threat isn't there. But the emotional damage is the same."

The corners of his mouth twitched. "Are we already practicing for closing arguments?"

I glared at him. "No." He widened his eyes and mock glared back. I folded my arms. "Okay, maybe. But that doesn't mean it's not true."

"Hey, I'm cool. Practice all you want." Alex stared at the jail building again, a searching look on his face. "Do you really think Tiegan was planning to have Cassie move in with her? That's just crazy. What were they going to do? Say they were sisters?"

"I don't know." It seemed crazy to me, too. "But that doesn't mean it can't be true. Mary Kay Letourneau moved in with her eighth grader."

Alex rolled his eyes. "That one was just a bridge too far for me. Thirteen years old. That woman was *loca*. And they had babies? Please. I get that some teenagers can look pretty grown up—especially when they get to be sixteen or seventeen. But I just don't know how you get past the fact that you can't talk to them." He gave me a frank look. "Speaking strictly for teenage boys, they're all idiots."

That pretty much fit my memory of them. Then again, I'd never dated anyone less than twenty years old—even when I was fourteen. "Well, in the name of full disclosure, teenage girls aren't exactly material for the Algonquin Round Table, either." I was ready to shift gears and talk about the murders. I'd had enough pedophile talk for one day. "You have the crime-scene photos?"

"Yeah." Alex pulled up the photos on his iPad and put it between us so I could see. "Looks to me like her story fits."

I'd known it would fit. I'd just wanted to look for places where Tiegan's prints might show up. I pulled out my cell and tapped the phone number for Emmons, hoping I'd be able to deal with him instead of Rusty Templeton. The call went to his voice mail. I couldn't leave a message. Technically, what I was about to do was a little unethical. I wasn't allowed to divulge what Cassie had told me. But if I just "helped" the investigation along with a little—okay, a big—tip, without saying where I got the information, I wouldn't exactly be *violating* the privilege. Just bending the corners a little. "Let's head over to PAB." Maybe Emmons was around and just hadn't heard his phone.

Alex pulled out of the parking lot. "Do you buy Cassie's story?"

"I don't know." I don't buy much of anything my clients say until I see some corroborating evidence. Especially clients who'd already lied to me once before. And it didn't matter. It wasn't my job to believe. It was my job to make the jury believe. "Let me put it this way: I think it's buy*able*."

But a lot depended on whether there was any physical evidence to back it up. Without that, it'd just be a "she said, she said," a credibility contest—which really translates to a popularity contest. If it came down to that, I liked Cassie's chances. Who's the jury going to believe? The poor orphan kid? Or the predatory pedophile? But juries are strange, unpredictable beasts. You can never be sure whose ox they'll gore.

What I did know was that now, I stood a real chance of winning this case. Not just getting a lesser conviction for manslaughter, but an actual acquittal.

When we got to the PAB, I asked the officer at the reception desk for Detectives Emmons and Templeton. I chanted to myself, "Let it be Emmons, let it be Emmons, let it be . . ."

So of course, Detective Rusty Templeton stepped out of the elevator.

"Detective Templeton, it's a pleasure." Alex wisely took the lead.

I nodded to him. "Hey, Rusty."

He gave us a look that managed to be both weary and suspicious. "Don't tell me, let me guess: you've got more leads for me. Pardon me if I don't break out the bubbly. Your last lead's still threatening to sue me."

I'd heard that Danny was pretty worked up about getting arrested "just for standing on a goddamn sidewalk." I shrugged. "He looked good for it at the time. And you should thank me. Hauling in suspects helps the image. Makes you look like you're actually doing your job."

Rusty looked like he wanted to take a swing at me. I kind of hoped he would. I could use the money. But Alex, the killjoy, stepped in close and distracted him. "We just wanted to suggest you run someone's prints. I assume you have some unidentified strays?"

Rusty stared at Alex and spoke with a mouthful of sarcasm. "Nope, not a one."

I couldn't stand it; I had to take a shot. "Come on, Rusty. This one's so easy, even you can do it. Run Tiegan Donner. She's a teacher; her prints are on file."

Rusty gave me an incredulous look. "Are you friggin' kidding me? That hot little English teacher?" He gave a loud bark of a laugh. "And so what if we do find her prints? She's probably been there to meet with the mother. That girl had to be one helluva problem child." Rusty snickered. "I've heard of some desperate moves, but this one beats all. I'm gonna post it on our idiot page."

"Otherwise known as your Facebook page?" He drilled me with an ugly glare. "Let me just warn you: if you don't run her prints, I'll dance you all over the courtroom with it. I'll wrap it around your neck so tight, the jury will have you swinging from it. So by all means, don't run her prints. Then get ready to hear 'Not guilty' on the biggest no-brainer you ever mangled."

Rusty's face got so red I thought his head was going to blast off his shoulders. He leaned in and spoke in a low voice. "Better drive carefully, Counselor." He turned and clomped over to the elevators.

I called out, "They say it's better for your heart if you take the stairs." He ignored me.

Alex gave me an exasperated look. When we got to the parking lot, he asked, "Why do you have to get into it with him?"

"Fish gotta swim, birds gotta fly. I've gotta call a lazy-ass cop a lazy-ass cop." We got into the car. "And if he were smart, he'd have played nice to find out why I was asking him to run Tiegan's prints."

"Would you have told him?"

"Of course not." But I did need to tell him where to look for her prints. I'd text Dale a list of the places I'd noted during Cassie's story and tell him to take credit for the ideas. If Rusty Templeton knew that list had come from me, he'd wipe his ass with it.

Alex gave me a look out of the corner of his eye. "Where am I going?"

"Atwater."

Alex made a U-turn and steered us toward the freeway. "Who're we going to see?"

"Not who. What." I gave him Tiegan's address.

Luckily, Tiegan's apartment building had open carports that were visible from the alley. I told Alex to drive slow. I'd noticed the car Tiegan drove when we'd met for drinks at Firefly. The memory reminded me of how she'd played me—and it pissed me off all over again.

I pointed to the blue Toyota Corolla. "Pull up next to that one." I got out, looked around to make sure no one was watching, then took photos from every angle. When I got back in, I told him to drive to the crime scene. "If we're lucky, someone around the neighborhood will remember seeing the car that night."

Alex gave me a weary look. "But we already canvassed that 'hood. Everyone we talked to said they didn't see a thing."

"No. They said they didn't see a *person*." I did a mental review of the people we'd spoken to. I wasn't crazy about more hours of door knocking, either. "Let's start with that retired Loomis guard. He'll come through . . ."

Phillip Bryer shook his head. "'Fraid I can't help you there. I'm never up past ten o'clock anymore." He sighed. "Used to really tear it up, going to clubs, parties, and whatnot. Now I'm lucky if I can make it to one bowling night a week."

So much for Phil.

We moved on. Over the next hour and a half, we hit twelve houses. We got no answer at four of them, and the folks at the other eight houses either hadn't been awake or hadn't seen anything.

When we got to the thirteenth house, we could hear the music from the sidewalk. Fast, heavy bass, head-banging metal. I couldn't place the band. When a young male answered the door, the music washed over us like a tidal wave and flowed down the street.

And he was a sight to behold. I'd never seen so many piercings on one person. Earrings ran up and around the perimeter of both ears, he had a ring in his nose as well as studs in both nostrils, his eyebrows were lined with tiny rings from one end to the other, and when he spoke, I saw that his tongue was pierced with a giant stud. Under his thin black T-shirt, which featured—what else?—a skull with piercings, I saw that he also had nipple rings. The man scored an A for consistency, I'd give him that.

He glanced at Alex, then at me. "Whaddaya need?"

His tongue slithered over the giant stud and made his speech sound like he was licking a melting Popsicle. I doubted he could hear much over the cacophony coming from his stereo, but I gamely introduced us and said we wanted to ask him a couple of question about the murders.

He said, "What?" I repeated it all again. He said, "You want me to do *what?*"

I couldn't take it anymore. I gestured for him to step outside or turn down the music. He thought about his choices for a few seconds. As he mulled it over, I thought that maybe I should let this one go. But finally, he told us to wait and left us standing on the doorstep. A few seconds later, the music got lower. Now it was just deafening. He motioned for us to come in, and we entered a very tame, standard-looking living room with the usual sofa, coffee table, and twin chairs. This was clearly his parents' place. He sat on one of the chairs, so Alex and I opted for the sofa. I ran through my spiel again, then said, "We just want to show you some photos of a car to see if you recognize it. Okay?"

He shrugged. "Yeah, sure."

I held out three photos showing different angles of Tiegan's car. He tilted his head from one side to another, pondered each one for longer than I've taken to decide who to sleep with, then gave a solemn nod. I didn't know what it meant. "Does this car look familiar to you?"

"Most definitely." A little bit of drool leaked out of the side of his mouth.

I tried not to look at the drool. "When did you see it?"

"That night. When the murders happened. I was playing *World of Warcraft* with a friend, and I went out to the garage to get a beer."

Do you remember what time it was?"

He slurped back the nascent drool and tried to furrow his brow—as much as his pierced eyebrows would allow. "Around one? Something like that. I remember because it was parked almost directly across the street, and I'd never seen it around here before."

Which put the car half a block down from the Sonnenbergs' house, on the opposite side of the street. Perfect. Tiegan wouldn't have wanted to leave her car any closer.

I didn't know whether to cheer or bang my head on the wall. We'd finally found a witness who could ID the car. And he was . . . this.

"Thank you so much. You've been extremely helpful. Can I get your name?" I knew it was going to be something exotic, like Eoghan or Zayn.

"Stewart. Stewart Smith."

The name sloshed all over his mouth before it managed to come out. No. Just, no. I bit down on my lower lip to keep from laughing and got his phone number as well.

Alex thanked him again, and we let him get back to his music. Which started to blast the moment we left the doorstep. When we got far enough away, we couldn't take it anymore and had to stop. I laughed so hard I got a stitch in my side, and Alex had tears rolling down his cheeks. It was probably as much from stress as it was from the comic relief of Stewart, the human pincushion.

When we recovered and caught our breath, I sighed. "Well, we finally got us a witness. Such as he is."

Alex looked back at Stewart's house. "I do believe him, though."

I nodded. "Me, too. I think he's solid. I just don't know what a jury will make of him."

Alex looked glum. "Then I guess we move on?"

I nodded. "Sorry, but yes. We move on."

FORTY-SEVEN

I pointed across the street to the area where Stewart had said he'd seen the car. "Let's hit that side."

We started at the house closest to the spot Stewart had identified. The older woman who answered the door said she'd been out of town visiting her son and his family in Colorado Springs the night of the murders. She looked at us with a puzzled expression. "Isn't the case solved? The daughter confessed, I thought." I said there were still some outstanding questions. She looked skeptical. But I wasn't about to take the time to explain. We had a lot of ground to cover before it got too late to knock on doors. I thanked her, and we moved on.

The occupants of the next two houses had been home, but no one had seen any strange cars in the area. At the third house, a young mother with long blonde hair answered the door, a towheaded baby on her hip. She frowned when she saw us on her doorstep. "I'm not buying anything."

She started to close the door. Alex flashed his trademark smile. "We're not selling anything. We just need a moment to talk to you about—"

"I'm not joining your church, either." She started to close the door again.

I held up a hand and talked fast. "Wait! We're not thumping any bibles. It's about the murders. We just have a couple of questions—"

She gave us an angry look. "And I don't talk to reporters!" *Slam!*

I took a step back. "I don't think I've ever had a door slammed that hard in my face before." Inside, I heard the baby start to cry.

We headed back to the sidewalk and moved down to the next house. "Have I told you how much I love this part of the job?" Alex asked, his tone sarcastic.

"I'm very glad to hear that, because we've got about twenty more houses to hit tonight."

Alex muttered under his breath as he rang the doorbell. This time, a boy no older than nine answered the door. He was wearing a dirt-smeared Little League uniform and socks, but no shoes, and he was chewing on a hunk of multigrain bread. A healthy choice. Maybe that was a good omen.

I smiled at him. "Hey, slugger. Is your mom or dad at home?" I didn't think he'd have been up late enough to see Tiegan's car, but I wasn't above asking him if no one else in the house panned out.

He stared at us for a moment, then, still facing us, he yelled over his shoulder. "Mom! Some lady and some guy want to talk to you!" He waited one second, then bellowed over his shoulder again. "Mom!"

The front door opened straight into the living room, and I could see that there was a tall glass of milk, now half gone, on the coffee table, and a pair of baseball cleats underneath it. The television was playing a *Futurama* cartoon. I deduced that the boy was currently the sole occupant of the living room. "If your dad's here, we could talk to him until your mom's ready."

The boy shook his head. "Dad's not home yet." He aimed his mouth over his shoulder. "Mom!" He took another bite of his hunk of bread and chewed as he looked from me to Alex and back again.

Finally, a pleasant-faced—but harried-looking—woman rushed to the door, pulling off a pair of rubber kitchen gloves. "I'm sorry, what can I do for you? Are you collecting for something?"

I shook my head and told the white lie we'd used before. I wasn't in the mood for any more door-slamming tonight. "We're helping with the Sonnenberg investigation, and we just wanted to show you a photograph."

She brushed her dark-brown hair off her face with the back of her hand and gave a disappointed sigh. "Oh, well, don't bother. I didn't see anyone." She shook her head. "I still can't believe that little girl did it."

It was too soon to start trumpeting the possibility that the little girl hadn't done it. "We're just asking about a car. Can I show you a photo?"

She looked a little uncertain. "I'm not really good at cars."

"That's okay. Just take your best shot." I showed her the photo. "Did you happen to see a car that looked like this on the block that night?"

She leaned closer and frowned at it. After a moment, her face showed mild surprise. "Actually, I think I did. I got home around one a.m. that night, and I believe I saw it heading in the opposite direction."

I asked whether she knew where the Sonnenbergs lived. She said she did. "Was it heading toward their house? Or away?"

"Toward their house. I remember noticing it because I'm usually the only one driving at that hour. It's a pretty quiet neighborhood."

I couldn't believe it. A normal person *and* a great witness? We were on some kind of streak. But I had to make sure she was kosher. "I hope you don't mind my asking, but had you been out to dinner or something?" If she'd been out drinking, it'd dent her credibility.

She rolled her eyes. "I wish. No, I'm a nurse. I was just getting home from work."

Booyah. Right in the middle of the ten ring. Just to see whether I could beat the odds to a pulp, I asked about her husband. But he'd been out of town.

I got her name—Allison Swanson—and all her contact information. "Allison, you've been a tremendous help. I so appreciate this." I told her I'd give her statement to the detectives and that they'd call her right away. I gave her my most ingratiating smile. "And if you wouldn't mind, when they call you, could you maybe put in a good word for me? It'd really help my chances in the department."

"I'd be glad to. Always happy to help a woman in a man's world. What's your name?"

"Samantha. Samantha Brinkman. Thank you so much." I couldn't resist the chance to give Rusty my one-finger salute.

We told her to have a great rest of the night, and she told us to do the same.

When we reached the sidewalk, Alex raised his hand for a high five. I shook my head. "You know I hate those."

He dropped his hand down by his waist, palm up. "How about now? Come on, even you can't miss that."

"Fine." I dropped the back of my hand into his palm.

But I wasn't going to shove these witness statements in Rusty Templeton's face just yet. They were a great start, but by no means were they proof positive that Tiegan had been in the house that night. A blue Toyota Corolla isn't exactly a unique car. And even if it were hers, we still needed proof that she'd been inside the house—and in Abel's room—that night.

The prints would be the real deciding factor—assuming Tiegan hadn't been in the house at some point before that night. And the location where the prints showed up would be key. It'd be one thing if her prints showed up on the coffee table in the living room. But it'd be quite another if Tiegan's prints showed up on Cassie's bedroom window—or in Abel's room.

For now, we'd just have to wait and hope the cops did their job and ran her prints. I had a good feeling about that. The threat of getting reamed on the witness stand can be a great motivator. And in Rusty's case, I had a feeling he'd had some very up close and personal experience to draw on. He'd do the print run. I just needed to make sure I got the results sooner rather than later so I could start planning my next move.

But we were riding high after scoring Allison Swanson. Even Stewart would come off well when we paired his testimony with hers. So I was in great spirits as we headed back to the car.

Unfortunately, I made the mistake of checking my cell phone for messages. Michelle had left three urgent voice mails: "Sam, you need to call me." That was at five p.m. "Sam, please call back right now." That was at five thirty. "Sam! Where the hell are you? Call me!" That was at six. I looked at the screen. It was almost eight.

I called her on her cell. When she answered, I said, "You'd better not still be at the office—"

"I'm definitely not. The Orozcos were all over me. They called four times asking where you were."

What the . . . ? My chest tightened. I'd just given them one hell of a gift—a chance to get some payback they'd been wanting for a long time. Granted, it wasn't the payback for Ricardo's death, but still. It should've bought me a lot more time than this. On a scale of one to ten—ten being the worst news possible—this was a twenty-seven. "What'd you tell them?"

"That you'd be back any minute. 'Cause, you know, that's what I was led to believe."

I had to get rid of those jackals once and for all. "Do they want to come in?"

"No, they're *coming* in. Tomorrow morning, first thing. I plan to come in at noon."

Damn it. "Okay. Sorry, Michy. Come in whenever you want. I'll be there by seven thirty—"

"Make sure Alex is with you. Or Dale."

I promised her I would and ended the call. I told Alex about our new game plan for tomorrow.

Alex didn't seem at all perturbed. "Well, I do have a hot lead. I'll work on it some more tonight. If I'm right, if that custody bus driver does have a cousin who's a Sunnydale Creeper, we might just have our man."

Something must've happened to make the Orozcos turn like this. They'd left my office happy after our last visit—as well they should have. Anxiety spread through my body like a thousand tiny knives. Even my hair hurt. I was out of time. There was no more *mañana*. I had to find a way to deal with this right now. In the meantime, I needed to pull Alex back. "Yeah, well, until we know for sure he's our man, I can't give his name to those piranhas."

"Understood. But you can tell them you're making real progress."

Except I'd already done that song and dance for them. I spent the rest of the evening trying to come up with variations on that theme that would sound different enough to back them off.

By the time I unlocked the office the next morning, the best I'd been able to come up with was a vague reference to a deputy who worked in transpo who might be connected to the Creepers. But I couldn't give them any specifics. Which meant I was in for big trouble. They wanted a head to roll. Now.

Alex made a point of opening the door when they buzzed. I made a point of keeping my left hand just above the open drawer that held my fully loaded Smith and Wesson. When they walked into my office, I stayed seated so I wouldn't have to move that hand.

They didn't even bother with hello. Ernesto lowered his solid frame into the chair in front of my desk, his eyes cold and hard. Arturo remained standing behind his father, his arms crossed over his chest, his hands tucked under his armpits. Fury swirled in the air around him as he fixed me with a stare that could melt iron. He took the lead. "We been talkin' to someone who knows the clerk in that courtroom."

I thought my heart was going to burst through my chest. I did my best to stay cool. "Okay. So?"

Arturo narrowed his eyes at me. "So the clerk says you were over by the bailiff's desk that day."

I forced a patient sigh. "Arturo, the bailiff's desk is two feet from where I sit at counsel table. I'm always over by the bailiff's desk."

He took that in for a moment, but his expression didn't change. "She said you wasn't sitting. You was standin'."

I met his gaze, but it was so fiery, I had to let my eyes go out of focus to hold it. "I always have to stand when my client enters a guilty plea." I shifted my gaze to Ernesto. He was as close as I could get to a reasonable mind. "Are you seriously accusing me of getting Ricardo killed? I'm the one who got him the sweetheart deal."

Ernesto stared at me for a long, very uncomfortable moment as I forced my eyes to stay on his. He finally gave a very small nod. "What you say makes sense. But we don't know if maybe Ricardo hurt a person you care about. When it is personal, business is not so important."

I could answer this one truthfully. "Ricardo never did anything to me or anyone I know. Now, if we're through with this . . . unfortunate mistake, I can give you an update." I looked from Ernesto to Arturo. The latter threw out one last hair-burning glare, then gave me a curt nod. "There may be someone in transpo who has a cousin in the Creepers." I fluffed it out a little but declined to give them any specifics.

When I finished, Ernesto stretched his neck. It gave an audible *crack*. "Then we should have a final answer very soon." He stood up.

It wasn't a question. It was an order. No answer required. But I nodded anyway, a lame effort to save a little face. I waited for them to move toward the door before standing and following them out. Alex, my guardian angel, was in the reception area. He watched them closely as he escorted them out. When he'd closed the door behind them, he said, "That was intense."

"You heard them!"

He nodded. "I was standing right there." He pointed to the wall just outside the door to my office. "They're getting crazier by the minute. If you don't mind, I'm going to stay on this full time until I have an answer for them. Whoever I land on, you'd better make sure the guy gets protection from the cops before you say anything to the Orozcos. He won't last twenty-four hours."

"Absolutely."

I went back to my office and flopped on the couch to catch my breath. I was out of time and out of options. I had only one hope of getting out of this alive.

I reached for my cell phone.

FORTY-EIGHT

It was almost seven thirty by the time Dale got to my apartment. When I'd invited him to dinner last night, we'd agreed on seven o'clock. He was apologetic. "Sorry. The traffic was—"

I waved him off and stepped back to let him in. "Horrible. I know, there's no good time to drive anymore. What're you drinking?"

"I'll take a shot of tequila on the rocks if you have it."

"As a matter of fact, that's what I'm having. I'm throwing steaks under the broiler, and I picked up a Caesar salad and mashed potatoes. Sound good?"

"Sounds perfect."

I nodded toward the couch in the living room. "Go sit down, I'll be right there."

I'd tuned the television to a music station that played a relaxing blend of soft rock and pop, and now I poured him a triple shot of Patrón Silver with as little ice as I could get away with. I needed him to be in a pliant mood. As I came in with our drinks, I saw that Dale was looking out at the view through the sliding glass doors. It was a clear night, thanks to the wind that'd kicked up again that afternoon, and the stars sparkled like flecks of silver in the night sky.

I handed Dale his glass, and we clinked and said, "Cheers." I sat down in the chair across from him and tried to act casual. But judging by the way he was studying me, I could see I wasn't fooling him. I'd just decided to get down to business and tell him why I'd asked him over when he set down his drink and said, "Did you get a nice thank-you note from the Orozcos?"

I tried to keep the shock off my face. How the hell had he figured it out? I put on a puzzled look. "What do you mean?"

Dale tilted his head, his eyes still on mine. "Are you really going to make me spell it out? I was hoping you'd show a little faith."

Now a sliver of anger pierced my facade. He was the last person who should be talking to me about honesty. "You mean, the way you trusted me with Jenny Knox?"

Jenny Knox was a prostitute who'd threatened Dale's teenage daughter, Lisa, nearly two years ago. Dale had snapped and killed her. The murder had gone unsolved until it'd surfaced during his trial. Dale swore he didn't do it, but Alex found damning evidence that proved otherwise. I'd kept the information to myself to see whether Dale would come to me with the truth. But he'd kept the lie going for quite a while—right up until he'd realized that we had no chance at a relationship if he didn't come clean.

Now he was turning the tables on me, letting me know that he was onto me—and demanding that I tell him the truth. I got his point. Fair is fair. I'd demanded honesty from him, and now he wanted the same from me. But I'd never told anyone about my . . . extracurricular activities, and I didn't like the idea of starting now. I wasn't worried that he'd bust me. I'd covered my tracks well. I just really didn't like having my hand forced this way.

Dale had been watching me carefully. Now he took a page from my book. "Look, Sam, if we're going to be in each other's lives . . ."

My exact words to him after he'd finally confessed to killing Jenny. And now I got the full picture. Dale had surmised this wasn't just a social call, that I needed his help. The quid pro quo was clear: if I wanted his help, I'd have to give him the whole truth. The problem was, if I pulled this thread, Dale might be able to unspool everything else.

And even if I found a way to prevent that, once I told him what I'd done, would he still want to be a part of my life? Dale was the closest thing to a real parent I'd ever had. Even though I still couldn't bring myself to think of him as "Dad," the connection had—surprisingly—come to mean something to me. I hadn't realized that until just this moment.

Dale spoke again. "Let me help you with this: I found out Alex was digging into the background of one of the missing deportees."

That told me I really had no decision to make. If Dale knew that, then he knew it all. "How?"

Dale's tone was ironic. "By accident. I'd called to give Alex some information on that custody bus driver whose cousin belonged to the Southside Creepers, and we got to talking." Dale swept a hand toward me. "Your turn."

I took a deep breath, then exhaled. "That missing deportee was a cousin of the Orozcos—Arminta Juarez. I recognized the name because Ricardo had mentioned her to me during one of our interviews. She'd just disappeared at the time, and the police investigation wasn't turning up any answers—which gave him yet another reason to hate *los puercos*. You guys." Dale nodded. "So when I saw her name on the list of missing deportees, I realized I could buy myself some time with the Orozcos and take care of our Hausch problem in one fell swoop. So I told the Orozcos that Hausch was the one who'd sold her to the MS-13." I'd expected that would generate enough gratitude to buy me at least another couple of months. And it probably would have if that damn clerk hadn't opened her mouth.

Dale didn't seem particularly surprised. "So who'd you use for security when you met with Hausch? Orozco's gang? The Grape Street

Boyz?" I nodded. Dale looked me in the eye. "You cut me out so you could use the Orozcos to take care of Hausch *your* way."

I returned his gaze with a defiant look. "With Santiago in the wind, we'd never have gotten Hausch convicted."

Dale's expression hardened, but he didn't argue. He couldn't; he knew that was true. He stared down at his drink for a moment. When he looked up, he asked, "Did Hausch pay up?" I nodded. "What'd you do with the money?"

This was it. This was where I had to tie a knot or the whole story would unravel, and I'd have to tell him about Deshawn and the dope I'd taken from him and . . . I came up with a fast lie. "I gave it to the Orozcos." I watched Dale absorb it all. Would he understand why I'd done it? He had to see the poetic justice of nailing Hausch that way: live by the gangbangers, die by the gangbangers.

Dale sat back and sipped his drink, then lowered his glass to his lap and searched my face. "How are you feeling about it?"

That wasn't the reaction I'd expected. I was confused. "About what? Giving them the money?"

Dale looked into my eyes. "No."

What did he want me to say? That I felt bad about setting up an asshole who'd fried ten people, had another one murdered—and who'd probably disappeared countless others? Fuck that. I wasn't sorry, and I wasn't going to put on some weepy act to please him. Besides, it's not like I did it myself. "I didn't pull the trigger, Dale. I just gave the Orozcos the opportunity to do it. It was their choice to make."

Dale gave me another searching look, then took a slug of his drink and stared out at the view through the sliding glass door. I held my breath as I waited for him to speak. Was he going to help me? Or was he going to cut me out of his life? I wanted to tell him he was no better than me, that I knew he thought what'd happened with Jenny Knox was different—but he was wrong. Killing her might've been impulsive, but the cover-up, the denials, weren't. No, Dale was a lot like me. And

I had a feeling he'd kept many more secrets than Jenny Knox. But I didn't think he was ready to hear any of that. It'd just make him pull away—maybe for good. So I said nothing and tried to act calm as I waited for his decision.

Finally, he turned back to me. I looked into his eyes. "And?"

Dale leaned forward, his elbows on his knees. "What do you need?"

He was in. I held on to my cool and tried not to let him see me exhale. I took a full, deep breath as my stomach unclenched. "The Orozcos are starting to lose their minds. Now they're pointing the finger at me, claiming the clerk said she saw me near the bailiff's desk. I either have to find out who did it or give them a believable fall guy."

Dale's expression darkened. "And if you don't?"

I tried to keep my tone even. "They'll kill me."

Dale ran a hand over his face, then put down his drink and gazed into my eyes. "Tell me the truth, Sam. Were you the one who messed with that custody list?"

I'd known that was coming, and I was ready. I'd decided ahead of time that this was a bridge I was not about to cross—at least, not tonight. But lying—especially to a practiced lie detector like Dale—is an art. The trick is to keep it tight and not embellish. And outrage wouldn't fly either, especially since I'd just admitted to setting up Hausch. So I didn't get angry or self-righteous. When I spoke, my voice was firm but calm. "No. I'm not sorry he's dead. But no, I didn't do it." I fixed Dale with a steady gaze, knowing everything hinged on selling the lie. If he didn't buy it, it could turn him against me forever. But there was only so much honesty I could stand. I'd hit my limit.

Dale watched me closely for a long moment, then stared down at his drink. I couldn't tell whether he believed me or not. When he finally looked up at me, he said, "You know whoever you name is a dead man, so if you're asking me to set up an innocent guy for this—"

I raised a hand to cut him off. "No, absolutely not. I have a plan."

FORTY-NINE

I had to be in court downtown by eight o'clock the next morning. Judge Franks likes to put in a full day, and he hates—I mean five-hundred-dollar-fine hates—when lawyers are late. I dreamed of the day I'd be rich enough to come in late on purpose, just so I could show him I didn't give a shit. But that day was not today. I was on the road by seven.

I still wished I hadn't had to tell Dale how I'd set up Hausch. I knew it'd rocked him. Or maybe it was the fact that I couldn't make myself say I was sorry. Maybe I should have tried. But then again, if I was going to be honest, shouldn't I let him see who I *really* was? Otherwise, what was the point? I sighed. It was useless—and way too late—to worry about that now. There was no way to know how this would play out. I'd just have to wait and see.

All I had in Judge Franks's court was a trial setting on my torture murder case. The DA wasn't making any offers, and it didn't matter if he were, because my client was adamant that he hadn't "tortured" anyone. Killed the guy, sure. Tortured, no. Whatever. All we had to do was pick a date. Such a simple thing, right? But the custody bus was late—one of the inmates in lockup had vomited, and they had to clean it up before they could spare the manpower to bring out the defendant whose case was before mine. And then that attorney argued endlessly—and use-lessly—that his client, a serial rapist, deserved to get bail. I pressed my hands together and imagined them wrapped around the lawyer's neck.

It took a friggin' hour, which of course made me late to my next appearance, because I always stack them up for maximum efficiency. But that always puts me on the horns of a dilemma because efficiency and courtroom management are oil and water.

I'd intended to go see Cassie after I was done in court, but a bailiff told me Twin Towers was on lockdown. Some inmate had been stabbed. That meant no visitors would be allowed until it was lifted. I got them to let me have a confidential call with her instead.

By the time I'd finished, I was ready for a drink. And it wasn't even lunchtime. I was on my way to the elevators when my cell phone buzzed. No name, but I recognized the number. It was either Rusty Templeton, in which case he was calling to gloat that none of the stray prints in the house matched Tiegan's, or it was Westin Emmons. If it was the latter, the call could go either way. My hands instantly got clammy. This was it. I answered the phone. "It's Sam."

"Hey, it's Emmons. Can I meet you somewhere? I've got some questions and answers for you, and I don't want to do it on the phone."

I told him to meet me in the courthouse cafeteria. "I'll be on the far left end, near the window."

"Be there in ten." Emmons ended the call.

I was anxious as I headed downstairs. If the print run put Tiegan in Abel's bedroom, I stood a chance of walking Cassie out the door. But if not . . . I didn't know that Cassie could sell a jury on Tiegan's guilt. She'd changed her story so many times.

After viewing the culinary offerings in the cafeteria, I decided on a cup of coffee and a bag of Doritos, then found a relatively isolated table next to the windows.

Three minutes later, Emmons strode in and scanned the room. I waved to him, and he nodded as he moved toward my table. He must've run out the door the moment we ended the call. I watched him weave through the growing lunch crowd like a running back—if the running back were built like Fred Astaire. He seemed like the type who ran track in high school or college.

When he got to my table, I saw what the case—and probably working with Rusty Templeton—had done to him. His eyes were bloodshot, the corners of his mouth sagged, and the furrows between his eyes—or as the Botox babes call them, his "11s"—had deepened. I even thought I saw more salt than pepper in his hair now.

He took in my chips and coffee. "That it?" I nodded. "Mind if I grab a bite?"

I wanted to seize him by the throat and make him tell me what came out of the print run, but just on principle, I didn't want to let him see me sweat. I glanced at the row of steaming trays. "I don't if you don't."

He gave me a quizzical look and floated over to the food counters. I watched him scan the steaming trays and tried not to laugh as he finished the circuit with his plate still empty. Even from where I sat, I could see the pained expression on his face. He came back carrying a bottle of water and a plastic-wrapped turkey and Swiss sandwich. "This has got to be safe, right?"

I lifted my hands and shrugged. "Your call. *Bon appétit*, brave warrior."

"Tell my kids I went down in the line of duty." Emmons unwrapped his prize with a wary expression. "We got the print run back."

My heart gave a hard thump. "And?"

He opened his bottle of water. "We've got Tiegan's prints at the doorway to Abel's room." He took a bite of his sandwich.

This case had just turned into a winner. I suppressed the urge to yell and do a fist pump. "What about on Cassie's window?"

He shook his head as he swallowed. "We couldn't lift any latents off the window. Too wet."

That's right. It'd been raining that night. "I've got something else for you—"

He took a swig of water and gave me a knowing look. "We already spoke to Allison Swanson. She gave you a glowing report."

I'd forgotten that I told her to do that. Just another fun "in your face" prezzie for good old Rusty. I gave a short laugh. "Did Rusty tell her he was giving me a promotion?"

Emmons pressed his lips together, but the corners of his mouth turned up. "Uh, something like that."

"I have another witness who identified her car, too." I gave Emmons the contact information for Stewart Smith. "You going to get a search warrant now?"

Emmons took another bite of his sandwich. When he'd swallowed, he said, "That's what I wanted to ask you about. I can make the logical guesses about what we want to seize, but I'd like to know if there's anything we should look for that's off the beaten path. I promise, whatever you tell me goes no further. I just want to get it right."

I smirked. "So now I'm . . . what? Your CI?"

He took a long gulp of water. "Not even. We would've had to talk for that to be true." He looked me in the eye. "And we never did."

I scanned the cafeteria, which was now packed, complete with lines of unsuspecting victims at the food trays. The likelihood that any of those poor souls would remember seeing me with Emmons—assuming they survived—was probably nil. "First, promise me you'll keep me in the loop and tell me what you find."

He raised two fingers. "Scout's honor."

I supposed that'd do. "I doubt I'll be able to tell you anything you wouldn't have thought of. But check Tiegan's car for blood. It's possible the murder weapon was there, though I'd be surprised if you found it now."

Emmons nodded and spoke around another mouthful of sandwich. "You never know. It's on the list."

I tossed out a few more ideas before I got to the most important part—the part Cassie had just given me during our confidential phone call, "And get a female cop to check Tiegan's butt for a rose tattoo and a mole on the inside of her upper left thigh." I'd been glad that I'd had to ask Cassie about any "unusual markings" on Tiegan's body over the telephone. Asking a fifteen-year-old to describe the body of her pedophile "girlfriend" wasn't something I'd have enjoyed doing in person.

Emmons had just taken another bite of sandwich. His chewing slowed, and he stared at me. When he swallowed, he started to ask, "Why would we—"

The cops didn't know about Tiegan and Cassie yet. I shook my head. "That I can't tell you. And if you can't justify it now, I'll get a court to order the exam later, so don't sweat it."

Emmons nodded, still looking at me, trying to figure out what I was up to. "If we bust her, we can handle it in the booking search."

Emmons balled up the rest of his sandwich in the plastic wrapper and polished off his bottle of water. I picked up my briefcase. "We good?"

He nodded. "I'll be in touch. We should be hitting her place in about an hour."

As I walked back to my car, I thought about my phone call with Cassie. When I'd asked her about any markings on Tiegan's body, she'd been silent for a long time. She'd asked in a small voice, "Why do you need to know that?" I said I just needed to know everything so I could be prepared for . . . whatever. She'd insisted, "You can't tell anyone about us!"

I'd assured her I wouldn't, but I'd warned her that at some point I might have to. And she was going to have to get onboard. Her life depended on it.

I called Michelle and gave her the good news about Tiegan's prints. She gave a giant "Whoot!" and then told Alex, who called out, "Fantastic!"

When I got in to the office, I saw that Alex and Michelle were watching something on her computer. Michelle waved me over. "Check it out. More Cassie love from another victim advocate group."

I watched over her shoulder. It was one of those daytime talk shows. A young woman in a smart business suit was telling the host, Tyra Banks, about the lifelong impact of childhood sexual abuse. "People don't realize how it stays with you forever. It's been fifteen years since my uncle molested me, and he only stayed with us for a few months, but I'm still not over it. So imagine how someone like Cassie suffered, being abused like that for so long."

Tyra's face exuded sympathy as she nodded. "It's impossible to overestimate the damage that can be done to a young person who suffers this kind of abuse. I hope you're getting therapy, because I don't know how you deal with trauma like that on your own."

The woman said she'd been in therapy for three years now. Tyra shook her head. "And yet you still suffer from the aftereffects."

The woman nodded, her expression weary. "Less than before, but yes." The camera zoomed in on her face. "That's why I'm speaking out on behalf of Give Children a Voice and asking that they remember what Cassie Sonnenberg has been through before they pass judgment."

Tyra threw to a commercial, and Michelle hit the mute button. She sat back and stared at the monitor. "You think they'll turn on her when they find out about her and Tiegan?"

Great question. It was one I'd been pondering ever since Cassie told me about the relationship. "You never know. But it could get her even more sympathy."

Alex nodded. "They'll see Cassie as a vulnerable young orphan kid who got preyed on by a pedophile teacher."

I told them the cops were searching Tiegan's car and apartment as we spoke. "We might know something more by tonight."

Michelle leaned back in her chair, her expression troubled. "But one thing's been bothering me. Since Tiegan was obviously there, how come Paula didn't see her?"

I'd thought about that, too. Paula had only accused Cassie. But maybe that was because Cassie was the only one she'd been able to see. "Paula got attacked from behind, and according to the medical reports, she went down fast. I don't think she ever had a chance to see who'd stabbed her."

Alex stood up and pushed the secretary's chair he'd been sitting on back into the corner. "That's right. Didn't Paula admit that the only time she saw Cassie was after she went down?" I nodded. "Then maybe that was when Cassie tried to help her?"

That's the way I saw it. "So both things can be true: Paula did see Cassie, and Cassie was not the killer."

Michelle leaned against her desk. "How's Paula doing now?"

"Last I heard, not too well. But she's still hanging in." I looked at my watch.

Michelle saw me checking the time. "Nervous about the search?" I nodded. "Why? They've got her prints in Abel's room. What more do you need?"

"Tiegan can say those prints got there any time. And even if Paula says Tiegan never visited them at the house, Tiegan can just say Paula wasn't around that day."

Alex frowned. "Then we need more."

I moved toward my office. "Right. So now I plan to go do some serious angsting about that."

Alex followed me into my office to tell me he'd finished putting together the background information and support letters on a burglary case that was due for sentencing next week, then left me to my own devices. I did my best to lose myself in those devices, but I kept darting glances between my desk phone and my cell phone, hoping to hear from Emmons.

I didn't get the call till six thirty. I fumbled with my cell and almost dropped it before I managed to hit answer. I could feel the pulse in my throat. "Tell me."

He spoke in a low voice. "We've got traces of blood in the trunk of her car."

I raised a fist in the air. "Good enough for DNA typing?"

"Don't know yet. But we took Tiegan into custody, and she just went through booking. We found the mole and the rose tattoo. Right where you said they'd be."

FIFTY

During the next seventy hours, the whole case swung around. And Emmons, true to his word, gave me the updates.

The day after Tiegan's arrest, he and Rusty visited Paula. Emmons called me from his car that night. "Tiegan never came to visit them as far as she knew."

"So the prints had to have been from the night of the murders."

"Seems so. I asked her whether it was possible Tiegan was in the room that night. She said no at first, that Cassie was the only one she saw."

"But she got stabbed from behind—"

"Yeah, so I pointed that out, and I asked her whether someone else could've been in the room. She said she didn't think so, but she admitted it was possible. We'll see what the DNA shows."

The following Tuesday, we got the results: the traces of blood in the trunk of Tiegan's car were a mixture of all three: Abel, Stephen, and Paula.

The court appointed a public defender for Tiegan. I'd known Fred Hamer when I was in the public defender's office, and he was good. Very good.

And he gave the lie to the notion that juries love the lookers. Fred had the body of Stick Stickly—he even walked like a stick figure, stiff-legged and jerky—and he had a frizzy brown comb-over that always looked untamed. He had an uneven, ruddy complexion—pale around the eyes and jawline, flaming on his cheeks and nose—and skin so dry the flakes showered the shoulders of his jacket. But he had merry blue eyes, a great sense of humor, and an overall kindness that made juries not only love him but also trust him. If anyone could pull Tiegan's bacon out of the fire, it was Fred.

But Tiegan seemed determined to thwart that effort. The day the DNA results came in, and against Fred's strenuous advice, she'd insisted on talking to the police.

And over Rusty Templeton's vociferous objection, I'd insisted on being there to watch. Emmons knew how to repay a favor; he'd over-ruled Rusty.

I sat in the darkened observation room with Dale and looked through the one-way mirror. Fred was already in the room, a legal pad and pen in front of him on the table. He twirled the pen around and around on the pad, his expression miserable. Even though Tiegan had let Cassie take the fall, I couldn't help but sympathize. Having a client who insisted on putting her head in the noose was every law-yer's nightmare. A few minutes later, a patrol officer brought Tiegan in and sat her down at the table. The orange jumpsuit gave her skin a sallow glow, and the circles under her eyes were so dark she looked as if she'd been in a bar fight. Her blonde hair, always so smoothly styled before, hung in bedraggled, oily clumps. The guard secured her ankle chains to a bolt in the floor and asked her which hand she wrote with. When she held up her right hand, he chained her left hand to the table.

Fred spoke to her gently. "Is there any way I can talk you out of doing this, Tiegan?"

She shook her head. Though her sunken chest and hunched shoulders made her look beaten, I saw defiance in her expression. "I want everyone to know the truth."

Fred opened his mouth to say something, but in that moment, Emmons and Templeton walked in. Emmons greeted Fred, then stated the date and time, listed the parties present, and read Tiegan her rights in a soft voice. Tiegan waived them, looking like someone who was about to step off a cliff.

Emmons sat back. "Since you were the one who asked to talk to us, why don't you go ahead and tell us in your own words what happened that night?"

A smart move, that. It made a record of the fact that Tiegan had been the one to reach out to them and set a laid-back, nonconfrontational tone. I knew Fred wanted to bang his head on the table; there was no way he'd get this statement thrown out.

I sat forward, my face just inches from the window. The cops knew nothing about her affair with Cassie. That meant Tiegan had no way of knowing Cassie had told me about it. Would Tiegan admit it? And what would she say about the blood in the trunk of her car?

Tiegan inhaled deeply through her nose, then closed her eyes as she exhaled. After a moment, she began to talk, her eyes focused on the wall between Emmons and Templeton.

Her voice floated through the speakers, soft but clear. "I didn't kill anyone. Cassie called me that night in a panic. I'd never heard her sound that way. She said something terrible had happened, that I needed to come over right away. I asked her what was wrong, but she didn't answer. She was breathing hard, like she'd been running."

Emmons broke in. "Was she calling you on her house phone or her cell?"

Tiegan paused for a moment, then said, "It wasn't her cell phone. I didn't recognize the number."

I remembered that Cassie had made the call on Abel's phone. Emmons nodded for her to continue. She took a deep breath and then exhaled slowly. "I was scared; I thought . . . a thousand things. Maybe a burglar had broken in or her father had a heart attack. I told her to call the police. She said that would only make things worse. She started to cry, then the line went dead. I didn't know what to do. I was afraid to call the police after hearing that, but I was worried out of my mind. I had to find out what was going on. So I went to her house."

Rusty broke in. "'Scuse me, Tiegan. Just to clarify, you'd never been to her house before, right?" Tiegan shook her head. "How'd you know where to go?"

"I have all my students' contact information on my computer."

He nodded.

A much smoother move than I'd have expected from Rusty. He'd just gotten Tiegan to admit that her prints could only have been left that night. And it was interesting, the way the detectives behaved toward Tiegan. They treated her like a doll made of spun sugar, and their tone was almost apologetic. I'd never seen anything like it before. Even when my clients were cooperating, in fact even when they were helping to clear open cases, I'd never seen detectives be that deferential.

Tiegan was silent for so long, Emmons prompted her. "You went to Cassie's house. How did you get in?"

"I knocked on the front door, but no one answered, and it was locked. I got really freaked. I thought something must've happened to Cassie. I ran around the house, looking for an open door or window. I found one window partly open."

Rusty broke in again. "Was it Cassie's bedroom window?"

The distraction seemed to throw her off. Her eyes darted to him, then away again. "I—I don't know. But it was the kind you push up, and it didn't have a screen." Tiegan started to breathe through her mouth as she relived the events of that night. "I climbed in and called out to her. I heard her say . . . something, I don't remember what. I followed the sound and . . ." Tiegan stopped and shook her head. When she spoke again, her voice was low and ragged. "It was horrible. There was blood everywhere. Cassie was just standing there. Abel . . . Paula . . ." Tiegan dropped her head to her chest and began to cry.

As her weeping filled the room, Fred looked at her with concern. But the detectives seemed poised between skepticism and confusion.

When the sobs began to subside, Emmons spoke. "So it was all over when you got there?" Tiegan wiped her face with her free hand and nodded. "Did Cassie say anything? Tell you why she did it?"

Tiegan looked at him through swollen eyes. "She just said she couldn't take it anymore. But I didn't know what she was talking about."

Rusty asked, "Then she never told you about the molestation?"

She stared down at the table. "No."

"And you would've expected her to?" Emmons leaned back and studied Tiegan.

Tiegan nodded, her expression perplexed. "We talked about every-thing—every argument she had with Abel, even the little dustups with her mother."

Emmons continued to study her for a moment, then he asked in a voice so soft I could barely hear it, "What happened next?"

"I—I know I should've called the police. But all I could think of was that I had to protect Cassie. I told her I'd get rid of the knife. I told her to give me ten minutes and then call the police." Tiegan bit her lip and looked at Emmons. "I know I shouldn't have done that. But you've got to believe me, I didn't kill anyone!"

Emmons nodded, but I could see it wasn't necessarily because he bought her story. He was just placating her. "What did you do with the knife?"

Tiegan exhaled and sank back in her chair. "I put it in the trunk of my car and then threw it down a sewer drain."

"Do you remember where?" Emmons asked, more out of habit, I was sure, than with any real hope of finding it.

Tiegan looked spent. She shook her head. "It was all a blur after I saw the . . . the bodies."

The room fell silent for a long moment. Emmons and Templeton exchanged a look. Templeton said, "Give us just a minute. We'll be right back."

I knew they were going to talk over what she'd said and figure out whether they'd covered everything. I knew they hadn't. I stood up.

Dale looked at me. "Bathroom break?"

"No, I need them to ask her about one more thing."

I hurried out. Dale caught up with me and nodded to the hallway on our right. "This way. I know where they are."

I followed Dale and found the detectives standing together at the end of the hall. "You need to ask her why it was so important to protect Cassie."

Rusty put his hands on his hips and glared at me, then shot a look at Emmons. "I thought you said she'd stay out of our way."

Emmons started to speak, but I moved in closer. "Come on. You've got to be wondering why she didn't just call the cops—"

"No shit, Counselor." Rusty was red in the face. "A blind rhino could see there's something wrong with that story. But if you want to tell us why she covered for the girl, I'm all ears."

I couldn't tell him. All the information about Cassie's involvement with Tiegan was privileged, and there was no way around it this time. I had to back off. "Sorry. Can't help you there."

Rusty gave me a look of disgust. "Then stay out of my way." He turned on his heel and headed back to the interview.

We got back to the observation room just in time to watch the detectives settle in at the table. Rusty sat at an angle, twisted slightly to the left. He led off. "I have a bit of a problem with your story, Tiegan. I don't get why you'd go to all that trouble to protect a girl who'd just killed her whole family." He frowned at her. "It doesn't make sense. Not for a smart lady like you. Not for a good citizen like you. You've never even gotten a speeding ticket."

I heard a faint clinking sound. At first, I couldn't figure out what it was. Then I realized—it was Tiegan's chains. She was shaking like a telephone wire in a windstorm. "I . . . uh, you know she was adopted, right?" Tiegan looked from Emmons to Templeton, then ran a tongue over her lips. "She's had a hard life, and I . . . just couldn't stand the idea of her spending the rest of her life in prison." Tiegan raked her free hand through her hair. "Look, I know I did the wrong thing. I'm admitting that. I should've called the police." She looked from Emmons to Rusty, her expression desperate.

Rusty shifted in his chair to face her squarely. "You want us to believe you, but you're trying to sell us a BS story about why you covered for a girl who just sliced up her whole family. So you need to come clean right now. This is your last chance. Why'd you cover for her?"

Tiegan stared at the wall, looking numb. When she spoke, her voice was thin, as though it were being squeezed through a straw. "Cassie and I . . ." She stopped and swallowed. "We were . . . involved." No one moved. All three men were frozen, as though time had stopped. A faint crackle of static came through the speakers in the observation room.

After a moment, she continued. "I was afraid if she got arrested, she'd tell about our, ah, relationship, and I'd lose my job." Tiegan bent over, as though a lead weight were on her shoulders.

Emmons finally cleared his throat. When he spoke, I detected a darker note in his voice. "How did that . . . come about?"

Tiegan didn't respond at first. Finally, she lifted her head. She stared at the wall between the detectives as she spoke, her voice soft. "Cassie used to stay after class a lot. That was before I became her counselor. At first, we'd just talk about assignments. She always seemed to need me to explain things more than the other students. She'd ask me to repeat my instructions three or four times before she felt like she knew what I wanted."

A sign of insecurity and neediness in my book. But Tiegan made it sound like it was Cassie's way of showing romantic interest. It was a typical pedophile mind-set. I knew the syndrome well. Tiegan continued. "After a month or so, Cassie started to tell me about her life. How she'd been tossed from one foster home to another before the Sonnenbergs adopted her. How she'd always felt like a misfit in the family, how her mother said that she was lucky to have them." Tiegan gave a heavy sigh. "Anyway, a couple of months into the school year, Cassie's counselor went out on leave, and the school asked me to take on some of her students."

Rusty asked, "So that's how you became Cassie's counselor?"

Tiegan finally looked straight at him, and there was a smug note in her voice. "No. Cassie asked me to be her counselor." Her eyes slid back to the space between the detectives. "She started coming to my office every day after school to talk about . . . everything."

Which was why she'd been surprised that Cassie hadn't told her about being molested. I was not so surprised by that. I'd been afraid to tell anyone after my own mother refused to believe me. And I'd completely given up after the police dusted off the housekeeper's report and apologized to Sebastian.

Emmons prompted, "How did that lead to a physical relationship?"

Tiegan tilted her head, and her voice grew so soft I had to strain to hear her. "She was upset at the way her mother always seemed to take Abel's side. I can't remember what the exact issue was that day. I just remember that she was more depressed than usual. We stayed until almost five o'clock, and when I moved toward the door, Cassie reached out to hug me. I—I hugged her back, but then she started to kiss me, and . . ."

After a long pause, Emmons asked, "Was that the first time you'd ever had physical contact?"

Tiegan dropped her gaze to the table. "We—we'd hugged, but nothing like that had ever happened before."

I sat forward, hoping Emmons would ask the questions that lined up like dominoes in my head. The questions that would expose Tiegan for what she was. Surprisingly, it was Rusty Templeton who zeroed in.

He'd shifted back to his diagonal position. It might have been partly for comfort. His bulk didn't fit easily under that metal table. But it might also have been a psychological ploy, a way to seem more relaxed and put Tiegan at ease. Now his tone was light, casual. "Before that day, how'd you help Cassie when she was feeling low? She sounds like a girl with a lot of problems."

Tiegan nodded and gave Rusty a grateful look. "She was. What did I do?" She paused for a moment. "I'd buy her little things to cheer her up. A Betsey Johnson charm bracelet with little skulls on it—she told me she liked Betsey Johnson stuff. A red Swatch. Nothing big. I took her to the movies once, a sci-fi film she wanted to see. Little stuff like that, nothing special."

Actually, it was classic grooming behavior, the way pedophiles inch their way into the victim's life, ingratiating themselves by doing little things like that, taking them places—the park, a restaurant, the movies—and buying them presents. And Tiegan's attitude, implicitly putting the blame on Cassie, making her out to be the aggressor who initiated the whole thing, was classic, too.

As Tiegan talked about her relationship with Cassie, I could feel Dale throwing me sideways glances. I figured he was worried about how I was reacting to Tiegan's story.

But her situation with Cassie was different. Sebastian's behavior had been far more brutal, almost sadistic actually, and it had none of the pretense of being a mutual relationship. And yet, as I thought about it, I had to admit that at base, there was a similarity. An adult in power and a vulnerable child with nowhere to turn—in Cassie's case, because Tiegan was her lifeline.

When they ended the interview, I reached for my purse and noticed that my hands felt slick. I hooked my purse over my shoulder and looked at my palms.

I'd dug my nails into them so hard, I'd drawn blood.

FIFTY-ONE

Tiegan's arrest blasted on every news channel. The media liaison for the police had issued a statement saying that they were "refocusing the investigation" to explore "new leads" that indicated Tiegan may have been "the actual perpetrator" of the murders.

From the very beginning, although Cassie had found champions in some of the child victims support groups, she'd also attracted some vocal antagonists. And lately the opposition had been gaining ground. One spokesperson for the opposition had even called her a "blight on the cause" of child abuse prevention.

Now the Cassie supporters were claiming victory. Their "I told you so" campaign struck me as odd, since they'd backed Cassie as a child who'd cracked under the strain of long-standing abuse and committed homicide because it was her only means of escape. Their logic seemed to be that Cassie's actual innocence—far from proven yet, but I was okay with that particular rush to judgment—was just further proof of her victimhood.

Whatever. If the pretzel logic of those vocal campaigners helped to push up our stock with the jury pool, I wasn't about to quibble.

Right now, the cops were holding her as an accessory after the fact, a crime she'd freely admitted. The substance of Tiegan's statement hadn't come out yet. But if they decided to charge her with the murders, Fred would probably leak as much of her denial as he could without tipping the part about her relationship with Cassie—I knew I sure would if she were my client. Tiegan's story was believable. And Cassie had a pretty strong motive to kill.

Until I could shore up my case, find something that more definitively pointed to Tiegan as the killer, I was glad to keep things quiet.

And I had enough problems with Cassie right now without the pressure of even more public exposure. She'd been enraged when I told her Tiegan had been arrested.

At first she'd stared at me, frozen. Then she'd screamed, "No! What happened?"

I had to bite the bullet. No one but me had any reason to look into Tiegan's possible involvement. "I never told anyone what you said to me. But I told them to check the crime-scene prints against Tiegan's. I had to, Cassie."

Cassie jumped up and screamed. "You promised you wouldn't tell! You promised! And you lied!"

"I'm sorry, Cassie," I said, though I really wasn't. "But I have to do what's best for you."

She started to cry, big, choking sobs. "I hate you!" She slapped the window. "I trusted you! How could you lie to me?"

I saw the guard on my side give a signal. "Cassie, you need to calm down right now—"

She wouldn't listen. "You bitch! You lying bitch!" Her body shook as she stared down at me.

A guard had hurried in and taken the phone out of her hand. He muscled her out of the room.

I hadn't seen her since. I knew she'd forgive me eventually, but the last four times I'd visited, she'd refused to come out.

In light of all that, I'd been very glad to keep the story about Cassie and Tiegan quiet for as long as possible.

Unfortunately, that didn't turn out to be very long at all. The following Monday, just six days after Tiegan's arrest, a former student at Mission Viejo High School came forward to say that she knew Tiegan had seduced Cassie because she, too, had been Tiegan's victim.

Michelle played the girl's media moment for me on the computer. Natalie Borowitz was a less pretty, more butch version of Cassie, with short blonde hair and blue eyes but a heavier brow, a thicker build, and a tougher demeanor. She stood at the podium next to her fawning, press-hungry lawyer and read from a prepared speech in a bitter, angry voice. "Like Cassie Sonnenberg, I, too, am Tiegan Donner's victim. I, too, was an inexperienced young girl who was flattered that this pretty, popular teacher took an interest in me. And I, too, was pressured into a relationship I was afraid to reject, because Tiegan occupied a position of power and trust, and I was just a student."

Obviously, the lawyer had written that clunky speech. And her outrage somehow didn't ring true. "Let me guess: she's suing the school."

Michelle nodded. "Figures, doesn't it? But if Tiegan really did come on to her, the girl has a right to be compensated. Doesn't she?"

"Sure. I'm just not a hundred percent this one's going to be able to collect."

I told Michelle that the principal at Mission Viejo had said Tiegan left the school because a student had been stalking her. If that was true and Natalie was that stalker, it'd be a messy lawsuit with lots of finger pointing about who the real victim was.

It took just one day to find out I was right; Natalie was the stalker. The kids who'd known about her "affair" with Tiegan came forward to say that when Tiegan tried to break it off, Natalie went off the deep end. She'd left messages on Tiegan's phone threatening to kill herself, put angry letters in Tiegan's mailbox, followed Tiegan home, and parked in front of her house for hours at a time. And just in case anyone thought it was Tiegan's fault that she'd tipped over into stalker land, one of Natalie's former girlfriends said that when she and Natalie had broken up, Natalie had done the same thing to her.

And now, predictably, reporters and commentators were speculating that Tiegan and Cassie had been "romantically involved."

We'd all been watching the news in my office. Alex leaned back on the couch, his arms folded behind his head. "How do you think this plays for us?"

Michelle picked up the remote and turned down the volume on the television. "I think it makes Tiegan look even guiltier. I don't care if Natalie's a stalker. Tiegan still got involved with a student. Correction: *another* student. To me, she looks like a garden-variety pedophile."

Alex considered that. "If that's the kind of reaction we can expect, then it might be a good thing to let it come out."

I shook my head. "Right now, Fred probably figures he's better off laying low and keeping the story about Cassie and Tiegan quiet. But if I jump on this bandwagon, Fred might decide he's got nothing to lose and blast Tiegan's story out there. We don't want that. Not until I can find a way to shred it. So I don't think I'll hold any press conferences just yet."

And frankly, I had the best of both worlds right now. Speculation that Tiegan had preyed on Cassie would earn her some sympathy whether I confirmed it or not. Whatever additional support we might get by saying it was true wasn't worth the downside.

My cell phone quacked. It was Emmons. "What's up?"

"Can you get down here? I've got something you should see."

His voice sounded fairly ominous. I looked at my watch. "I can be there in an hour."

I ended the call and grabbed my coat as I told Alex and Michelle what Emmons had said.

Michelle looked worried. "What do you think it is?"

I shook my head. "No clue." I picked up my briefcase. "Wish me luck."

Emmons met me in the PAB reception area and took me to a room set up with seats facing a large, pull-down screen. "We had the jail deputies put your client and Tiegan in adjoining cells."

I felt the blood drain from my face as I sank down on one of the chairs. "And you recorded them."

"Right." Emmons took a seat next to me.

It was such an old trick. Why hadn't I thought to warn Cassie about this? I felt sick to my stomach. "Have you shown this to Fred yet?" Emmons nodded. "Who comes out worse, Cassie or Tiegan?"

He paused and stared at the screen. "I'll let you be the judge. Ready?"

I braced myself. "I guess."

Emmons lowered the lights with a remote control, then started the video. Cassie was sitting on the bed, her back to the corner. Her knees were drawn up to her chin, and her face was turned to the wall.

Tiegan appeared on the right side of the screen, being escorted by a jail deputy. She shuffled along, head down, but when she passed by Cassie's cell, she did a double take. She started to say something to the deputy, but he ignored her. The door to her cell opened, and she stepped inside.

When the door closed, Tiegan turned back to the deputy. "What about my attorney visit?"

"You'll have to reschedule." The deputy walked off.

Cassie lifted her head and studied Tiegan. After a moment, she moved off her bed and went to the bars separating their cells. Tiegan turned to face her but stayed where she was, near the door.

Cassie gripped the bars. "I'm sorry, Tiegan! I told my lawyer not to tell! You've got to believe me!"

Tiegan seemed dazed as she peered at Cassie. "Why are you doing this to me?"

Cassie was wide-eyed, her voice a little hysterical. "Doing what? I told you—my lawyer did it! She totally screwed me!"

Tiegan put a hand to her forehead. "I can't believe this." She let her hand fall back down as though it were a lead weight. Her head tilted to one side as she peered at Cassie through the bars. "You fed Sam a bunch of lies, and she bought them all." She stopped. "Wait. Did she put you up to this? That's it! This was all *her* idea, wasn't it?"

Cassie looked bewildered. "What are you talking about? Sam didn't put me up to anything." She leaned her head against the bars. "But she promised she wouldn't tell. I'm so sorry, Tiegan."

Tiegan looked incredulous as she took a step toward Cassie. "How could you? I was always there for you. I risked everything for you! And this is how you repay me?" Her chin trembled as tears welled up.

Cassie stared at her, then bit her lip and started to cry. "I'm sorry, Tiegan! I shouldn't have told her; I didn't mean to! But I was so upset when you said we couldn't be together." Cassie wrapped her arms around her waist. "It was the only thing that kept me going—knowing that you'd be waiting for me. When you said we were through, I just didn't want to live anymore." Cassie hunched over and shook her head. "I . . . I couldn't take it." After a moment, she looked up at Tiegan. "I'm sorry! I wish I never told her!"

Tiegan backed up, her expression confused. "What are you talking about? I never said we couldn't be together, Cassie. I just said we had to wait until everything cooled down."

Cassie glared at Tiegan, her expression cold. "Yes, you did. And you made me so depressed I tried to kill myself. Don't lie about it!"

Tiegan rushed toward Cassie, her eyes wide and furious. She reached through the bars. If Cassie hadn't jumped back, those hands would've done some serious damage. Tiegan screamed, "Don't lie? I'm not the one who's lying, you little bitch! The only thing I ever did was cover for you!" She clutched the bars. "I should've called the police and let you rot in prison, you fucking murderer!"

Cassie stood a few feet back, well out of reach. When she spoke, she sounded puzzled. "I'm the murderer? But that's crazy. Why would *I* kill them? I'd have no place to go! No one would adopt me. I'm too old!"

Tiegan's voice was sad, broken. "But you've been telling everyone that *you* did it because they molested you—your father, your brother. Was *any* of that true?" Tears rolled down her cheeks.

I couldn't see Cassie's expression, but after a brief pause, she covered her face with her hands and began to cry. "Of course it's true! You know it's true! But I never meant for you to kill them!"

Tiegan's tears stopped. Her eyes now glittered, icy and hard, as she spoke in a voice that was low, menacing. "You played me and you used me. But you're not going to get away with it." Tiegan squeezed the bars as though she were wringing Cassie's neck. "You hear me, you little bitch? I'm going to make sure you go down for this!" Then Tiegan began to scream, but the words were indecipherable. Cassie backed up to the farthest corner of her cell, crouched down, and put her arms over her head. Her body shook with deep, choking sobs. Deputies came running, and then the screen went dark.

FIFTY-TWO

Emmons brought up the lights. "So there you have it. We'll have a transcript prepared in the next month or so."

I wasn't sure what to make of it. "Can I get a copy of the DVD?"

"Sure. I'll e-mail it to you."

It arrived shortly after I got back to the office. I played it for Alex and Michelle. Now that I knew what was coming, I could study it more carefully. It was only a few minutes long, but it was searing. When it ended, I asked, "What do you think?"

Michelle's chin rested on her hand, her eyes narrowed. "Cassie accused Tiegan of saying she was breaking up with her. She said that was the reason she tried to commit suicide, right?" I nodded. "But Tiegan denied it. She said she'd just told Cassie they had to be cool. Why would Tiegan lie about that?"

I'd noticed that, too. "I don't think she did. I think Tiegan said one thing and Cassie heard another. Cassie's in a wigged-out state of mind to begin with, probably already worried that Tiegan might fade away. And"—I sighed—"I didn't help matters." I told them how, early on, back when we thought Cassie had a secret boyfriend, I'd warned her that he wouldn't hang around and wait for her even if I got her the best verdict possible.

Alex looked concerned. "They both come off pretty bad. I'm no fan of Tiegan's, but she does kind of make me wonder about Cassie."

Michelle folded her arms. "Well, I'm still Team Cassie. I think Tiegan's fury is all about the fact that she finally got busted—and outed as a pedophile."

I circled a finger around Alex and Michelle. "And if I'm lucky, I'll get a jury to split up like that."

But that's the best I thought I could hope for. Because I agreed with Alex; they both looked bad.

Alex got off Michelle's desk. "I'm not exactly saying I'd vote to convict Cassie. I'm just saying . . . I don't know what I'm saying. This case is such a nutcracker." He looked at me. "What's your vote?"

"I just don't know. I can't call this one."

A *ping* sounded on Michelle's computer in the reception area. She stood up. "E-mail. Be right back."

I sat back and replayed the footage in my head. Cassie's face, her reactions, Tiegan's face, her reactions . . . A few seconds later, Michelle came back in. "More discovery on the case. Just photos from the search of Tiegan's apartment. I forwarded it to you."

I opened the e-mail and downloaded the photos. There were two separate batches. I started with the smaller one. It seemed to consist of the photos they'd seized from her apartment. The first one was of a picture in a frame. It showed Tiegan and a friend standing in front of a bookcase, holding wineglasses. I scrolled through the rest of them, hoping to find a picture of Cassie, but no such luck. The only photograph close to being of interest was a picture of Tiegan with three other girls who looked like they were high school age, but then I saw that it was taken at a school open house. No issue there.

Alex saw me pause over that photo. "I know what you're thinking. You're not gonna find it. The cops sent over a report yesterday saying they'd checked her computer and her cell phone and found 'nothing relevant to this investigation.'"

"I didn't expect to find kiddie porn." Tiegan didn't seem to roll that way. "But wouldn't you think there'd be something? I mean, at least photos of her with an arm around a girl?"

Alex shrugged. "She might just be the careful type. But the cops hardly found any photos in her apartment. So maybe she just wasn't into taking pics."

True, they'd seized only six photographs. Come to think of it, I wasn't such a big shutterbug myself. "Moving on." I opened the second, larger batch of photographs. These had been taken by the cops when they served the search warrant. Tiegan's apartment was a small one-bedroom. The initial photographs, taken before the search began, showed that it was spare but tidy. The photographs taken after the search showed the police had been very thorough in their search—and not so thorough when it came to putting the place back together. They'd taken the residence apart; cupboards were open, drawers were emptied, cushions were thrown off the couch, and the bedroom was completely torn apart.

I heard Alex typing on his iPad behind me. "Anything else come in?"

"No, I'm just putting these on our discovery list."

I clicked through the photographs taken just before the search again. The color scheme in the bedroom—a duvet of pink and red roses, a matching dusty-rose curtain—showed the room clearly belonged to a woman, but there were no knickknacks on the dresser, no photographs on the nightstand, and no mirrors. The living room was just as bare-bones. The only decorative touch beyond the standard couch, chairs, and coffee table was a floor-to-ceiling bookcase, where I noticed some unimaginative mementos from trips abroad—a photograph of the Eye of London, a spoon from Paris, a Celtic cross from Ireland. That was the bookcase Tiegan and her friend had been standing in front of, holding wineglasses.

But something about the bookcase looked different now. I clicked over to the photo of Tiegan and her friend and studied the background. Then I clicked back to the photo taken by the cops, just before they started the search. "Alex, check this out." I pointed to the bookcase. "See that?" I pointed to the area between the Parisian spoon and the Celtic cross. It was packed with books.

Alex leaned down to get a closer look. Then stood up, his expression confused. "Yeah, so?"

I pulled up the photo of Tiegan and her friend again and pointed to the bookcase behind them. "Now look." I pointed to that same spot—where a knife with a vicious-looking blade was on display in an open box.

"Holy crap."

"You have the autopsy report handy?" Alex nodded and opened his iPad. "Tell me if it could be the murder weapon."

Alex peered at the photograph. "It has a straight edge. Looks like it's about twelve inches long." He read the autopsy report. "Damn. Yeah, it definitely could be."

At last, I had my smoking gun.

I put in a call to Emmons. "You have any leads on the murder weapon?"

Emmons sounded annoyed. "What are you, my captain? Our deal's over with. I only said I'd give you the heads up on our search at Tiegan's place."

"And the answer is . . . ?"

He sighed. "No. We don't. Why?"

"Because I have a very hot lead for you. But first, you've got to promise me that if you talk to Tiegan again, I get to be there."

Emmons gave an even deeper sigh. "Rusty'll put my head on a spike."

"Tell him he needs to show a little gratitude."

He gave a sarcastic snort. "Yeah, I'm sure that'll work." Emmons swore softly. "Okay, fine. We talk to her again, you're in. Now tell me."

I told him about the knife I'd seen—and then not seen—in the photographs.

"Seriously? Damn. We only just got her photos put on a disc. I haven't had the chance to see them yet. Hang on." I heard keys being tapped, then a few seconds of silence. "You're right. I've got to get the search team back out there. Okay, I'll be in touch."

The line went dead. I looked at my phone. "You're welcome."

Alex smiled. "Nice catch, boss."

"I get lucky every once in a while."

He gave a little chuckle. "If that's what you want to call it. Think this'll do it for Cassie?"

I turned to look out the window. When had it gotten dark? I'd lost all track of time. "Unless Tiegan has some kind of amazing explanation for that disappearing knife."

After Alex and Michelle left, I pulled up all the photos that showed Tiegan's bookcase and enlarged them so I could examine every inch. Something else had caught my eye. An hour later, I headed home.

FIFTY-THREE

It didn't take long for the cops to confirm that the knife was missing. It was a small apartment, and they'd already given it an intensive going-over when they'd served the first search warrant. I had a feeling I'd be hearing from Emmons soon, so I went downtown to visit Cassie. This time, she agreed to the visit.

Cassie seemed to have gotten some rest since her meltdown with me. The dark circles under her eyes were lighter, and she sat up straighter in her chair. As we picked up the phones, I said, "Thanks for seeing me."

She sighed and dropped her eyes. "I didn't want Tiegan to get busted, and I felt like you betrayed me. But after a while, I realized you were just doing your job." Cassie's expression was soft. "You were doing what was best for me. I just wasn't . . . used to that."

I looked into her eyes and nodded. "I'm glad you understand. Now I want to warn you about something that happened here, so you'll be ready if it happens again." I told her about the fight between her and Tiegan that'd been captured on camera.

Cassie gaped at me, her eyes wide. "No! Can they do that? What did I say? Did I say anything bad?"

"Yes, they can do that. You have no right to privacy in a jail cell. And no, you didn't say anything bad. You're okay. But don't ever forget: you can't trust anyone. Always remember, you have to act as though someone's watching."

We talked for a little while longer, but I had to cut our visit short. I got a text from Emmons. Tiegan had agreed to talk again, and they were going to start the interview in half an hour. I decided not to tell Cassie. I said I had to get to court and that I'd be back to see her tomorrow.

I was alone in the observation room this time. Dale was tied up in a meeting. Tiegan and Fred were already seated at the table; Rusty Templeton sat across from them. A few seconds later, Emmons glided in and took the seat next to him. They read Tiegan her rights again, and she waived them.

Emmons led off by telling her they'd found some new evidence that made things "look pretty bad for her." He gave her a semisympathetic look. "So we wanted to give you the chance to explain it."

Fred held up his hand like a stop sign. "Again, I want it clear for the record that my client is doing this against my advice."

Emmons nodded without looking at him. He held up the photo of Tiegan and her friend standing in front of the bookcase. She glanced at it, then looked back at Emmons. "Do you remember when this photo was taken?"

Tiegan hesitated for a moment. "In February, I believe."

"Of this year?" Emmons asked. Tiegan nodded. "When, exactly? It's April third now. Would you say it was around February twentieth?"

Tiegan shook her head. "No, later. Probably toward the end of the month."

"Who's the other woman?"

"Shana Pohler. She's a friend from college."

He pointed to the knife displayed on the bookshelf behind them. "Where'd you get that?"

Tiegan blanched. After a long pause, she said, "India. I went there after I got my teaching credential, to celebrate. But it's—"

Emmons pulled out the photograph taken during the search and pointed to the bookshelf where the knife had been—where there were now only books. "So it was there about a week or less before the murders. But it disappeared after the murders. Want to tell us where it went?"

Tiegan's face got even paler. She stared at the photograph, her expression frozen. "I meant to tell you. I—I just forgot. Cassie took it. She stole it from me."

The detectives watched her in silence for a few seconds. Then Rusty said, "So you're saying Cassie planned this in advance? She stole the knife, because she was planning to use it to kill her family?" His tone was even, but there was a hint of incredulousness.

Tiegan raked her free hand through her hair, her expression confused, desperate. "Yes! Or, wait . . . no, maybe not. I don't know." Tiegan leaned forward, her elbow on the table, and dropped her head into her hand. "I know I should've told you this before. But the thing is, she used to steal things from me all the time. A comb, a pair of earrings. Once, she even took a sweater." She let her hand fall on the table, palm up. "So I don't know if she planned it. Maybe she did, but maybe she didn't. At least not when she took the knife."

Emmons didn't try to hide his skepticism. "And that never bothered you? You just let her keep stealing from you?"

Tiegan's voice was now ragged, bitter. "When I told her I knew that she was taking my things, she said it made her feel closer to me. Like a part of me was always with her." She shook her head. "And I just thought it was kind of sweet."

Emmons studied her for a beat. "You thought stealing a knife—a *dagger*—was sweet?"

"No! I didn't realize she'd stolen it until that night, when she . . . when she gave it to me."

"You have her over to your apartment often?" Rusty asked.

Tiegan looked haggard. "A couple of times a week."

Emmons watched her closely. "What about the week of the murders? Did she come over then, too?" Tiegan nodded. "You got anyone who can verify that?"

Tiegan stared at him, then threw her head back and made a grinding sound that seemed to come from deep in her core. "Oh God!" She shoved her fingers into her hair. "Why can't you see it? She lied about . . . everything! She set me up. I've been thinking all along, why wouldn't she tell me they were molesting her if it were true? She told me every little thing that happened every single goddamn day. Every ugly thing Abel said, every time Paula stuck up for him. Why would she tell me all that but not that her brother and her father were molesting her? Don't you see? It's all a bunch of lies! No one molested her!"

Emmons did not look impressed. "Maybe she didn't tell you because she was afraid you wouldn't believe her. You should know as well as I do that there're a lot of reasons why victims don't report."

Tiegan sat back in her chair, looking broken, defeated. Then, suddenly, she sat up. "Wait! Did she tell you Abel was blackmailing her?"

This was a new wrinkle. I felt my mouth go dry as I leaned forward and studied Tiegan. She was straining toward Emmons, her eyes fixed on his.

Rusty tried to sound casual, but I could feel the intensity in his voice as he spoke. "No. Why don't you tell us about that?"

Tiegan faced him, her speech rapid and pressured. "She told me she couldn't take it anymore. That Abel had found out about us, and he was making her do . . . horrible things."

"When was this?" Emmons asked.

Tiegan paused, stared at the table for a moment, then said, "It was just a few days before the murders."

Rusty's eyes hadn't left her face. "What was he making her do?"

Tiegan swallowed and shook her head. "I don't know; she wouldn't tell me." She rubbed her chained hand with her free hand so hard it left angry red streaks. "She said she couldn't live there anymore, that we had to run away together."

I stared through the glass at Tiegan. She was clearly too unhinged to realize that she'd just put the noose around her own neck. Cassie had told Tiegan about getting blackmailed, and a few days later, Abel wound up dead. I'd wondered about Tiegan's motive from the first moment Cassie told me Tiegan was the killer. It wasn't that I *couldn't* believe she'd get crazed at the thought of what Abel and Cassie's father were doing to her. But it'd been a stretch. Now I understood.

Rusty tapped a thick finger on the table for a moment. "When she said she wanted to run away with you, what'd you say?"

Tiegan seemed to vibrate with agitation. She looked at him as though he were crazy. "I said no, of course. How could I possibly let her live with me? That's insane."

"Did she tell you what Abel had on you?" Emmons asked.

"She said it wasn't really a big deal, that all he saw was a text she'd sent me, saying that she missed me. I couldn't tell if that was true or not. But it didn't matter. I had to put some distance between us, so I told her we had to back off and that she probably shouldn't contact me for a while."

Emmons had a skeptical expression. "How'd she take that?"

Tiegan's knee bounced under the table, making her ankle chains rattle. "Badly. At first, she said to forget about it, that she could handle him. But when I told her I meant it and we couldn't see each other for a while, she fell apart."

"Meaning what exactly?" Rusty asked. "What did she do?"

"She cried, then she yelled at me, called me names."

Rusty raised an eyebrow. "She called you names. That's it? She didn't threaten you, get violent with you?"

Tiegan shook her head, then looked from Emmons to Rusty, her expression frantic. "But don't you get it? That's why it all happened! She killed Abel because he was the reason we couldn't be together! She did it to be with me!"

The room was silent for a long moment. When Rusty spoke, his tone was casual, but I could hear the underlying intensity. "You said Cassie used to tell you everything?" Tiegan nodded. "Then I guess you knew her folks were celebrating their anniversary that night."

Tiegan looked numb, tired. "I think she may have mentioned that."

Rusty nodded. "Then you knew her parents were supposed to be staying in a hotel that night."

Tiegan stared, openmouthed, as the import of what he'd said sank in. She leaned across the table, her face inches from Rusty's. "No. She never told me that! You've got to believe me!" Tiegan turned to Emmons. "Why don't you get it? It's so obvious! She had to get rid of Abel so she could come live with me!"

Rusty tilted his head toward her, and his voice was hard. "But you were telling her all along that you couldn't live together, so why'd she all of a sudden decide she needed to kill that boy? And *she* wouldn't be ruined if people found out about you two." He faced Tiegan and poked a finger at her. "*You* would. If Abel talked, you wouldn't just lose your whole career, you'd go to prison. Know what I call that? Motive. One of the best I've ever seen." His eyes bored into hers. "You killed Abel, and then you had to kill the parents. And you left Cassie there to take the fall."

Tiegan shook her head vigorously. "No! No! You're wrong!" She yanked the hand that was chained to the table. "She did it! She's the one!"

The detectives stood up and motioned for the unis to come get her. As they walked out, Tiegan threw her head back and began to scream.

FIFTY-FOUR

Tiegan's screams were still ringing in the distance as I hurried out to intercept the cops. I caught up with them at the elevator. "You've got to cut Cassie loose."

Rusty gave me a weary look. "No, we don't."

"Come on, are you kidding me? You've got your killer. You can't hold Cassie."

"Sure we can." Rusty turned to hit the up button. "Far as I'm concerned, those two might've cooked it all up together. And even if your girl isn't the killer, she's at least an accessory after the fact."

I folded my arms. "Really? You saw that video of them in jail. Do they seem like they 'cooked up' *anything* together?" Not that crime partners don't turn on each other. They do. All the time. It's actually a shocker when they don't. But there was nothing about either Cassie's or Tiegan's behavior that fit the picture of co-conspirators.

They'd never be able to sell that theory, and we both knew it. That meant they had to pick a killer, and they'd need one of them to testify against the other. Tiegan was looking better and better as the perpetrator. But Cassie wasn't completely in the clear. So I had to strike now, while the tide was turning in my favor, and get them to commit to a deal for Cassie's testimony.

Rusty leaned back and rubbed his chin. Behind him, the elevator dinged, and the doors opened, but he ignored it. "I take it your client's been telling you Tiegan did it." I nodded. "What about that blackmail bit?"

I looked him in the eye and lied my head off. "She confirms that, too." Or more accurately, she would when I got done with her.

Rusty gave me a narrow-eyed look. "You got any witnesses to back that up?"

Cassie might be able to help us out there. But I had no way of knowing for sure. I was really stepping out on a limb now. What the hell; in for a penny . . . "Yeah, I do." Rusty started to speak, but I knew what he was about to ask. "And yes, she'll testify."

Emmons and Rusty exchanged a look. Rusty hit the up button again. "Tell you what, you put together those witness statements about the blackmail and get me a summary of what Cassie's gonna say. If I like it, I'll take it to the DA."

Shit. I'd have to move fast. "Nothing's in writing, so I'll have to go back out and talk to everyone again. Give me a week."

The elevator dinged, and as the doors opened, Rusty stuck out a hand and grabbed one of them. "You've got forty-eight hours." He and Emmons stepped inside. "If we've gotta change horses, we need to do it fast."

I got it. The longer it took to resolve this, the worse they'd look. But I was really up against it now. I put on a confident smile. "Shouldn't be a problem."

The moment the doors closed, I took off at a gallop and didn't stop till I got to the car. I grabbed my cell phone and punched in Alex's number. I was still winded when he answered. "We've got maybe forty-eight hours to dig up some witnesses." I gave him a brief sketch of Tiegan's statement and what we needed to do. "I'm going to go see Cassie right now."

I ended the call and headed to Twin Towers.

"Was Abel blackmailing you?" I leaned across the counter, the phone clutched in my hand so tightly it made my fingers hurt.

Cassie shook her head. "No. She's lying. And she's full of shit that I didn't tell her about them molesting me. I totally told her that!"

Whether she'd told Tiegan about being molested wasn't our problem. "Cassie, you need to focus. Do you want to get out of here?" She nodded. "Then tell me what was going on with Abel."

Cassie frowned and stared down at the counter. Her hair had grown out a little. It now reached her chin. She tucked it back behind an ear. I was about to prompt her again when she finally said, "He saw our texts."

"What did they say?"

"I said that I loved her tattoo. I thought it was so sexy." Cassie refused to meet my eyes. "And I—I sent her the photo I'd taken of her the weekend before. She was in bed, all wrapped up in a sheet."

"Did Tiegan text you back?"

Cassie nodded. "She said it was a great night."

I noticed that Cassie had a guilty look on her face. "What's wrong?"

She hung her head. "I messed up. Tiegan always told me to delete our texts. But I didn't." Cassie met my eyes, her expression pleading. "I needed them! They kept me from going crazy."

"So how did Abel get those texts?"

Cassie hung her head again. "He took screenshots of them on his phone."

"What happened to the screenshots?"

Cassie swallowed. "I deleted them that night, right after I called the police." Cassie bit her lip. "I was just trying to protect her!"

"And those texts, that photo of Tiegan? Did you delete those, too?"
Cassie nodded. "The second Abel showed me the screen shots."

"I don't suppose you backed up any of the texts or photos—"

She wore a disgusted expression. "No. It was bad enough I didn't delete them to begin with."

It figured. Having physical evidence right there at my fingertips would've been too easy. Still, I'd check with Alex. Maybe Abel backed up his screenshots in the cloud or . . . something. Tiegan had claimed the text just said that Cassie missed her. Pretty innocuous. I'd wondered why Tiegan would get so worked up about that. What would it prove? But what Cassie had just described was damning evidence. And I definitely believed Cassie's description. Abel couldn't have done much with a text that just said Cassie missed Tiegan. No wonder Tiegan had given the cops that watered-down version of the blackmail material. Her motive had just gotten ten times stronger. If only Cassie hadn't deleted everything . . . I sighed. That brought me to my next point: possible witnesses. "What did Abel make you do?"

She told me. It was much worse than I'd expected. When it came to sheer nastiness, Abel never failed to disappoint. I tried to get details. The cops weren't going to take Cassie's word for this. I needed witnesses. But Cassie had almost no memory beyond the general outlines. So we had very little to work with and just forty-eight hours to deliver. Perfect. Just once, I wished something could fall into my lap.

I waited to call Alex until I got into my car. I told him what I'd learned from Cassie. "Can you see if Abel backed up those screenshots to the cloud?"

He gave an impatient huff. "Does Beyoncé rock the casbah? Of course. Piece of cake."

"That's only the beginning. How long would it take you to set up interviews with the kids in Cassie's classes?" We'd already spoken to her friends and Abel's friends. None of them had said a word about the incidents Cassie had described. Rain and Tawny in particular surely would've said something about it if they'd had solid information. In any case, I could call them and find out pretty quickly. But what would be better than friends—who might lie for Cassie—were witnesses who didn't know her well. If I wanted this deal to happen, I had to do everything I could to sweeten our side of it.

"I've got a bunch of cell phone numbers. I can probably line them up by Friday."

It was only Wednesday. By Friday, they might decide to pull the deal. "Not good enough. It's got to be tomorrow. Split it up with Michelle. I'm on my way back. I'll pitch in when I get there."

I was going to find platinum backup for Cassie's story if I had to squeeze every kid in that school.

FIFTY-FIVE

The next day, Alex and I rolled into Glendale at two p.m. With all three of us working the phones, we'd managed to set up thirty-four interviews for today and Friday morning. And Alex had checked the cloud last night: Abel hadn't backed up anything. So these interviews were a make-or-break situation. If we didn't score some awesome witnesses, Cassie's deal would go down the shitter.

Alex had suggested we meet the students at the Starbucks near the school. That way, it'd be convenient for them, and we could bribe them with muffins and Grande lattes. Michelle hadn't been wild about the idea. "They only get one latte, and no muffins. It's gonna cost a fortune."

I'd promised her we'd keep expenses to a minimum. But there was no way I'd cheap out if a couple of muffins bought us a good witness. When we got to the Starbucks, we found it fairly empty, so we were able to commandeer a couple of tables at the back. Shirley, our first interviewee, showed up ten minutes late. She wore black leggings and a knee-length sweatshirt. We had sixteen others stacked up after her, so I introduced myself and got right to it. "Before everything happened, when Abel and Cassie were still in school, did you hear any rumors or gossip about either of them?"

"I heard Abel was nice, but I didn't know him or Cassie. I can't believe she killed her own family. I mean, even if he did molest her, so what? Who'd do a thing like that?" I was about to tell her we clearly knew who'd do a thing like that when she leaned in and whispered, "Is it true what they're saying about Tiegan and Cassie? Did they really hook up?"

Next.

A white boy in dreads and a Bob Marley sweatshirt called Abel a "wannabe" (oh, the irony) who was always "sucking up to the jocks." But Cassie "seemed kinda cool." No clue about any rumors at all. But "If that nutsack really did mess with her, he totally had it coming."

I hoped I'd get more like him on my jury, but . . .

Next.

A class nerd—black-framed glasses, pencil neck and all—didn't know Abel, hadn't heard anything about Cassie, but thought her story was "inherently incredible" because Abel "could get girls." He thought Tiegan was hot, and he, too, wanted to know whether she and Cassie "hooked up." He managed to punch down two muffins.

Next.

A girl who looked like a Janis Joplin wannabe, with long, wild frizzy hair and dangling feather earrings, had always felt sorry for Cassie because "Abel could be, like, a real dick, you know?" But she didn't know Cassie that well, and she'd never heard any stories about her. If Abel was molesting her, that was a real drag, but she, herself, "couldn't imagine ever stabbing anyone."

And on and on. Until we hit our tenth, a cute little brunette cheerleader who showed up in uniform—a very short, pleated blue and gold skirt and matching crewneck sweater, a high ponytail, and pink lip gloss.

Hillary Placker licked her lips and glanced around the coffee shop. She spoke in a voice so soft I had to lean in to hear her. "I feel really bad about this. I know I should've said something at the time, but I didn't want to talk bad about Cassie. And really, I didn't even know if it was true. You know how people are."

Finally. I was not in a patient mood—not that I ever am—but I was in a "talk fast or I'll shoot you in the head" mood right now. I reined myself in and forced a calm voice. "Everything you say to me will be confidential. I promise you." Unless you give me something I can use. In which case I'll tie you to my bumper and drag you all the way to the courthouse.

But the unsuspecting Hillary nodded and thanked me. "After Cassie and Waylon broke up, I heard some guys talking about how she'd do . . . anything."

This was it. What I'd been hoping for. "What guys? And when?"

She played with the cuff of her sweater as she thought for a moment. "The first time was a few months ago. I heard a couple of guys on the junior varsity basketball team talking about her. It was totally by accident. I was in the locker room, and they were just outside in the hallway. After that, I heard some of the other guys on the team talking about it."

"Definitely during this school year, then?"

"Oh, for sure. Yeah."

"Did they give any specifics? Say what Cassie was doing?"

Hillary blushed. "The junior varsity guys talked about how they were at a party and she . . . uh"—she glanced at Alex, then looked down—"she gave one of them a BJ in the bedroom."

She was so uncomfortable, I had to help her out. "Was that the gist of the rumors you heard after that? That she'd do those kinds of favors for guys at parties?"

Hillary nodded. "Pretty much. The guys laughed about it, but I thought it was kind of sad that she felt like she had to do that stuff."

"Did you know these guys?" Hillary shook her head. "Did you happen to get a look at any of them?" And I thought, *Please, oh please, don't just tell me they're tall.*

Hillary gave a reluctant nod. "I peeked out the door when they passed by the locker room. The one closest to me had thin, scraggly brown hair and a tattoo of a pyramid on the back of his shoulder." Her brow wrinkled as she stared off for a moment. "I think it was his left shoulder."

Alex had his pen poised over his notepad—just our usual show for the witness. The recorder hidden in his jacket pocket was catching every word. "How long was his hair?"

She gestured to the bottom of her neck. "About here."

Alex made a note. "Can you remember his build? Was he super skinny? Medium?"

"I'm not good at height. Everyone's taller than me." She was five foot two if she stretched real hard. Probably one of the squad's fliers. "But I remember he had really skinny legs."

"What about the others?" I asked. "You said there were two?"

Hillary nodded. "I think one had blondish-reddish hair, cut in a fade. He was a little bit shorter, but I don't remember anything else about him. And I couldn't really see the other one."

Alex asked, "The one with the fade, how long was it on top?"

Hillary held her hand an inch or two above her head. "About like this."

Alex opened his iPad. "I'm going to show you some pictures, okay?" He pulled up the school photos for the junior varsity basketball team and scrolled to the photos that looked most like the boys she'd just described.

Hillary looked frightened. "You're not going to tell them that I—"

I shook my head. "Absolutely not."

Alex showed her the photographs. She studied them for just a few moments, then picked them out. She pointed to a boy with a long nose and shoulder-length hair. "I think that's the one who was bragging." Then she pointed to a boy with a blondish-reddish fade. "And that's the one who was laughing."

I smiled. "Thanks, Hillary. You've been a big help. By the way, how did you know they were junior varsity?"

"Because the day I heard them talking was a Thursday, and that's when they have practice." A flash of anger crossed her face. "I know it was Thursday because I was having a fight with my *ex*-boyfriend."

I gave her a sisterly nod as I thought, *Thursday—as in today.* Time to wrap this up. "Thank you, Hillary. This was very helpful."

Hillary's chin trembled. "I feel so bad. I knew I should've said something."

"Hillary, it's not your fault. If you'd reported it, the boys would've just lied and denied. You're doing the right thing now. That's what counts. Okay?"

She tried for a smile and half succeeded. "Thanks, Ms. Brinkman."

"Sam. Call me Sam." Or any other damn thing you want. And I'll call you Star Witness Number One. But no need to bring that up right now. "Do you think we can still catch them at the school?"

"They practice till at least five."

I looked at my phone. It was only four thirty. We were in luck.

FIFTY-SIX

It took us just ten minutes to walk to the school, so we killed some time strolling around the campus, revisiting shitty memories. Shitty for Alex, because he went to "a ghetto school where gay was not okay." Shitty for me, because I'd been a mess. The bleachers off in the distance reminded me of the bleachers I'd hidden under back in the day, where I'd snort coke, smoke cigarettes, or polish off half a pint of Jack Daniel's. Good times.

We headed for the gym at five and waited in the hallway outside the basketball courts. At a quarter after, the first players started to leave. We'd decided to split up. I'd take the first one we saw; Alex would take the second. We'd have to catch the third guy, who hadn't said anything—and might not even be involved—another time.

We were in luck. Jason Lichter, the one with the long brown hair, came floating out with a towel over his shoulder, and right next to him was our number-two target, the blond guy with the fade, AKA Owen DeMayne. They both had that ripe smell of sweat and dirty gym clothes long overdue for a washing.

Jason was at least six foot one, with a long nose and thin lips, but the high cheekbones and strong jaw saved him from the Ichabod Crane look. His hair and tank shirt were soaked, and his face was flushed.

I took the lead. "Hey, Jason."

He stopped and looked me up and down, a little bit interested, a little bit suspicious. "Who're you?"

His buddy Owen had stopped, too. Alex greeted him. "Hey, Owen."

I introduced myself as just Samantha—no lawyer stuff yet. Alex did the same.

I looked up at Jason. "Can you give me a sec? I've got something I think you'll want to hear." Hoping that was intriguing enough, I stepped across the hall to a small round table in an alcove and gestured for him to follow. Behind me, I heard Alex ask Owen to join him on a bench farther down the hall.

When I reached the table, I turned and gave Jason a friendly smile. He hesitated for a moment, then slowly ambled over. I could almost see him thinking, *What the hell, why not?* No girl would ever stroll over to a stranger with that kind of nonchalance. Not even if the stranger was a woman.

I kept the smile going. "I hear you and Abel Sonnenberg were friends."

His nostrils flared as if he'd smelled a fart. "Not really. I mean, I knew him, but we didn't hang out or anything."

I threw my sucker punch. "But you knew him well enough to get a beej from his sister."

He pulled back, his eyes wide. "Whoa, what now?"

I dropped the smile. "Cut the crap, Jason. I've got witnesses."

He ran a tongue over his lips and darted a quick look over my shoulder as he spoke. "I didn't do anything wrong. She was into it."

I lifted an eyebrow. "That's not what I heard."

Jason sat up, his expression alarmed. "What?" He leaned forward and spoke in a harsh whisper. "Well, whoever said that's a friggin' liar!

382

I'd never force a girl to . . . to do anything! Who said that? Is she saying that?"

I watched him carefully, "Why don't you tell me what happened?"

He frowned at me, but the frown was laced with fear. "Who are you?"

"I'm her lawyer." I handed him my card.

He glanced at the card, then looked back at me. "What's she saying? That I forced her and that's why she killed everyone? That's crazy! Besides, I wasn't the only one!"

"If she gave consent, then you need to tell me about that. I just want to hear your side of the story." Actually, it didn't matter if she gave consent. It was still a criminal offense, even though both of them were minors. But his legal exposure wasn't my problem.

His Adam's apple bounced as he swallowed hard. "I saw Abel at this party a couple of months ago. He was all bragging about how he could get his sister to do whatever he wanted. Said he made her give handies to some guys on the football team and asked if I wanted one." Jason made a face. "Like we were friends or something." He worked his jaw. "I was pretty drunk; I thought it was a joke, you know? So I told him I wanted a BJ." Jason slouched down in the chair and spread his legs.

His BO, his manspread, what girl wouldn't drop to her knees? "What did Abel say?"

Jason had a sullen look, as though it were all Abel's fault that I was bracing him up now. "That she'd be waiting for me in the back bedroom if I wanted to go for it." He stopped and glared at the floor as he clenched his jaw.

Come on, dickweed, speak. "And?"

He blew out a breath and spoke fast. "And a few minutes later, he gave me the sign, and I went to the bedroom, and she did it." Jason's face turned crimson. "I didn't even do anything. She just . . . took over. She did it all. I didn't even hardly touch her!"

"Did she say anything to you?"

Jason shook his head. "I don't think so. Like I said, I was pretty drunk. But she wasn't, like, crying or anything." He leaned in, his expression pained. "Look, I know I shouldn't have gone along with it. I probably wouldn't have if I weren't so buzzed. But you've got to believe me, if she'd been acting upset or scared or . . . or anything, I wouldn't have done it." He slouched in his chair, his eyes on the floor.

I wasn't sure what to believe. Was he the laughing asshole who'd bragged to his buddy? Or the relatively decent guy in front of me who felt bad about his part in that ugly scene? I supposed he could be both. He was a teen boy. "Did Abel tell you why Cassie would do whatever he wanted?"

Jason knitted his brow as he shook his head. "No, but now, from what I heard about Ms. Donner and all, I'm guessing she and Cassie were . . . together, and he found out about them?"

I nodded. "We think he might've been blackmailing her."

His expression was a mixture of pain and disgust. "Seriously?" He shook his head. "What a dick."

I guessed I didn't need to point out that he'd gone along for the ride with "that dick." "You said there were others. We already know about Owen. Who else?"

Jason sat up and gave me a pleading look. "Does it really matter? You know about Owen and me. Isn't that enough?"

I could well understand that he didn't want to rat out his buddies. But that moral dilemma was none of my concern. I spoke with sarcasm. "What do you think, Jason? Two guys versus twelve—or maybe twenty. You think it was all the same to Cassie?"

He hung his head and sighed. "I think maybe Ronnie and Beck did something with her. That's all I know."

I thought I recognized the names. "They on the team, too?"

He nodded, looking like he was about to cry. "I'm not gonna have to testify, am I?"

"I'm not sure. I'll let you know." I told him we were done. For now.

Jason hooked the towel around his neck and paused as he stared at the gym door. "Will you do me a favor?"

"Depends."

He looked at me, his eyes sad. "Tell Cassie I'm sorry. Okay?"

Alex and I swapped stories on our way back to the office. Owen's story was similar to Jason's.

Alex sighed. "Owen was a douche at first. Made it sound like he was this irresistible stud and Cassie had gotten lucky. When I told him that this 'lucky' girl was being blackmailed into servicing him, he got upset. Said he had no idea. He seemed pretty embarrassed about the whole thing, for what it's worth. But he said after that, Abel tried to get invited to one of their parties and offered to bring Cassie with him. He told Abel to fuck off."

"Abel came back to him for seconds, and Owen turned him down?"

"That's what he said. I guess he could be making that up." Alex shook his head. "But it didn't feel that way. Owen said he had a sister. When he'd sobered up, he got to thinking that the whole situation was sleazy and wrong, and that he'd never have done a thing like that to his sister."

I was glad to hear it. "But no one ever turned Abel in."

Alex glanced at me with a rueful expression. "The law of the pack. No one wants to be the snitch. And empathy is so uncool." Alex pulled off the freeway and stopped at the light. "But don't forget, Cassie never said anything, either."

I definitely hadn't forgotten about that. "Did Owen give you any more names?"

Alex nodded. "Two on the basketball team and one on the football team."

"If we can't catch up with them tonight or early tomorrow morning, we run with what we've got."

Alex pulled into the garage under our building. "You don't have to come. I can handle those interviews. I'll get to the school at zero hour and snag whoever I can find."

He probably could handle it alone. All he had to do was tell them we already knew about Jason and Owen. They'd cave in like a cardboard box in the rain.

As Alex drove, I mentally revisited my conversation with Cassie. After she'd told me how Abel had blackmailed her into servicing all those boys, I'd asked, "Why didn't you tell me?"

The skin on the knuckles of the hand that gripped the phone had stretched tight. She'd been shaking with rage. "Because it's humiliating, that's why! Isn't it bad enough that I was the family fuck doll—I also have to let the world know that I got pimped out by my brother?"

I'd backed off. That wasn't the most important question. My next one was. "Did you tell Tiegan what Abel was doing to you?"

Cassie gave a long sigh. "Yes, the day of the—the day they got killed. That's when I told her about everything. My father, Abel . . ."

I told Alex about that conversation now. He shook his head. "That girl's had one heck of a life."

"'Heck'?"

"I'm trying out the understated approach."

I saw a Kentucky Fried Chicken up ahead. Just the sight of it made my mouth water. "Want to pick up some morsels of greasy delight?"

"Absolutely."

When we got back to the office, we spread out our feast and brought Michelle up to speed while we ate.

"Abel sounds like a friggin' sadist." Michelle had finished her extra-crispy chicken thigh and was wiping her face and hands with a napkin.

Alex balled up his paper wrapper and napkin and tossed them into the trash can. "I'm not a big fan of jock-asses, but I got the impression that these guys really didn't know what was going on."

I'd been chewing on my drinking straw, pondering the question I'd had on the ride back. I posed it to the troops now. "The problem is, this blackmail business is a double-edged sword. Now that we know what Abel put Cassie through, I'd say she had one hell of a motive to kill Abel, too."

"But Tiegan's still got more," Alex said. "At the end of the day, Cassie's just a victim. If she rats Abel out, even if she tells everyone about her and Tiegan, nothing happens to her. But Tiegan's totally screwed."

I couldn't argue with the logic. "I just wonder why Cassie never told me about it."

Michelle tossed her soft drink cup into the trash can. "Did she tell anyone? Ever?"

I shook my head. I'd called Tawny and Rain from the car when we were on our way to Starbucks. They admitted they'd heard a few rumors about her, but when they asked her point-blank, Cassie had said it was a lie, probably spread by her asshole brother. "Not as far as I know. Other than Tiegan."

Michelle shrugged. "Then it's maybe not so strange that she didn't tell you. Obviously, it's humiliating. And like you said, it does give Cassie a motive. She was probably afraid it'd make her look guilty."

I supposed that made as much sense as anything else in this weird case. "Well, I think we've got the proof the cops wanted." I sighed. "Let's just hope they agree."

FIFTY-SEVEN

The next morning, while Alex trolled the campus for the other boys who'd been serviced by Cassie, I cleaned up the statements we'd taken from Jason and Owen and typed up my interview with Cassie.

At eight thirty, Alex called to tell me that he'd been able to catch up with two of the other guys. "It's almost the exact same story, Sam. Alex pimped her to some jock-asses to try and ingratiate himself, get invited to the hot parties. I can give you details, but there's nothing new here."

"No need. Just text me their names and contact information."

By nine thirty, I'd e-mailed everything to Rusty and Emmons. It was out of my hands. Now all I could do was wait.

I went out to Michelle's desk. "Can you set up a meeting with the Orozcos? Make it as soon as possible." Michelle gave me a look of disbelief. "This might be the last time."

She was wary. "Promise?"

How could I promise anything when it came to those scorpions? "There's a hope."

I went back to my office and distracted myself with work on my other cases. Ten minutes later, Michelle buzzed me. "They'll be here at two thirty. Jeez, Sam. Don't these guys have jobs?"

"Sure. Beating, stabbing, shooting, and selling dope. It doesn't always pay all that well, but the hours are flexible."

Michelle gave an exasperated sigh. "You're not funny, you know. We'd better make sure Alex is back by then."

In fact, when Michelle told him who was coming, Alex got back to the office so fast I thought he must've flown. I'd gone back to work, with an eye on my e-mail and phone, hoping to hear from the cops about Cassie's deal. But by a quarter after two, I'd still heard nothing. I closed the file of the trial brief I was working on and prepared for my meeting with the wildebeests.

At precisely two thirty, the buzzer at the outer door sounded. Alex had insisted on escorting them in this time, so I stood up, my left hand hovering over the open drawer where my Smith and Wesson rested— locked and loaded.

As usual, they brought a dark cloud of malevolence with them. It felt like a slow, heavy mass around the older Ernesto but a fast-buzzing mini cyclone around Arturo. And now that they'd started to put me in their crosshairs, it was worse than ever. I could feel my breath catch in my chest, but I pasted on a cool, confident smile as I sat down and opened the file. "Gentlemen, I have good news. I've found your man." I took out a photograph of a man in a sheriff's uniform who was standing next to a custody bus.

Ernesto picked it up and studied it, then passed it to Arturo. "This is the driver you told us about?"

"No. He's a deputy who works the local jails. Lazaro Estevez. He was working Twin Towers when Ricardo was there. But on the day Ricardo got bused to prison, Lazaro was working backup for the driver." I waited for them to absorb this. "That means he had complete access to the custody list."

Arturo dropped the photograph on my desk and gave me a skeptical look. "Why do we believe he's the one?"

"Because of these." I handed over three more photographs of the deputy, which showed him dressed in the typical gangbanger uniforms of tank tops and sagging jeans—and specifically sporting tats that said "SC" and "Creepers Forever" and the usual three dots that stood for "My Crazy Life." Then I passed them two more photos that showed Lazaro throwing gang signs with a whole group of Southside Creepers.

Ernesto's chin drew back into his neck; his eyes were slits of mistrust. "What is the date on these pictures?"

Stomach acid boiled up into my throat as I gave a shrug that I hoped was nonchalant. "I'd guess they were pretty recent. His face looks pretty much the same to me in those gang photos as it does in that photo with him in the sheriff's uniform."

Ernesto did not look convinced. "This is all you got?"

My throat was on fire; I cast a longing glance at my bottle of water. But I didn't dare reach for it. I was afraid my hand would shake—or worse, that I'd choke if I tried to drink. "No. I also found this." I took the last page out of my file folder and handed it to Ernesto.

He glanced at it, then passed it to Arturo—as I'd expected. Arturo was the literate one. He scanned the page, then frowned at me. "This is from his Facebook page?" I nodded. He read it once to himself, then, his voice low and shaking with rage, he read aloud for his father's benefit. "It says, '*Homie, you put in great work on that Grape Street piece of shit. Respect.*'"

Ernesto gripped the arms of his chair, and Arturo's nostrils flared as the paper shook in his hand. His eyes bored into mine. "Where can we find this son of a *puta*?"

I took a moment to make sure my voice came out steady. "That's the only problem. A month after Ricardo was killed, Lazaro took off. Said he needed sick leave. But no one's heard from him since." I sat back and slid my left hand across my desk, closer to the open drawer that held my gun. "Now you have a choice. I can certainly take this evidence to the sheriff's department and ask them to look into Lazaro

Estevez. But if I do, you run the risk that they'll wash it out, claim he had nothing to do with Ricardo's death. Or I can—"

Arturo jumped in. "No! You give this information to us. No one else."

Ernesto glanced at Arturo and gave a slow, deliberate nod. "We will look into this. No disrespect, Señorita Brinkman, but we will check this out. We must make very sure before we send out *soldados* to find him."

I mustered up a calm nod. "Of course. I understand. But I have confidence that this is your man. So as of now, I'll consider your case to be closed." I stood up and handed them the file folder so they could pack up the photos and Facebook page printouts. As always, I ended on a complete lie. "It's been a pleasure, gentlemen."

Arturo helped his father up, then looked down his nose at me, his gaze cold. "We'll be in touch."

Anger overrode fear. I wasn't about to let that dickweed have the last word. "I'll certainly be glad to hear from you"—I paused and met his gaze—"if you have new business for me." I walked them out, and the moment the door closed behind them, I told Michelle to send out their closing bill, then I went into my office and collapsed on my couch. It took me a good ten minutes to get my pulse to ratchet back down to normal.

Michelle and Alex came in just as I was making serious plans to stand up and get back to my desk. Michelle looked at me lying on the couch like a beached whale and shook her head. "Are we sure that's the last of them?"

I sighed. "As sure as we can be."

"Nothing yet on Cassie's deal?" Michelle asked.

I sat up slowly and put my feet on the floor. I shook my head. "They might be getting pushback from the captain." I didn't think the DA was the problem. Gideon had been worried about the case even before we found out that the murder weapon belonged to Tiegan.

But even so, Tiegan's story wasn't bad. She'd have trouble getting a jury to like her—juries don't usually show pedophiles a lot of love. But she wouldn't come off as predatory. If Cassie didn't testify, there was a decent chance the jury would believe Tiegan's story. So Gideon was probably in favor of the deal.

I didn't really have the focus or the energy for more work. Between the Orozcos and my anxiety about the deal in Cassie's case, my brain felt like it was filled with static. But I did my best, because the alternative was making myself queasy with nonstop pacing.

It was five o'clock before I heard back from the detectives—a terse e-mail saying, "Nothing yet. Should have word tomorrow."

Dale and I had planned to have dinner tonight so I could tell him how the meeting went with the Orozcos. But I didn't feel up to cooking, so I'd suggested we meet at Barney's Beanery for dinner, then go back to my place, where we could talk safely.

We'd planned to meet at six, which meant I had about forty-five minutes to kill.

I did what I'd been doing ever since I first saw it: I pulled up the video of Cassie's jailhouse confrontation with Tiegan. There was something about it that bugged me; I just couldn't put my finger on what it was. I hit the play arrow and sat back to watch it again.

FIFTY-EIGHT

Dale and I both showed up early at Barney's Beanery, and we made it a fast dinner—we couldn't really talk there. But back at my place, I made us tequila sodas and held up my glass. "Kudos, Dale. You did a great job. Amazing, actually. Where'd you get all those computer skills?"

Dale waved his hand. "That was nothing. The hard part was finding a fall guy who fit our timeline."

The truth was, Lazaro Estevez had never been involved with any gangs, let alone the Southside Creepers. And he'd actually died when he got hit with a stray bullet during the gang wars that ensued between the Grape Street Boyz and the Creepers after Ricardo's death. He'd been off duty, visiting an aunt and uncle who happened to live on the outskirts of Creeper turf.

I took a sip of my drink. "The only thing that worries me is the possibility that one of those Grape Street Boyz has some underground connect to a Creeper. A Creeper who'd take about ten seconds to figure out that Lazaro was never a *compadre* of theirs."

Dale nodded. "Nothing we can do about that. But the *sort of* good news is that they're still at war, so it's not going to happen now. Probably not for some time. And Lazaro's real Facebook page got taken down a while ago."

I stirred my drink with my finger as I thought about that. "You know, with any luck, by the time their war's over, the Orozcos won't be a problem."

I looked at Dale with a steady gaze to see whether he knew what I meant. He met my eyes and nodded slowly. We were on the same page. Excellent. Then I'd been right. I'd been waiting to see whether he'd press me again for an answer as to whether I'd set up Ricardo. He hadn't. And he'd just helped me cover it up. Ergo, it was fair to assume that he knew I'd done it.

I'd been wanting to find out whether Dale would be willing to take matters a little—okay, a lot—further if the Orozco problem didn't go away. Because if they figured out that we'd duped them, more drastic measures would be necessary. The kind that'd make Dale's help come in handy. I hoped I'd guessed rightly that Dale's reaction just now indicated he'd be willing to take that next step.

Of course, if it came to that, it'd mean letting Dale get further into my . . . personal form of justice. A dangerous proposition. But I'd wait and see what happened. No need to make any decisions now. Especially since the Orozco problem might have finally been solved.

And as I went to sleep that night, I savored the possibility that I'd seen the last of those cretins.

That possibility should've made for a great weekend. It didn't. I worried nonstop about whether the cops would give Cassie the deal. I woke up at six on Monday morning, both dreading and hoping for the call from the cops. It came at ten o'clock.

"Meet us at PAB in an hour," Emmons said.

"Do we have a deal?"

But the line was dead. Damn those guys. I told Alex and Michelle. "This is it, kids."

Alex offered to go with me. "Just to make sure you and Rusty Templeton don't wind up in a shootout."

I thanked him, but I declined. "No restraints necessary. I think they've got to give me the deal, and that means I'll get to have the fun of watching Rusty eat shit."

"I hope you're right," Michelle said. "Okay, break a leg."

"You mean theirs, right?"

But by the time I got to the PAB, I wasn't so confident. With every passing minute, I worried about what might've gone wrong. What they might've discovered in the last forty-eight hours that I didn't know about. I sat in the lobby, sweating it out, for almost half an hour before they brought me up to the captain's office. Rusty and Emmons were standing against the wall; Captain Hales was sitting at his oversize desk.

He had the standard cop mustache and short blond hair. His dark eyes had the typical cop suspicious look under his thick eyebrows. He did not look happy. "Have a seat, Ms. Brinkman."

I wanted to refuse, just for the hell of it, but my client's life was on the line. I sat. "You've read my witness statements?"

Hales gave me a deadpan look. "No, I never bother with evidence." He sighed. "Of course I read them, and we checked them out. They look solid."

"Then we have a deal?"

His gaze was direct and hard. "I'm not dropping our murder investigation on your client. But for now, given what we know, I'll agree to let her out with an ankle monitor. We'll have a uni watching her, so let her know she needs to keep her act together and stay clean. If we can't turn up anything new in the next month or so, we'll go along with the deal. And the deal is, your client testifies against Tiegan Donner, and she pleads to accessory after the fact for low term."

I shook my head. "She gets time served."

Hales exchanged glances with Rusty, who gave him an "I told you so" look. "Fine. Time served. But she signs a binding agreement to testify."

I nodded. "And she processes out today."

Hales sat back. "To where? Her adoptive relatives won't have her." He shook his head. "She'll have to go into foster care."

I'd spoken to Cassie about this. She was adamant about not going back to foster care. "No foster care. Barbara Reeber said she'd take Cassie back."

Hales raised an eyebrow. "For how long? Is she planning to adopt the kid?"

"Not that I know of. But Cassie can stay there until we've at least had the chance to find the right foster home."

Hales didn't seem to like it. The muscles in his jaw bulged as he stared at the paperwork on his desk. Finally, he spoke. "She stays with Reeber for now. But she gets into *any* kind of trouble, she gets foster care." He pushed the papers toward me. "Your client can start processing out after she signs and initials."

I took the plea forms and headed to Twin Towers.

Cassie was so ecstatic she dropped the phone and jumped out of her chair. "You saved me! I can't believe it!"

I waited for her to calm down and pick up the phone. "Remember, though, you have to testify against Tiegan."

Cassie nodded, but she didn't look all that perturbed. She'd already moved on to the next issue. "Where am I going to go? Am I going to stay with you? Please?"

I shook my head. "Sorry. Not an option."

Cassie gave me a pleading look. "Why? I know how to cook, and I wouldn't bother you, I promise!"

"Barbara Reeber's agreed to let you stay with them—"

Her face was anguished. "No! I hate it there! Please don't make me go there!"

I waited for her to calm down. "You can always stay here. I'm sure the cops wouldn't mind."

That sobered her up. She dropped her head. "Okay, I'll go to Barbara's."

I waved to the guard to pass the plea forms to Cassie for her signature. Once she'd signed and passed them back to me, I told her what the captain had said about keeping her nose clean. "A uniformed officer will be watching you. And you can't get in any kind of trouble. That means you can't litter, you can't jaywalk, and you can't cross the street on a Don't Cross light. Got it? Squeaky clean from here on out."

Cassie gave me a solemn nod. "Got it."

I called the guard to say we were done. Cassie hugged herself and pointed to me, giving me a hug through the glass, and hung up. I watched as the guard led her away.

I asked Alex to drive Cassie to Barbara's house that night. I didn't want to give Cassie a chance to start in again about living with me. But the case was over. And I'd won. When Alex got back, we all shared a drink—courtesy of the minibar I kept in my bottom drawer—to celebrate our victory.

FIFTY-NINE

For the next several days, I worked on my other cases and managed to pull in a couple of new ones—a twenty-two-count credit card fraud case that screamed "plea bargain" and a case involving a woman who'd killed her abusive boyfriend that screamed "sympathy verdict."

A few of the child victim groups who'd supported Cassie asked me to speak at their functions. I turned them down. But I hadn't stopped thinking about the case. And I still had some unanswered questions. Those never sit well with me, but they'd especially gotten under my skin this time.

In short, I knew I wasn't finished. So I kept digging, quietly—and way under the radar—but steadily. One thing that'd always bugged me was Tiegan's story about the knife. Tiegan had claimed Cassie liked to steal things from her. She'd insisted that Cassie must've stolen the knife during one of her visits. I'd thought that was pretty far-fetched at the time. Now I wasn't so sure.

But I thought of a way to check out Tiegan's story. I called Fred and asked him to have Tiegan look over the photographs of the items seized from Cassie's room. Tiegan identified a pair of earrings, the sweater she'd mentioned during her interview, and a bracelet. Then, I had Alex track down Tiegan's friend Shana—the one in the photograph. She'd confirmed that the items had all belonged to Tiegan. Was that proof positive that Cassie had stolen the knife? Not necessarily. But it showed Tiegan's story wasn't as far-fetched as I'd initially thought.

Two weeks later, I got a phone call that resolved another doubt—one I'd had for some time. It was from Waylon Stubing's mother. "I'm sorry this took so long," she said. "I only just heard about it from Marina's mother last night."

Apparently, Waylon had unburdened himself to his new girlfriend, Marina. Marina had told her mother, and Marina's mother had called Waylon's mother. I went to see Waylon that same day. We met in his living room. His mother sat next to him on the couch, her expression stern. When she spoke, her voice was angry. "Tell her everything."

Waylon looked pale and guilty. He laced his fingers together and squeezed so hard I saw the skin on his knuckles turn white. "I—I lied. Cassie never told me she'd been molested by anyone."

Hardly the shocker of the century, but he deserved to feel shitty. I nodded. "I figured."

Waylon's mother nudged him. "That's not all. Tell her the rest."

He took a breath, his eyes on the floor. "After Cassie got out of jail, she called me. She wanted to get back together, but I told her I was with Marina. I asked her if I'd still have to testify. She said no, and she thanked me for backing her up." Waylon swallowed and finally looked at me. "Anyway, I asked her what was up with that? Were they really molesting her? She laughed and said, 'Don't worry about that shit.'"

Don't worry about that shit. I pondered that statement all the way back to the office.

That Cassie had put Waylon up to lying for her was really neither here nor there. I could see how a victim might be desperate enough to ask someone to back her up. But a victim being that cavalier about what she'd been through . . . that was a different matter. That statement played over and over again in my head as I drove, my anger growing with every mile.

And that's when I realized what it was about the videotape of Cassie's confrontation with Tiegan in the jail that had pinged me. Just to be sure, I decided to rewatch it.

It was late by the time I got in—eight thirty—and Michelle and Alex had gone home. Given the mood I was in, it was probably a good thing I was alone. I sat down at my computer, pulled up the e-mail from Emmons, and clicked on the attachment. This time, I knew what to look for. I sat forward and watched carefully as Tiegan asked why Cassie was doing this to her. I studied Tiegan's demeanor. Then I studied Cassie's reaction. I stopped the footage each time Tiegan's emotions shifted, then stopped it again when it got to Cassie's reaction. And by the time I got to the end, I knew what had always bothered me about this scene.

Tiegan cried. Cassie cried. Tiegan cried. Cassie cried. Monkey see, monkey do. But when Cassie accused Tiegan of abandoning her, she was cold as ice. And when she insisted she hadn't committed the murders, her reason was equally as cold. It wasn't because they were the only family she'd ever known. It was, "Why would I kill them? I'd have nowhere to live." Nowhere but foster care, which she'd vowed never to endure again. And at the very end, when Tiegan became enraged, Cassie had known better than to react in kind—I'd always warned her not to say or do anything she didn't want the world to see. So she'd begun to sob. But when she turned toward the camera, I could see there were no real tears.

And now, with the benefit of time and distance, I realized what it told me about who Cassie might really be.

I wasn't 100 percent sure, and there was nothing I could do about it now. But I needed to know, just for my own peace of mind. As I turned off the computer and left the office, my mind began to work on the problem of how to determine once and for all whether I'd finally gotten it right: that Cassie was a psychopath, that she'd lied about the molestation. And that she'd decided to kill Abel because he was going to ruin her relationship with Tiegan.

Over the next few days, I found myself preoccupied with the question. Was my new perspective on Cassie the right one? Or was I making too much of the recent revelations? I had to admit that those revelations didn't necessarily have to mean Cassie was a liar. But it did seem clear to me that she had an antisocial personality disorder and was likely a psychopath. After my last viewing of the jail footage, I'd gone back over her behavior with me from the first time we'd met, and I'd been forced to recognize that the signs had been there all along. It was in the way she talked about others, with a near complete emphasis on what they could do for her; it was in her manipulative behavior—with Barbara, with Tiegan, and with me—and it was in her emotional reactions. The undying love and affection for Tiegan when she thought Tiegan was her ticket out of the Sonnenberg house, and the shift to total indifference when she learned that testifying against Tiegan was her ticket out of jail. The abrupt shift from profound sorrow and remorse to cold accusation when she'd accused Tiegan of abandoning her. And there'd been many times during our visits when her emotional outbursts felt like fake soap-opera melodrama.

But even so, that didn't necessarily mean she hadn't been molested. And if she had been telling the truth about that, the rest of her story—that Tiegan had gone off the deep end when she found out and committed the murders—stood a good chance of being true, too. Mostly true, anyway. I thought Cassie's claim that Tiegan had become unhinged when she'd heard about the abuse was a bit of self-puffery. The blackmail undoubtedly played a bigger part in Tiegan's motive to kill Abel.

But if Cassie hadn't been molested, the case took on a whole different blush.

I needed to keep digging. Maybe there was something I'd overlooked. I went back to the police reports, the crime-scene photos, everything I had on the case, to try and figure out what I'd been missing. But it wasn't until I happened to take another look at the photos of Tiegan's apartment that I hit on a possible solution. It wasn't really a "Eureka!" moment. It was more like a "Hey, that's an interesting idea" moment. But I needed Emmons's cooperation. It was Friday, and everyone likes to take off early on Friday afternoon. But when I looked at my watch, I saw it was only two thirty. I might get lucky. Emmons was a hard worker who was trying to make a good impression. I'd heard he was hoping to transfer to LAPD. I called his direct line.

He answered. "Emmons."

I asked him whether Tiegan's apartment was still being held as a crime scene. He said they were about to release it tomorrow, actually. I had to act fast. "Can you let me in? There's something I need to check. I promise it won't take long."

His voice was suspicious. "Your girl's out of it. What more do you want?"

"Please, humor me. Just this once."

After a longish pause, he said, "I'll send a uni to let you in. Be there by three thirty. I'll give you one hour."

That should be more than enough time for what I had in mind. I thanked him, told him I'd head over there right now, then went to get Alex. Two pairs of eyes would work faster than one.

We flew out the door and got to Tiegan's place at three thirty on the dot.

The uni let us in, and we headed straight for the living room.

One hour later, I had the answer I'd been looking for.

SIXTY

I spent the weekend catching up on laundry and housework, mindless chores that helped me sort through what I'd learned about Cassie. When I got in to the office on Monday, I found a message from Cassie on my voice mail. She thought her ankle monitor was supposed to be taken off by now. I consulted my calendar and saw that it was actually due to come off tomorrow. I'd just picked up the phone to call and tell her when it rang in my hand.

It was Rusty Templeton. He'd called to tell me that Paula had made an unexpected recovery. She was fully lucid, and she wanted to see Cassie. He asked whether Barbara or I could bring her to the hospital today. I said I'd do it, but I wanted to know whether Paula had given them another statement.

Rusty was noncommittal. "We'll question her again. But I'm not sure she'll have much more to say. Anyway, you don't need to hang around. You can just drop her off; we'll bring her home."

I called Barbara, who was at work, and asked whether I could pick up Cassie and take her to see her mother. She was happy to have me do that and said she'd take a break so she could meet me at the house. I told Alex and Michelle about Rusty's call, then headed out to Glendale.

The drive gave me a chance to think—about a lot of things. My first thoughts went to Cassie's jeopardy. I considered the possibilities. Could Paula now claim to *know* that Cassie was the killer? That didn't seem likely. Paula had been attacked from behind, and she'd gone down fast. No, if she remembered anything new, it'd more likely have to do with hearing Tiegan's voice—or maybe seeing another pair of feet—before she totally blacked out. If so, that'd be a big plus for Cassie. I didn't see Paula as a viable threat. On the personal front, if Paula kept improving, Cassie would be able to go and stay with her in the not-too-distant future. I thought Cassie might be okay with that. I knew she'd had her problems with Paula—and some were legitimate. But I had a feeling Cassie wouldn't mind getting out of Barbara's way-too-normal household—a constant reminder of the kind of life Cassie could never have. And whatever my feelings about Cassie's psychological makeup, she was unlikely to harm the only person who'd put a roof over her head at this point. When I got to the house, Barbara Reeber—that long-suffering saint—had just pulled into the driveway. She seemed happy to see me. "How've you been, Sam? I haven't seen you in . . . Lord, it's been quite a while."

She ushered me in, and I thanked her for taking Cassie in again. I didn't see Cassie in the kitchen or the living room. "I guess she's in her room?"

"She must be. You can just go on in." She looked at her watch. "But I'll have to get back to work pretty soon. I just thought I should be here to let you in, in case Cassie didn't hear the doorbell. Sometimes she puts on those headphones and . . ." Barbara smiled. "A bomb could go off and she wouldn't hear anything."

Sure enough, I found Cassie sitting on the bed, listening to music on her headphones and swaying to the beat. Her knees were drawn up, and a math textbook was propped up on her legs. Just your average teen—who'd managed to beat a double homicide rap. When she saw me, she smiled and pulled off her headphones. "Sam! Hey!"

She started to get off the bed, but I motioned for her to stay put. "Cassie, I've got some news."

The smile started to sag. "Is something wrong?"

"Not at all." I pulled over the chair in front of her desk and sat down. "It seems your mother has gotten better. She's fully awake, and she'd like to see you."

Cassie looked stunned for a moment. Then her expression became puzzled. "But I thought the doctors said she wasn't looking that good?"

"They did, but she unexpectedly made a turn for the better." I watched her absorb the news. "Pretty wonderful, don't you think?"

Cassie nodded slowly and her smile returned. "I . . . yeah, it really is." Her smile grew hopeful. "Do you think maybe she'll remember seeing Tiegan there now?"

"It's possible." I gave her arm a squeeze. "What do you say? Want to go see her?"

Cassie's eyes were shiny. "Sure. Can we go now?"

I said we could.

Ten minutes later, we were on our way to Glendale Adventist Hospital.

The room in ICU was dark and quiet. The lights in the ceiling had been turned way down, and the monitors glowed dimly above the bed. I could barely make out Paula's face above the covers. She appeared to be sleeping. The steady *beep-beep* of the machine that registered her heartbeat was the only sound.

Cassie stood back against the wall, watching her. "Should I wake her up?"

I kept my voice low. "Maybe give it a minute and see if she wakes up on her own."

I watched Cassie closely. At first, when I'd told her that Paula was recovering, I'd thought she seemed worried. But she didn't look worried now. Her head was tilted to one side, and there was a little smile on her face.

She stayed focused on Paula as she whispered, "Will I get to go stay with her?"

"If she keeps making progress, I can't see why not."

A look of fear crossed her face. "We won't have to go back to that house, will we?"

That was unthinkable. "No, certainly not."

Cassie's face relaxed, and she resumed watching Paula with a fond smile.

A moment later, a nurse stepped in. "Ms. Brinkman?" I nodded. "We have an urgent call for you."

I frowned. "Did you get a name?"

The nurse gave an exasperated sigh. Her voice was low but irritated. "We're a hospital, not an answering service." She backed up, one foot out the door. "I'll tell them you're not available."

"No, don't. I'll take it." Cassie was still watching Paula, her expression wistful. I whispered, "I'll be right back."

Cassie stared at me blankly for a moment, as though she'd forgotten I was there. Then she blinked and nodded. "Sure, okay."

I took one last look at her, then hurried out.

I'd just reached the nurses' station when I heard a loud *bang* that sounded like a slamming door come from inside the room. I ran back.

Just in time to see Cassie leaning over the bed, pressing a pillow down on her mother's face. Cassie was fixated on Paula, her jaw set, her expression determined. Emmons, who'd just thrown back the door to the bathroom where he'd been hiding, grabbed Cassie and pulled her hands behind her back. "You're under arrest for the murders of Abel, Stephen . . . *and* Paula Sonnenberg."

Cassie jerked up as though she'd just been shaken out of a trance. She twisted around and looked at Emmons, her mouth agape, then turned back and stared at the body on the bed. Her lips moved, but no sound came out.

Emmons pulled her away. "Your mother died this morning."

I stared at Cassie, who stood there, frozen, as she tried to process what had happened. Then, all of a sudden, her eyes grew wild. She struggled against Emmons and whipped her head back and forth as she screamed. "No! You can't do this! It's not fair!"

She'd just been caught red-handed, but my lawyer reflex kicked in, and I barked, "Don't talk, Cassie."

Rusty Templeton, who'd been waiting in the room next door, rushed in and helped take control of her. As they half dragged, half carried her—still screaming—out of the room, I said, "She's invoking. No questioning until she has a lawyer."

He gave me a grim smirk. "Guess that's not going to be you this time?"

I glared at him. "No. Not this time."

I stood in the hallway and watched them leave. I'd had a feeling this was a setup when Templeton told me Paula was better and wanted to see Cassie. The tip-off had come when he'd told me I could leave once I got her there. And the confirmation had come when the nurse told me I had an urgent call—which, as I'd expected, turned out to be bullshit.

I didn't have to go along with it. I could've refused to bring Cassie—and I could've warned her not to go.

But I didn't, because I'd found the final piece of evidence that laid my other lingering questions to rest.

It'd been on Tiegan's bookshelves. When I'd studied the blowups of the photos, I'd noticed an entire shelf of books devoted to child psychology. One in particular caught my eye: *Child Molestation: Case Studies.* At first, it'd merely struck me as ironic that Tiegan would have books like that, though it made sense that a school counselor would need to be well versed on child-focused issues. But in that moment, I'd realized it might be more than just ironic.

When Alex and I went to Tiegan's apartment, I saw that the book was still there, on the upper shelf. And after fifteen minutes, I found what I was looking for. It was in the fourth case study. "Ann R." had reported that her brother would "come into her room while she was asleep" and that she'd wake up to see him "with his pants open." At first, "he only touched her," but after one week, he began to demand that she "touch him." Ann R. said she was always "afraid to fall asleep." The assaults quickly escalated as he demanded that she perform oral copulation on him, and then forced her to engage in anal intercourse.

Julie M. reported that her stepfather would come into her room at night and make her undress and lie on top of the covers "while he touched himself." And on and on.

It was all there—Cassie's story—with remarkably little variation.

I marveled at how well she'd pulled off her act, at how real her pain and embarrassment had seemed when she described what Abel and Stephen had supposedly done to her. But of course, psychopaths can always feel their own pain—even when it's imagined.

Truth be told, I'd always had my doubts about Cassie's molestation story, but they'd fluctuated. Sometimes I believed it; sometimes I didn't. But for the most part, I'd given her the benefit of the doubt.

Still, when she spoke to the reporter and neglected to say that her father had been abusing her, too, it sent up a red flag. It seemed unlikely that a true victim would leave out something that big— especially since, at that time, the molestation was her whole defense. Cassie had made it seem as though she'd left it out because she was too embarrassed. But she'd been pretty graphic in her descriptions of what Abel had done to her. And I'd seen how she behaved during that interview. She didn't look in the least embarrassed. She'd just forgotten her lines under pressure.

And so it was clear: Cassie had never been molested. She certainly had been tortured by that sadistic freak, Abel. But Cassie couldn't afford to bust him, because he'd out her relationship with Tiegan, which would have put an end to her dream of escaping from that house and going to live with Tiegan.

And that dream was real. Delusional. But real. Cassie had clearly been unhappy long before Abel started blackmailing her. I remembered how she'd complained right from the start that she'd never felt like she fit in, that Paula had always reminded her how "lucky" she was that they'd taken her in. Cassie may have exaggerated, but I'd never gotten the impression that she was lying. And Tiegan was supposed to be her way out.

Only it hadn't worked out that way—because of Abel. When Tiegan learned he was blackmailing Cassie, she'd immediately told Cassie to back off. Tiegan was a predatory pedophile, but she wasn't suicidal.

Cassie saw that her ticket out of that house was all but gone— unless she could eliminate the threat, i.e., Abel. Had Cassie planned it all long in advance? The fact that she'd stolen Tiegan's knife made it seem so—and the fact that she'd picked the night her parents were supposed to be away, at a hotel. But maybe not. Cassie did like to steal things from Tiegan. So it was possible Cassie took the knife with no plan in mind, that she'd only begun to conceive of killing Abel that same day, after Tiegan told her they had to "cool it."

Had I been playing hide-and-go-seek with the truth about Cassie's molestation because I'd been so bent on winning? Probably, in part. But so many victims suffer in silence, and so few ever lie about it, that I'd been willing to resolve my doubts in Cassie's favor. So even though my own ambition played a part, I cut myself some slack for letting myself get duped.

What I wouldn't do was cut Cassie any slack for lying about it. I have no sympathy for a faker. Even one facing life without parole.

But Cassie's duping me wasn't the biggest issue I had with her.

My biggest issue was that now, and for years to come, abusers would point to Cassie and say, "See?"

Even so, ever since Cassie's rearrest, I'd been asking myself why I'd allowed the cops to set her up. I'd been gamed by clients a million times before. And I'd certainly represented some truly depraved psychopaths before. What was so different now?

I'd given that some serious thought, but I was stumped until I remembered Michelle's remark—that she didn't like a kid who lied about being molested. And then I realized what was different. I'd told Michelle I didn't care about that. But it wasn't true. I cared a great deal.

And that's why I'd let the cops set Cassie up. Because this time it was personal. Too bad for Cassie.

EPILOGUE

The fallout from Cassie's rearrest, and the revelation that her molestation story had been a lie, was dramatic. And sadly, the children's advocate groups were taking it full in the face from the naysayers who'd argued all along that the molestation story was just an excuse fabricated by a killer so she could get away with murder.

I got requests to speak at the children's advocate groups again, and to be on a bunch of cable news shows, morning shows and afternoon talk shows. I accepted them all.

I had to do what I could to repair the damage. "I can't comment specifically on Cassie Sonnenberg, because she was my client. But I can say this: the overwhelmingly vast majority of children who report abuse are telling the truth. Our biggest problems are that so many children are afraid to report—afraid they won't be believed or that they'll be blamed—and the adults who turn their backs when children do report. And no one should doubt that sexual abuse can cause serious, permanent damage to a child's psyche."

The hosts always came back with a variation on the same follow-up question: "Serious enough to commit murder?"

And my answer was always the same. "Most definitely."

The shrinkers on those shows helped. But they also agreed that Cassie was a prime example of a psychopath—though they believed that she and her lies would've been exposed eventually.

I wasn't so sure about that. Tiegan was a great fall guy. No matter how sweet and petite she looked, no matter how soft-spoken and nonthreatening she seemed, the jury would've hated her. I thought they would've been more than willing to believe Cassie's testimony.

So why hadn't Cassie pointed the finger at Tiegan to begin with? I'd knocked that question around with Alex and Michelle over drinks in my office.

"I think she was still hoping to go live with Tiegan," Michelle said.

Alex polished off the last of his drink. "Maybe, but at first, I think she just saw no way out. They found her bloody clothes in the backyard, and her mom had basically said she was the killer. I think Cassie figured the only way out was to admit it and find an excuse."

Michelle set down her glass. "And then, when Tiegan started to back away, she finally saw that her dream of running away together wasn't going to happen."

I nodded. "So Cassie turned on her. I think that's when she realized she could put the blame on Tiegan."

Michelle asked, "Is Tiegan going to get a deal to testify?"

Tiegan was on the hook for being an accessory after the fact and for having sex with a minor. There was no getting around any of that. She'd given a full confession. "Fred's going to try and get her a deal. But just between us, she told him she'd testify whether they give her a deal or not."

Michelle raised her eyebrows. "No shit?" I nodded. "That is one pissed-off woman."

It really was. "Can you blame her?"

Alex shook his head. "Oh hell no."

I held up the bottle of Patrón Silver. "Another round?"

"No." Michelle gave me a pointed look. "Because, *driving*."

"I'm gonna Uber." I refilled my glass.

"Me, too." Alex held out his for a refill.

By the time we left, I was feeling very relaxed and a little buzzed.

So when I found my front door unlocked, I just thought, how dumb of me to forget to lock it that morning—until I saw the man who was sitting in the wingback chair in my living room. I stood frozen just inside the door as my knees began to shake. "Who the hell are you?"

The drapes were open, and the city lights glowed in the dark behind him. He looked to be in his fifties. His hair was thick and almost all white, as were his trim beard and mustache, but his eyebrows were still dark, and they matched his large brown—almost black—eyes.

He smiled and held up his hands. "I'm not armed, and I have no intention of hurting you, Ms. Brinkman. On the contrary, I've come to tell you that I have saved you from some serious trouble."

He spoke with a Spanish accent, but his English was perfect. I stood in the open doorway, scared and unsure of what to do, but getting angrier by the second. "Again, who are you?"

"My name is Javier Cabazon." He kept his hands up. "You can certainly stay over there if it makes you feel safer. But I'd close the door if I were you, because I don't think you'll want anyone to hear what I have to say."

I hesitated as I weighed the danger of being alone with him against the danger of someone hearing what he might say. The range of things I wouldn't want anyone to hear was painfully extensive. And it would be stupid of him to kill me and think he could get away without someone noticing him. It was early, and the people in the apartments all around us were awake. Plus, he had a very distinctive look. They'd remember seeing him. I shut the door but kept my hand on the doorknob.

"What exactly do you think you've saved me from?"

He lowered his hands and started to reach into his black sport jacket—it looked like it was cashmere. I started to take a step back. "No, no. Calm yourself." He brandished a pipe. "I hope you don't mind." I watched him without blinking as he lit it and inhaled. The smell of cherry tobacco filled the room. "You are familiar with Ernesto and Arturo Orozco, yes?"

My grip on the doorknob tightened as I nodded.

He took another pull on his pipe and leaned back. He looked completely at ease, as though he owned the place. "They work for me. And the other day, they came to me to resolve a certain, I will call it, *concern* they had about a man who supposedly set up the killing of Ricardo."

My heart gave a loud, painful thump. I was busted. I was dead. But I was going to go down fighting. "What do you mean, 'concern'?"

Javier raised an amused eyebrow. "They did not believe that he was really the one who'd altered the paperwork. They thought it was you."

My hand on the doorknob was slick with sweat, and my heart was beating so fast I could barely breathe. "They're wrong. It wasn't me." Even to my ears, my voice sounded strained and reedy.

Javier shook his head. "You have nothing to worry about. I am not at all sorry that Ricardo is no longer with us. He was an embarrassment, a disgrace to us all." A look of disgust crossed his face. "Killing that child. A terrible thing. There was no reason for it." He puffed on his pipe again and blew out a cloud of smoke, as though he were erasing the words from his mouth. "So I told the Orozcos that I would check it out myself."

I had no choice; I had to brazen it out. I lifted my chin and stared him in the eye. "Then you know that the deputy was the one who did it."

Javier raised an eyebrow again, but this time with no amusement. "Actually, I know it was a complete fabrication. I have contacts everywhere, including within the so-called rival gangs. This deputy had nothing whatsoever to do with the . . . Southside Creepers." His mouth twisted with derision as he said the gang name.

I let go of the doorknob and edged sideways, toward the kitchen table. I tried to keep my voice steady as I asked, "What did you tell the Orozcos?"

Javier lowered his pipe. "That this deputy—Lazaro, correct?" I nodded. "That he was most certainly the man who set up Ricardo to be killed." He drew on his pipe and spoke through a cloud of smoke. "You will no longer be bothered by the Orozcos."

But now he owned me. My days were numbered—and not in double digits—unless I did whatever he'd come to ask of me. "What do you want?"

"Now? Nothing. But it's good to have a lawyer in the family. Especially one whose father is a detective." He stood up and began to approach me. I backed away till I bumped into the kitchen table, but he moved past me, opened the door, and walked out.

When the door closed behind him, I turned and grabbed the back of a chair, faint from lack of oxygen. My stomach was roiling from the mixture of adrenaline and tequila. And in my brain, I kept hearing the old saying: out of the frying pan, into the fire.

The following evening, Dale and I were sitting on his patio, polishing off the last of a bottle of Adastra Proximus. I'd called him the morning after my visit from Cabazon to ask whether he wanted to join me for dinner. He'd suggested we meet at his place this time, and I'd accepted. Over spaghetti and salad, I told him about Cassie and what I'd learned. "That little girl is one scary psychopath." Dale stared at me. "What?"

He turned to scan the untamed hills behind his property. "Nothing." After a brief pause, he took a sip of wine. "You know, I'm kind of surprised you didn't see that little setup coming."

He suspected . . . but he didn't—*couldn't*—know that I'd not only seen it coming but also gone along with it. And he never would. I'd take this one to the grave. I shrugged. "Surprised me, too. Rusty isn't usually that smooth."

Dale raised an eyebrow, then reached for the bottle and poured the last of the wine into our glasses. "Anyway, however it had to happen, I'm glad the case is closed." He set down the bottle and picked up his glass. "Now, how about we toast to getting rid of the Orozcos?"

My heart gave a dull thud, and my throat grew tight. This was it. I searched Dale's face. I didn't know whether he was ready to cross this line. But I had no choice. "Yeah, about that." I set down my wineglass as I looked into his eyes. "We need to talk."

ACKNOWLEDGMENTS

As always, my infinite gratitude goes to Catherine LePard. Without her support, I would never have had the courage to reach for the childhood dream of writing crime novels.

Thank you, Dan Conaway, agent extraordinaire. You're the best in the business, and I'm so glad I found you.

Charlotte Herscher, you are one fabulous editor—there's no one better. Thank you for your fantastic notes and for being such a pleasure to work with.

Thank you, JoVon Sotak for believing in Samantha. Collaborating with you has been a truly great experience.

ABOUT THE AUTHOR

Photo © 2016 Coral von Zumwalt

California native Marcia Clark is the author of *Blood Defense*, the first book in the Samantha Brinkman series, as well as *Guilt by Association*, *Guilt by Degrees*, *Killer Ambition*, and *The Competition*—all part of the Rachel Knight series. A practicing criminal lawyer since 1979, she joined the Los Angeles District Attorney's office in 1981, where she served as prosecutor for the trials of Robert Bardo—convicted of killing actress Rebecca Schaeffer—and, most notably, O. J. Simpson. The bestselling *Without a Doubt*, which she cowrote, chronicles her work on the Simpson trial. Clark has been a frequent commentator on a variety of shows and networks, including *Today*, *Good Morning America*, *The Oprah Winfrey Show*, CNN, and MSNBC, as well as a legal correspondent for *Entertainment Tonight*.